BEYOND THE GRAVE

Also by Pierre Magnan and published by
The Harvill Press

THE MURDERED HOUSE
INNOCENCE

Pierre Magnan

BEYOND THE GRAVE

Translated from the French by
Patricia Clancy

THE HARVILL PRESS

LONDON

First published by Éditions Denoël in 1990
2 4 6 8 10 9 7 5 3 1
Copyright © Pierre Magnan, 1990
English translation copyright © Patricia Clancy, 2002

Pierre Magnan has asserted his right under the Copyright, Designs
and Patents Act 1988 to be identified as the author of this work

First published in Great Britain in 2002 by
The Harvill Press
Random House, 20 Vauxhall Bridge Road,
London SW1V 2SA

Random House Australia (Pty) Limited
20 Alfred Street, Milsons Point, Sydney,
New South Wales 2061, Australia

Random House New Zealand Limited
18 Poland Road, Glenfield,
Auckland 10, New Zealand

Random House South Africa (Pty) Limited
Endulini, 5A Jubilee Road, Parktown 2193, South Africa

The Random House Group Limited Reg. No. 954009
www.randomhouse.co.uk

A CIP catalogue record for this book
is available from the British Library

ISBN 1 86046 078 7 (hbk)
ISBN 1 86046 739 3 (pbk)

Papers used by Random House are natural,
recyclable products made from wood grown in sustainable forests;
the manufacturing processes conform to the environmental
regulations of the country of origin

Designed and typeset in Minion by
Palimpsest Book Production Limited, Polmont, Stirlingshire

Printed and bound in Great Britain by
Biddles Ltd, Guildford & Kings Lynn

For Marie-Laure Goumet
and Michel Bernard,
my friends.

She felt as though she had lost herself in the arms of a lover made of bronze, a statue, an image . . .

"And what's more," she said to herself, "that smooth face without a single line which he invariably presented to me . . . Where does it come from?" Then she asked herself the same question, but more precisely: "Who did it come from? Who had made him wear it? Or rather, who had put that mask on him?" For that is what she really felt: making love, she had encountered someone who physically concealed his true self, as though he were wearing a mask.

The Murdered House

AUTHOR'S NOTE

When an author has grown fond of a character he has to leave at the end of a book, he always finishes with more than a tinge of regret. Writing the words "The End" on the last page of a novel is like nailing down the coffin lid of a very dear friend.

There is naturally a great temptation to make another story emerge from the ashes of the one before. Even more so in the case of *Beyond the Grave*, as a lady one day at a book-signing encouraged me to do it. She asked me: "Won't you write a sequel to *The Murdered House*?" I laughed at the idea, but she had planted the seed in my mind, and as it grew, it soon began to disturb my sleep.

Séraphin's stature, his silence, his lack of interest in everything that is usually the delight of people like us, his compassion – all this convinced me that there was more than bare bones hidden under the skin of that body; easily enough to fill my imagination.

The story you are about to read is permeated with the common humanity of the character to whom I have given life beyond the grave.

Pierre Magnan

I

Haute Provence, 1921

WHEN MARIE CAME BACK FROM DEATH'S DOOR, THE FIRST THING SHE did was to ask for Séraphin. She was still weak and wobbly on her feet, and had to cling with both hands to the thick rope that served as a banister for the steep steps leading up to her bedroom.

"Don't be in such a hurry! Do you want him to see you like that? Just take a look in the mirror. You look almost as awful as I do! Your skin's sagging like an old leather purse! Get better first. Then we'll see . . ."

It was the biggest lie that her mother, Clorinde Dormeur, had ever told in her life. We never did see anything, ever. Séraphin had left without once turning back, taking with him his bicycle, the shirt he was wearing, and not a thing more.

"Not a thing more!" old Tricanote echoed in dismay.

He had left the key in the door, his shaving soap on the sink and his Sunday suit in the wardrobe. He had taken only the bare minimum to avoid being arrested by the gendarmes.

"Just the clothes he stood up in!" exclaimed Tricanote, raising her hands to heaven. "I ask you, how far will he get like that?"

"Perhaps further than you think," said Marie's godmother, the old Marquise de Pescaïré, still staring beyond the horizon.

Most people thought he must have gone off and thrown himself down a well, where some day a hunter would come across his remains.

Maître Bellaffaire, the notary, who never tired of praising Séraphin's unselfishness, summed up the situation the way we all hoped it would turn out.

1

"So," he said, "it would all be for the best in the best of all possible worlds!"

He had made all the necessary arrangements. It wasn't customary for a key to remain in the door of an abandoned house, even if there was nothing inside. And so, after a suitable time had elapsed, he called on the help of two gendarmes and, in the presence of the bailiff, affixed the seals on Séraphin's few miserable effects.

It was the second time in half a century that a member of the Bellaffaire family had barred the door of a house where a member of the Monge family had lived. He sighed as he did it, remembering the past. Like the Marquise de Pescaïré, he too scanned the horizon uneasily.

The Monges were creatures of this land, just like the rest of us. It was pure chance that a curse should fall upon them in particular. No one was safe from its ravages. We would still have to be on our guard: it would keep on affecting us in one way or another. If we had any doubts on that score, we only had to look at Marie.

Marie's health bloomed again in a week, like a plant soaked in water. Rose Sépulcre, who thought the girl's beauty was lost for ever, had the shock of suddenly coming face to face with it one morning at the corner of the street. She barely had time to put a smile on her lips.

"You'll be coming to my wedding," she said.

"Sure!" Marie said. "And you'll be coming to mine."

They confronted each other like two storm clouds, puffed up with pride in their loves, the poor little things, as though there were no such thing as fate. Tricanote, the Marquise de Pescaïré, in fact all of us felt for them as they stood there gloating to each other.

Taking her mother's advice, Marie looked at her reflection in the bakery mirror every day. By the end of the week, even her breasts had filled out again. She thought that now she looked presentable.

"You can send Charitonne back," she said. "I'll do the deliveries from now on."

Charitonne was an orphan who was doing her best to escape from her situation as a ward of the State. She hated Marie immediately with all her heart for having recovered so quickly.

"No!" Clorinde said in a panic. "You're still too weak. And besides, as far as Charitonne is concerned, I have an agreement with the orphanage to keep her until Christmas."

"Tell her to take a rest!" Marie said. "Can't you see that she's as skinny as a rake?"

Almost by force Marie grabbed the empty three-wheeler delivery bike from Clorinde, whose hands were gripping the handlebars. She turned it downhill, leaped on just as she used to in happier days, scarcely remembering that she had recently been at death's door, and pedalled off down towards Peyruis and, as she thought, to Séraphin.

We had all rushed over in a body to the stone rampart, our black clothes flapping in the wind like beating wings, for that year in Lurs we were all dressed in black as though sharing a common bereavement. Was it the effect of the war that had made us all either widows, wards of the State or old men before our time through the loss of our children? You think you remember the war, but it disappears into the past terribly quickly when you have to earn your living. Actually, our mourning habits had been too well made. It looked as though they would last longer than sorrow itself. The fact is we were poor and had to wear them out. But the most cheerful thing in our part of the world was the sweet smiles of our little girls – such a contrast to the black of their smocks.

As it happened, Marie Dormeur was one of the few who were not in mourning for anyone at the time, and we could follow her progress on the way down, through our well-kept olive groves, her summer dress a bright spot speeding towards the love of her life.

"*Aïe, aïe, aïe!*" Tricanote exclaimed. "Heaven help us!"

There were about thirty of us leaning over the *barri* – the stone rampart – who risked toppling over into space, so eager were we to watch Marie disappearing in the direction of Peyruis.

She was pedalling like fury, as though she had never been out of action for a whole month, imprisoned in her bed by Zorme's curse. The aquamarine ring, which Séraphin had put back on her finger, sparkled in the sunlight. Her hands gripped the handlebars tightly as she sped to her love with all the life force returning to her body. Behind their curtains – either of simple gingham or embroidered with cross-stitch – the population of Peyruis eagerly jostled for positions to watch Marie go past on the road to sorrow.

Marie arrived at the fountain square. The silence was so intense it was like thunder. She was seen getting off her bike, heading straight for Séraphin's narrow house, running up the five steps and banging on the door like someone who has a right to do so.

There were two or three gloomy old ladies like Tricanote who also exclaimed "*Aïe, aïe, aïe!*" as they pulled their black scarves down even more tightly over their hair. From behind their windows they could see Marie take a step back on the narrow space at the top of the stone stairs. She had just come in contact with one of Maître Bellaffaire's seals. They were brand new and the red wax had not yet faded. Marie took them for what they were: a decree of fate.

She was seen going down the stairs as quickly as she had climbed them. She crossed the square to the side with the fine houses. And this time, in spite of the howling wind, one could hear the gleaming brass knocker in the shape of a lady's hand that graced the notary's residence being struck against the door several times. It was Marie boldly banging at Maître Bellaffaire's door. They had to come and open it in the end, but they kept her between two doors, in the vestibule. The man or woman who spoke to her was not visible. Unfortunately no one could pick up the words that passed between them. They did see the door close in her face, not rudely but not gently either, and from the way they got rid of her, it was clear that she had no business being there.

She was hanging her head as she got back on her bike and set off towards Lurs. There were fewer of us now leaning over the *barri* because some of the women had to go and prepare supper and the men had to feed their donkeys. Those of us who were left saw her reappear among our olive groves which the tree pruners took pride in keeping so neat and tidy.

I remember it; we all remember it. The door with the glass panel shook in its frame when Marie pushed it open with all her might. One letter of the word "Dormeur" fell off and hit the ground with a clang like a metal saucepan. We could hear Marie shout "You lied to me!" to her mother who didn't know what on earth to do.

Ah, Marie! She was twice as beautiful as before, standing there banging the counter so hard with her two little fists that they made the Roberval scales jump.

"You lied to me! You lied to me!"

"Aren't you ashamed to raise your voice to your mother like that?"

"No, I'm not ashamed! I'm not ashamed! Séraphin is *my* husband! I chose him! I decided it! Who took away my illness, you or him? He's the only one I've no right to raise my voice to!"

As her mother unthinkingly reached over to weigh two loaves a neighbour had just ordered a moment or two before, Marie gripped her mother's wrists and held them rigid.

"Tell me where he is! I want to know where he is!"

"You're really getting on my nerves!" exclaimed Clorinde. "I haven't the faintest idea where he is!"

She had been on the point of saying, "He's dead! There! Are you satisfied now?" She was convinced this was a love Marie would easily get over, a love like so many others that would die by the end of the year or be buried by the next superficial infatuation. She had seen so many girls happy enough with that. How could she know, as she had never experienced any other kind of love herself. Heavens above! Poor Clorinde, when she was still very attractive, had yearned for the Marquis de Pescaïré, a resolute fifty-year-old, for a whole summer.

But something sombre, and heavier than a mourning veil, clouded her daughter's bright eyes, and warned Clorinde not to mention these words in her presence.

"You're lying and you know it!" Marie shouted. "I'll go and ask *them*. They'll tell me."

We could see her from our stone wall, pointing vigorously in our direction. She pointed at us with a tragic gesture through the words traced in tranquil white on the shining pane of glass: "Célestat Dormeur. Baker and pastrycook. Speciality: focaccia breads." Suddenly she came out of the shop. There were plenty of people clever enough to know what she was going to ask us, without having heard her talking to her mother. They had already retreated, dusting down their aprons or their corduroy britches. We were the only ones left, the slow ones, caught on the hop as always.

"My mother's not telling me the truth!" she said. "*You* know where he is!"

"I could ask you *who*," said Tricanote, "but I know it's not worth it."

She walked up to Marie and placed her hands firmly on the girl's shoulders.

"Forget him!" she said.

"No!" Marie said. "You're not the one he saved!"

"Forget him, you silly girl!" Tricanote shook her as she spoke. "Can't you see? He's a ghost of a man and he'll bring you nothing but grief?"

"Forget him!" the Marquise de Pescaïré begged, coming to the rescue. "He wasn't meant for you. He wasn't meant for anyone."

"Oh yes he was!" Marie replied. "He was meant for *me*!"

When our eyes met hers, they all expressed the one thought: "Forget him!"

But it was all in vain. Marie dropped us all there and then, like a tool that was no longer needed.

"Right!" she said, "I'll look for him on my own."

From that time onwards, she could be seen everywhere riding her delivery bike along the roads. She asked for Séraphin at shop doors and in municipal offices. She roamed around the whole of the Lure district, through the trees left from felling – in spite of the risk of being raped by love-starved woodcutters – calling for Séraphin in the empty, echoing woods on our mountain. She was seen stumbling along in her fine leather shoes through the furrows in the fields stretching as far as the eye could see at Paillerol or Les Pourcelles, asking for information from some ploughman who had been pointed out to her. She would have gone as far as Briançon, as far as Italy. With nothing! Pushing her bike in front of her, she, like Séraphin, was in the clothes she stood up in, without money, just a few bread rolls she had forgotten to deliver in the box on the back of the bike. We had never seen a love like that. It amazed and disturbed us. We questioned each other:

6

"Have *you* ever loved like that?"

"Never, thank God!"

There were noble though wrong-headed souls who ventured up to Lurs, through November floods and March mistral winds so strong they would blow your words back down your throat, to shout to Marie what they thought they knew.

"He's been seen in Malijai! He's been seen in Manosque! He was found wounded at the Dauphine Gate in Sisteron! He came down from the mountains with the sheep at Crau! He's in the St Charles prison at Digne! He's dead! He was buried at Noyers-sur-Jabron!"

Nothing could stop these odd souls from coming to offer their services to Marie and her passion, perhaps to have the pleasure of seeing this victim of love quiver before their eyes. Marie would dart off as though drawn by a magnet towards these lies whose origin no one could remember.

And of course, noble souls were not the only ones who presented themselves as messengers of fate. Certain sly fellows were not slow in coming forward, saying to themselves,

"Séraphin's gone. Good riddance! We'll never see him again. That doesn't change the fact that the girl's pretty and the Dormeurs aren't penniless. Let's move in!"

Before telling their made-up tales, these men would try to make Marie see them in the best possible light, holding her arms and standing straight in front of her so that their faces would be imprinted on her memory. She looked at them intently, but didn't really see them. She would then suddenly push them aside, jump on her bike and speed towards whatever improbable place they had mentioned. There was never anyone there.

People ran to warn the bakery that the girl had gone off once again. Célestat would leap into the truck at any time of the day or night, even if it meant burning the batch of bread. Clorinde would also drop everything and go, leaving us there with the shop door and the drawer of the till wide open, having just served a customer and given the change.

We waited there patiently, our shopping bags empty, the crust of the bread crackling as it cooled, looking more and more tempting the longer the baker's wife stayed away. In the end Tricanote gave up and took over, making sure everyone took note of the money she put into the till and the change she took out of it.

"Heaven forbid . . . !" she would say.

As if anyone had ever doubted her honesty! As if we kept our distance from her because we suspected her of anything like that, and not because of the power to cast spells, which she seemed to have inherited from her mother and which we never dared even mention. We watched her fearfully as she handled our bread and our money. But what could we do?

Then suddenly we would hear the truck sounding its horn down below at the Feignants' Gate. Out we'd rush. Clorinde, with her hat awry, would be squeezed up close to Célestat. Golden-haired Marie would be crouched down behind them next to the bike, indifferent, stubborn as a mule. Although not a word passed her lips, the determined expression on her face clearly said to us, "I'll do it again!"

They had caught up with her at Volx, or Sisteron, or Digne, wherever the barely-whispered name Séraphin had drawn her like a magnet. And we could see her flash with anger and pain. She was being hammered like the blade of a scythe before the harvest. Her cheeks and buttocks had grown thin. Fate had sculpted the lines of her face into something from a Greek tragedy. (You know: those heads that always seem as though they might suddenly begin to scream into the great emptiness.) We said to each other,

"She won't last six months! The state they're in, if the girl dies they'll pack up and leave, and then we'll have to traipse heaven knows where for our bread! *Aïe! Aïe! Aïe!*"

That was the reason – for our bread – that we were all so intent on watching this family in such distress.

It's not as though his daughter was the only thing that worried him. He'd never been fat, but now he was painfully thin. His cheeks stuck to his teeth. His moustache hung limp and uneven on his shrunken top lip. He didn't bother to trim it as he always had in the past. Yet he still went hunting. His bread still tasted as good. Eating it was like rolling in freshly mown wheat on a warm July day. He still smiled at us. He still went to Planche's every Monday at noon to have a glass of *pastis*. But if you really wanted to see how much he'd changed, it wasn't so much his face as his back you needed to examine. From the back, this scrawny man, who nonetheless could knead his hundred kilos of dough every night, seemed as though he was carrying the weight of the world on his narrow, hunched shoulders. Our long narrow street, which bumped downhill like a roller-coaster, is the backbone of our town and we're very proud of it. Célestat went down it every night, his hobnail boots making sparks fly from the uneven flints on the road. It wasn't unusual to hear him rather than see him. Behind our shutters, when we couldn't sleep and the clock struck two, we'd usually say,

"There he is! Célestat's on his way to the oven."

It gave us a selfish pleasure to know this man was awake and out in all weathers while we were warm in bed asleep. Since misfortune had struck him, we still listened to him pass by beneath our windows, but it gave us no pleasure. It seemed as though the hundred kilos he had to knead were being hauled to the oven on his back. We said amongst ourselves,

"Célestat's in a bad way. If he goes on like that, he'll kick the bucket for sure. Then what'll happen? What about our bread?"

And so we tried to bolster him up with our friendship. If we were awake, it wasn't uncommon for one of us to say to his wife,

"Don't worry. I'm going to the bakehouse to keep poor Célestat company for a while."

Two or three – God forgive them! – even used it as an excuse to scout around for some widow on holiday who might be receptive to a serenade. But that was the exception. At three o'clock the others were lifting up the jute sack at the entrance to the bakehouse. Three o'clock in the morning is the time when a man on his own, working or not, has the most tenuous grip on reality. If in danger he hauls in the anchor that attaches him to life. Everything lures him towards eternity. And especially our town baker, who was so miserable and had no water yet in the bakehouse, so that he had to go several times with bucket in hand all the way to the fountain.

Now all the rest of us who live in Lurs, whatever we do, as soon as we put our noses outside the door, we face the sky. It's our pride, and also our pain. There's no problem in the daytime: it's just the sky. It's cheerful even in December when the mistral blows back the branches of our shiny black

9

olives already gleaming with oil, so that they stand out against the blue. But at night! With its expanse clean and windswept, dark and deep, the sky reveals itself to man to show him what he is. A man alone with the sky looks at it first without thinking, then immediately gives in to the obvious and his arms go limp. He puts his over-flowing buckets down on the uneven pebbles. He looks up. He says to himself, "What's the use?" We've all known it. That's why we make sure the sky stays where it is. We have shutters of solid wood, not ones with louvres. We have rep curtains, surprising for people of such modest means, but you can't see through them. The baker is the only one who has to face the night and listen to all it whispers in his ear. And that's why, at this troubled time of his life when we can see him fading away before our eyes, we insomniacs – always the same ones really – took turns in spending time with the baker.

"Hey there! Célestat! I'm not disturbing you am I? I couldn't sleep. Have you heard the wind out there?"

"It's a solid wind all right!" Célestat would say. "Sit down on the sacks and warm yourself."

And that's the way it always was, apart from one particular time. Agaton Chabassut was on duty that night. He was a big, fat, awkward man. He never knew what to do with his height, his weight or his strength, which was considerable. He didn't know how to move through life. You always saw him with his arms dangling by his sides, doing nothing, looking like a top about to spin. I know how he lives, and I'm giving you all these details simply to explain how this same Chabassut never went through a doorway with a curtain the way he should. He always turned around and went in backwards. His big wide behind lifted the whole lot up and then he got tangled in it and could only struggle through, always a bit hot and bothered, by making wild rowing movements with his arms. It's because of this peculiar habit of his that we really only found out half of what happened and had to guess the rest.

And when I say we found out, you know what we're like: Agaton Chabassut had to be at death's door before we heard about it. It was then and only then that he got it off his chest. He was lying under the bedclothes that hung limply over his shrunken body. His feet were together, toes pointing upwards, ready for the coffin. It was in this state that he finally spoke.

"Victoria!" he called out.

She was busy in the kitchen, and thinking he was dying she rushed to his bedside. But she could see that his eyes were still bright as he directed his gaze towards her as far as it would reach, being unable to move his head.

"Victoria!" he said, his voice rattling in his throat. "Do you remember the night I went to see Célestat in the bakehouse?"

"That's what you're thinking about, eh? *Eh bé, vaï*! Well then, you've still got time to waste!"

She had decided to keep on nagging him right to the end to reassure him. And she was right.

"If she's still going on at me," he thought, "I can't be as bad as all that."

Nevertheless, he was still lucid enough to reply, "No, I haven't really."

She sat down by his bedside with a sigh, as she was busy cooking, making a tart for her grandchildren, and the dying man was keeping her from a task which, for the moment, he had no part in.

"That night I was as welcome as the rats under the house! Célestat who was usually so good-natured! I hadn't even had time to turn around and face him, as I was still fighting my way through the curtain, when he said point blank, 'What the hell are *you* doing here?' I didn't know what to do or say. At the same time I could hear the sound of a heavy shower of gold . . ."

"A shower of gold . . ." Victoria said.

"Yes. That's the best way I can describe it. Then I turned around, and there was Célestat frantically gathering up what remained of a pile of coins on the lid of the kneading trough. The coins were spilling into a kind of iron box that he was concealing under the table. That's where the noise was coming from."

"A shower of gold . . ." said Victoria, who had stopped kneading the pastry in the bowl.

"Oh! If you could have seen him! If looks could kill! Well, he calmed down after that. He could see he'd upset me. 'Specially as I've always been good to old Célestat."

"A shower of gold . . ." Victoria repeated for the second time.

"Oh, and then right away Célestat said to me, 'They're twenty sou coins.

11

They're twenty sou coins from the shop. Clorinde didn't have time to count them.' That's what he told me, but . . ."

He tried to shake his head, which already made a faint sound of bones clicking as he had no more muscles to support them.

"But to my mind," he went on, "those weren't twenty sou coins . . . They were too shiny and the colour was too warm. That set me thinking, that made me think Célestat was lying. My grandfather had two gold louis[1] coins he always kept aside. He would sometimes let them fall on to the tiles on the kitchen floor, and he'd say to me, 'If there were a thousand of them, they'd make a sound like that!'"

"What sound?"

"The very sound I heard that night at Célestat's! That sound, Victoria! I've never heard a shower of gold in my life, but I'm sure that was one."

Victoria sighed.

"What have other people's affairs got to do with us?"

"Oh, but wait a minute," Agaton said. "We are all part of this affair. When Séraphin left, he left us all!"

"Exactly! Do *you* know why he left? He had everything, if ever anyone did. Young Marie wanted him and we'd forgiven him."

"We'll never know," Agaton said, staring at his long hands, never good for anything much. "'Specially me. I'll never know!"

Yet it was thanks to him that we others, who were always full of fanciful ideas, eventually found out. After the funeral his tearful wife went round saying,

"My poor man said to me, 'That'll give you something to think about. That's why I'm telling you this. You'll need consoling, and something that intrigues you will help. When you see the misery of others, you forget your own for a while.'"

It was little enough to go on for such a great mystery. Did we really know this man Dormeur whom we called our baker? We could tell that something was gnawing at him inside, like the arch of hot coals that sometimes held the curved shape of the oven, as evanescent as a fiery skeleton, and then suddenly

1 Nineteenth-century gold coins with the head of King Louis Philippe.

collapsed in a mass of red stars. But Célestat, all eaten up like that inside, did not collapse. He was empty, he sounded hollow. Perhaps the framework of his body was only held together by the work of the Holy Spirit. Everyone had a theory. But now that we've been able to retrace the agony all these poor people suffered, thanks to several informants, we say with certainty: that's what made Célestat's life a misery – that unusually heavy sugar box that Séraphin Monge had held out to him and he'd accepted without thinking and without understanding what it meant.

"So that she'll forgive me, if she can, for having briefly come into her life."

What kind of talk was this? It was as though he had thrown Célestat's beloved Marie back in his face; as though there was such a distance between this big man framed in the doorway and the Dormeur family, Marie included, that contempt was the only possible attitude to take.

For weeks afterwards, in spite of Marie's recovery, Célestat felt Séraphin's gesture as an insult. Even more so when he lifted the lid.

"He spat in my face!" he said to himself.

He counted the louis. One by one. At night, in the heavy silence while the bread rose and cooked, he would stack them up in piles. He counted them many times, and sat there with his head in his hands, red with shame. The extraordinary sum this heap of gleaming coins represented cancelled out, in one stroke, all the patient, careful life savings of a worthy man, guilty of a single mistake. Their well-filled bank books – Marie's, Clorinde's, his own, – the odd shares he owned, the block of land he'd bought to build on some day, all that seemed paltry, looked meagre beside the mountain of money which that man who had nothing, that orphan, that beggar had thrown in his face.

He had totted up what the pile of louis represented on a clean sheet of the paper used to line the focaccia bread shelf. He had multiplied the number by the current value ten times over, scarcely able to believe his eyes. He knew the price of land and commercial property. He had counted it up on his fingers. With the contents of the sugar box he had enough to buy the Chiousse bakery in Les Mées, Gallant's in Peyruis, Dehais's in Reillanne, Pacalon's in Oraison, and the best patronized shop of all, Marius Blanc's in Manosque. And even then, it was only by overestimating the clientele of these businesses that you could come close to emptying the casket.

Célestat was appalled by it. The secret choked him. He didn't want to mention it to Clorinde. She was quite capable of saying,

"Think of what we can do with that! We'll buy a kneading machine, so that you don't have to wear yourself out doing it. We'll build straight away on our block of land. And hey! What a villa it'll be! And how about our girl! What a fine husband she can get with what's left over!"

Women are always more practical than men. He mustn't tell Clorinde about it. But this fortune thrown at Marie's feet like a final farewell, what a burden to bear, what a painful blow to his pride. Poor Marie searching everywhere for the man she loved; Marie who had enshrined him in her heart; Marie who could well stay an old maid if Séraphin didn't return. Célestat's blood ran cold at the very thought.

But what humiliated him above all else, to the point of overwhelming him with shame, was his awe of these gold coins, which made him powerless to do anything about them. Time and time again he'd been on the point of going to the river and throwing them to the bottom of the Durance. That very night he'd gone from Lurs to the river with the box in his game bag, but once he'd reached the edge and opened the lid, he just couldn't do it. A moonbeam striking the glinting louis had been enough to make Célestat give up, cowed by the power of that money. He came back to Lurs head bowed and back bent.

Time and time again he'd thought of hurling them into the oven, building up a huge fire to consume them until the louis melted into a lump of slag, unrecognizable as gold. This was easier to do – but no! The moment he opened the box to seize the coins, they would shine so brightly in the firelight that they dazzled him and filled his eyes with tears. No! You just can't burn or destroy the price of five or six bakeries!

But the louis weren't the only problem. There were the three promissory notes to remind him that one day he had almost committed murder. Didon Sépulcre and Gaspard Dupin were resting in peace under the ground while he, Célestat, was left here to brood alone.

What's more, he couldn't even bring himself to destroy these papers that bore witness to a dreadful moment in his life. They fascinated him, and while the bread was baking he would sometimes reread them, the two that Séraphin had cancelled with a big cross after the deaths of Gaspard and Didon, and his still in its original state: *I, the undersigned Célestat Dormeur, baker's assistant at Peyruis, acknowledge having received herewith and in cash . . .*

Célestat Dormeur, baker's assistant at Peyruis . . . When was that? Who was the man who signed that? Surely not the man he was today. Célestat felt his sides, then his legs. He stroked his cheeks where the stubble was growing, and even looked at himself in the little round, flour-stained mirror he hung on the oven door to shave himself sometimes when he looked too scruffy. But it was no use. Célestat couldn't recognize the baker's assistant from Peyruis who had borrowed 1200 francs to buy the bakery at Lurs. He'd written these words in another time, in another world, in another man's skin. And yet it was indeed the same being who felt humiliated by Séraphin Monge's generous disdain and tormented by all the memories that lived forever in that sugar box.

When he had had enough of these thoughts going through his mind as he stared at the pile of gold in front of him, he would tip it back into the box again, replace the folded promissory notes and close the lid. This is what he was doing when Agaton Chabassut and many others long since dead had sometimes caught him unawares.

Like a gravedigger, he had dug a hole in the beaten earth of the bakehouse, under the right corner of the oven, and it was there that he buried the casket, and it was there he went when he couldn't resist making sure once again that he and the wretched life he was leading were not just part of a nightmare.

He wasn't fat before this whole sorry story began; now he was frightening to look at. His eyes were hollow, his belt hung loose on his hips, his trousers were wrinkled all the way down, but the thing you noticed most was the limp, low-hanging seat where his behind used to be. We wondered what he could possibly sit down on.

Some of the more well-to-do amongst us began to think he was looking consumptive and kept their distance from him. Very discreetly they began to get their bread delivered from Brillanne's by the carter. Anyone who hasn't seen them out there in the torrid heat, icy cold or driving rain, waiting sometimes half an hour for the truck at the Saint Antoine turn-off, then taking the long way around the whole village to avoid going past the bakery, doesn't know what showing Christian charity means. Clorinde crucified them publicly in the middle of the street if she happened to meet them there.

"We never see you any more," she would say. Her sarcasm made them squirm like worms cut in two.

"My dear Clorinde, we'd love to, but Dr Jouve has told us both we have to diet. I have a thrombosis and poor Antonin has a blood sugar count of 3 grams 10. So, as you can imagine, bread is out of the question!"

For the rest of us, even tuberculosis would have seemed negligible compared with what we suspected. As a result of a few things we'd heard, we were inclined to imagine the worst, but it was the widow Chabassut who put us on the wrong track. After her Agaton's death, she could find nothing more pressing to do than pour out to us everything the dying man had revealed to her.

"Aïe! Aïe! Aïe!" she said. "If Célestat counts his money, and so often, he's got money worries. No doubt about it."

Money worries! So that was the trouble. And straight away we thought that Célestat's bread didn't taste as good as it used to. We were less worried about the future if, by some misfortune, he had to sell, went bankrupt or died from worrying about money. The insomniacs' dutiful visits dropped off and, within a few weeks, ceased altogether.

We knew that it was in these situations, cooped up alone in the silence of the night with a desperate man, that you were at greatest risk. And so once we had the idea that the baker's suffering had nothing to do with the heart, the mind or the body, but with money, we stopped coming and Célestat found himself alone every night at the bakehouse. We women, who don't often have money at our disposal, even we avoided the bakery so that we wouldn't have to talk to Clorinde, for fear she might . . .

Well, of course! It's easy to explain, now that we know! Now that we all know. But at the time how could we possibly have imagined that if Célestat had money worries, it was precisely because he had too much?

*　　*　　*

Then a man arrived. Who had sent him? What strange thought had directed his wandering to this place to live out his destiny. There were so many villages in the world with bakeries needing assistants. Why had this man chosen ours?

He arrived from God knows where on foot one Tuesday at five in the morning. When he raised the flour-sack curtain, there was thin, exhausted Célestat sitting down, feet splayed and head down on the bench. From what he saw, he too mistook the situation as we had done. "This baker," the man thought, "is worried about money." He'd have left if he'd been free, if fate hadn't already collared him.

"Do you need any help?" he said.

"Who are you?" Célestat asked.

"My name is Tibère Saille," he said. "I'm learning the trade. My parents have a bakery at Lodève, but I've got two sisters."

"Start now!" Célestat said. "Do you know how to unload the oven?"

The man nodded and picked up a paddle. He went to open the oven door.

"Hold on!" Célestat ordered. "You don't even know if it's done."

"Yes I do!" the man said. "From the smell. And what's more we'd better hurry."

And that's how the first person who went out that morning to sweep the front steps came across this completely unknown intruder filling both of Célestat's buckets at the fountain. The presence of this person at five o'clock in the morning was so out of the ordinary that three hunting dogs wandering about from one rivulet to another made a great nuisance of themselves as they harried him noisily all the way to the bakehouse.

His face made a strange contrast under his raven-black beard. He shaved every day but the skin on his round baby cheeks stayed blue, the colour of a plucked guinea fowl. His thick lips seemed to pout as though he was constantly about to cry. At least that's the way we saw him, and seeing him like that we couldn't take to him.

"I don't like the look of him!" we all said in our own different ways. "If *he's* the one who's soon going to make our bread, no thanks!"

We stood with pursed lips in his presence. Mind you, we'd have done the same with anyone. It's our way not to trust people. But with him, as it happened, perhaps we were right.

We waited for him to get down to work. Like a good apprentice, he took over the kneading from Célestat, who could sleep or pretend to, for the fact that he had an assistant didn't relieve the unhappiness that was wearing him down. Nevertheless, we were soon convinced that Tibère Saille was born to be a baker. If he was asleep on his pile of sacks, the smell coming from the oven alone would wake him at exactly the right time. We knew it from the very first time he baked the first batch on his own. This was when Clorinde and Célestat had to set off late at night to fetch Marie, who had ventured as far as Piégut, where it seems someone was supposed to have come across Séraphin in the forest.

On that day, families broke their bread rolls in silence as they made their judgment, and the contents were examined very closely.

"What do you think of our ugly newcomer's bread?"

"Well, I can't really see any difference. It's just as good as the boss's. I was wondering what you'd think of it."

He even made a good job of the savoury focaccia bread made with our olive oil, one of the special things we just must have at Christmas. From that time on we no longer paid any attention to Célestat's state of mind. And yet his mind was still in a state.

Once a week at least, when he had sent his assistant to take a rest in the loft where he slept for the moment, Célestat would dig up the box and give his obsession free rein, convincing himself as he stared at the glint of the golden louis that a whole life of honest toil was not enough to expiate five minutes of guilt. Oh, yes! He hadn't killed Séraphin Monge's family, but it was only because someone else had already done it. And that evil deed wasn't the only one. The pact between the three grandfathers – his, Monge's and Gaspard's – was a blood oath.

On his deathbed, Célestat's father had said to him, "If ever you're in need, just go and ask Félicien Monge. He can't refuse you. Do you understand? He can't refuse! His father would have said the same thing to him as I'm telling you!"

On the day Séraphin had given him the box and Célestat confessed that he didn't have any idea what his father meant, Séraphin replied,

"Go down the well. Then you'll understand!"

One moonlit Sunday night Célestat had gone down alone into the well at La Burlière. It was also on a Sunday thirty years ago that he, Dupin and Sépulcre had met at the La Burlière farm. Now the farm was nothing but an empty space shining in the moonlight between four cypresses softly mourning that strange absence.

The well had practically dried out apart from a whispering stream of rusty water shimmering in the dull light. All Célestat had found on the bottom was a headless skeleton embedded in the stone. It was the body of a young soldier from the old days – one of those who escorted the royal mail coaches when they were transporting State revenue.

So that was the blood oath: three peasants attacking a mail coach to rob it. And the proceeds of that crime were there in front of Célestat, who couldn't stop himself from unearthing it from time to time to gaze at it, enthralled. The fact that he had this treasure and couldn't bring himself to get rid of it preyed on his mind.

Now one evening when he had forgotten to weigh the yeast for the morning, Célestat sent Marie to the bakehouse to fetch it. There were only 200 metres between the shop and the bakehouse where the assistant slept, but he had never yet seen Marie. He was still on trial, which meant that Célestat himself brought his supper to him in the loft. He would only have the right to sit at the boss's table when it was certain he would *agrader* (be considered suitable).

He had sometimes heard the name Marie shouted at the top of the Dormeurs' voices when they went into action at the bakery because their girl had gone off again. But he asked no questions and didn't try to find out what was happening. Experience had taught him that bosses don't like people knowing what goes on in their lives. It was a good job and he'd been looking for one for some time. He was determined to keep it.

Marie threw aside the curtain at the door with the same abruptness she showed in everything she did recently. He saw her suddenly and was quite unprepared. He just stood there stunned, with his mouth open and hands still stuck in the bread dough.

At that time Marie had the face she would retain for more than thirty years. Misfortune had set her beauty, had crystallized it. Before then her beauty was everywhere about her, intangible and hard to define. But since her brush with death had been so prolonged, since love had said goodbye to her before it even said hello, the girlish smile on her lips was seen less and less. She had lost weight, and as a result, the dimples that gave her a charming naïve look had smoothed out at the corners of her mouth. They no longer appeared when she did smile. Even the colour of the iris in her eyes had changed. They now had scarcely perceptible streaks, as if the clear porcelain blue had been exposed to some harmful sun for too long. The complete withdrawal of Séraphin, when she thought she had him, left her tense and questioning, living the rest of her life with no interest at all.

The young man should have been on his guard. Her gaze had never been more distant. With him as with us her eyes were empty, like those captive animals who take no notice of you, refusing your compassion because you look too strangely similar to those who have enslaved them. Marie blamed the whole human race for having lost Séraphin.

Of course you needed time and great concentration to usefully observe what the new Marie had become. Now the young baker was struck full on, and all at once, by Marie's face, body and soul.

Apart from the sunset, which shone interminably on our windows, there was nothing exceptional or harmful happening in Lurs that evening. Nothing troubled our calm existence nor the silence, except for the hurried steps of the girl striding down the street she knew so well and which could hold no surprises for her.

Marie had just come across her godmother, the Marquise de Pescaïré. Since witnessing her goddaughter's resurrection almost from the dead, the old lady had dedicated her old age and her rheumatism to walking innumerable Ways of the Cross at dusk and in all weathers, from one shrine to another along the Bishops' Promenade.

She kissed her as she always did but the Marquise, like everyone else, received no more than Marie's vacant look in return for the sad concern her own eyes expressed. Marie was carrying a kilo of yeast to her father's assistant, that's all. Fate didn't seem to be concerned with anyone in particular.

And yet that evening, in the long street where the wind was blowing against the stone walls, the young baker who saw Marie framed in the doorway thought she was the personification of the whole of that part of the country, and he fell in love with them at once: both the countryside and Marie.

A strange connection also took place between them. A holly-oak leaf from a piece of firewood had flown up and settled in her hair without her being aware of it. The draught from the curtain being raised dislodged the leaf which drifted down to the kneading trough, slowly coming to rest on the fat belly of the dough where the young man's hands were still buried.

"Oh dear!" Marie exclaimed.

The bread dough was sacred. Nothing must sully it, not even an oak leaf. She put her parcel down on the small oven shelf. She leaned over, her hair wafting under the apprentice's nose. It smelled of the box bushes in Lurs, truffles from Les Jarlandes and the wind in the Lure district which whipped around the narrow streets with a sound like washing flapping on a clothes line. He knew then that he would never leave this land again. Marie's still bony hands, with the aquamarine ring loose on her finger because she was still very thin, were well within the young man's field of vision. The hand passed quickly in front of his face after she had seized the oak leaf.

In those days young men still thought *demoiselle* – a young lady – when they came across a girl in the street. He too thought *demoiselle* and his respect was so great that when she turned her back on him to leave, he didn't notice, he never noticed, that she hadn't even seen him.

After that he worked even harder, with even more zeal and dedication. One day Célestat put his hand on his shoulder.

"You'll suit me well!" he said.

"You too," his assistant replied.

"Fine!"

Their agreement was settled. That very evening, the man called Tibère Saille sat at the boss's table, and his serviette in its ring was placed in the drawer beside Marie's. She said good morning and good night to him, but never anything more. That was actually all she could manage to say to any of us.

People said, "No! That's not it! If Célestat has money worries, he wouldn't be taking on an assistant."

"Well then, it's cancer!"

"That wouldn't last so long!"

"And what about all they're going through because of the girl? Surely you don't think that counts for nothing?"

And indeed, the girl was relentless. At the slightest whisper of Séraphin's call carried on the morning breeze, she would leave her delivery round and be off. She would be found with the orders still in the box on her bike in front of some café or going into a church, always enquiring, asking, begging for information. We were beginning to say between ourselves that she would never come back to earth. We began to say that she wasn't right, that her illness had left her with something.

The Marquise nodded her head as she confided in Tricanote,

"Oh dear! Just look, Tricanote. You can see he's taking back all the good he did her!"

What with his daughter and the box, poor Célestat was at his wits' end. He was withering away. He was scarcely fifty-five, but when he put on his clean shirt to go to Planche's of a Monday, the skin of his sunken cheeks sat in folds on his stiff collar.

He was in this state when he noticed that his assistant was suffering too. His eyes were shifty when he sat at the meal table. He ate the least possible and as properly as he could. When Marie leaned over at his side to serve him, which she always did, he sat up stiff and straight as though on inspection, holding himself in as much as possible so that she wouldn't have to brush against him.

"It's not possible!" Célestat thought.

A fairytale idea began to form in his mind. He looked at it from every angle for months before being sure that it was a good one. He observed his assistant when they emptied the coals out of the oven and rubbed over the damp cloths. Actually, Célestat now only came on Saturday night to help with Sunday's double batch. Sitting on piles of empty flour sacks, at five in the morning they would slice some sausage, open the bottle of wine from Les Mées, which Célestat was particularly fond of. They talked about bread and olives, or some sudden unexpected misfortune that had befallen people of the region. Seeing him so thin and hollow-eyed, the young baker was many times on the point of asking him what was troubling him. And just as many times he decided not to, out of respect.

What brought it all to a head was that one morning when they were sitting like that under the dim light of a weak, floury light bulb, they suddenly found themselves staring at each other. They had both carefully avoided it until then, out of a sense of propriety, not wishing to read what was in the other's eyes. That morning, finally, Célestat clenched his fists to strengthen his will and managed to hold his assistant's eye.

"Do you love my daughter?" he asked point blank.

"Yes," said the apprentice.

"Then go out and win her!"

"How?"

Célestat got up and closed his pocket knife.

"Wait!" he said. "Outside under the stone steps, you'll find a mattock. Bring it here."

The young man did what he asked and when he came back he found his boss in the dark corner where the poles for the damp cloths were put against the wall. He stamped on the beaten earth with his heel.

"Dig there!" he said. "But do it carefully!"

"It's not hard . . ." the apprentice said.

Célestat nodded his head.

"I do it often," he said. "Be careful! Lift it up! The hole's not deep."

He had knelt down. With his floury hands he pushed away the loosened earth, which was full of broken pieces of blue orange flower water bottles. He lifted the sugar box over to the sacks. It still looked the same, still blackened by the years it had sat in the smoke on the small ledge at the back of the fireplace in the demolished La Burlière farmhouse. Once the lid had been wiped, there was the picture of the Breton woman still standing at the foot of a Calvary cross, looking out to sea.

"Open it!" Célestat ordered.

The apprentice obeyed immediately.

"Oh Lord!" he said.

He looked at his boss over the top of the box with something like terror in his eyes. Both of them had pale faces the colour of badly cooked bread, the typical complexion of those who work at night and sleep during the day.

"Sit down and listen!" Célestat told him.

He filled a glass with wine and handed it to him. Then he told him the whole story from beginning to end, without omitting anything.

"Oh Lord!" the apprentice repeated from time to time.

Completely enthralled by the contents of the box, he couldn't take his eyes off the golden light that played about the pile of gold in ever-changing shimmering waves, which would suddenly darken as though it had gone cold and just as suddenly glow red like coals from the oven.

"And then . . ." Célestat said.

His voice faded like a lamp about to go out. He could see Séraphin's moonlike face as though it were yesterday as he pushed the sugar box towards him. Célestat remembered how Séraphin's eyes had looked through him, through the walls, seeking another horizon perhaps not of this world. Could there be any greater insult than that indifferent gaze, that complete lack of interest in anything in the world.

"You see," Célestat continued in a hollow voice, "this man Séraphin had none of our appetites, none of our desires, none of our . . . our vices! Even strangers were more like our brothers than this . . . this being who came from the heart of our own race."

"But," the apprentice said, "after all's said and done . . . He never really did anything but good to you, did he?"

Célestat shook his head.

"No," he said. "Before he came, I could be justly proud. All I owned I'd earned. He's made me look small. He's brought me lower than the earth. When he pushed that box full of gold towards me, I could hear him even though he said nothing. He was saying to me, 'There you are! Since that's what's most important to you! Since you're content with that! Take it! Wallow in it! All your holidays have come at once!' If I'd been the only one to suffer . . . but no! My daughter had to be tainted by it too. Do you know what he said as he left? 'Give it to her when she gets better, so that she can forgive me, if she can, for having briefly entered her life.' That's what he said to me. At first I didn't understand what he meant. You see, Marie was at death's door. I was confused. It was only afterwards, when I thought about it, that I took it to be what it really was: an insult."

Célestat stopped speaking. You could hear the emotion in the apprentice's heavy breathing. Both of them had their eyes riveted to the glow of the gold.

"My parents have a few of these coins," the apprentice said gravely, "oh, maybe ten . . . or twelve . . . hidden in a wardrobe. But there's enough in there for . . ."

"To buy at least five bakeries," Célestat said. "I know. I've counted them."

"But this Séraphin you've been talking about, he must have owned something else?"

"No, nothing! He had nothing! He left with what he stood up in: his pants, shirt and jacket. That's all. And his bike. I tell you, he had absolutely nothing!"

He was silent for a moment.

"And that's the main reason," he said, "why the weight of that insult is so hard to bear alone."

"But why are you telling me all this?" the apprentice said. "I only work for you."

"Do you love my daughter?"

"I said yes."

"Then take that!" Célestat ordered. "No! Wait!"

He sank his hands into the pile of gold. The stream of coins clinked as he pulled out the only promissory note he hadn't destroyed: his own.

He took a wallet, white with flour, out of the deep pocket in his baker's apron. In it he kept two 1000 and one 500 franc notes folded in four. He intended to surprise Marie at Christmas with a motorized delivery bike. That was the money he had set aside for it. Too bad! Marie would have to pedal for one more year. That would do her a lot of good, given the state she was in. He always kept that money on him for fear that Clorinde would do something more sensible with it.

He spread the promissory note out on the marble used for rolling the focaccia dough. And there, with the miller's thick pencil, he swiftly drew two lines across the document that Félicien Monge had written more than thirty years before, and between them wrote: *Paid in full.* He folded the document over the money and put it on top of the pile of gold. He snapped the lid shut, saying to his apprentice,

"There! Take this box. Take it! Go and look for Séraphin Monge."

"But where?" said the bewildered young man.

Célestat thought for a moment.

"He worked as a woodcutter for a while when he left the State orphanage. He said it was somewhere up there around Enchastrayes or Fours, I'm not too sure. Anyway, it was somewhere in the Barcelonnette Valley. Go and look. It's very likely he went back there – without even thinking where he was going. You see, he didn't know anything else. Go and look. I'll give you 500 francs over and above your monthly wages. And when you find this Monge fellow, throw his damn box back in his face. From me! Don't forget to tell him, 'It's from Célestat Dormeur!'"

"But what about the bread while I'm away?"

"I did it before you arrived. I'm a bit off colour, but I'll do it again. Anyway, I don't want to see you again until you've found Séraphin!"

"What if I can't find him?"

"Then don't come back! And keep the lot! That'll console you!"

"You're not being very kind ..." Tibère said with a sigh. "When do I leave?"

"Straight away. Go up to your room and pack your bag. I want to see you disappearing around the corner of the street before sunrise."

Célestat was there, standing in front of the curtain at the door of the bakehouse, when the first rays of the sun struck the shutters on the presbytery windows. Further down the street, the dark silhouette of the baker's assistant was disappearing into the distance at the bottom of the steep incline.

"With *him*, Marie will have children," he thought. "And fine ones at that!"

Now he could entertain such positive thoughts. Once the box had left the bakehouse, his conscience was clear at last.

II

WHEN SÉRAPHIN MONGE ENTERED OUR LIVES FOR THE FIRST TIME
we were all sitting around the wood stove at Auphanie Brunel's. The
door opened and there he was. He looked as though he'd come from the
Champanastay river, which was carrying as much stone and earth as
water.

We all turned around and watched the patch of mud form on his trousers.
His clothes were in a dreadful state. He stood there, a large figure framed in
the doorway. He was the only thing between us and the storm, and our only
thought was to get away from it. He didn't say good evening, neither did we.
We shouted,

"Come in or go out, but whatever you do, shut the door!"

He stepped in and pushed the door shut.

His eyes didn't settle on anything, but his gaze seemed lost somewhere
between the air and our bodies. As he moved he left traces of the rainstorm
in the sawdust on the floor, and the glasses trembled on the marble tabletops
to the sound of his footsteps.

Auphanie was leaning against the counter, her breasts cradled in her
folded arms. She was stunned, staring wide-eyed as though this was the
first time in her life she'd ever seen a man. But for the rest of us, it was once
seen soon forgotten. We had other things on our minds. We were engaged
in the serious business of comparing which were the worst incidents on our
mountain the community could remember. We were arguing hotly and not
very amicably about the exact date when the iron bridge was finally swept

away. It had been deteriorating there across the river for thirty years, and in all those thirty years our river had never regained the crystalline colour it offered us like a gift.

We had got to the stage in our discussions of arguing over a few additional gaps in the pines that the flood waters had uprooted in such and such a year, or a few tons more or less of aggregate dumped along the dike that been built more than a century ago to stop the water undermining the banks.

There's nothing worse in our part of the country than not making good use of your hands. We'd herded the cattle and loaded the hay into the racks. The women were busy with the milking. Now we were there around the stove, repeating and emphasizing to each other the fact that no, we'd never seen anything like this. It was no use the more rational among us shrugging their shoulders and saying we were too close to it to judge, we put our faith in what we'd heard when the stranger came in. The continuous roar of the Champanastay in flood had reached us, even in this haven of tranquillity: a café with oak parquet floor, marble-topped tables, decorated glasses, green rustic scenes painted on the oval panels of the gold-painted counter, between the burlesque male figures supporting the framework. It had reached us despite the comfort of the huge stove, taller than we were, with its pipe disappearing into the high ceiling. It had reached us despite the familiarity of the Claquescin poster and the notice proclaiming the law against drunkenness in public places.

It wasn't for nothing that we were smoking so heavily in the morning as soon as we got up that the coughing and spitting made our chests red-raw. It wasn't for nothing that we were drinking enough to shorten our lives by ten years. And last but not least, it wasn't for nothing that we furtively watched the sway of Auphanie's glorious arse as she moved about the café. We drank more than we could afford, more than usual, more than was reasonable, just to have her presence more often in the air around us when she brought our drinks. We did it because out there we couldn't get away from the noise of all those crushing forces of nature.

Although it was never more than 500 metres from where we lived, for the last twenty-two days we'd had to use our umbrellas to get to Auphanie's each evening, and we hated that. Most of the time we'd take off our jackets and put them over our heads. An umbrella looks sissy. Except when the relentless downpour had lasted for twenty-two days! All our clothes were damp, so we just had to use an umbrella.

To begin with, the Champanastay had made its usual grumbling sound when the south wind scatters the snow over the forests and feeds the river with new water. But now it was roaring. It lashed the banks with a thick brown flow in which twenty-kilo rocks struck the granite boulders dividing the current, making sparks fly.

At that time of year it should have been snowing as far as 1500 metres, as far as the outskirts of the village. The people of Pra-Soubeyran, whose fields are up above us, should already have been walking on new snow when they went out of their doors. Instead, it was raining up to 3000 metres. You could hear the almighty, all-encompassing song of the rain right up to the furthest limit of the larch forest. You could hear it much higher in the sky than the last trees. It moved unstable rocks; it undermined the tunnels under the marmots' nests.

Sometimes, when a hole in the sky drew up the mist from deep down below, you could see the hard glacial snow dwindling at the top of the pyramids and leaning towers that form the jagged line of our strange mountains. In the hollows you could see crevasses with patterns of dark snow appearing, and water trickling through the ravines still sparkling clean.

One man who was greedy, keeping his flocks for as long as possible in the sheepfolds up on the Lauzanier, had just got back. He was like a solid block of mud. Auphanie had made a terrible fuss when she saw him turn up, hurrying behind him with a floor cloth and a bucket of sawdust.

He told how, in the mountain stock routes, the sheep slipped on the woodsmen's timber chutes and caused a mudslide; how two lambs had died rolling one after the other into that teaming torrent; how, if we didn't believe him, we only had to go and take a look up there under the shaky roof of Krüger Jauffret's ruined barn, where he penned 5000 animals.

He also told us that the Ubayette creek was absolutely prancing along. (That was the word he used.) He said that normally you had to go right up to the stream before you could hear it, but now – (and in fifteen years of taking the sheep up into the mountains for the summer, he'd never seen that) – it was five metres wide and two metres high, and it was black. He also said it was all right for him, as he was taking it slowly down towards the Crau and the sheep would get a wash on the way. He said he wasn't worried for himself, but that *we* should definitely be wary.

He repeated the word *wary* three or four times with a rather threatening look on his face. He had the red face of those who look to Nature for everything. They're as cruel as she is. Whenever they can, they use her weapons, thinking nothing of lighting fires in her forests to get better grass. They pay her back for all the bad things she does to them, blow for blow. We could hardly wait for him to go, this bird of ill-omen in league with the bad weather. We're peace-loving but determined people, and there were even a few of us ready to help him on his way across the threshold. He must have sensed it. He didn't wait any longer. Shaking all the mud he could on to the floor, he went out and slammed the door behind him.

We were still laboriously pondering the shepherd's words when the stranger entered, and you can imagine how little attention we paid to him, given the state of mind we were in at the time.

He walked in slowly without saying a word. If we weren't interested in him, he was hardly interested in us either, for he went up to the counter without looking to left or to right, as if we ten or twelve strapping fellows sitting around the stove, each weighing between eighty and a hundred kilos, were no more substantial than a puff of smoke. We like people to greet us, even if we don't reply, so it was at that moment we started to pay the man some attention.

And yet . . . I've been going over that moment in our collective lives for twenty years. Now that they're all dead or departed, now that there's scarcely anyone left here apart from myself, today as on that day, I feel as though I never really saw him.

Actually, he already had his back to us. He was at the far end of the room, in front of the counter. Auphanie was the only one looking at him in the face.

There is often a lone woman at the crossroads in our part of the world, a woman who arrives here, leaving her past behind, preferring once and for all the fear of loneliness to the fear of men. Ordinary, reasonable people could never understand her.

We told our wives she had a long nose and a shock of blonde hair that hid her face. We told them that when she leaned them on the counter, her breasts must have weighed three kilos each, and they can't have been a pretty sight wobbling about under her nightgown. We also told them that she had an under-arm odour you could recognize ten feet away. As they hated Auphanie because she was a free spirit, they still believed she was ugly even when they met her. Our consciences were clear.

If we hadn't seen Auphanie change to a pillar of salt when she saw the stranger, then run her eyes all over his face as he stood in front of her, perhaps . . . But no. I'm just trying to find some excuse for us. To tell the truth, we took a dislike to the man from the moment he came in. But who knows? If only she hadn't said to him the moment he reached the counter,

"You're wringing wet."

She always spoke to everyone with the familiar *tu*, but she had used the polite *vous* to him, even though the fellow standing there dripping water all over her floor didn't look to us the sort who would make a huge impression on her. Thinking back on it later, it seemed to us she had always been waiting for him.

"I'm sorry," the man said.

"No. Don't apologize! That's not what I meant. I meant you! You're wringing wet!"

It was true. We were seeing him from the back and he was steaming like a horse after a long haul.

"It's a long time since I set out," the man said.

She had already filled a small glass which sat clear and trembling on the lead counter-top.

"No," he said. "Give me a hot coffee, and then I'll be on my way."

"Are you going far?"

"Oh," the man said, "perhaps . . ."

He searched in his pockets to pay her. He pulled out a small coin which rang on the metal counter. Auphanie stopped looking at the man and looked at the coin.

"Is that gold?" she said.

"It's all I've got," he replied. "I'm sorry . . . I left in such a hurry . . ."

Dirt had become encrusted in the engraved portrait of Louis-Philippe, the king of France, when it had lain in the soldier's pouch at the bottom of the well at La Burlière. It had been sitting there deep in Séraphin's pocket from the time he had gone down to see what was there.

"Keep it . . ." Auphanie said. "What can I do with a gold coin? For one cup of coffee . . ."

It was at this point that Polycarpe made his entrance. Whenever he came in he almost knocked the door down and you could almost hear him saying the words that summed up his whole attitude, "I'm a man of importance."

He *was* a man of importance, and to look even more important he never went out just in hobnail boots like the rest of us: he extended them with leather gaiters.

His eyes looked innocent enough but the innocence ended there. That clear candid gaze came from his mother and we all hoped that up there in heaven she was now being severely punished for it. There were countless occasions when we shouldn't have trusted him, but in spite of everything we still fell for that guileless expression in his eyes. We still weren't sure whether it didn't reflect his soul. For example, when he was just about to trick us, he'd say,

"What? Don't you believe me?"

Our faces went red with shame and, with a heavy heart, we assured him to the contrary.

Added to that, Polycarpe was a man who supported his family by killing trees. He owned forests of spruce trees and he made his fortune by having them destroyed. We're not actually as sensitive as all that, and we only put it in those terms deep down in our hearts. All the same, we wouldn't have invited him to have a meal with us without consulting others and making the fact known, any more than we would willingly have the wholesale butcher who came to choose our calves, the slaughterman who came to kill the pig, or even Calixte Dépieds, who took away our dead and then put them neatly into their boxes and into our family tombs.

There are trades we know are necessary, but we still don't want to be forced to look at them. The men who exercise them are given a wide berth in the street, as even brushing against them seems shameful, above all when they arrogantly pride themselves on their profession, as Polycarpe did.

Yet at that time the man was in a critical situation. He was losing more than any of us. Losing that money was like a wound, a mortal wound. The rest of us from up there had been anxious for the last three years. Our land was slipping away from under our feet.

Who knows what they thought down in the valley. You couldn't really blame the weather. It had been what it always was – unreliable, controversial – perhaps a little more than usual. There had been 1200 millimetres of rain the year before, and this one was shaping up the same way. But it wasn't the first time this anomaly had occurred in our region. From time to time the land here reminds us that it's still very young. No. The real worry was what was happening up there in a locality called Pra-Colombelle, which happened to belong to this same Polycarpe.

Up there were certain family parcels of land that had never been touched and we didn't know why. It was an amphitheatre of purple beeches, which the old people called *fayards*. Planted in rows on the mountain side, they quietly watched us go about our lives as though they were at the theatre. When you were beneath these trees, they whispered to you familiarly because they knew your forebears, who had been hunting in their shade for 300 years. Their branches sat like sails on a ship, and when the wind imitated the sea swell you thought you could hear them driving the land in front of them forward on its eternal voyage. There were easily 400 or 500 of them. The smallest were twenty-five metres high.

In the autumn they rolled out a carpet of gold under our feet, and when the setting sun carded its light through the small branches, the trunks lit up green as young shoots of wheat. Neither brush nor forest plants grew in their shade. We never went up into these beeches in a group. When one of us took that path it was because his heart was heavy and he needed to be alone. We let him go up and languish a while in that profound peace.

They were the last trees growing below the mountain tops. They backed on to an army of rock pinnacles with sharp ridges which sometimes crumbled with a sound of shattering glass. These were trunks of stone in the same terraced formation on the slope as the real trees. They were the face of a moraine. No glacier had moved it for a very long time, but one had left the sunken imprint of its weight in the hollow of the mountain. The large bed was crushed and folded as though kneaded by the heaving of some gigantic coupling, and it seemed to be recently deserted. All that was left was the tiny trickle of a stream disappearing stealthily between the stones.

About two years ago someone bold enough to go looking for a sheep had had the fright of his life there. It had been quite a while since we'd killed the only animal we had a legal right to hunt for all year. The wardens of the reserve never tired of warning us whenever they came to Auphanie's for a drink,

"Don't forget. Five hundred to a thousand francs fine and twelve to eighteen months in prison! A warning to anyone wanting to try it!"

There was always someone wanting to try it, and the one we're concerned with now was no angel. He knew the mountain like the back of his hand. You'd have to, going out like that at three in the morning when it was pitch black to catch the herd of deer at dawn as they were going up to the pass, 3000 metres high.

When he appeared again he was encased in a crust of mud. He told us that when he was leaving the cover of the trees at the part of Pra-Colombelle where the rock and the forest were usually one unbroken piece of land, he had fallen in a hole – he, the gun, and the rolled up bag holding the knife and the cleaver for breaking the bones. It took him till morning to get himself out of that hole, and it was only then he discovered it was a fissure that went all the way around the face of the moraine, clearly outlined, deeply indented and gaping wide.

"Just like when you start to lift up the skin of a hare after you've skinned the feet," he explained.

That's when we took to wandering around under Polycarpe's beeches for other reasons than just wanting to see them again. We had the awful feeling that the small amount of land bequeathed to us was being ruined. The fissure against the pinnacles of the moraine got wider by the month. (In our panic, it seemed more like by the week.) Strange swellings came up in the ground under the trees like suspect patches of mushrooms, then they began imitating white-capped waves on the sea. It was as though moles the size of oxen were arching their backs under the moss. One day a beech tree was lifted up on one of these mounds slowly sliding down the slope. Sometimes the heavy swollen abcesses seemed unable to drag along any further and burst open with a gush of clear water. Then, shining deep inside, you could see the same flesh of blue clay that was tearing apart higher up on the face of the moraine.

"Good for business!" Polycarpe thought.

He had just been hopefully eyeing that hundred-year-old beech beginning to lean its top towards its neighbour. He had several times intended to knock down these trees, but the parcels of land were marked out in mauve on the plan of the commune and the Forestry Commission maps. The word *marmenteaux* – mature forest not to be felled – was written in full right across each plot. That meant that this forest was classified as a historic monument and no-one, not even the owner, could lay a finger on it.

"You can't call the place your own any more!" Polycarpe sighed. "Talk about the Revolution! A lot of good that did."

A warden came down one morning covered in clay up to his thighs. He left marks behind him all the way to the post office where he made a telephone call.

"You should come and take a look at what's happening up here!" the post mistress heard him say.

They came – a whole pack of men from the Forestry Commission landed in the district with their green caps and gold braid. With remarkable agility for people with silver hair, they went up among Polycarpe's golden trees, following close behind a man in leggings who could climb like a monkey, apparently keen to get there before anyone else. This man seemed to be anticipating with indecent relish what we most feared. We heard he was a geologist. He was very short-sighted and, apart from his aubergine nose, you wouldn't have given him a second look. And yet he was the one who intimidated us. He was the one we'd clapped our eyes on, the one we watched suspiciously.

We saw the group go up past the long-deserted hamlet of Les Aupilles, and then we lost them as it was misty. It had been raining during the morning, and the evening looked as though it would be no better. However, a few of us who had brought back a pair of binoculars from the war were watching the area where they were working. And when the group came out of the mist they were there, ever-watchful, to tell us what they saw.

"They look as though they're coming from a funeral!"

"Well!"

"They've got faces a mile long!"

"And what about the geologist?"

"He's writing something in his notebook."

"*Aïe*! And what about Polycarpe?"

"He's laughing his head off!"

"*Aïe, aïe, aïe!*"

We peered as hard as we could as the procession of men descended the mountain. In spite of the slope, they seemed to come down more slowly than they went up. Now there were some among them who loved trees. I saw one or two who were almost weeping. They left the geologist behind with us. He would take the bus the following day.

Using a table raised to the right incline and three kilos of flour kneaded by Auphanie, he explained this "purely local and superficial telluric epiphenomenon" to us as well as he could. He showed us three times, making the fat mound of kneaded dough roll down the bed of dry flour he had scattered over the marble tabletop.

"There you are," he said, "that's what it is and that's not what it is. You're not specialists, so I won't go into the details. But *grosso modo*, that's it."

There were lots of objections.

"*Grosso modo*! That's easily said! What about the trees then? We've been told a hundred times not to take out the trees because they hold the soil together. They've even had us plant thousands of them! And aren't there trees here? Trees more than twenty metres high, what's more! With trunks like barrels!"

He had a sympathic smile and nodded as we spoke.

"Elsewhere, yes. Here, no. It's a pocket of clay rolling on a plate of shale.

Water has got in between the plate and the clay moving over it. There you have it! As for the trees, here they are!"

He took a box of Swedish matches from his pocket.

"To scale!" he said.

He stuck ten, fifty into the dough. He stuffed the fat mound full of them. He didn't need to tilt the tabletop any further. The spongy mass rolled at the same speed right to the abyss, which was the edge of the table. We could hear the wooden matches cracking. We looked on, aghast. Polycarpe's smile was so wide you could see all his false teeth.

"Well then! There's only one thing to do!" he was saying. "Cut them down! Tomorrow I'll go and work something out with the people of La Drôme. They've been looking for wood to make good beams for ages!"

That was not what was worrying us. The floury mound dragging the trees along might perhaps be going to rush down into the valley where we clung precariously on the slopes with our church, our cemetery, our houses and our café.

"But where will it stop? When will it stop?"

The geologist opened his arms and shrugged his shoulders. It was no use putting to him arguments about building dams, jetties, walls, trenches – all of which would have cost more than the lot of us put together with our flocks, barns and woollen socks. He just stood there with his arms wide open, nodding his head. No, no! We could throw all the money in the world at his feet. He explained that it was already useless. As for the rest, he wasn't God the Father.

"Clay is a neutral substance. Nothing comes of it. It's the pus of the earth, it's festering. We don't know if it's one or fifty metres thick. It's a substance that only can do one thing: press heavily, let itself slide down the incline. That's what we're dealing with: clay!"

The geologist left the next morning. We'd been anxious to find out all about it. Now we knew the worst. We knew, and there was no solution to the problem. Only Polycarpe was happy, standing there rubbing his hands and flashing his gleaming teeth in that greedy, lustful smile. He looked around him for someone to offer their services, but we just stared into space.

One day he went down to Barcelonnette, coming back that evening with a man he kept holding by the shoulder, no doubt for fear that he might escape. He was a squat, strapping fellow who planted his legs solidly on the ground as though he had just killed a snake, turning a little on his heel with each step to crush it and affirm his supremacy. He certainly crushed all of us with his scornful attitude from the very first day.

He was from Piedmont and thought he was stronger than everyone else because he was just that much poorer than we were. And so, this Piedmontese joyfully spat into his hands shouting *Porca Madonna!*, an oath from those parts. We saw him stride away like a defiant conqueror and disappear into the mist of Pra-Colombelle.

He came back three days later at about four o'clock with his axe on his shoulder and the steel wood-splitting wedges in his sack jingling like mad. He was still shouting *Porca Madonna!*, but this time it was at the top of his voice and it was directed at Polycarpe. As he thought Polycarpe was in here, he nearly kicked the door down to get in. Auphanie remonstrated with him as soon as he entered.

"What's this! Where were *you* brought up! Trying to frighten everyone, are you? Well, you don't frighten me!"

She had rushed out from behind her counter, brandishing the wooden rolling pin she'd been using on some pastry. The look in her eyes meant business behind the curtain of dishevelled hair. She looked like a gorgon, with her two breasts as the line of first defence.

The Piedmontese sighed and sank into a creaking chair. The sack of wedges clanged on the floor when he put it down. He said,

"I saw a wave of earth as high as a wave on the sea, *corpo d'un accidente*! I swear to you! I'd just started felling the tree. I'd just given it about three chops with the axe! And small ones, I swear to you! Absolutely no reason for it to fall on me! I had just enough time to get out of the way to avoid the wave! I heard it crash like a real wave when it breaks! And while this was going on, the tree had lifted me up on its roots. I was clinging on to my axe still stuck in the trunk, and when it was horizontal I fell on it face first. And just as well! If I'd jumped backwards the wave would have buried me! All the roots of the tree were standing out behind me like a wheel. It's no joke! Just go and look! The beech had been pulled out by the roots like a leek! Like a leek, I tell you!"

He suddenly dashed forward, dragging us along with him for a metre or two, as we had grabbed hold of him by the belt.

"Get out of my way. I'm going to kill him!"

"What? Didn't he warn you? Didn't he tell you that our ground moves?"

"No, he didn't warn me! No, he didn't tell me!"

He grabbed his axe. Murder was not only in his eyes but also in his muscles. Four of us could hardly hold him down on his chair, and we're no weaklings. Those who were the weakest, plus the priest who had arrived on the scene took him to task and tried to reason with him. On the pretext of trying to comfort him, they slowly but surely got him drunk on Fernet-Branca (a drink Auphanie despaired of selling and which she gave us at a special price). We stayed with him until he fell asleep. The six of us carried him to Krüger Jauffret's barn and left him there between four bales of hay to sleep off his Fernet-Branca.

This was just at the time when Polycarpe usually came to drink a few glasses of his favourite, Clacquescin.

"Ah! There you are. Do you ever owe us a big favour!"

He looked surprised.

"Me? Do I owe you something?"

"Oh, hardly anything at all! You haven't seen your Piedmontese for a while, have you?"

"Actually, I'm looking for him. I have to pay him his wages."

"Don't pay him anything at all! And if you take our advice, you'll stay indoors until he leaves!"

So fond were we of deluding ourselves – as everyone does – that we hadn't gone up Pra-Colombelle way near Polycarpe's beech trees for quite some time. After hearing the report of the Piedmontese, who disappeared without a warning, each of us in turn stealthily made our way up there on the pretext of getting branches to have some roaring fires in our hearths. We went as soon as our work gave us a bit of free time; but we went there alone, just as we did when that forest was our place of meditation.

It was winter then and we could easily see that the bare trees embossed in the snow were trapped in the earth they could no longer trust. They began to lean over on the slope, drawn by the hole being left as the clay slid on the shale plate way down in the depths. From one day to the next they were like tangled masts of ships moored too close together in too small a port. They were pushed up and compressed this way and that by the slow swelling that raised the earth up like dough. It was an armada of beech trees with flags flying, saluting each other for the last time before being forced into battle or breaking up as they collided. Sometimes at night in a stormy wind, only too happy to knock them down at last, we could hear them cracking as they clashed with a noise like a naval battle.

We came down the mountain filled with a terrible sadness. We came down the mountain blocking our ears so that we couldn't hear any more of the deep moan of the tree trunks as they laboured with each other, cracking with pain. We came down the mountain sick at heart because we could do nothing about it. We didn't mention it to anyone, but deep within us, we had heard the pitiful call of those beeches saying to each of us individually, "And what about you men? What are you doing? You who think you're so strong? What now? Are you going to let us die? We could make trees to supply your wood for more than a thousand years!"

We went to drink at Auphanie's and watch the sway of her hips simply to drown our consciences imploring us in vain up there among the trees.

It was in those dark days that Polycarpe began to spy on us. He closely watched those who had least money, those who had the most debts and those who had the largest families. He always had money in hand. He offered advances, loans without interest. He didn't even mention the trees, but we knew what the bargain would be if we accepted anything he offered.

That day when Séraphin came into our lives (and we didn't know his name or even if he had one), Polycarpe Coquillat hadn't yet been able to con anyone. He wasn't any more intelligent than us, but no-one could equal him in quick thinking when his own interests were involved. He saw immediately that the man was desperate and, that being the case, he could be ruthlessly exploited. Polycarpe knew it without seeing his face, just by looking at the set of his shoulders, which were wider than his, and his height, which was taller.

"Now, *this* fellow . . ." he thought, and touched his arm. Auphanie was still standing in front of Séraphin, not sure what to do. Séraphin was still holding the cold coin he was going to use to pay for his coffee.

"It's on me!" Polycarpe said. "Are you looking for work?"

And inspired by a phenomenal stroke of intuition, he added straight away,

"Do you want to work alone?"

It was at that moment that Séraphin began to nod his head. Polycarpe tapped him on the back.

"Fine!" he said. "You can have a farm in the forest all to yourself. Nobody wants to live there any more. I've got 400 beech trees to fell. What do you say? They're as high as pillars in a cathedral. What do you say?"

Séraphin kept on nodding his head in agreement. Polycarpe gave the assembled company an imperious look, as our silence was indicating disapproval. But we were used to being afraid of him. We wouldn't have budged, even if he had a knife in his hand to kill the man.

At the same time as he noticed the downpour that was drowning the whole region, Polycarpe suddenly realized the man was wearing a vest. He exclaimed in alarm,

"Is that your bike outside? But where's your bag? Haven't you got anything else?"

He made as if to take off his jacket, as he would have done for a sweating mule just before a storm. Séraphin lowered his eyes and stared at the bottom of his coffee cup.

"I left in a hurry . . ." he whispered.

"Have you something to change into?"

"No," Séraphin said.

"Give him . . ." Polycarpe said.

He reached out his hand towards the man's vest. He felt it and then, with a look of surprise, crushed it between his fingers as though he wanted to test the quality of the material. He had just realized that it was strangely dry.

41

"Auphanie!" Polycarpe called in a voice of authority. "Give him something to drink, give him something to eat, and give him a bed!"

"No!" Auphanie replied. "What about my reputation?"

"Your reputation's as bad as it can get. You know what you can do with your reputation!"

"You can't give me orders! You've never been able to!"

We were used to it. They always spoke to each other at the top of their voices and as rudely as possible. They delivered vicious home truths to each other with a murderous look in their eyes. The waves of hatred constantly battered the walls around them.

"I'll see you tomorrow," Polycarpe said to the man.

He left, with the echo of his footsteps on the wooden floor still ringing in the air. It was as though crushing others wasn't enough for him, as though he had to tell himself all the time that he was crushing them, as if he could only feel that divine sensation by constantly talking himself into it.

In spite of the deluge outside, Auphanie made us clear off very quickly. Until then she'd been taking twenty minutes to wipe one balloon glass, as she gazed into the man's face. Admittedly, since the rain had started coming down so relentlessly on to the riverbed of the Champanastay, we had to be driven away from the stove.

What happened next behind the closed window of the café, when the room, the kitchen, the corridors, the whole house dangerously perched above the torrent, were dark and filled once more with the roaring sound of the waters? Auphanie Brunel's memory is the only source. She alone can tell the story.

"I gave him something to eat and drink," she said later. "I kept talking. He never replied. I kept looking at him, but he still managed to avoid my eyes. Holding the lamp, I led the way to his room – the electricity had been off for a week. I closed the door firmly behind him. I began to suffer. Everything that was happening outside made me think how precarious life was. Have you never heard that sound? Everything had forced me to think of it for the last week, plainly, forcibly. I could see the faded gold letters against the starry blue background on the top of the rotting entrance to the cemetery: you can still read it: *You who pass by, remember that what you are, so were we, and what we are, so you will be.* On the day I go under that porch feet first and start becoming what they are, will what I dared not do carry much weight? I stood it until two in the morning. Then I got up as I was and went to his door. I didn't knock; the door scraping against the floorboards was enough to wake him. He looked at the candle held high in my hand and perhaps also my face, perhaps . . . Do I know? He was in the shadows, black against the white wall, still and quiet. Not a sigh came from him. And I assure you, at that time any man I stripped for couldn't do anything but reach out his arms to me, and the rest!

"Oh, you can laugh now," she said to that group of gloomy ghosts from whom no human joke or human suffering had ever drawn a tear, a smile or an expression of surprise from time immemorial.

"To laugh, or not to laugh. Is that really the question?" was the reply from the depths of the shadows. "Our man could have been impotent. What was he doing alone there with you?"

She shut her dazzled eyes. She saw herself throw back the sheets covering Séraphin, who was as naked as the day he was born. She saw him, his cock raised eagerly towards her, but at the same time he was calmly shaking his head, meaning no, no, no. She let herself fall towards him with all the weight of her seductive body. She was stopped short by his outstretched arms holding her away from him. His arms were enormous, cold and disheartening; his huge hands were spread to push her away. She re-enacted that unequal struggle, which she finally abandoned, defeated, exhausted and humiliated.

"I'm telling you that he didn't *want* to make love, you bunch of weaklings! You've got no balls, any of you! I never said he couldn't!

"He pushed me away," she repeated to herself, "in the same way as you won't fondle a wet dog, but by the sheer force of his arms! He pushed me away – not because he was horrified, revolted or mean – but with a kind of pained compassion."

And the following morning, you had to admit that Auphanie didn't have the exhausted look of a woman who has just experienced a night of love. There was no happiness in her eyes. She was like the rest of us: watching

43

the mountain, the mountain soaked with water, the mountain that seemed to be dissolving.

We came out early to find out what had happened. And the sky invited us out of doors. It had cleared. When the fog had disappeared, a wonderful expanse of blue and white was spread out over the land. When it reappeared we hardly recognized it, and this time only twenty days of rain were enough to make us forget what it could be like. It bathed our eyes; it revealed itself to us with the brazenness of a seductive woman, but at the same time it also revealed that menace hanging over our heads we'd been able to forget for a while. It showed us Polycarpe's beech forest: now a gigantic shipwreck.

"Anyone who goes to work up there," said Peyru with the crooked mouth, whom we called Cassandra, "anyone who goes to work up there won't make old bones."

And yet there *was* someone who was going up there; someone who was slowly climbing up the alpine hunters' path; someone who seemed scarcely a metre high from down here; someone we couldn't take our eyes off as he made his way up the mountain, even if our bums froze on the railing of the bridge, our best observation point. Auphanie was with us. The percolator could whistle its head off down there behind the counter. With our hands shielding the bright light from our eyes, we all looked as though we were giving a military salute to some hero who had already died.

"Didn't you tell him" someone asked Auphanie. "Didn't you tell him what happened to the Piedmontese?"

She nodded her head dispiritedly.

"I even exaggerated it! I told him about the wave of earth. I even told him that for the price of a cup of coffee, Polycarpe was sending him to his death. That's it exactly!" she cried. "To his death!"

She had just noticed the man in question, who was more than a head taller than the rest of us. As usual, he had crept quietly into the group. Auphanie stood there defying him, with her hands on her hips and a dangerous look in her eye. We'd only once or twice seen her anywhere as angry as this since she landed in our midst. But Polycarpe was used to her bad moods. That wasn't what was worrying him.

"And what did he reply to that?" he asked.

44

She lowered her head.

"He shrugged his shoulders. He moved me aside, as I was in his way. He said to me as he left, 'I'm going to a place where they're calling for me.'"

"A good lad!" Polycarpe exclaimed. "An example to us all! But," he said suspiciously, "surely he's said something more to you since last night?"

Auphanie swallowed three times before replying.

"He told me he was an orphan and his name was Séraphin Monge."

This is what he had repeated like a litany all through their long confrontation. For the rest of her life she would never forget those eight words of the objection he so patiently put to her time after time:

"I'm an orphan. My name is Séraphin Monge."

We were all staring at her unflinchingly, shamelessly: Polycarpe still suspicious and us with our imaginations slowly becoming heated at the sight of this woman who was so familiar but now, suddenly, so enigmatic.

"That's enough! You're getting on my nerves!" she shouted.

She pushed her way through the group, her breasts brushing us as she passed. We watched her march into the café and slam the door behind her. Then, as the noise of the percolator faded, we heard the sound of an axe chopping up there in Polycarpe's beech forest. It was the echo in the winding valley sending us the sound of that steady work high above. That sound was so familiar to us that we usually took no notice of it, but now it seemed to affect us for the first time.

We listened to the streams of water running down the mountain side. You could sometimes see them flowing over mounds of rainwash coated with velvety thick grass. The cows were coming out of their sheds and their bells rang through the pastures as if invisible choristers were asking people to stand back before the holy sacrament. The three eagles from Pra-Bertrande which solemnly greeted us three times a year had just passed. For a whole hour at sunrise they had hung there in one place with their wings outstretched like black stars in front of Parpaillon, before gliding back and forth like dead leaves in the empty sky. The weather had definitely cleared.

And there we were, standing on the endless carpet of autumn crocuses that grew everywhere: in the fields, on walls, cliffs, the roof of the church, on the rotting bales of straw at the public weighing station. It was a strange thing to see and hear the contrast of our dismal faces and dismal words with all the exhilaration and joie de vivre springing from the earth.

We were fearful, holding our breath. The gendarmes had been sent to prepare us for the worst. A meeting was organized in the Town Hall. The word *evacuation* was mentioned. A good eighty per cent of us, men, women and children, didn't believe it. Eighty per cent were ready to let themselves be swept away or submerged by this epiphenomenon of local erosion rather than leave.

During all this time you could hear the regular sound of the axe up there in the heights, in the very heart of the danger area. Those who stayed in the village at that time – the women, children and old folk – never saw Séraphin Monge again, for he never came down there again.

Those who ventured out, often in the hope of seeing the sight so well described by the Piedmontese, reported – from a great distance, mind you! – that they'd seen a man struggling in the clay, his arms whirling about like a bird stuck in lime, and that they'd seen him haul on his boots with both hands to pull them out of the ground.

Polycarpe Coquillat went to help him, taking his mule to carry the timber. When first he climbed up the alpine hunters' path, he was whistling at the top of his voice and merrily cracking his whip, but he became visibly more serious as time passed. He changed. He no longer humiliated anyone with his self-importance and his big laugh, the symbol of his success. He still rubbed his hands together, but he did it without bragging, as though from habit. We could see his disappointment growing each evening in the café. We began to fear him less.

At first we thought it was because of Auphanie, for she was the only one to venture out into the woods where Séraphin was working, the only one to regularly bring him a mess tin of hot food to prove her love. We never knew if Polycarpe even thanked her. We thought . . . But if she and Polycarpe had ever slept together, it had left them with a visible, vindictive resentment that left no room for jealousy. And besides, we were quite aware – we observed her closely enough – that Auphanie had been well and truly rejected by Séraphin Monge.

We soon had the impression, although we didn't have to time to verify it, that if Coquillat Polycarpe was more and more submissive, it was due much more to that man whom he was exploiting than to nature which was oppressing him.

And indeed, whenever anyone hesitantly ventured near the dangerous area where this strange couple were working, all they ever heard was one person talking, waiting in vain for some reply, giving up, then starting to talk again, even if it was only to the mule or to fill the silence. There had been no wind for some time to either trouble or brighten that silence, a silence suddenly filled with the rumblings of the earth barely holding itself back from shifting and sliding.

You had to admit it was impressive: a man who never said a word, except thank you when Auphanie brought his food, a man who was content to stay for hours wheeling his axe above his head and bringing it down with amazing precision into the cut in the swaying trunk he was cutting down.

In the beginning Polycarpe never tired of singing his praises.

"By heaven, I've found a good one there!"

He gave the thumbs up to show his enthusiasm. But before long he stopped talking about it. Triumph and jubilation gave way to dejection and doubt. He made himself take more and more risks working beside Séraphin, as though it were some sort of challenge. He'd been seen taking his turn at swinging the axe at a beech tree with a lean like the Tower of Pisa and half its roots dripping with that treacherous clay already pulled out of the ground.

One day he arrived at the café and said, out of the blue,

"He's not a man who doesn't want to talk, he's a man who's been forbidden to speak."

He was silent for a good minute. No-one replied. We all knew whom he meant.

"For good and all," he added with a sigh.

That's what we thought too. That day, for the first time in his life, Polycarpe paid for all our drinks. You'd have thought he'd worked out how to square the circle, but we never did know whether the discovery pleased him or not.

Shaken by a deep fear, he clung to his love of money like a lifebuoy. He went down as far as Carpiagne where there was a large yard of rusting war equipment. He brought back a truck you could hear labouring up our steep mountain road for an hour before you even saw it.

We'd never seen a real truck in these parts, apart from during the war, but all the same it seemed to us that this vehicle had been through the whole campaign and would never last another. The tyres were eaten away to the rims. The vibration of the engine made rust fall in a fine powder from the struts and mudguards. Chalk from the miserable Champagne countryside was still clinging like a tragic memory to the moth-eaten brake shoes.

As soon as he saw it Peyru, known as Cassandra, called out to Polycarpe, "You'll kill yourself on that poor excuse for a truck!" he said.

"You know what you can do . . ." muttered Polycarpe.

He went up to the site in the old thing, all its loose bolts and rivets making a noise like an alarm bell. The tethered mule pricked up its ears when it came into view. Séraphin didn't hear a thing. He continued chopping away further down in the depths of the beech wood.

Loaded down with huge logs, the contraption made three trips to the sawmill at Romeyer, way down in the Drôme. He could well have met his end in some unknown ravine far from our village. But no. He chose the Combe-Madame stockroute, which is long and straight through the spruces, finishing at the big bend at Aulan. This straight line cut through the evergreens is so long that from a distance it seems to rise whereas it is still really going down.

Something eventually had to give in that worn-out machinery. It was a part that weighed scarcely twenty grams. One day the pin that held the drive chain broke. It jumped out of its housing and was found uncoiled like a snake that had been run over in the middle of the road. Without the engine to regulate their rotation, the only thing that could control the free-spinning wheels was the brakes. The completely worn-out linings smoked for some time as they ground against the wheel rims. You could hear them screeching for a mile around through the forest. Séraphin himself heard them, put down his axe and came to the edge of the forest to see what was happening. Polycarpe had plenty of time to feel death approaching.

We were all out of breath when we got to the bottom of the ravine where everything had stopped, and we had a good idea of what to expect. Polycarpe's body had been cut in two. The bottom half was intact as it had been protected by the framework of the truck. The top had been squashed between two beech trunks. We had to take the pitiful remains of that half back to the family. One of us followed, carrying two milking buckets full of what we'd been able to scrape from the logs and squeeze from the grass. The whole lot was hopelessly mixed up with splinters of beech wood.

It was on this occasion that we saw Séraphin again for the last time, in the cemetery above our village. He walked with us all as we made our way there. He had offered to carry the coffin up the small steep streets, but he was too tall and would have unbalanced the rest. He made the sign of the cross when the coffin disappeared into the hole.

"He's a Christian!" we thought with some satisfaction.

But that didn't explain very much.

"He'll be leaving!" we thought hopefully.

We couldn't work out why this man who didn't speak should make us feel so ill at ease. He didn't leave. Polycarpe had only been buried for two days when we started hearing the sound of the axe coming once again from deep in the beech forest. Auphanie, who still kept taking his food up to him, said,

"But he won't be paying you! He's dead!" But it made no difference.

Seraphin just shook his head.

"I have to finish it!" he said.

Winter came. It was rainy, mild and without snow for the fourth year in succession. The alders never lost the madder colour, which shows on the bare branches as a sign that spring is coming. This festive red lit up the pale thickets. Now Polycarpe's beech forest began to fall flat like a field of corn ravaged by a blast of wind. The uneven, swollen ground looked like the back of a toad.

In the autumn whole patches of lovely little cep mushrooms popped up underneath. No-one dared go and pick them.

The rain and the muck even got the better of Séraphin. He stayed up there in the empty farmhouse Polycarpe had given him as a refuge, but to tell the truth, it had been cracking for the last hundred years like a bridge about to break. We said to each other, "The rain and the winter will bring it down." But no, it didn't come down. We could see the light through the windows in the distance. The baker, who was bringing back a load of branches for his oven, said he'd seen a lamp moving from one empty room to another in that house no-one until then would willingly go near. The kerosene lamp stayed lit all night. We could see it shining like a beacon from afar. We didn't know why.

Auphanie still brought him food but we knew she did it out of the goodness of her heart. The way her mouth turned down at the corners revealed her disappointment. And what's more, we fantasized less about her since we knew there was a man who resisted her.

As soon as the rain stopped, we heard the sound of Séraphin's axe once again, in spite of that part of the beech forest becoming such a mud heap.

Overcoming her grief, Polycarpe's widow went up to find out what was happening. We watched her groaning, dumpy, awkward figure disappear under the cover of the condemned trees. She came down again biting her nails to the quick from the frustration of not knowing what to think.

"Well, you wouldn't believe it! He won't stop! He won't let me send help. He won't let me pay him! It's unnatural! There's something fishy here, I'll be bound!"

It was three hours later that the other man arrived. He was as wet and muddy as Séraphin Monge had been on that famous evening when we'd seen him come out of the rain, but this man had no effect on Auphanie. When he came up to her she just looked him up and down and asked what he'd like to drink, as she did to all of us.

He had a coal-black beard and eyes like a frightened pigeon. We knew straight away he was a regular sort of fellow. He kept his eye on his bag all the time, putting it down on the marble tabletops as though he was handling the holy tabernacle. In spite of that, he couldn't stop it making a jingling noise like a sheep bell.

"I'm looking for someone," he said.

"Who?"

"A man about this size."

His short arms drew a cube in space, but much taller than himself, so he had to stand on tiptoe.

"Well, that's what I was told. I've never seen him myself."

We knew straight away that it was Séraphin he was looking for. We described him.

"What luck!" he exclaimed. "Where can I find him?"

We told him.

"But you're surely not going up there tonight?" we argued. "You don't know what it's like. Haven't you noticed the weather? We don't want to go looking for you!"

"But where can I sleep?"

"If you're happy enough with the seat over there, you can stay next to the stove until tomorrow," Auphanie offered.

She had locked forever the bedroom where Séraphin Monge had appeared to her on that famous night. She didn't want to sully that memory with any other presence, and she had no other bedroom to offer.

"I'll go up there tomorrow," he said.

He didn't even look at us or ask for anything to eat or drink. He stretched out on the seat Auphanie had shown him.

As it happens, he should have set out then in spite of the storm. He could still have thrown the sugar box in that Séraphin's face, as Célestat Dormeur had told him to. He should have gone up there that same evening. But who can tell what fate has in store?

He woke up to the smack of a shutter banging. The front window of the café looked out over the whole mountain. It was vertical like an open book to the bleary eyes of the man who had just woken from a deep sleep. It was the first time Tibère had ever seen a real mountain. It seemed to be trembling in the wind storm raging across the forlorn valleys, the giant fir plantations and the bare spindly larches. It pushed the fast-flowing river water back in little white waves. Through the fanlight in the café window, you could see patches of snow clinging to the sides of the peaks. They swirled up and swelled out into veils of mist concealing the summits. The sky was blue.

Standing behind the counter with her arms crossed, Auphanie showed no particular friendliness as she watched the stranger shake himself. They were alone. We others had hardly started to roll our first cigarette as we thought that we'd soon have to go out and see to the cattle.

"What do I owe you?" he said.

"Nothing," she replied. "Why are you looking for Séraphin? Do you want to do something for him or to him?"

"Why would I want to do something to him?"

"Usually, when people are looking for someone . . ."

"No," he said, "it's neither. It all depends how he takes it. I've been asked to do something, that's all."

He thanked her and left. Deep in thought, Auphanie kept on wiping the same glass she had just washed for some time, instead of doing the next. She was listening to the squall which was twisting the skeletal branches of the small elder tree on the stone wall and making the glass shake in the front window.

It was midday and this time we were all there around the stove, warming up after our morning's work. Suddenly there came a short, sharp tearing sound like a fart. The flue from the stove was shaken from top to bottom as if by a boilermaker's poker. Soot fell down inside it making a terrible din. Jets of smoke shot out in our faces from all the joins of the furnace. We couldn't see each other any more. Tears came to our eyes and we started coughing. Over behind the counter, all Auphanie's glasses began to tremble like chattering teeth.

"What's happening?" we said, wide-eyed.

Then we rushed outside, Auphanie included, as you do without thinking in an earthquake. We'd already had one in 1907, and it had done a great deal of damage. The cracks zigzagging across the foundations of the Fouillouse bridge date from that time. But no, that wasn't it. There was the squalling wind, the roar of the waters pouring down all the stockroutes on the mountain. You could see plumes rise into the air as the water hit the thick grassy patches growing on the rainwash under the snow line. But the walls around us, the barns and the houses were still intact.

Then we looked up towards Polycarpe's beech forest. Apparently nothing had happened up there either. Standing anxiously at the wall we scanned all around us, our eyes sweeping over our countryside etched by abnormally high waters for several consecutive years. But apart from the Pra-Lombard trench which had been gaping there for years and didn't worry anyone, there was nothing new on the sides of our mountains.

We could have gone happily back under cover, as the wind was going straight through us in spite of our heavy jackets and the jerseys knitted by our women. But it was a habit with us never to believe what we saw. When you live in a region prone to unpredictable upheavals, given how young it is, you must always be on your guard. And then the geologist had said almost apologetically: "From time to time, the phenomenon may be liable to some acceleration."

So we called by the firemen's garage to get some coils of rope used when the alarm was raised on high walls of rock. There were twelve of us plus Auphanie. She was so worried about that Séraphin, who offended all of us by his prominent place in her heart, that she had followed us without even taking the lever handle out of the café door. There were twelve of us making the stones roll on the alpine hunters' path that morning. The south wind was whistling around our ears and as we climbed a strong smell of freshly opened earth came to meet us.

We had just left the grasslands full of nettles which always grow on former paddocks where sheep had grazed for a long time. It was there, coming around the Combassive huts, right between the two fences of the race that guides the lambs down into the disinfecting trough, that we suddenly came face to face with him and stopped short, as much through fear as surprise.

It was the man who had arrived the previous evening. He was covered in mud from head to foot. His trousers were slimed all over with it. He even had it on his eyebrows. He was like a rough, unfinished clay statue. He was coming down the slope with his arms waving. His mouth was opened to give a cry that wouldn't leave his throat. His bag was banging against his side with the jingling noise we had all noticed. Yet it seemed to all of us that it was much bigger than the night before.

When he saw us the cry came at last and didn't stop. It was the long piercing cry of a woman in labour, which made us tremble with panic the longer it went on. We shook him to make him stop. We said to him,

"Say something! What's wrong?"

But he just kept on screaming. His arm running with soaking mud was pointing to something up there, much higher up, at the place we were going to. Someone hastily shoved a piece of sugar soaked with brandy into his mouth to shut him up. He stopped yelling then, but began to speak as though he was vomiting.

"Up there!" he said. "Séraphin! He's dead! I saw it. He was cutting down a tree as solid as he was! I saw him make one last swing! I saw him bring down the last blow with his axe! I saw his body straighten up covered in mud!"

"Did the tree crush him?"

"No! Not the tree! The mud! The tree didn't fall. The whole tree lay down. I saw it! Its roots! They looked like a white octopus. I heard them popping in the mud! It went over on its roots as though someone was pulling it out by the branches . . . with a ball of earth as big as a house! And all that slid down on top of Séraphin. I saw it, I tell you! He held up his arms to hold back the wave of earth that was falling down, but at the same time he was sinking into the ground! And it was soft, and yielding! It fell like a rain of mud, but with drops weighing fifty kilos! I saw Séraphin struggle against the thing that was swallowing him up, pinning his arms. It was like a shroud of earth which finally turned him into a statue! I dashed forward to help him. Without thinking! But I was held fast by the mud around my legs. I had to pull them out to make each step. And he, he was forty metres away. I was done in. I gave up. I came down to fetch you."

We were scrambling up behind him as we listened. But in spite of the rising incline, someone had run to the front. Someone was speeding around the zigzags of the hunters' path.

"Auphanie! Come back! What do you think you can do?"

There were perhaps five of us yelling at her to stop. The others were already finding it hard enough not getting out of breath.

We arrived one after the other at the edge of the disaster area behind the mud-covered man who kept pointing at a precise spot higher up under the tangle of huge sword-like trees that used to be Polycarpe's beech forest.

"Look up there! The tree is disappearing! The axe is still stuck in the trunk!"

But we weren't looking at that. Things had changed radically in the twenty or thirty days since we'd been here. Even the hundred or so tree trunks which Séraphin had felled and put safely out of the way of the land slide, or so he'd thought, even these huge logs were scattered over the slope like matchsticks and heaved up by the swelling earth breaking through the large patches of moss.

In some of the fresh crevasses, the clay was coloured the same blue as the enamel on coffee pots. For my part, whenever I made coffee for the whole family, even five or ten years later, I could never help thinking of that blue, that gash, that man.

It was all that blue clay spewing out and surging down the steep slopes which pushed up the mountain like a muscle detached from the bone by a skilled surgeon. The trees still standing held each other up in the tangle of their trunks and branches. They moaned in the fierce wind with ominous creaking and cracking.

We were on the edge of that blue moving clay which seemed to take on animal shapes the better to swallow us up, as if the earth really did have bowels that had been taken out and exposed to the sun.

The sky took no part in this suffering, nor in ours. It stayed an almost sacrilegious, joyful blue. It seemed to flap in the evening wind like a victory flag. And there we were standing beneath it, overcome, clinging on to each other, holding each other back.

"It's over there!" the man shouted. "The top of the trunk and the branches are starting to go down into the ground! Can't you see it? It's almost horizontal. Look! All the roots are spread out in a circle. And all that mud stuck to them! He's underneath it! He's dead!"

"No!" Auphanie screamed.

She had got there before us. She was already over among the fissures of blue clay, her arms flailing as she staggered forward, struggling at each step to pull her feet out of the clay holding her in the earth. We were shouting,

"Auphanie! Come back! What are you doing? There's nothing anyone can do! You'll get killed up there!"

But did we help her? Did we go after her? We were thinking of our wives and children. We saw her hitch up her skirts. We could see those buttocks we dreamed about so much. We saw her rip off the pink ribbons holding her stocking and firmly tie them twice around one of the branches of the beech where Séraphin's axe was still planted. We saw it all, standing there rigid with fear and apprehension, expecting any minute to see the tree roll over and bury her alive. She was already in the clay up to her knees. Both arms were searching under the huge tree slowly sinking into the mud. We could hear her shouting "Séraphin!" hysterically, like a madwoman, but we all knew her cries were useless.

Finally though, when we realized that she wouldn't be able to get out alone, when we realized that if we let her sink, we'd see her disappearing shouting Séraphin's name every night of our lives, we made a move, but with great trepidation.

The ropes were uncoiled and tied around the tree trunks that seemed most stable. We took the risk . . . finally. Three risked sliding through the mass of beeches, leaving about ten of us on the edge of the slip to keep a firm hold on them. They reached the roots under which Séraphin had disappeared. Auphanie, suddenly overcome by an instinct for self-preservation, reached out her arms to them. They managed to catch hold of her and get a slip-knot under her arms. One of us lost his footing during the rescue operation. He grabbed something he thought was a branch. He said later that it was Séraphin's axe still wedged in the wood. He also said that he had grabbed the handle in wild desperation, with all the strength of his 80 kilos. Normally the axe should have given way under his weight and he should have joined Auphanie in the mire. Now the axe hadn't budged, and that wasn't natural. We didn't believe him, then or since. The others said afterwards that they were all tied to the tree trunk as though they were on a raft at the mercy of the waves, and they feared the worst.

We passed Auphanie from one to another of us. She had no more pride, no more interest in her appearance; in fact she was just a heap of mud. We had only as much contact with that body of our dreams as was strictly necessary. No-one had any desire to lay their hands on her. The tears which washed her eyes left their tracks in the dirt on her face.

We had to link our arms under her and carry her to the Combassive huts. It was only then we noticed that the man who had sounded the warning had also disappeared.

Dawn was just breaking when an exhausted Tibère Saille reached Lurs. Coming out of the Pra-Combassive woods, he had found Séraphin's bicycle leaning against a tree. He had recognized it, because that very morning while trying to catch up with him, he had seen him leave it and continue up the path on foot. At that time, Tibère Saille was not yet really firm of purpose. He kept going over in his mind the curse Célestat had pronounced as he thrust the sugar box into his hands:

"And then throw it in his face! Throw it in his face!"

He had repeated the phrase four times to burn it into his memory. But fate had decreed that Tibère Saille should never see the face of the man he was told to insult in that way. The only things he knew of him were the swing of his shoulder as he brought down the axe, the calm way he walked up to the eerie forest where the trees no longer stood upright and where Tibère saw him struggling with the treacherous clay.

Then there was that gut-wrenching sound he'd never forget for the rest of his life, the whirling of the tree thrown like a top into a spiral of earth, dragging up the roots, and the man caught in the blue whirlpool of the thick mud that engulfed him. Tibère could no longer suppress the urge which made him go to help the man. No. He'd never seen him from the front. That unknown face had never appeared to him, and yet . . .

He had pedalled like mad all night, with fear at his heels. The bag suddenly weighed very heavily and its strap cut into his neck.

Célestat saw him come in looking like a ghost. A stale odour of something dug up from the earth overpowered the good smell of well-cooked bread all around him. He had been too near the bowels of the earth and he smelt like it. He was still in a daze, having witnessed that disaster and having only escaped from it himself by the skin of his teeth.

"You look awful!" Célestat said. "Did you find him."

"Yes."

Tibère had just taken his bag from his shoulder. It was too heavy. He let it fall on the bench holding the scales, which gave out the same metallic sound as the gold pieces in the box.

Célestat stared at the bag.

"You didn't give it back to him?"

"How can you give something to a dead man?"

"Is he dead? I don't believe you!"

"I knew you wouldn't."

"How can I believe you? You've said to yourself, 'I'm not going to give the box back, now that I'm going to marry his daughter.'"

"He's dead, I tell you! Here's proof!"

He opened the bag, pulled out the sugar box and then a carefully wrapped parcel, placing it gently on the work-bench.

It was one of those white cloths for carrying bread that used to be woven out of hemp as thick as jute. Tibère Saille's fingers trembled as he unfolded the cloth.

Since the previous evening he had felt the need to picture Marie's face in his mind, but not as she had appeared to him that first day. Then she had been standing in the doorway of the bakehouse, showing no reaction to his presence, as though he didn't exist. No. He wanted her radiant, smiling at him at last, as he'd always imagined it. And yet, in spite of what was at stake, in spite of that hope, he couldn't look squarely at what he'd just done. When he lifted off the last corner of the cloth, he closed his eyes.

"Here's proof!" he said again, almost in a whisper.

Célestat didn't cry out, but he breathed in sharply with a sound like a last gasp, then stepped back two paces.

"You killed him!" he said in a low, gutteral voice.

He hid his head in his hands.

"No!" Tibère exclaimed. "It was the earth that killed him! It wasn't me!"

"Get that out of my sight!"

Tibère wrapped up the cloth again. Célestat, shaken to the core, watched him do it as though hypnotized.

"Quickly, quickly! Before somebody comes!"

He rushed out to the shed to get a pick and shovel.

"Bury the thing!" he cried. "No! Wait!"

He reached for the box. He opened it, then took out the notes he had set aside to buy Marie a motorized delivery bike. Those he stuffed in his pocket.

"Quickly!" he cried.

He spat into his hands and began to dig with the pick at the beaten earth at the right foot of the oven where the sugar box had been buried. But this time he had to make a much bigger and deeper hole, a hole where no-one would think of looking.

That morning the Dormeurs' bread was a strange roasted-coffee colour. It was because Célestat had stayed more than ten minutes stamping down the earth where the two men had just buried the box and the bread cloth. It was an exhausted Tibère who had taken the bread out of the oven; Célestat was incapable of doing it. He stood with his feet riveted to the soft earth, not daring to move, as if he was afraid that once his weight was removed, the secret would burst out and reveal itself to all.

III

WHEN ROSE SAW PATRICE FOR THE FIRST TIME AS HE REALLY WAS, it was on an autumn evening when the tall trees behind him hurled their chorus of curses over the plain. The Pontradieu wind was blowing. This particular wind howls over a few square kilometres south of the Durance river and nowhere else.

No-one ever hears it further away. It's not like the mistral or the tramontana. It's a deafening wind. People give you a funny look when they come out of it or talk about it, as it seems so strange to the ordinary folk that a wind of any kind can blow exactly where it likes, in this precise part of the country.

Patrice had just pulled the chain on the big bell which jingled merrily each time he returned home.

"He's forgotten his key again," Rose thought, smiling indulgently. Her mind was at peace and her body, which had tormented her only once in her life, was also at ease.

She had wanted a big wedding: large rooms where the skirts of her wedding dress could flow out proudly around her, well clear of any furniture, bathed in the light from the large windows and their fanlights. And that is what she had.

She had wanted candelabra, chandeliers, Charmaine's black piano as a contrast to the white of her tight bodice with its thirty little buttons to undo from neck to navel. Although she was impatient to be married she had asked for some partition walls to be demolished before the wedding. And she had everything she asked for.

She made her entrance among the vulgar masses, and in Dupin formal attire, in a room eighteen metres long, under four Venetian glass chandeliers as heavy as crowns of thorns. One hundred and fifty people were crowded between the brightly-lit walls, under the intricate panelled ceiling. Her mother, Thérésa Sépulcre wept with pride.

"If only her poor father could see her now! He was so proud of her," she confided to Clorinde Dormeur.

"You're all I want!" Rose said to Patrice. "This luxury is just to make sure that people remember."

He had made an effort to look handsome for the occasion. The empty socket of the eye he had lost now held a shining agate behind a monocle. The plaster he had used to smoothe out his scars gave him a more or less normal face, as long as he stayed in the shadows.

He glanced surreptitiously at himself in his wife's eyes as she stood there with her imperturbable smile. "She loves me," he thought. "She has chosen to have those thirty tiny buttons on her bodice because she knows that what we have to offer each other tonight is something anyone can have. It's the subtlety we bring to it that will make it unique. She loves me! I'll bring her slowly to my desire, as you tame a bird. I'll take hours to undress her. I'll show her how extraordinarily gentle, considerate and self-effacing I can be. What I am will cancel out what I look like and that is all she will ever see."

Her love put new life and energy into Patrice. When he saw her, even more beautiful in the flower-like dress which seemed to flow out over the floor and keep the men's feet at a respectful distance, he suddenly felt a great urge to paint her. He was dying to cut the image into several pieces, to portray her upside down with her tiny foot and gartered leg draped across her body like the sash of the Légion d'Honneur. A single eye with its lid closing over a sly gleam would outline her right breast and illuminate the whole picture like a clear conscience. He would crucify her on canvas in a surreal portrait that would be more real than the conventional symmetry of her soul within, more real than her disconcerting beauty in all its poignant fleeting glory.

"Wait a while," Rose said. "I want them all to take a good look at me. After all, my glory is your glory."

He was about to speak then thought better of it. It had just occurred to him that her thought processes were different from his, that she had not spent time in the same wilderness, and that she had not grappled with the same feelings of helplessness. There were things he could never come right out and say to her, never share with her as he had with his sister Charmaine. He could never say to her: "Because you think, my love, there could be any glory in all that for me? But my love, even if God laid his hand on my face and changed it back to what it was before 3 November 1916, when a shell burst on the top of the trench, even then there would be no glory! I'll whisper it to you my love: I paint, I'm a painter, I want to paint, and I'm not succeeding. Well . . . I succeed more or less. But I haven't that spark of genius, my love. I'm sorry for your sake that I have a face like this, but if having one more hideous still could give me what I lack, I'd slash what is left of it with the greatest joy!"

But how could he confide his bitterness to a fiancée on the evening of her wedding? He knew she would find those words much harder to cope with than the scars on his face.

He still had that burning desire to paint her first. He had a feeling that it would be the best work of his life. It had to happen. She put her hand on his wrist.

"Wait a while!" she said. "Let me go and mingle with all those chattering guests. After that, you can paint me as much as you like!"

He stood there amazed by her reply. A vision of Charmaine went through his mind like a bolt of lightning, her face frowning bitterly. "So," she seemed to be saying, "I won't be the only one to share even that with you." He silently begged her pardon. He understood what Rose meant by glory. His feet hardly touched the ground for the rest of the evening.

Meanwhile Marcelle, Rose's spiteful sister, sat huddled in a corner daintily eating her ice. Several times she had refused to dance with men excited by an ugly girl with an Aphrodite bottom. She liked to play the part of Cassandra, the prophet of doom.

"One day," she said, "she'll see him as he really is, and that'll be the end of that!"

"Aren't you ashamed?" Marie said, "You don't even like your sister."

"Well people don't like me!" Marcelle replied.

Her features crumpled for a moment with the effort of suppressing a sob. Marie left her and went over to Rose who was talking to Clorinde.

"I don't dare kiss you," Marie said, "in case I tread on your dress."

"Tread away!" Rose said "You have a right to!"

They looked each other straight in the eye with beaming smiles, then gave a heart-felt hug which they both understood. They were alone in that crowd of a hundred people. They felt that Séraphin's shade was protecting both of them under the lights of those dazzling chandeliers.

"But you'll be getting married soon too, won't you," Rose asked.

"So it seems . . ." Marie said without any enthusiasm.

"Tibère's a good-looking man!"

"Oh . . . him or someone else."

Rose secretly took hold of Marie's hand among all the lace.

"Do you still think about it, about him?" she whispered.

Marie blushed and looked away.

"Is that any of your business?"

"So do I!" Rose said softly. "But it's not for the reason you think."

"In my case, it *is* for the reason you think!" Marie retorted.

Patrice was making his way towards them through the groups of guests. He had been walking from one to the other with newly-opened bottles of champagne sending sprays of bubbles fizzing into the air.

"Marie!" Patrice said. "I must drag her away from you! I must paint her, there, now! In another hour it might be too late!"

"Patrice . . ." Marie said, "do you know what has become of Séraphin?"

"No," Patrice replied.

"Do you think of him?"

"All the time. As much as . . ."

He stopped short. He was going to say: "As much as I think of Charmaine." He had just remembered that Marie had suffered because of her.

He took Rose's hand and pulled her after him. Groups of respectful guests stepped back to make way for the huge bell of her skirt. The wife of the deputy mayor of Les Mées, who had not moved quickly enough was suddenly confronted with Patrice's beaming face. She clapped her hand to her mouth to stifle a cry, at the same time collapsing noisily on to a chair.

"Heaven help me!" she exclaimed to Councillor Mme Dupuy. "I wouldn't be in the bride's shoes tonight for anything in the world! I think I'd faint dead away!"

Mme Dupuy nodded her head in assent, but she was thinking that apart from the bride, the deputy's wife already had quite enough to make her faint: her husband weighed 105 kilos, strands of varicose veins stood out all the way down his calves and he smelled like a goat.

At Pontradieu, Charmaine's apartment and Patrice's studio were now one. No-one had touched the huge low bed, the fireplace, the flowers, or the wrought-iron railing that seemed to be protecting a tomb. Patrice liked to indulge in the memory of his sister whose perfume still lingered in the air.

The way his wife had immediately accepted this was another surprising thing about her that he admired. He expected that Rose would want to get rid of any trace of Charmaine. After all, she had witnessed Patrice's extravagant behaviour when his sister died: the revolver she had to snatch out of his hands; the coffin where he had wanted to lie next to Charmaine and have the top nailed down over their intertwined bodies. All this morbid passion should surely have left its mark on Rose. But no, she had agreed of her own volition to come and live among Charmaine's furniture, in the atmosphere Charmaine had created even down to her perfume.

He had impetuously dragged her along to this studio, starkly lit by lights which were never turned off. He had dragged her from one room to another through doors that were too narrow for her dress, and had thrown her, white and panting, on to the sagging divan which usually held the various things he needed for painting. The air smelled of turpentine and Indian ink. The sumptuous gown which set off Rose's face took up the whole space, spilling over on to the palette and the rags used for cleaning the colours. She partly hid Patrice's largest painting in which an army of dead men, slashed with grey, were climbing up and disappearing into a coal-dark sky.

Patrice knelt down among the lace. Rose's hands gently cupped his broken face, which she drew towards her own until they touched. She planted a tiny kiss on the lid of the eye he had lost.

"Do you know why I love you?" he suddenly asked.

"Because you want me!" she replied softly.

"No."

"What do you mean, no?"

"Well, yes. But do you remember what you said to me a while ago?"

"I said so many things!"

"You said to me: 'Let me mingle for a while with the guests chatting over there. Then you can paint me as much as you like.'"

"And that's why you love me?"

"No. But do you really understand? You're not pretending to understand that I want to paint you *before anything else*?"

"Why then, didn't you love me before that?"

"Yes, but it wasn't the same love."

He stood up again and took hold of a medium-sized canvas already prepared. He enthusiastically sketched some bold lines on it with what seemed like a sure hand, full of hope that this time would be different, that the painting would miraculously take on a life of its own, and in the end, not look like anyone he knew.

She timidly watched him working, not understanding anything of his passion but having an infinite respect for it. She whispered absurd, child-ish, risqué things to him; he was not looking at her but within him-self, far back in the past where he could see Charmaine, loving sensual Charmaine. He had begun cutting up the image of the bride in good faith, but it was slowly being transformed into a hymn to the features and colours of the dead young woman, just as it always did. The eye he had wanted to depict as crafty and knowing was assuming abnormal proportions at the top of the picture. It was Charmaine's eye gazing at the pool in the garden on an autumn evening, imagining that she would die young.

"Show me!" Rose exclaimed suddenly.

She tried to extricate herself from the sofa and her flounces and frills.

"No!" Patrice said sharply.

She stood up quickly. He took the canvas and put it with the others, painted side to the wall. He caught Rose in his arms.

"Come!" he said. "I don't want to paint any more now. I want you!"

He led her into the bedroom where a fire was burning in the grate. It was only September, but Rose had made sure there was a fire. Patrice was still holding her. He was trying to make her out, to define her features in the midst of all that profusion of material swamping them both. The effort began to tire him and take the edge off his desire.

"Wait!" she said.

She had realized how silly, inappropriate and old-fashioned those thirty little covered buttons on her bodice were. The idea had come from the minds of a mother and a dressmaker who had never had enough imagination to see further than what they had been told from mother to daughter for perhaps a thousand years.

"Wait!" she said once again.

She went into the bathroom and tore off the dress she had been so proud of two hours earlier, thinking it would make Marie, Marcelle and all the other girls die with envy. That wish, even fulfilled, now seemed of no importance.

When she reappeared before Patrice, she was wearing something transparent and revealing, such as the free and easy young things of those days wore, a dark green dress clinging to her figure, which shimmered and slithered like a skin with every movement and, as she was well aware, was more shocking than her bare skin. She sat down gracefully on a high-backed chair. Slowly raising her right leg, she rested her ankle on her left knee. The silky dress slipped back like a snake skin.

Patrice watched as she held out her arms to him. He gazed at the naked triangle she had revealed to him. Without moving or speaking they held on to the moment which would soon become the past, before venturing to doing what everyone else does. Until then they were entitled to think that something extraordinary made them different.

Below their windows, cars and buggies parked on the wide paths of the formal garden were setting out into the night with a flurry of farewells and bawdy jokes.

It was then that the wind in the branches blowing over the plain made them realize they were alone at Pontradieu, alone with the tall trees, alone with the rococo fountain at the end of the pool, alone with ghosts who were patiently waiting for them, alone with the enigma of how to live, given all that was working against them, inescapably alone. Outside their room, beyond their solitude, they could feel all about them the land which had made them what they were: the murmuring waters of the Durance, the poplars standing guard in serried ranks, the badly-lit villages with their black fountains under sloping roofs, the abandoned farms in the distance, the thriving farms close by, the mountains hanging like a white garland at the far end of the plain. That world was summed up in the anxious expectation of their bodies. They could not forget any of it when they finally came together. They felt that the whole happy land would experience their delight.

"Shall I turn out the light?"

"No! I want to see us!"

But all through that terrible night and the following nights, days and weeks, the overwhelming sense of expectation never left Rose. Everything remained unresolved like a puzzle, like a question with an answer that could not be found. Yet they did not tire, they never gave up. They forgot the world for months; they held each other tight, gazing into each other's eyes in the vast rooms of Pontradieu. The only thing that made them shiver was the judgmental chiming of the relentless clocks at the end of long corridors, making the two of them all the more aware of their failure. When they gave up and turned away from each other out of breath, they did it with a wry smile, still holding hands. They could not believe, they never believed that it would always be like that, that they would never be able to really be one.

During the day, they were happy. He left to manage the factory near Manosque, where thirty people depended on him for their livelihood. He had inherited business acumen from his father and knew all the tricks of the trade that can make a man rich buying or selling, especially in iron, cement or wheat, as he had discovered a flour mill among the things he inherited from his father Gaspard. However, he never used these tricks in his domestic life, with his employees or those close to him. The only people treated with this cool, pragmatic approach were his equals or superiors. To them, he gave no quarter. He had not a friend in the world since Séraphin Monge had decided to keep his distance.

Rose waited for him while he worked. It took many years before she began to lose enthusiasm for Pontradieu, its rooms, its furniture, its innumerable drawers, the indoor plants that needed attention, the cats that wandered about at the end of the park and were fed in the sheds. On the other hand, she demolished the enclosure from which the savage dogs had escaped and killed Charmaine.

She discovered the library and took up reading. With the same subtlety and tact he brought to educating her in love, Patrice guided and advised her. But she went too quickly, wanting to show how anxious she was to please. Sometimes when he came out of his studio, his face looking discouraged and more disfigured than ever, she would tactlessly ask him:

"Well then? Are you happy with what you've done? Tell me about it," she would ask him earnestly.

But he found that thought repulsive. He could accept their intimate problems with a smile, but it took all his self-control not to shut the door in her face when she tried so obviously to infiltrate his secret garden. He was happy to cover her with emeralds and mink. He wanted to receive everything she was capable of giving, if that were possible. He did not want her to enter that small secret place of unhappiness where he alone could wallow in the certainty that he did not have the spark of genius.

She insisted, thinking that her energy and conviction would surely have some effect.

"Sell the factory!" she would tell him. "Sell the mill! Sell everything! Be happy just with painting and with me!"

He laughed, finding her candour disarming in spite of himself.

"That wouldn't give me what I lack."

He took her in his arms.

"And you, you need a jewel box. You need to be shown off."

"I'm too small," she said to him crossly. "I'm invisible to you!"

Then she would burst into tears.

"I'm stupid!"

At those times he did not try to convince her to the contrary. He treated it like an illness.

"It won't always be so," he would say to her. "And when that moment comes, you'll wish it hadn't."

These were bitter words and she would remember them all her life.

A long time afterwards, searching the abyss of hours and days when she was no longer what she had been and not yet what she would become – this interruption in her life when her feelings, her personality were those of another person – she whispered to herself as she gazed in the mirror:

"It's not possible! I said that to him! I was that for him! He did that! I waited for such a long time! Why? And why that sudden panic, that terror? Why did I only see him as he really was after one precise moment in time, when I'd been living with him like a lover for years? Before that moment, only ten hours earlier, his broken face was still dear to me: I kissed it, I touched it, I tried vainly to make him forget it. Yet he was certain, and I too was convinced of his certainty, that I would never manage to forget that mutilated face, and that my coldness was the result. But that wasn't true! I know now that no-one has ever been able to give me an orgasm. I don't even know what it is!

"All the same! I didn't come to his bed like a naïve young girl. I'd found out all I needed to know. And he'd had two mistresses before the war when he was only twenty, before his face was destroyed. They were jealous and one had accidentally shot the other and blinded her in one eye during a hunting party. I don't know and I've never wanted to know how they consoled each other during their lonely childhood. When he spoke of her during his last years, the horror of the way she died had lessened, and what I saw shining in his one eye was a kind of poignant regret. So he could certainly be a lover. It was obvious in the amount of time he could hold back while vainly waiting for me to come. I was the one who couldn't be a mistress."

Things were like that between them for a year or two, or perhaps three. They were sure that one day, maybe that night, they would be both able to fall asleep together, both exhausted but eager to hold each other again, to have each other again.

He forgot his key almost every evening during this time, perhaps for the constant delight of seeing the obvious affection in her greeting. She would play the maid, open the door wide and bob a curtsey holding out the hem of her skirt. Behind her wafted the homely smell of dishes that her grandmother used to make. She inherited her skill as an excellent cook of peasant food from her mother, Thérésa Sépulcre, and thanks to her, Pontradieu had become a house filled with the most delicious smells.

He would have liked her to have staff in the house, a maid, perhaps even a cook, but she always said:

"No, later! I'm not a lady yet. I wouldn't know how to give orders. And besides, I just want to be alone with you!"

That ill wind blowing through the trees in the park had blown through them many times before and nothing had happened. Why then on an evening no different from any other, why, when she opened the door as usual, should she suddenly see in front of her not her well-dressed husband pleasantly smelling of expensive after-shave, but the ghost of a someone dug out of the earth alive, covered in chalk and bleeding, his flesh horribly torn apart and his eye hanging out of its socket, barely attached to the optic nerve looking incongruously like the ribbon of a monocle. Why had that thoroughly familiar face suddenly appeared hideous to her?

Right up to the time of her death, with the regularity of planets coming into alignment, her obsession would drive her to turn this question around and around in her mind, as a fly slowly makes its way to the edge of an impenetrable window pane. There was no answer to be found in this life. Even when the situation had long been irreparable but also pardoned by the passage of time like an amnesty, what upset Rose most in her obsessive quest was her inability to hold on to its main subject.

Apart from a portrait of him as a child wearing a sailor-suit, there was no other photo of Patrice as he was while he was alive. His disfigured face no longer existed in Rose's memory either. She vainly tried to picture what was so hideous in that poor, crazily-patched head that it could make her recoil with such sudden revulsion.

She never perceived him again other than the way he was when he appeared out of the blue that first time at the house Séraphin was knocking down, when she had said hello to him, just as she would have to any ordinary-looking boy.

Why then that evening rather than any other? Nothing had happened that day which could explain such a shocking revelation. Nothing material. No new event. None? Well, yes. But even years later Rose could scarcely admit it in the deepest recesses of her soul let alone face up to it squarely.

The previous night, beside Patrice who was sleeping quietly, she had dreamt that Séraphin had lain down on top of her, that he had made love to her in torrid heat, and that she had cried out, she had gasped, she had come. Then she woke up distraught, not because of what had just happened, but because she felt sure that Patrice must surely have known. But no! She turned on the bedlamp and, leaning on one elbow, looked long and hard at the good right profile of her husband's face as he slept peacefully. No. He showed no emotion at all, just as she had probably shown none while the insubstantial ghost of Séraphin held her in its arms and she felt herself penetrated by that cock which had no physical existence but which could make her utter cries of joy and bring her to the only orgasm that had ever swept through her.

And so the fate of these two beings lying side by side was sealed in the silence of the night, quite independently of any wish of theirs, without the slightest disturbance to their slumbers, without a sigh of anxiety. Years later, Rose often thought about these twenty-four hours long ago as she lay wide awake, unable to sleep. However, when she had woken next morning in the cheerful sunlit bedroom after such a wonderful dream, reassured that Patrice had no inkling of it, nothing had warned her that a radical change was going on inside her, to be revealed that very evening.

She could picture herself as she went over the scene hundreds and thousands of times in her mind, trying to understand the moment that shaped her life forever.

"The bell rings. I'm in the kitchen, not thinking of anything in particular. I'm rolling out pasta for the ravioli I'm making. My hands are floury. I wipe them on the cloth hanging at the side of the oven. I say to myself, 'He's forgotten his keys again.' I hurry to the door so that he doesn't have to wait. I fling it wide open as usual. Do I only see the trees that I love so much behind him, even when they whisper misfortune? No. I really *see* him! And

71

it's a sudden shock, as though I were meeting him for the first time in my life. I'm terrified! How did I manage not to stagger back? How did I manage not to clap a hand over my mouth to stifle a horrified cry? The look in his only eye envelops me with love. And I? How do I look at that instant?

"Luckily, and probably unbeknown to me, my mind had been alert and prepared for this confrontation for a long time, perhaps forever. I swear that I could still fully respond to the impulse that sent me into his arms every evening. There wasn't the slightest hesitation, the slightest interval, I swear, between my usual happy surprise and the moment when I was clasped in his arms. Perhaps the only thing might have been that instead of my offered lips, he might have only had my hair to kiss, but even then I was already turning my face to him with a willing mouth and eyes wide open.

"But how could I hide that first look from him? I couldn't take it back and change it. And besides, Patrice must have been expecting it for months, for years. Oh my love, could it have been you, who eventually, knowingly, caused that look?

"I said to myself, 'Be very careful. If ever he detects the slightest sign of revulsion, he'll kill himself.'"

Yet nothing of any significance changed between them. They continued to try and reach some mutual satisfaction in their failed sexual relations, playfully, with laughter, as though it were something of a joke not to be taken seriously. They encouraged each other with words of hope and gentle, tender gestures.

She thought, "I'll keep control of myself. He'll never suspect anything. He'll die or I'll die in the certainty of our love for one another, sure that I've never seen his disfigured face, and that for me at least, his features have always been intact. Even if it should last for 50 years."

But it's impossible to resist the truth when it's determined to come out. Even the sacrifice of a life cannot halt it. Rose must have often said to herself what Thérésa Sépulcre, that ordinary woman of very little brain, used to repeat whenever possible: "Truth is like oil; it always comes to the surface!" She would proclaim it triumphantly as if this irresistible thrust of truth could only lead to the liberation of all the peoples of the world, whereas it usually brought in its wake nothing but disaster, heartache and grief.

Truth has treacherous ways of revealing itself to whoever should not know it, for the person who is hiding something is not always on his guard, while the one who is dying to find out is always on the watch. Patrice was always watching. Like Marcelle, he too was convinced that one day, instead of looking at him through the eyes of love, Rose would really see him as he was, and then that would be the end of that . . .

And yet, the day when it happened, when the door opened wide to greet him and revealed his wife standing there disconcerted – oh, it might only have been for a thousandth of a second, no more, if that is possible! – on that particular day, he was not expecting it. It was such a good evening to be together. The autumn air promised many pleasures for a long time to come. Patrice was so happy to be home. And Rose had done so well and for so long now that he had forgotten about his disfigured face.

She had suddenly reminded him of it. All that patient work had been destroyed in a flash. Nonetheless it took months for Patrice and the stupid insistence of the truth to "come to the surface" in spite of Rose, in spite of himself, to crystallize in his mind those words which would cut short his life. "She can't love you, because you're hideous to look at."

He would stop, taken aback, in front of all the mirrors in Pontradieu. Charmaine had put them up everywhere to remind her at every turn, when she was a widow some time in the future, what love had lost when it lost her. Rose could see that this involuntary confrontation was helping to destroy Patrice. Later, when she tried to work out just what she had to reproach herself with, she would say to herself: "I couldn't take any of them down. He would have noticed it straight away. He would have known why I did it. The truth is that, well before me and in spite of me, he had never got used to the face he'd been given, patched up as best they could. He wore it like a carnival mask. Sometimes, when he thought he was alone and nobody was watching him, he couldn't look at himself without laughing. I imagine it must be a terrible thing to have to laugh at the sight of your own face in the mirror."

And so Rose lived in a state of some tension, ever attentive to a single objective: "Above all, he mustn't know! He mustn't suspect anything!" But now she inwardly screamed with terror each time he bent over her with all his love to give. No matter how well suppressed these silent, secret cries deep within her may have been, Patrice could sense them. They were like stab wounds, but he was able to put on such a front that she didn't notice. Willing and well intentioned though she was, she had no experience of guile or hypocrisy, and saw no significance in certain instinctive gestures of his, which he himself found so full of meaning.

One night, having given up the effort, he was making love for his own pleasure with no reaction from her, she saw that his eye was closed and thought that at last she could turn out the light so that she would no longer have to look at him. A long time afterwards, when everything was over, her obsessive remorse forced her to confront that furtive, innocuous gesture: the hand leaving the beloved shoulder, reaching out beyond the sheet, feeling for the cord, then quickly pressing the switch. For a long time during her life, Rose heard the click as the light goes out, often waking with a start as if that minute incident had been enough to reveal to Patrice that she hadn't the courage to face what he looked like.

But those we no longer love do not so easily believe what is in their hearts, and when Patrice wanted to weigh up losses and gains, he did not look for futile details such as these. Always trying to work out the enigma that Rose represented to him, he added up her advances on the one hand and her retreats on the other. Similarly, Rose tried to keep up the role of the person she had been before the incident at the front door, so that he should not see that she no longer loved him. Besides, it was not true. She no longer loved him as a lover, but she felt pity for him, compassion, and she was willing to sacrifice anything for him for as long as she lived. Wasn't that also showing love?

Nevertheless, her brightness and her surges of affection had a hint of something studied and forced. Of course when she opened the door to him she could still hold out the hem of her dress and curtsey as if he were still her lord and master. The good smell of grandma's cooking still filled the air behind her at Pontradieu, but there were little lapses in her tenderness of which she was not aware since she no longer loved him.

She always sensed one of these a few seconds after he had. On one such evening, sitting by the fire, she suddenly said:

"It's been ages since you played the mandolin for me."

"It's been ages since you asked me."

"I didn't have to ask you then. You just played!"

They were both well aware that their words rang false, and were dismayed by it. In the course of the social gatherings they had to attend, Rose and Patrice had heard so many similar conversations from couples well on the way to separation. The words were spoken in a casual, cynical tone, expressing mockery or polite disenchantment.

Whenever they were witnesses to these frosty sparring matches, they would say to each other,

"Did you hear the way they speak to each other? They're not going to last long."

They would hold each other tight in the night and laugh quietly. And they would hurry to their bed to cling together for fear of losing each other. There was still that physical distance between them, but it did not stop them from appreciating how much they were partners against the disorder of the world. And they were proud to say that no matter what happened, they would never leave each other.

Then they too used a number of these almost automatic expressions, because if they didn't fill the silence with something, the truth would have burst out between them with a force that could have shattered the peace and quiet of the drawing room, put out the fire, opened the windows wide to the moaning of the trees in the park, which would then have been entitled to whisper in the wind: "Patrice has a disfigured face!"

Yet it seemed only yesterday, on the moonlit banks of the Lauzon, that he had banished the ugliness of his face from her eyes by intoxicating her with his beautiful serenades. It was only yesterday that he tried to share his pleasure with her, never tiring of trying to discover the puzzling hidden, silent, delicate spots he should have aroused. It was not because of indifference on her part. She enthusiastically joined in all the little tricks and games that usually have the desired effect. What is more, she did so still, ever since looking at Patrice's face had become unbearable.

Only she no longer excited him every night or every Sunday afternoon, when, with the shutters closed against unwelcome visitors, they never tired of being alone together.

It had no doubt been a mistake to give her a taste for reading, as she now read far too much. He had great respect for the enthusiasm of the new convert, but she read with an application and desire to understand that made him frown. When he went to bed after doing everything he had to, or after wrestling with a new painting he was trying to bring to life, as he did with Rose, he would find her reading with great concentration, propped up against the pillows. He would gaze for a long time at the suggestive outline of her breasts under the lace, but he knew that they were inert, unresponsive to every approach, every appeal. She offered this alluring sight to his senses while quietly reading like a little girl of eight or an old woman of eighty, studiously turning one page after the other.

He would run his fingers and his mouth over this tranquil body. In earlier days, before his face was disfigured, they had the power to excite women and make them cry out their enjoyment to him. In the end he fell asleep like that, his hand still at last after having once more given up trying to elicit any response from her.

Slowly edging her way to the side of the big low bed that Charmaine had occupied, she managed to make the heavy hand preventing her from dreaming slip off her without waking Patrice. Then she would cross her hands over her breasts and in her imagination call to Séraphin. But here too, there was nothing, no response. Only once, and it was so long ago, had she been able to capture him in her dream. Only once had he lain with the weight of his ethereal body upon her, and just a few centimetres away from her face she had seen the sad, compassionate expression in his eyes, which did not even blink when she was faint with pleasure for the only time in her life. Since then, she kept waiting for him, hoping he would come.

It happened that one night when she had fallen asleep like that, lying straight, her expressionless face contemplating the unknown like a pious recumbent statue on a tomb, her unconscious was troubled by an alarming sensation which slowly drew her to wakefulness. She opened her eyes and took a long time to make out what was disturbing her.

It was summer, and through the open window the song of the nightingales high in the tall trees was accompanied by strange crackling sounds. Darting gleams of light coming through the gaps in the shutters were playing around the scrolls and beams of the ceiling. Still heavy with sleep, Rose looked at the glowing lights dancing on the plaster roses. Her arm reached out to the place where Patrice should have been sleeping. It was empty and cold. Rose was suddenly fully awake.

"My God, fire!" she said.

Fire and earthquakes are the two things that propel people out of bed with the same surge of energy: sheets and blankets flung aside with one instinctive sweep of the arm to be ready as quickly as possible. Rose was on her feet in the middle of the room in an instant, struggled into whatever clothing was lying over the back of a chair, then rushed out of the room. She made her way to the hall door and flung it open. The château was dark, quiet and tranquil as usual, but the same glow that was on the bedroom ceiling was dancing on the eighteen windows of the façade.

It was coming from somewhere beside the ornamental pool. A tall blaze of fire was reflected upside down in the pool and the undulating line of the little waves was like red festoons around the rim.

Everything was quiet that night. Not a bird rustled the branches as it flew off into the night; not a breath of wind murmured in the trees. Down behind the clipped box hedge a fire was burning away, its candle-like flames darting straight up towards the foliage.

Rose crept down the avenue of lilacs, their romantic perfume wasted on the air. Patrice was standing fully clothed on the raised path between the plane trees. Next to him was a pile of frames which Rose initially thought were just lengths of wood, but an acrid smell of turpentine and linseed oil quickly made it clear to her what he was doing. She pressed her hand over her mouth, rushed towards Patrice and shook him as if to wake him up.

"What are you doing?" she exclaimed.

"As you can see . . . I'm burning my paintings!"

"But why?" she asked.

He shook his head.

"They're worthless!"

Later, when she thought of that night and many others, she thought:

"Who knows when I killed him most? Was it the day when I opened the door and saw him at last as he wanted me to see him? Was it the evening I turned out the light to forget his face? Was it the night he burned his paintings? Who knows if he wasn't expecting me to rush forward and pull some from the fire even if I burned my hands? Who knows if that wasn't ultimately the night I destroyed him by not saying or doing anything? There were still seven or eight canvases untouched at his feet. He said to me: 'Even Charmaine. And yet she loved this big portrait of the widows.' He held it up to me, and no doubt he expected me to say: 'Not that one. At least keep that one!' But no. I remained silent. I'd so often had the impression that painting was his secret garden where I, poor ignorant thing that I was, had no right to enter. But no! I'm trying to justify myself! It's an excuse. That night there was no more pride left in him. He was like a pleading beggar. He no longer had any thought for my ignorance. He no longer had a secret garden. He no longer had any artistic superiority over me. Patrice hoped for my verdict like a dying man waiting to be reassured that he is going to live. And I kept my mouth closed, taking refuge in my incompetence. My silence condemned him. I knew it and I said nothing."

But he had not said anything either during all this. It was later that she imagined the words he should have said if he had had the slightest wish to save himself. They were both too intelligent to use words they didn't mean. At that moment they were both overwhelmed and paralysed by the truth, as unquenchable as the flames.

The strange fire shot through with blue and yellow streaks of burning paint was reflected in an inverted pyramid across the pool. The swans, awoken by this untimely light, glided out of the shadows and were bathed in a rosy glow from the flames as they swam swiftly in and out of the darkness and the half-light. They clacked their beaks as if whispering the truth to each other. Sometimes they rose up on their webbed feet, beating their wings and hissing to chase away the untimely blaze robbing them of their night. The draught of air they created flattened the flames on the autodafé.

The swans, the trees, the perfume of the lilacs, the Olympian calm of the château with its badly filled crack on the wall like a gash caused by some ancient thunderbolt, the château itself that had witnessed so many other tragedies, they all appealed to the two of them to submit humbly to the mystery of existence and appreciate its small joys. Everything whispered to them that no matter what happened, they did not have so very long to live and that it was useless to cut short these pleasures, which would vanish soon enough of their own accord leaving no trace behind them.

When all was said and done they were not so unhappy together, except for the fact that love had become a chore to one of them and the other had become aware of it. How important would the disillusionment they felt today seem 30 years hence, when their bodies would be so familiar that they would no longer feel any emotion at being close? But wisdom was preaching in the desert: they had chosen truth over happiness.

Rose searched for something to say and found nothing. Her silence meant that she agreed with everything he thought he had discovered about her and which he might have wanted her to deny. But she stood there in her transparent nightdress, her body revealed in the brazen light, her unresponsive beauty mocked by the tragedy of the moment.

Only once did she show any reaction. It was when she saw the fragile musical instrument lying on the gravel, the fire reflected on its upturned belly: it was the mandolin he used to play so well on the banks of the Lauzon in front of the creaking shutters she used to open just a little to show him she was listening.

"Are you going to burn your mandolin *too*?"

He turned towards her and she could see that his eye was full of tears.

"It's no longer my friend," he said, his voice choking. "It has lost all its power to move you."

He seized the instrument and threw it on the fire. She did nothing to hold him back but she never forgot the sound made by the wood as the strings broke, like a live animal shrivelling up. The whole thing twisted and turned, disappearing finally in a long pink flame.

When it was all over and nothing was left, they put out the flame together with buckets of water from the pond. The swans had turned their backs and were floating gently on the water with their heads under their wings, moored in the gulf of darkness that had returned at last.

Rose led Patrice back to Pontradieu by the hand. She undressed him, put him to bed and tucked him in. She then lay down naked beside him, pressed herself to him, kissed his face, his lost eye, his good eye, his soft chin, the crevasses of his badly rebuilt cheeks. She tried to arouse him, made herself seductive, offered him her tongue, even tried to make him take her by force, did everything she could to try and make him forget. But he knew through bitter experience what she was trying to do, and he had destroyed too many precious things that evening without Rose lifting a finger to believe that the love she showed him was anything more than profound pity. Giving up the struggle, she cradled him in her arms all night long.

They had all the unhappiness in the world for company.

Patrice was slowly dying all through the summer and the heart-breaking autumn which followed. We people from Lurs and Les Mées – the farmers, passers-by, the old men who stood back cursing his red car – we took his despair to be arrogance and his distraction disdain. The rich rarely inspire pity: we would be much more satisfied with our lot if we could imagine that they also had to endure, submit, and turn away to avoid looking fate squarely in the face, just like the rest of us. Besides, Patrice was so rich compared with us that we didn't even see his disfigured face. We thought he was happy; we envied him. We all watched Rose Sépulcre change from a devilish beauty to a heavenly one. There was not a curve that wasn't soft and shapely. Her lower back was slightly flat when she was 16, but now it had filled out. Her hips swayed regally when she walked and her come-hither eyes were always the perdition of her soul. "When you have that in your bed every night, how could you complain about your lot?" we'd say to each other, thinking about our own wives who were either too skinny or too well-endowed.

When we heard the gunshot in November, we thought: "Who is out hunting so late?"

Smoke from the fires in the plain had just been dispelled by the evening wind. The sun's rays were slanting across the town rampart. The Briançon train was leaving Peyruis, its whistle blowing. Tricanote was keeping a disdainful distance from us as she crossed the Place des Feignants, balancing on her head a big bundle of olive twigs guaranteed to set her goats' teeth on edge.

Peace reigned. We were humble happy people living quiet lives. We took pleasure in watching time pass. How could we have imagined that someone of our race would want to escape from our serene anonymity?

Have you ever seen misfortune strike a middle-class house on a November evening? The flames on the black cooker glow under the saucepans of food which are almost ready to be served. The roast is sizzling in the oven, demanding to be basted. Guests are expected, three, perhaps four. Some bottles of ten-year-old wine have been opened and cautiously sniffed by the lady of the house before being decanted into long-necked carafes. Grandmother's embroidered cloth and the etched crystal glasses in front of the bouquets of flowers wait to be admired. Everything is ready. Such comfortable preoccupations tend to keep premonitions at bay.

In a scene like this, nothing is more startlingly out of place than the sudden appearance of two gendarmes in the doorway, the evening wind blowing behind them. It was bitterly cold in the dusk of that November evening. When the bell rang, Rose hastened to the door as usual to avoid Patrice having to wait in a draught. Her hands were still floury as she had been making gnocchi for her guests. Traces of it remained for some time on the big front door key she had just turned in the lock. She saw the blue uniforms and the caps. She never had any memory of the faces beneath them. When she was a child during the war she had seen it too often: two gendarmes resting their bicycles against the threshold of some house in the village, straightening their uniforms before knocking at the door, while everyone in the neighbourhood trembled and shut themselves away in their own homes. When they arrive unexpectedly you immediately think the worst and stand there stiffly as they salute. Rose understood why they were there before they began speaking.

"You are Madame Dupin née Rose Sépulcre?"

He had killed himself with the same pistol used by a comrade in arms with facial injuries like his, who had shot himself and left the weapon to Patrice in his will. This was the gun he had used to finish off the two huge dogs that were dragging the body of his father, Gaspard, around the freezing water of the pool. He had kept this weapon of war for years in his glove box, taking it out and stroking it from time to time like a friend always ready to be of service.

He had left no note of explanation for his action. Even if the gendarmes and the population were puzzled by the place where the body was discovered, Rose on the other hand had immediately interpreted it as an admission he had got from her. What use had it been to keep resolutely silent about her secret? So, during all that time when they hid the thoughts behind their words, he had quite correctly interpreted her responses when she remained silent or failed to mention something. Perhaps he had arrived at the only possible explanation even before she did and with greater understanding. What stood between them was the ghost of Séraphin Monge, all the more powerful because it was not of flesh and blood; it was an insubstantial but enduring absence, and therefore it could not be accepted or attacked or resisted.

He had killed himself on the clean open space of La Burlière where grass had begun to grow amongst the gravel that Séraphin had spread over it. He had no doubt stared for some time at that empty space where the farmhouse used to stand, where he had so often watched his friendly rival demolishing his obsession with a sledgehammer as if it were a man he was trying to flatten. His rival? He had not loved Rose, just as he had not loved Marie nor himself, Patrice. Her beauty, like all the rest, had left him unmoved. But no doubt Patrice had killed himself standing before the phantom of La Burlière to explain to Rose that he had lovingly understood her and that he was moving aside for the ghost.

His raincoat and scarf were found carefully folded over the marble coping of the well, the last surviving witness to so many tragedies, as though he had wanted to throw himself in it but had recoiled at the thought of all the things he would encounter on the bottom.

He was no more disfigured by the shot he had fired into his head than he was when he was alive.

The wind in the four cypresses standing sentinel around the ghost of La Burlière blew no more strongly when it heard him arrive than when he was nothing more than a small still bundle of flesh lying face down against the earth, shielded by their long evening shadows.

IV

EVERY NIGHT WHEN THEY WERE FACE TO FACE AT THE OVEN, BESIDE the hole where their secret lay buried, Célestat would say to Tibère as they waited for the bread to bake:

"You killed him! I know you did!"

"No!" Tibère replied.

He would keep shaking his head vigorously from side to side to emphasize the sincerity of the "no". Célestat looked at him still unconvinced; Tibère held his gaze. They sat on either side of a large heap of empty flour sacks which served as a table. They ate stale bread and *filetti d'alici* or goats' cheese. There was half a litre of wine opened in a lemonade bottle. They were very careful how much they took as Clorinde would not allow them any more.

Tibère could not get used to the profound silence of Lurs, a silence without water. In the Cévennes where he was born, the sound of a rushing stream could always be heard within the walls of the bakehouse. Apart from the occasional barking of a fox seeking the warmth of the village, there was nothing here but the wind to keep them company. And if there was wind, then he preferred silence. When the wind entered the long winding street in Lurs, it was greeted with the mournful humming of the electric wires. It would often whistle softly like someone calling and expecting a reply. The jute curtain scarcely separating the bakehouse from the street would wave and sometimes flap like a flag. Tibère could never get used to that wind.

This was the time when Célestat's strange behaviour made him feel ill at ease. The baker's eyes were becoming more and more sunken in his head. In the feeble light of a weak electric bulb you could be excused for thinking sometimes that he no longer had any eyes at all. The people of Lurs were becoming increasingly alarmed by his hollow cheeks accentuated by a growth of black beard.

For a few weeks it seemed that he was improving, but then he went back to looking just as bad as before. Now bakers are already pale people, but him, if he stood against a whitewashed wall, you wouldn't see him at all. He gave up playing *boules*. He no longer went hunting, which we are all mad about.

We needed to be reassured by the sight of Tibère's rude good health and the knowledge that the bread had never been so good, to keep giving him our custom. And of course we didn't know everything then. If we had . . .

Sometimes when Célestat had his mouth full of food he would suddenly stop chewing. It seems that the sound prevented him from hearing if someone was coming, as he had been constantly on the lookout lately. A big ball of food would stay there like a swelling in his cheek. His gaze stopped at the jute curtain and he would not take his eyes off it. Tibère felt a chill run down his spine. He had to stop himself from suddenly turning around. He had his own worries and his own haunting visions. He would not have been surprised either if someone had grabbed him solidly by the shoulder.

"What's wrong?" he would ask. "You look as though you're seeing a ghost."

"I'm afraid of seeing one . . ." Célestat replied gloomily. "The same wind was blowing the night he pulled aside the curtain."

"He's dead," Tibère said.

"Yes, he's dead. You killed him. You killed him so that you wouldn't have to give him back his box. And now I'm the one who's got the box."

He put his index finger to his forehead and twisted it as though he wanted to screw a hole in his head.

"No!" Tibère exclaimed in a quiet but exasperated voice. "I've told you that the earth was swallowing him up. I just had time to . . ."

"That's enough!"

They would both turn anxiously towards the right corner of the oven where a heavy drum of charcoal and ashes had been pulled over the hole they had dug. It was never moved.

There was no animosity when they spoke to each other. There was no bitterness in Célestat's accusation that Tibère had killed Séraphin, and no resentment in the way Tibère reacted to it. He willingly admitted that appearances were against him. They were men who were not used to expressing their thoughts or even to formulating them. One single thing had happened in both their lives: one had received a fortune from a person he detested; the other had seen this same man being dragged into a whirlpool of earth as if he had been in a whirlpool of water. At least that is what he claimed, what he was tired of repeating:

"I just had time to . . ."

"That's enough!"

And Célestat wouldn't believe it.

"You didn't want to give the box back to him. Tell the truth!"

"How can you give anything back to a dead man?"

During nights of silence or howling wind, whether one was kneading and the other weighing the flour, or they were packing or unpacking the oven together, they always came out with the same accusations and objections, but there was no hatred or anger in their voices. Whenever the wind blew, Célestat would say:

"He lifted up the curtain. He was twice as broad and as tall as I was. He took up the whole doorway! What would you have done if you were in my shoes. I took aim at him, but he kept on coming towards me. He said to me: 'Give it to her when she's better.' He said to me: 'So that she can forgive me, if possible, for having come into her life.'"

"But why didn't he want Marie. A beautiful girl like her!"

And Célestat would reply:

"Because . . ."

But he stopped short and would never go any further. The reply he whispered deep inside, no torturer could have extracted from him. He would have bitten off his tongue rather than say it. There are certain things you mull over between your conscience and your soul, which you never have the right to tell. You must keep them to yourself from the cradle to the grave. Something you believe deep in your heart can no more be expressed than it can be shared. And that is what Célestat Dormeur managed to do for the rest of his days: he kept that belief to himself until he died.

So, seeing that he'd get no more out of him on that score, Tibère Saille tried another angle:

"But given that fact, the gold belongs to Marie, doesn't it?"

"Given that fact, yes. But you haven't a hope. You'll never see it."

"Me, no. But what about Marie?"

"Marie has even less chance. It's murderer's money! I don't want my girl soiling her hand with that! Because . . . you see, I also went down into the well as he asked me to . . ."

We people of Lurs, one or other of us, at some time or another over the years came and stood behind the jute curtain trying to get some clue to the mystery of that family. Sometimes it was the wind, at others the noise of the shovels that prevented us from quite hearing what was being said inside. All we ever gleaned about the story were bits and pieces of various importance, scraps we had to piece together laboriously using our imagination. This wasn't easy. Whatever one person heard, that information was not shared with the rest of us. It was only when we were in a group expressing our frustration, when one of us was too confidently asserting something false to ferret out the truth, that in spite of our own self-possession, we would suddenly find some vital piece of information issuing from our usually tight lips. No sooner had the words escaped than we regretted them, and our husbands or wives bitterly reproached us for having carelessly given in.

"You great ninny, you know, do you, what Célestat and Séraphin said to each other on the night Séraphin came looking for him? Do you know what happened in Marie's bedroom when he went up there to make her better, or so they say? Would *you* have let a stranger into your daughter's bedroom? And *alone*, mind you! With her! As far as I'm concerned you'd have to rip out my liver before I'd allow it. Especially Séraphin! With his reputation!"

Lying in the conjugal bed, the beloved would let out a sarcastic laugh that echoed in the dark.

"Anyway, Tibère Saille doesn't seem to be in any hurry to marry the girl. We've waited a long time for the wedding. There's something fishy in all that, believe you me!"

We circled around this family, but also around Patrice and Rose Sépulcre, with a stubborn curiosity which we really couldn't help. We were in the shadows, while they were in the spotlight, struck by the hand of fate. The hand moves on and one day it could be us in the centre of the arena suffering our destiny. But for the moment we were simply in a good position not to miss a scrap of someone else's. Nothing, almost nothing, turned our attention away from it. We were hardly aware of ourselves growing older. As we made our way home every morning, the warm bread held against our chests, we reflected on the snippets of information gleaned around the counter in the bakery while Clorinde – who had always been so good – weighed out our order.

All the same, you musn't think that our curiosity was idle or unfriendly. In the same way as we had observed the transit of a comet 20 years earlier, we were simply observing the strange phenomenon of this family who had not given us a single smile since Séraphin left the village. So although we quietly kept our heads down to escape being noticed, we were perfectly aware that one day a Séraphin could descend upon us, turning our lives upside down and taking the smiles from our faces forever.

Something strange was going on. It was Marie who kept saying no in spite of the heart-shaped brioches Tibère made her on Sunday mornings or the chocolate bell – he dared not give her an egg – which he put on the family table at Easter. When he lifted it up, a shower of gold coins made of chocolate fell out of it and scattered between the wine glasses. Célestat turned pale and left the table. That evening he collared Tibère.

"Don't ever do that again! Never show a gold coin to my daughter again! Or I'll throw you out!"

"But they're made of chocolate!"

"It makes no difference. Even chocolate coins! Remember she knows nothing about it. We're the only ones who know! I don't want her tainted with gold!"

When Marie noticed Tibère was looking sad, she took him aside at the end of the meal.

"Listen Tibère. I'm telling you the truth. I'll never marry. I'm going to stay single. I'll not be a bride for any man. You'll be lucky if I don't become a nun!"

"You have . . ." Tibère began, but his voice choked.

Marie shook her head sympathetically.

"No, I *don't have*, if that's what you're thinking. Why should it be necessary *to have*?"

Tibère hadn't got over his boss grabbing him by the collar like that. That same night as they shared their bread and *filetti d'alici*, he said to Célestat:

"I spoke to Marie. Or rather, Marie spoke to me."

"Oh? What did she say?"

"She said she would never marry me."

"Oh? What do you expect? Women are like that sometimes. What do you expect? That's life!" Célestat said philosophically.

"She told me she would never marry anyone. That we would be lucky if she didn't become a nun."

"Good grief!" Célestat exclaimed. "That girl!"

From the time Marie began to grow up he had imagined himself at the centre of a gaggle of grandchildren she would present him with. For that reason he was quite pleased to grow old. And now Tibère had destroyed his dream with just a few words. He shot a baleful look at the right side of the oven then stared at the earth he would have liked to dig up there and then and remove from it what it would not allow him to forget. He even shook his fist at the container he and Tibère had dragged over to the excavation they had made.

"All because of that . . ."

Fear or prudence stopped the word on his lips. He calmed down little by little. He was panting like someone who had just made some great physical exertion. Tibère watched him and slowly regained some hope. He was wrong. Marie still said no. Célestat, however, continued to harass her.

"Why won't you marry Tibère?"

"Because I don't want to marry anyone."

"And what then? What about us? What about your mother? Are we going to grow old like this? After all we've done for you? And what about our land? The house? And everything we've earned? And the business? And the olive trees?" he exclaimed with an edge of panic to his voice. "What about the olive trees? Will they go to strangers too?"

"Well then!" Marie exclaimed in exasperation. "You should have had a boy!"

Now it was Clorinde's turn to groan.

"You know that I couldn't have any more after you!" she whimpered.

Marie got up and put her arms around her, to console her and say she was sorry. Plain Clorinde was sobbing into her plate.

"After everything we've done for you! You! The apple of our eye!"

All this was happening with Tibère sitting at the table, as if the family had closed in around him in spite of Marie's constant refusals. There were also heavy silences when the meal progressed as if the four of them were in complete agreement and one more family in Lurs was enjoying the peaceful evening around the meal-table.

Marie seemed docile with her parents and with Tibère. Occasionally she would even lay her hand on the apprentice's shoulder. He would hold his breath and remain stock-still, as if it were a bird that had landed there and would fly away again at the slightest movement. But he soon realized that she also put her hand on her mother and father's shoulders.

"It's a sign of affection," he thought. "It's all over. She's got used to me like a brother. She'll never see me as a man."

At night in the bakehouse his attention would turn to the corner of the oven and he would stare at it for a long time until Célestat realized what was going on and guessed his train of thought. When their eyes met, Célestat said:

"If you ever say anything to Marie about what you brought down from the mountain, I'll split your head in two with my hatchet!"

"Why?" Tibère replied quite taken aback. "If she knew that Séraphin was dead, she would give up hope and then . . ."

"I warn you . . . with my hatchet!" Célestat repeated through clenched teeth. "She's my daughter. The apple of my eye! She's already suffered enough. Besides, don't you understand that she'll immediately think you killed him? You don't really think she could accept you after that?"

"But I didn't kill him!" protested Tibère.

"You'll never get anyone to believe you."

He went out for a piss. The jute curtain had just fallen back behind him when he jerked it up again.

"Never! No-one!" he shot these words at Tibère, who slumped in his seat.

It was then that we saw Célestat and his workman begin to waste away. They looked haggard, exhausted, dull-eyed. People said of Tibère:

"What a pity! 'Specially as he was such a good-looking fellow!"

As for Célestat, well, the stones in the road are set edgewise in our part of the country and he continually stumbled on them. Watching him walk, you'd swear he was carrying a sack of flour. The business about Marie not wanting to marry had taken all the strength from his legs.

He deliberately set out to make her feel sorry by indulging in all kinds of dissolute behaviour he actually loathed. Normally as sober as a judge, he took to all kinds of excesses, drink obviously, but also food, especially game. He made a great show of salting his food at mealtime. He also showered it with pepper. He ground chilli into his soup on the pretext that nothing had any flavour. In short, he did everything a human being could to ruin his health. Clorinde watched him anxiously on his path to self-destruction.

"Don't drink so much!"

"What business is it of yours if I drink?"

Clorinde collapsed on to the table, her hair trailing among the noodles in the soup.

"You'll kill your father with your pig-headedness!" she would shout at Marie.

The two of them seemed to be putting on an act to force her to give in. But that was not the case: they meant it. Marie, however, did not give in.

One evening in the depths of winter, in spite of Tibère's efforts to stop him, Célestat went out to the bakehouse dressed in a flannel vest open at the neck, his arms bare up to the shoulder. He strolled over to the fountain to fill his buckets with water for the dough. When the night wind blew on the jet coming out of the spout and sprayed him with water, he took it full on the chest.

The following day he took to his bed. Dr Jouve said that he had pneumonia and he would reserve his diagnosis.

In fear and trembling we repeated this phrase which we knew did not bode well: "Dr Jouve has reserved his diagnosis." We heard nothing but bad news about Célestat in all the places in Lurs sheltered from the mistral. We gathered around the scales at the bakery where a mournful Clorinde still managed to serve the bread. We didn't greet Marie, but always stared at her so that she would be aware that we held her responsible for her father's illness. Marie, Clorinde, the women customers, everyone was in tears.

Célestat sank very low. Marie watched over him by day and Clorinde by night. All the baking fell on the shoulders of an anxious Tibère, who worked conscientiously. But when he was alone in the bakehouse the silence, only broken occasionally by the crackling of the coals, became more and more difficult to bear. He was not a man with much imagination and yet, like Célestat in recent days, he found himself looking towards the corner where they had both buried their secret. "What'll happen," he wondered, "if the old man dies? What should I do? What should I say?"

One night when Célestat had taken a turn for the worse, it occurred to Tibère to call in at the bakery on the prextext of finding out if he was needed there.

The door was open. Clorinde had fallen asleep from exhaustion behind the Roberval scales, still fully dressed, slumped on the stool where she usually just rested her knee. In the room behind the shop, normally so spick and span, everything was a mess. The day's dirty dishes were still in the sink and on the waxed tablecloth, bottles of Célestat's medicine were scattered among sticky spoons that had been used to pour the potions through his clenched teeth. The mess everywhere gave the dismal impression of someone who had given up the struggle.

Tibère, who was wearing rope-soled shoes, crept quietly upstairs. The sound of Célestat's breathing filled the stairwell and all the rooms in the house through their wide-open doors. You felt that he could be heard from the attic, from the street. It was as though he had to steal everyone's air to survive.

Marie's head was resting on the top of the walnut bed-end, her father was lying under an eiderdown. She was sobbing, her head hidden in her arms. Tibère would have given all the gold in the box to console her. He couldn't bear to see her unhappy. She had become the apple of his eye too. She stammered something he couldn't pick up.

"I was sitting further away," Tricanote said later, "in an armchair with its back to the bed, and not only that, it was dark in my corner of the room and no-one could see me. When I heard Tibère whisper 'Marie', I turned around. He was reaching out his hand towards her but he didn't dare to touch her."

"And she, Marie, what was she doing? What was she saying that Tibère couldn't hear?"

"She was saying: 'Séraphin! Oh Séraphin! Why have you forsaken us?'"

"But that was terrible blasphemy!"

"May I be struck down dead on the spot if that wasn't what she said!"

When Tricanote was daring death to take her with these words, she was almost ninety-three years old. She and the Marquise de Pescaïré, who was a recruit of hers, fought neck and neck as to who would bury the other. Tricanote gave up at 100 and the Marquise, perhaps because her soul was more at peace, outlived her by four years.

"Well then," we said, "you must have been in a good position to know what they were going to say to each other."

"Yes, I was in a good position. And I know what they said."

"Tricanote, aren't you ashamed, spying on lovers like that?"

"First of all they weren't lovers, well, at least she wasn't, and furthermore if I'd shown myself, they never would have been! The truth is that after about twenty-five minutes when Tibère finally touched Marie's arm, she turned around as if he'd stung her. She said: 'Oh, it's you. What are you doing here? Go back to the oven or the bread will burn!' 'Mistress,' he said humbly, 'I didn't want you to be alone in these sad times.'

"Then Marie threw back her hair – you know that proud swing of the head of hers – and she said: 'Oh, but I'm not alone. Don't worry about that!'

"'Yes mistress. You are alone.'

"'No. Séraphin is by my side.'

"'No mistress. Séraphin is dead.'

"'It's not true! He isn't dead!'

"'Yes he is mistress. I assure you he's dead.'

"'You silly fool, how would you know whether he's dead or alive? Eh? How would you know?'

"She was shaking him like a plum tree. That was our Marie all right: spirited, forceful, passionate.

"And," Tricanote said, "I remember that there was silence, a silence that lasted at least a minute or two. A silence troubled only by the laboured breathing of Célestat lying there dying. At the end of that long, wordless lull, Tibère replied: 'Nothing mistress. I know nothing about it. You're right. Nothing at all.'

"'Get back to the oven then, or the bread will burn!' Then she turned her back on him to give all her attention to her father. Then I heard Tibère dragging himself to the door on his rope soles. That's when she called him back: 'Tibère!'

"'Yes mistress.'

"'Tibère, if you can prove to me that Séraphin really is dead, I'll marry you then and there! Do you hear me? Then and there!'

"He didn't reply. He went silently down the stairs, in the same way as he'd come up.

"But," Tricanote reported, "it was after those words that Célestat's death rattle suddenly stopped. They didn't even notice. But I said to myself straight away: 'That's it! He's dead!' Then I went up to the bed. I took hold of Marie's arm and I said to her: 'Marie,' I said to her, 'remember what you've just said! It's a solemn promise! And you've just made it in the presence of your dying father!' I was sure then that he was dead. We both went up to the head of the bed and leaned over the dying man. But no. He wasn't dead. He was sleeping peacefully."

It was the following day that Marie went off to see her godmother. She never forgot that winter day when she went to meet her destiny at the Phare du Soleil, the Lighthouse of the Sun. The Marquise's house was called the

Phare du Soleil because it stood like a cube on its promontory, exposed to winds from all points of the compass. It was built on an angle with one of its corners facing the edge of the cliff like the bow of a boat, so that the fourteen windows on each of its sides glowed with the first and last rays of the sun. Because of them Lurs, high on its mountain ridge, heralded the morning and evening for thirty kilometres around.

It was formerly a seminary of the bishops of Sisteron, acquired some time in the past by the parents of the Marquise, when they had had enough of catching their death of cold in their draughty Château de Bel-Air in the Sigonce area. But people who cannot conceive of corridors shorter than twenty metres have no hope of avoiding draughts. Although they were austere and without the ancestral portraits, the corridors at the Phare du Soleil were every bit the equal of those in Bel-Air. The parents of the Marquise had draughts aplenty which eventually killed them. The Marquise herself from the age of sixty, made the empty spaces echo with the creaking of her old bones, for she was as crippled with rheumatism as a sailor on a Cape Horn clipper.

It was scarcely 400 metres from the bakery to the Phare du Soleil, and those of us who saw Marie pass by that day wondered what was making her walk so fast. Could the reason have been, perhaps unconsciously, that there had never been so much hope in that poor heart of hers, which felt the presence of death on all sides!

A bunch of pretty clouds was blossoming in the sky. It made Marie think of new beginnings and eternity. The poor girl was only twenty. How could she not feel hope reviving?

She pushed open the swinging door to the main corridor. Slanting rays of sunlight beat down through the window on the west side of the corridor. Marie was dazzled by them and had to shield her eyes with her hand to see where she was going. She called out:

"Godmother!"

Her voice echoed down the hall. The Marquise's reply came from far off and in the sharp tone she used since she had become a little hard of hearing.

"Here I am! Come down here!"

Here was a large panelled drawing room at the end of the corridor Three rays of light from the three windows passed lit up the faded blue of the armchairs, crossed the open space and hit the fire in the hearth, making the flames appear to vanish into thin air. A tearing sound came from behind the open double doors. The Marquise, who was trussed up in an ugly dress of worn flannelette, was tearing long strips from a pile of unfolded sheets coming up to her knees. From twenty ancestors, direct or by marriage, she had inherited the trousseau linen that had been gathering dust ever since in wedding chests never opened.

Marie kneeled down to kiss her, for the Marquise had shrunk as she got older and the armchair was now too big for her.

"What are you making?" Marie asked.

"As you see: bandages. You know Marie, there will always be wars. I'm preparing bandages for the wounded of the future."

She looked at her goddaughter's face. At the time we are speaking of, she was a shrewd old lady who said little but who humbly devoted herself to alleviating the misfortunes of others. We didn't know whether she had ever been young, whether she had known love. It seemed as though she had always been the way she was then: wise and respectable, hair always neatly done, extraordinarily pale, with eyebrows always arched as though eternally surprised.

"I hardly see you these days," she said to Marie.

"I've been very worried about my father."

"I know you've been worried about him, but that's not the reason why you've stopped coming."

"No. That's not the reason. I didn't want you to keep telling me to forget him. That's all you seemed to say: 'Forget him! Forget him!' I didn't want to hear it any more."

"And now?"

"Now I want you to tell me if he's alive. Everyone says he's dead. But I won't believe it! I won't have it!"

She had seized the wrists of the Marquise who was desperately trying to avoid Marie's eyes.

"You won't have it! You won't believe it! Who are you not to have or believe?"

"Someone who loves him! I beg you. You know, don't you? Tell me if he's alive or dead?"

"What's it got to do with you? What good will it do you? Marie, listen to me. He never looked back, not once! Oh, we were watching him, believe me! As soon as he started down the hill on his bicycle, Tricanote and I went out. We rushed over to the ramparts. And it was windy and cold, I can tell you! But no. He never turned his eyes from the road in front of him, neither towards us nor the village. Now if he had loved you Marie, if he had loved us even a little, even if he had forced himself to leave, wouldn't he have looked in our direction one last time?"

She shook Marie by the shoulders and looked deep into the eyes of the girl kneeling before her. She said softly as she rather clumsily tore her bandages:

"Listen, if I weren't afraid of blaspheming, I'd say that his kingdom was not of this world. Even when he was born, Marie, he should not have survived. He didn't fit in with us. He had no special regard or love for us."

"But he saved me! He fought with death for a whole night for my sake!"

"He would have done the same for anyone, my poor Marie! That's what's so heart-breaking for us! For you! Oh, believe me! Tricanote and I have talked about it endlessly and . . ."

"I beg you! Godmother, just tell me if he's alive or dead!"

"Tricanote, what would you have done in that situation if Marie had asked you that question? Well, I must confess to you that it pained me to see her poor parents fretting so much and the man who loved her so full of anxiety. He's a good young man from an honest family – I made enquiries. And then there was Marie, so full of life. It oozed out of every pore. It was all very well her talking about becoming a nun; she wasn't cut out for it. She'd have been one of those sisters who writhe in pain every night. What would you have done? As for me, I have to admit it: I lied! I lied on purpose!"

This is what the Marquise said to Tricanote the following day when they saw each other, and Tricanote replied:

"No, you didn't lie! He's dead! He's dead! I can feel it here."

96

She placed her arm firmly across her chest with a gesture that expressed the certainty of Séraphin's end.

The Marquise had taken Marie's hands in hers and, looking her straight in the eye, said to her:

"Marie, listen to me carefully: as truly as my name is Marie du Cental-Lozière, Marquise de Pescaïré. I swear to you he's dead. You shouldn't think about it any more. On my oath. You know Marie, I've never sworn an oath by my whole name. And believe me, I've been through a lot in my lifetime!"

She put her hands on each side of her goddaughter's head and stroked her hair:

"There's only one thing you can do for him now, and that's to pray. Pray for the repose of his soul. He must need it, believe me! As for the rest, there's no more you can do for him and he can do no more for you."

That's what the Marquise de Pescaïré said to Marie, who didn't believe her for a moment.

"They haven't a hope!" she said to herself. "They want me to stop loving a ghost. They want me to be normal again. They want me to give in to them. They haven't a hope!"

But the sublime is not an attitude that the ordinary run of mortals can proudly maintain for very long. One day nature would get the better of her, and she would have to give in. When nature first makes itself heard in a girl's heart, it rumbles like a distant storm: nothing to worry about. But then it grows, it thunders and sweeps away the small store of good sense she prided herself on. One day it cannot be contained any longer. Trying to stop it is like trying to stop the bud of almond blossom from coming out in winter. Marie felt flattened by a strange fatigue, something like the way she felt when her illness literally fell away from her.

We all noticed the irrational way Marie behaved during that spring. Tibère still looked just as bad with the black stubble on his unshaven face. His bread was as good as Célestat's; there was no argument about that. But going from that to marrying Marie! Since her misfortunes, we all took something of a proprietorial interest in the girl. We were quite offended to see her taken from us by someone who looked so bad. People said: "They're not suited!" This judgment obliged them not to marry.

Nevertheless, one evening at the dinner table Marie said to Tibère:

"Tibère! Look at me!"

Since Marie had told them that she would rather become a nun than marry anyone, and as everyone in the family and in Lurs knew about her decision, Tibère, Clorinde and Célestat had taken to keeping their noses down in their plates. They were a sorry sight and there were no more smiles around the table in the Dormeur household of an evening, although the meal was still as good.

Tibère, therefore, timidly raised his eyes to Marie sitting opposite him. In front of him was the very picture of beauty he had always imagined. He still couldn't imagine himself catching hold of her by the waist or squeezing her around the hips. He never saw her as a simple country baker's daughter. She stood out against the cold fireplace and the red-tiled *potager*[2], unreal and inaccessible, as she would to a love-struck suitor. He didn't consider that what he had done to get her, those acts that would permanently weigh on his conscience, bound Marie in any way. He had never once thought of saying to Célestat: "You promised her to me."

"I'll live in her shadow," he thought. "I'll never demand anything."

There she was, looking at him across the table with those impenetrable clear blue eyes. She had raised the silver mug she had drunk from since she was a child, since her godmother had given it to her as a christening present with the silver cutlery set and the Dresden knick-knacks sitting on the dressing-table in her bedroom.

She was looking at him from behind the mug with a slight smile on her face. He couldn't decide whether it was friendly or just mocking. She said to him:

"Tibère! Get your nose out of your plate. Look at me, straight at me! You wanted me to marry you? I'll marry you! Are you happy?"

He obeyed her and looked up. He stared at her for several seconds without saying anything. They had only reached the soup course. The food was simmering on the stove over the embers. Tibère quietly folded his napkin

---

2 A *potager* is a tiled stone or brick construction found in Provencal kitchens, usually next to the fireplace. The top surface is both a work-bench and a stove, with one or more openings fuelled by charcoal underneath.

instead of putting it into the wooden ring. It was the only one on the table without a name engraved on it, and suitably anonymous for a journeyman doing his tour of France, one day here, somewhere else the next. He got up slowly and turned his back on the family. He raised the curtain between himself and the shop, then raised the curtain to the street. They could hear the sound of the beads as it fell back behind him.

"*Voï!*" Clorinde exclaimed. "What's wrong with him? What did you do to him, Dormeur?"

"Me? Nothing," Célestat said, "but our girl threw that 'I'll marry you' at him like a bone to a dog."

"*Beau diou!* Good Lord, he *is* a touchy one!" Clorinde groaned.

Marie said nothing. She stared dumbfounded at the empty seat opposite her, got up and also left the room. Down in the direction of the bakehouse Tibère was disappearing up the ladder leading to his loft. Marie went that way. She stopped for a moment in front of the open door to the dark corridor. She called out:

"Tibère!"

He didn't reply, so she went up the stairs as determined as she always was, with a confidence that came from her whole personality.

Tibère had his back to her. He had spread out his bundle of clothes on the bed. It was a real bundle: a big unbleached linen cloth brought from Lodève, which had already served three generations of Sailles on their journey around France. It took no time to count the contents: two shirts, three underpants, four pairs of socks, and that was it. And his mother's picture in a small black frame that he usually stood on the bedside table.

"What are you doing?"

"As you can see mistress. I'm going away."

"Oh!"

She knew that if he uttered these offhand words without replying, it would be true: he would go away. But if he engaged with them, if he had the misfortune to add other words to them, he would stay, and for good.

"Do you think you are the only one who has their pride? I have mine too.

You are marrying me like someone going to their death! You are marrying me because you've lost everything!"

"Yes," Marie said.

"You don't love me."

"No," Marie said. "But I'll get used to you. I don't love anyone. I loved Séraphin Monge, full stop, end of story."

"Well then, why do you want to marry me?"

"Because my parents are miserable. They want grandchildren. I'm their only child. I must give them what they need."

"You'd find plenty of others to help you do that."

Marie clenched her fists and shouted:

"What do you want of me? My body? You'll have it! What are you complaining about?"

He was going to reply: "Do you think I did all I did simply because I wanted your body?" He too clenched his fists to stop himself from blurting out those words that could never be taken back. He could quite clearly see before him Séraphin Monge, just as he was a few seconds before he died, looming up out of the mist as if he were slowly taking flight, covered in mud, raised up on the crown of the tree roots turning like the spokes of a wheel dripping clay, then swallowed, buried alive with his arms raised up to the open air like a drowning man. It was at this moment in his vision that he was the most tempted to tell Marie the truth. If he had spoken, nothing would have happened and he could have just gone on making up his bundle.

"Tibère," Marie said deliberately, "make up your mind. I told you this evening that I would marry you. I won't say it again."

She went out. Taking her place at the table again, it seemed as though her father and Clorinde had been there all that time with their soup spoons stopped half way between their plates and their mouths. She slipped on to her chair, then took a good drink from her mug, which was all she drank.

"He'll come back," she said.

And come back he did. He lifted up the curtain to the room behind the shop and sat down in his place opposite Marie. Clorinde got up to put the pot of food in the middle of the table. She removed the lid. Used to her role as servant to all, she was about to serve everyone else before herself, beginning with Célestat and Marie. Marie stopped her arm, nodding in the direction of the baker's assistant.

"Serve him first," she said "This evening he has a right to it."

There was pain in Tibère's eyes.

The wedding took place three months later at the Phare du Soleil, which the Marquise let them have while she went on her annual retreat to the nuns of Sylvabelle.

Members of the Saille family came from Lodève in the train. By chance their eldest daughter had also just married a baker, allowing them to leave the shop, otherwise they would not have been able to come. They were a couple who never left each other's side, and there would be a great hullabaloo if one of them happened to lose sight of the other. They were always leaning against each other like two shaky columns. If they let go, they would both fall down.

"You'll come to mine," Marie had said to Rose. This wedding was the only time when the two Lurs girls could imagine that they had put a grain of salt on happiness' tail and that it would stay there, tamely, curled up between them.

Patrice's face still wore the expression of a happy man waiting patiently. Rose had not yet seen him as he really was. Her feet scarcely touched the ground. In the presence of Marie, who had never managed to look Patrice in the face, she made a deliberate show of her happiness and exaggerated it. Séraphin was still so much in her heart that she was not yet resigned to see Marie as anything but a rival. Marie, who felt the same aversion, had outdone her. Rose had thought of the Venetian glass chandeliers for her wedding but not of providing music. Marie had the Varieties jazz band from Manosque. The guests danced until four o'clock in the morning in the Marquise's drawing room.

For their wedding night, the Marquise had given the keys of Bel-Air to her goddaughter and Célestat those of the truck to Tibère. They slipped away as soon as they could.

"It will be cold at Bel-Air at this time of year," the Marquise thought. "All to the good. They'll cling to each other. The cold will throw them into each other's arms more surely than love. They'll have nothing but each other. It's a life-raft I'm giving them, not a château."

Yes indeed. It was cold at Bel-Air. The chestnut trees twined the lace of their bare waving branches around the old building. The evening air seemed to echo with the thunder of disapproval, already foretelling the future.

It was a country château where the air smelled of wild savory. It used to be pink. Large ochre patches of it sometimes turned dark when the rain whipped across it from the south.

"I've had the bed set up in my parents' bedroom," the Marquise said.

A tester bed with floral hangings stood in the middle of a room in which everything was pink. The door curtains beneath the coffered ceiling were pink; also pink were the poufs, the armchairs, the writing desk with ten little drawers and the 36 square metre carpet with a medallion picture in the middle. It showed a pink, muscle-bound Aeneas, still wearing the plum of Troy in his helmet, astride an unrealistic, flesh-pink Dido who, despite her baby face, welcomed the warrior's attack with an ambiguous smile.

"As soon as they see that room, they'll be so impressed they'll forget their soul-searching and their wariness of each other," the Marquise thought. "They're not used to looking at tapestries, let alone erotic tapestries. They were given by the Marquis de Sade to my ancestor from Lozère, as a tribute to her sexual skill – God have her soul, if it's within his power."

This Marquise from a bygone age had her weavers imagine what had taken place between these two giants, half-god, half-human, after Virgil had created them. It resulted in the finest series of erotic scenes that one could imagine, encircling the room, finishing in triumph at the centre of the carpet. One could almost hear the joyful cries of those flesh-pink embraces in which everything was subtly suggested by the lovers' eyes raised heavenward. The charming convulsions of their amazingly muscled bodies were frozen in full play, but it was impossible not to imagine them tensing.

"Look!" Marie whispered. "You'll never see anything like it again in your life!"

She drew him by the hand to look closely at each painted scroll.

"I want you to do that to me!" she said.

Her finger was pointing in very definite fashion at Dido's revealingly displayed buttocks. By the time they had gone around all the painted medallions, Marie's veil was hanging over the pink writing desk and half their clothes were strewn over the carpet. They leaped into bed with a cry. The Marquise had had the bed made up with satin sheets, which were also meant to be cold. There was nothing else to be done but cling tightly to each other to keep out the cold and loneliness. The Marquise was right: she was giving them a life-raft.

"Turn out the light!" Marie ordered.

Then she touched the muscles in his arms. They were as big as Aeneas'. For a long time now she had needed to make love: seven, perhaps eight years, she couldn't count how many years she had felt this desire, so frequently repressed. All Marie had to do, with eyes closed and hands firmly gripping Aeneas' muscles, was to call up Séraphin in her imagination and concentrate all her attention on him.

Swapping Tibère for Séraphin was a difficult exercise. It was also a dangerous exercise to hide from a living man the fact that a dead man was being superimposed upon him. But Marie was made to accomplish this transubstantiation quite naturally. The passion of her embrace was never feigned. Tibère never had any reason to doubt.

It was more than 100 years since those walls had heard anyone make love. The last time any cries had rung out in that house they were death throes, and they were soon replaced by the dull sound of a coffin adorned with a blue coat of arms being bumped into one doorway after another along the grand corridor.

That night the walls were rejuvenated and came to life again. As the newly-weds knew they were alone in the whole empty, icy building, they had not even bothered to close their door. Tibère kept his eyes open, straining to see Marie; Marie had hers closed, looking at Séraphin. But they each made up for the torture endured by their bodies for so many wasted years when they had been cut off from the only pleasure that obliterated everything.

Yet their lips never uttered a Christian name nor a term of endearment. It was more like a battle they were waging. The jerking movement of the canopy on the bed and the tassels on the hangings bore witness to the energy of their lust. Yet that night and those that followed, Tibère never said anything but the formal *vous* to Marie, even when she climaxed, squeezing his neck with all her might as though she was strangling him. He would have to use all the strength in his hands to unlock this vice-like grip. At those times he had the feeling of ill-treating her. Once he even heard Marie's bones crack and the next morning her wrists were still red.

"I'm sorry," he said, "I've hurt you."

She rolled her eyes and shook her head to show she understood. And yet she never forgot her wedding night in the tester bed, the satisfaction of her flesh luxuriously accompanied by the silent lovemaking of Dido and Aeneas, frozen in the frustration of timeless immobility. She always believed that her first child had been conceived that night during those hours when she had at last had her fill of Séraphin in the mystery of the château with the smell of wild savory in the air.

Later she wanted to tell Tibère the truth, but they were ill-matched, except at night. There was no tenderness in their love. They spent their days, taciturn and uncommunicative, trying to forget their lovemaking. Whenever their eyes were likely to meet, they looked away, as if gravely offended.

Old Clorinde, who still served in the bakery until she died, would groan and say a long time later: "What can come of a marriage like that?" For, not wanting to be separated from their daughter by a floor or even a few metres, the Dormeurs had simply changed the bed in Marie's room. As a result, they kept up the frenetic activity they had begun in the château in that maidenly bedroom, where their frenzied bouts made the trembling Dresden figurines rattle on the marble top of the chest of drawers for hours on end. Two rooms away, Clorinde's heavy slumbers would suddenly be interrupted by the glass on the kerosene lamp which shook even more steadily than during the Venelles earthquake of 1909. Clorinde turned over towards the wall and clamped the pillow over her head, trying not to hear. Even though she knew that the arrival of the grandchildren she wanted so much depended on it, she felt that such immodesty in their intercourse could only bring down the wrath of heaven. She was not wrong.

Not yet knowing the real situation, we poor fellows heard something about this lovemaking. but could only imagine it with heavy hearts. What happened to the tremendous love we had all witnessed? The all-consuming love that made us fear that the whole thing would end in tragedy and that Marie might throw herself into the waters of the Durance? We were full of bitter thoughts against fate, which had transformed the poor girl's tragic destiny into a natural but banal happiness. There was even something rather indecent about it.

Clorinde shared her fears with the Marquise.

"Do you think it's normal to make such a racket?"

"So much noise, you mean? Don't worry, Clorinde my dear. They love each other, that's the main thing!"

But one day Marie came to see her and confessed:

"Godmother, I'm pregnant."

"Goodness, how wonderful! How wonderful! Do your parents know?"

"Yes, but I don't want to deceive you. It's Séraphin's child."

"What did you say?"

"Yes. Oh, I know. You say he's dead, but he's alive every night for me. I think of Séraphin every night, otherwise I could never do it!"

"My poor child! What about your husband? It's worse than if you were unfaithful to him!"

"No! He's happy. How could he know? What more does he need?"

"But," said the Marquise, who was frightfully curious, "what do you do? How do you do it? And first of all, how do you know it's Séraphin?"

"He envelops me. He's between me and Tibère, as if he was protecting me all the time we're making love. Do you think I'm imagining it?"

"One day you'll say his name aloud, and that will be the end of everything. It has happened to stronger women than you!"

"No. I never say a word. I cry out, that's all. I don't want to talk. I don't talk. Did you?"

"You'll say his name in your dreams!"

"What of it? Tibère knows that I've only loved one man in my life and that it's not him."

"No doubt he knows, but he must always be trying to forget it."

"He has my cries. He has my body. I don't hold back. I'm as energetic as he is. He'll have children. He has his job. I give him every reason to be proud. What more could he want?"

"Your heart."

"My heart? Séraphin took it with him."

"But can't you forget him? Everyone forgets in time. A dead man's a dead man! You would do better to think of what he must be now, rather than imagine him alive!"

"I don't believe he's dead," Marie exclaimed. "You all keep repeating the same thing! But surely I have the right to something in my life too?"

She turned away sobbing and began to leave.

"Marie!" the Marquise called to her.

"What now, Godmother?"

"Do you sometimes go to confession?"

Marie shrugged her shoulders without turning around.

"At Easter, like everybody else."

"Well, never confess that!"

Time sharpens remorse and allows it to thrive. After that day the Marquise began to entertain her own.

"I've been very thoughtless," she said to herself. "What right did I have to tell Marie that Séraphin was dead? How do I know? Now, as far as she's concerned he's dead and she resurrects him every night! What a situation! Who would have thought that this straightforward girl would become so secretive in herself and to us?"

Séraphin's ghost repeatedly disturbed the Marquise's dreams at night, like a copious meal that makes one pay the consequences of having indulged in it. But he also haunted her during the day. Since she kept watching for it so intently, a draught shooting down the corridor was enough to make her think that he was there walking slowly, as huge and solid as he was on the day when the Marquise on her knees with Tricanote watched him leave for another destiny.

She often felt, in fear and trembling, that he was about to appear at the open door of the drawing room, taking up the whole doorway, his eyes pale and without expression – Good Lord, so like her own mother's – and that he would ask her to justify herself.

"Why did you tell Marie that I was dead?"

At times the illusion was so gripping that the Marquise's mouth went dry with terror, her knitting needles stopped in mid-air if she was knitting, or her scissors wide open if she was cutting up her endless bandages. She only managed to reassure herself through her piety and powers of reason.

"If he were alive," she thought, "he couldn't come down my long corridor so silently. It's quite simply his ghost who wanders among us whenever we think of him."

It was at this time one evening that a breathless Tricanote was rushing up the street driving her goats before her.

"Clorinde! Clorinde! Where are you? Rose Sépulcre's husband has blown his brains out!"

"Good Lord!" Marie groaned. "She must be suffering terribly!"

They couldn't hold her back. Even with her large belly, she didn't wait for her father who was struggling with the crank handle in the car. She left them all standing and got on the delivery bicycle as if she were still the slender Marie of old.

She arrived at Pontradieu just after the gendarmes. Apart from the anxious farmers standing there hat in hand, thunderstruck, suddenly without a master, Rose was the only person in the drawing room with its chandeliers who had seen her so triumphant. Bathed in tears, she rushed towards Marie crying:

"You know, don't you Marie! You know that I wasn't pretending! You know that I really did love him!"

"Of course, my dear Rose! Of course I do. Don't worry! I do know!"

They hugged each other, hampered somewhat by the size of Marie who held centre stage in these tragic circumstances, almost mockingly in control, as if thumbing her nose at death's moment of triumph.

"They'll bring him back to you! You'll be here alone!" Marie exclaimed. "I'm staying with you!"

"My sister . . ." Rose said defensively.

"Your sister!" Marie replied, rolling her eyes. "My dear Rose, she hates you."

From that moment on, Marie with all her bulk took over the running of Pontradieu. She was everywhere, giving orders to all and sundry. She stood like a rampart in front of Rose when the farmers brought back Patrice's body on a stretcher with the shroud covering his head, and put it down on the same spot where Gaspard Dupin and Charmaine had been laid several years before.

"Rose! Don't look! You mustn't see him! I beg you!"

"Oh, Marie. You mustn't look either! You'll harm the child you're carrying!"

But Marie presided over the preparation of the body without flinching, assisted by the farmers. She went to bed fully clothed with Rose, who lay there with her teeth chattering all night. She fell asleep and woke up freezing cold. Rose was going down the main staircase in the dark when Marie caught up with her and put her arms around her, enveloping her in her dominating love.

"No Rose! You mustn't! You mustn't see him!"

"One last time!" Rose sobbed. "He loved me so much! Spoiled me so much, if only you knew!"

But she let herself be held back without too much resistance, worn out by the shocking tragedy. "If I see him," she thought, "he'll appear to me every night. But it will be my punishment. You mustn't take that away from me!" That is what she said to Marie who was firmly holding her back and pushing her upstairs with her arms and her belly. And it was then, staggering up towards the bedroom, that Rose also confessed to her that one day the sight of Patrice had become intolerable to her and that he had noticed it straight away.

"I killed him!" she said.

She slipped from Marie's grasp, collapsing on the stairs and crying more than she had ever done in her life.

"I'm here!" Marie said. "I'm here! I'm like you! There, there. I won't leave you."

When the coffin arrived, she was there. When the wheels of the hearse crunched on the gravel of the path, she was there. She supported the widow walking unsteadily behind it in the rain, stumbling through the puddles. The tall trees were also in mourning above the Dabisse cemetery set among the cornfields.

No-one was there. Well . . . apart from the factory people, the farmers, Rose's mother and her other, unmarried daughter.

"I told you so," Marcelle murmured to Rose. "The day that happens, it's the end of everything!"

"Get away!" Marie whispered. "Aren't you ashamed, you dreadful creature!"

"All the same, I was right!" Marcelle insisted.

No-one was there. Rose had not let people know. She had wanted to be alone as much as possible with the man she had brought back to life and then reproached herself for killing him.

"I should at least have saved the mandolin," she said, "the day he burned everything. You know, Marie, the mandolin he played to serenade me during those evenings on the banks of the Lauzon? I should have torn it out of his hands, told him he was mad, that the mandolin was mine not his, and protected it with my body so that he couldn't get at it. What would it have cost me? He would have understood then that I loved him, that I still loved him! Then he would still be here. And then he would still be with me! That's what you'd have done, Marie!"

Marie patted her, held her more closely, but said nothing. She couldn't say to her: "No, I wouldn't have done it." She remembered too well the day she had torn Séraphin's cradle from him when he was about to throw it on the fire. She had sworn to herself that her first child would sleep in that cradle every day. Clorinde would wring her hands in despair.

"You're out of your mind! A cradle that's been part of a murder, a cradle still stained with blood!"

"Marie," the Marquise de Pescaïré said, "I beg of you! I have a family cradle in the attic. The Duchesse de Berry put the Comte de Chambord in it one day when she was fleeing! I'll give it to you Marie! I'll make you a present of it! Your children will sleep in a royal cot!"

But Marie just shook her head.

"It will be Séraphin's or a straw mattress on the floor!"

Tibère also went on the attack, after being lectured by Clorinde.

"Mistress, mightn't it be better to . . ."

He got short shrift:

"That's enough from you! You have no rights over my children, apart from making them!"

Tibère said no more. He watched Marie's belly with great delight. She could say what she liked: she was carrying the proof that they had made wild love.

"Rose . . . I wanted to say to you . . . I don't know how to ask you . . . Well, you're part of the social world now and we, Tibère and I, we're no shining lights."

"I belong to the world of the lonely," Rose replied bitterly.

"Would you be godmother to our first child?"

"Is that what you wanted to ask me?"

Marie flung her arms around her neck.

"Oh, I'm so happy! If it's a girl we'll call her Rose, and Rosin if it's a boy."

"Oh, no! It's awful! Why wouldn't you call him –?"

Marie put her hand over Rose's mouth.

"No!" she said. "I'd never call him that!"

Rose gently removed Marie's fingers from her lips.

"You knew what I was going to say?"

Marie nodded.

Immediately after Patrice's death, Marie was all Rose had. No-one came near her. She had committed the cardinal sin of not formally informing people.

"I didn't know! I wasn't informed!"

It didn't matter that the announcement appeared in the paper or that the postman had been spreading the terrible news everywhere. His legs were so tired that he had to sit down frequently on his rounds as he repeated the same words each time:

"Patrice with the disfigured face has blown his head off!"

No, that was not enough. As far as we were concerned, a person was not dead until the family itself, specifically, had knocked on our doors individually to inform us of the bad news. The narrow-minded village, of which we were all a part, gave its verdict on every occasion:

"*Eh bé vaï*! She can't have thought much of him if she didn't even inform us of his death!"

A woman from Entrevennes who had always thought she was related (she brought them tommes cheeses every week) still had raised eyebrows on the subject.

"Patrice Dupin? He's dead? That's the first I've heard of it! *I* wasn't informed."

The widow encountered the severe faces of people like these who only recognized grief once it was made public.

"Look at her!" they said. "She's not weighed down with grief! She didn't shed one tear at the cemetery!"

It's difficult not to get the reputation of being a merry widow when the person in question has a château, for anything with more than ten rooms, a pond and a hectare of ground around it is called a château here. It's difficult to acquire the reputation of an inconsolable widow when one has an income that arrives regularly and increases from year to year with very little attention paid to it.

Patrice had left his will with the notary. It could not have been simpler: *I leave all the goods I possess and will possess at the time of my death to my wife, born Rose Sépulcre on 3 May 1906.*

The mill carried on as usual, overseen by old servants who voluntarily kept on working for the sheer pleasure of living with the colour of wheat and the warmth of flour until they died. They never mentioned this strange passion, but Patrice had guessed it: "When you are very old Père Lambert," he would say to him, "we'll buy you and your wife a bath chair so that you can move around among the machines!"

When he died, with the fine example of a mutilated veteran that he had steadfastly shown to all, the Lamberts transferred the great love they had for him to his widow. As for the factory, Patrice had said to Rose:

"If something should happen to me, Antoine will be there. He's my foreman. He knows scrap iron better than I do. He's better at figures than my accountant. You can have absolute faith in him. But please don't ask to meet him. He's a handsome man!"

It was hard not to set men fantasizing when we women went shopping in summer in Peyruis, Les Mées or at the Forcalquier market, dressed in light clothes, although they were black. But there was little under them and the rising sun shining through the silk clinging to your legs left you defenceless against the desire of all those who saw you.

Rose had become the symbol of lust for all the road workers, bus drivers and cyclists, the pale, badly-paid salesmen in the general stores and bank employees, who sometimes had the luck to speak to her.

Everyone thought that she would break out, that once the minimum acceptable time of mourning had passed, she would plunge into eroticism, if only to forget death. After all, she had experienced it so often for one so young.

Everyone was wrong, the most perspicacious men as well as the most jealous women. Although it was silent, secret and never actually expressed, the hatred our wives felt for her weighed on her as surely and as heavily as if it had been shown in curses or cruelty.

Far from wishing to cling to life, Rose was preparing to cherish her dead. They had had such an effect on her that no living person could come between her and them. Only those individuals who had been close to them or who had witnessed what they did seemed worthy of her attention.

Rose changed nothing at Pontradieu after Patrice's death, just as she had changed nothing after Charmaine's, but an idea was slowly taking shape in her mind. She soon believed it came from the dead themselves and she lost no time in putting it into practice as soon as she had organized the help she needed.

At that time Marie went into labour and Rose rushed to her bedside. Marie screamed a good deal. On that oppressive September day, as hot as August, you could hear her from one end of Lurs to the other.

"*Eh bé vaï!*" the people thought. "Well, she shouldn't make such a fuss! She certainly went about getting into that condition with a will!"

There was much pursing of lips and nodding of heads. The pleasures of love are what we most want for ourselves and what upsets us most in others. That's the way we are: the joyous cries of our neighbours always seem artificial and theatrical. And so we took these cries of pain (so close to cries of joy, if we'd thought about it) as the inevitable punishment for so much immodesty.

Rose would love to have taken the midwife's place, putting her hands where she put hers, drawing towards her that long twisting shape, as wet and white as a sheet from the fountain, that thing that would be a man. She felt a kind of holy amazement at this mystery that she would never have wished for herself, but which seemed so right for Marie.

Marie lying in childbed and Rose dressed all in black acted quite strangely. Marie had her bedroom door shut in her mother's face. They stayed for an hour leaning over the swaddled newborn babe in Séraphin's cradle and listening to his cries.

It was a boy, duly weighed like a wholesome loaf of bread on the Roberval scales, with the cast iron weights, plus the little copper ones to be quite exact, piled on the other pan. Clorinde proudly announced to her amazed customers: "Four kilos 200 grams!"

There was at least one charitable soul who exclaimed:

"Good Lord! I'm not surprised she screamed so much!"

"Come closer!" Marie said hoarsely, "I screamed so much I haven't any voice left . . ."

Rose was squeezed on the pillow close beside Marie who was beginning to feel her milk coming in.

"I've called him Ange." She said. "I couldn't possibly find anything better. Of course they didn't want it, but I insisted!"

"Good for you! You're wonderful!"

Their words were inaudible beyond the walls of the room as they kept whispering. Neither father nor grandparents were allowed to be part of the mysterious understanding between the two women. When they tried, all they met were blank faces.

These two innocent women kissed each other tenderly. They looked at each other like lovers, but with the ardour they had felt for the same person. Now that his flesh was no doubt turned to dust, they could peacefully share his dead embraces.

"As soon as you're on your feet again," Rose whispered, "come to Pontradieu. I've something to show you. Come! You'll be glad you did!"

"Oh, tell me what it is! Tell me now!"

"No. I want to surprise you. Come as soon as you can."

She put a finger to her lips and left the room. Marie was up in no time. The dresses she had before she was married, with the pale colours she liked so much, still looked wonderful on her. The effects of pregnancy had left no trace at all on her face, her flat stomach or the skin on her legs.

In spite of work at the shop, where she was still busy, Clorinde had confiscated the baby, aided and abetted by Tricanote. Our alarm increased to shock as we looked on helplessly as this old sorceress, with her strange powers, took this blameless child in her hands and held him high above the rampart.

After scarcely two months Marie was back on her delivery bike. However, as she had to feed the baby at regular times, she began to take her father's cattle truck (they hadn't been able to find a baker's cart and Célestat had decided that the cattle truck would do just as well for storing the bread baskets).

We found that quite scandalous, for at that time there were hardly a dozen women in the whole *département* who could drive a car, and they all had bad reputations. Notable among them was Rose Sépulcre. Nonetheless, this is how Marie also arrived at Pontradieu one day in a cloud of dust.

"I couldn't wait," she said. "You promised . . ."

"Come and see!" Rose said.

She led her friend with an arm around her waist. They slowly crossed the park, down the paths with their neatly clipped box hedges. Their light tread passed over the place where Charmaine's body had left its mark in the immaculately raked gravel, when she had been killed by the dogs. The wind and heat had obliterated all trace of it and their minds were on other things. They went around the shimmering pool where Gaspard Dupin's body was found. Their nice shoes were dirtied as they walked on the ash that the rain had blended with the earth at the spot where Patrice had burned his paintings before destroying himself. They left the park which merged into the vineyards without a fence between them. The countryside was magnificent: you could see the hill right up to the Var beyond Oraison. You could see the Ganagobie plateau, which always looked as though it were about to come to life. At the far end of the plain where it widened out, dominating the Digne mountains, you could make out the ghostly shape of the Tête de l'Estrop spread out like a white butterfly. We could never tell whether it was the rock or fresh snow splashed on its white stone shroud. The wind in the poplars made a noise like the sound of the Durance.

"Look, Marie!"

On a rise at the end of a vineyard, Marie could see a small pink building shimmering through a curtain of poplars. It was brand new and shone in the morning light, which was also tinged with pink. Her companion, who was still affectionately shepherding her, gently pushed aside the last curtain of reeds separating them from the mound.

"Look!"

"But . . ." Marie said. "Is it a chapel?"

"No," Rose replied. "It's a tomb."

The door had only recently been forged at the factory and had not yet been painted black, so that you could still see the colours in the metal from being wrought while it was white-hot. It seemed that someone had brought much more than skill, much more than art to the elegant design in all that iron. It was like a resplendent ciborium guarding the entrance.

The chapel sat on top of the knoll whose sides sloped down towards the vines on all sides. The place was a warm sunny spot in winter. Tall silky grasses grew there, and in November they made you think of the harvest. The gentle wind whispered along the ground through their stalks, making their heavy heads wave as it passed.

"Touch it!" Rose said. "It's marble! It cost as much to build as a house for the living!"

She had erected this sepulchre between four cypresses, which she wished were already tall and straight, but they bent, still obedient to the wind's caprices.

"A tomb!" Marie said with a shiver.

With her breasts full of milk and her lust for life, there was no room for even the idea of a tomb.

Rose had wound the cord of a key in her hand around her index finger. She put the key in the lock and with all the strength in her small hands pushed the wrought iron door, which opened silently. Marie had thought it would grate.

"Come in!" Rose said.

But Marie was still standing, disconcerted, on the threshold.

"Come in!" Rose said once again. "Don't be afraid. It's still empty."

Marie timidly followed her. The interior smelled like a new house, with the cement still a creamy-colour and the roughcast scarcely smoothed over.

"Be careful! Don't come too far."

Marie could see four holes gaping in the marble floor. The gravestones to seal them were propped against the back wall.

"It was my idea," Rose said hesitantly. "What do you think of it? I go to the Dabisse cemetery every day. I could come here several times a day. Luckily the property is very large, otherwise I would never have been allowed to do it."

"What are you going to do?"

"I'm going to have Charmaine and Patrice's bodies brought here. I think they would have liked the idea."

"But there are four places!"

"The third is for me," Rose said.

"Good heavens!" Marie said. "You think of your own death! You could remarry. You could have children, too, and you're thinking of dying!"

"It'll come," Rose said. "There's nothing one can do about it."

"And the fourth?"

"Come," Rose said. "Let's go outside and sit on the grass in the sun. It's cold in here."

She gently led Marie outside again to the golden grass moving in the wind. She sat her down on the slope, lowered herself beside her and drew her close against her shoulder.

"Can't you guess the other?" she whispered. "They were close in life. Patrice was his only friend. Charmaine is the only woman to whom he almost succumbed."

"Séraphin!" Marie exclaimed.

Rose nodded her head.

"You still love him!"

These words were said with the same sarcastic bitterness she used to feel when Rose and she fought over the same man who didn't want either of them.

"What about you? Don't you still love him?"

"But it's not certain that he's dead! Why are you already appropriating him? Can Séraphin really . . . die?"

"What does that mean?"

"I don't know," Marie said. "It still makes me shiver to think of it. Sometimes when I'm making love with Tibère it stops me from . . . I owe it to you to tell you the truth Rose. I think about it too often. I stop for weeks, I'm happy, I'm walking on air. The people in Lurs can't get over it. And then suddenly it comes over me. I'm frightened. My teeth chatter. I look at the world as if it was hunting me down. But it's a fear that stirs me, a fear that isn't natural. How can I explain it to you? You're completely thrown by it. The mind can't cope."

"A feeling of terror . . ." Rose said pensively.

"You're reading my mind," Marie said with admiration.

"But why are you afraid?"

"That such a thing can exist in the world."

"What thing?"

"Remember! His hands! He always kept them closed. We always saw fists, never hands! Even that time when the dogs bit him so badly. The time when I saw him kneeling beside your sister-in-law they had torn to pieces. I wanted him to open his hands so that I could pour arnica on them. Everyone tried to persuade him, but it was quite useless! He kept his fists clenched. I only saw his hands open once and that was when he fell asleep at my bedside, on the night he saved my life."

"Marie! On that night! Nothing happened between you, surely?"

"How could it? I was dying. I could feel nothing within me but my bones. I could already feel myself decaying!"

She stopped speaking and gave a furtive look behind her in the direction of the tomb. She had already seen this profusion of pink marble when she was delirious.

"I'm going to tell you something I've never said to another soul: his hands were lying open and defenceless on the counterpane. I swear to you Rose, they were smooth!"

"What do you mean, smooth?"

"They weren't like yours or mine. Destiny was not written in them."

Rose was speechless. She looked closely at her friend, laughing Marie with the dimpled face, Marie Dormeur, the Lurs baker's daughter. She gazed deep into eyes that she found extraordinarily beautiful. She shook her head.

"You must have imagined it," she said. "You imagined it when you were delirious."

"No," Marie said. "There was a smell of death in the room. The box twig above my head had turned yellow-gold and dry. It was still fresh when I lapsed into the coma. Did I ever give you the impression of having a lot of imagination?"

"What was the use of all that anyway Marie? You know it as well as I do. He still had his own destiny. The proof of it is that he's dead, Marie my dear. He's dead! Tell yourself this: if he wasn't dead, we would feel it here!"

She made a gesture with the side of her hand as though she were cutting her chest below her breasts. She added:

"We couldn't feel this affection for each other if he weren't dead. Because I'll say this to you, Marie: I've never loved anyone but him."

Marie suddenly moved away from Rose, who was looking at her affectionately with a sad smile.

"Do you realize Marie what we're arguing about?"

Marie shook her head, which she kept determinedly turned away.

"I can't help it," she said. "Your words hurt me. Because, you see, I've never loved anyone but him either."

They pulled out a stalk of the grass that waved in front of them and chewed on it to stop themselves from saying more. All the unhappiness in the world shone in their eyes, despite the brilliant sky on the November day.

V

WHEN ANTOINE MAUJAC SAW ROSE FOR THE FIRST TIME, SHE WAS standing still and straight as a tree trunk in front of Patrice's open grave. Her features were hardly visible under the widow's veil covering her face and much of her body.

Patrice had never shown his wife to the man who was closest to him. Patrice had never explained this to anyone else or even to himself.

Antoine was a rough man, who kept himself to himself. His features showed no emotion. People said that he had shirked active service for the whole of the war by pretending he was deaf. The gendarmes had had their eyes on him for two years. They threw coins behind him to provoke a reaction so that they could bring him before a court-martial. In the end, they threw coins under his heels. Not once did the imperturbable Antoine turn around, stop walking or allow a single quiver to run over his immobile features. His two brothers had been killed in 1914, one on the Marne and the other on the Meuse. The second did not die instantly. When he was taken to the field hospital with a gaping wound in his abdomen, he still had enough strength to write a postcard to his mother: "I die so that France may live". Antoine, who was seventeen, had seen it stuck in a corner of the kitchen mirror beside the Post Office calendar. A suspect stain still remained between the two lines of the address. He couldn't be sure it wasn't blood. Antoine had decided that two lives lost in one family was enough.

The first time he saw Rose full-face in front of him, he had been signing papers and telling her about negotiations with important clients he was trying to steal from another firm. He continued to feel uneasy in his role as manager. Like Rose, he was still haunted by the image of Patrice's broken face.

One day when the two men were together, having just helped each other to earn a lot of money in a single deal, he had said to Patrice:

"Nobody makes me feel guilty about not having gone to the war. Nobody can make me hang my head. But with you, I feel ashamed."

"Why?" Patrice replied. "The first on the scene could just as easily have copped it. I'm living proof!"

Antoine's grief at Patrice's death made him more silent than ever. Although Patrice never once confided in him, he immediately suspected that the cause of his death was this widow standing there so still and straight that when people saw her they didn't realize straight away why Patrice had killed himself.

One evening he could not put off going to Pontradieu any longer, resolving to put between them the maximum distance possible between an owner and her workman. Normally women were intrigued by the chronic absence of a smile on his expressionless face. He was in the thoughts of more than one between Lure and Durance, where he travelled constantly.

Rose could see that he had been devoted to Patrice as soon as he came in, and that he also held her responsible for his death. The called each other *monsieur* and *madame* for the whole quarter of an hour their conversation lasted. Patrice's name was never mentioned. Not a single word was ever said on any other subject apart from iron and flour. She didn't thank him. They didn't shake hands. Then he left.

He had never come to Pontradieu before but he knew about the tragedies that had taken place on that tranquil estate. When he was still very young and shy, he had just once seen Charmaine dressed all in black at the Oraison marketplace. This image together with that of Rose, now also a widow, became strangely superimposed in his mind, so that both their faces became blurred and finally neither had a face at all. Only their silhouettes haunted the paths in the park, much too big for their lonely existence. But one was a ghost and the other was alive.

After having seen Patrice's widow that evening, he wondered if the living woman had ever met the dead one, and what they could say to each other. It was this absurd thought, inspired by the total solitude in which he had found Rose, that made Antoine come back to Pontradieu. She had not asked him to come; he had nothing to tell her. He was alone in the world, his only home the factory where he was continually reminded of Patrice. He knew that she was also alone and isolated in her widowhood. He was tall, thin and lithe. He made no sound as he arrived, rang the bell and saw her standing before him.

"How did you know that I needed you?" she said.

"I didn't know. I wanted to come back, that's all. It seemed to me that you were alone."

"I am, but it doesn't worry me."

"Do you read?" Antoine asked.

"Yes. All the time. It was Patrice who taught me. Before I knew him, I never even opened a newspaper."

She poured him a drink without asking, but nothing for herself.

He raised his hand to refuse it.

"No," he said, "I don't drink either."

He was conscious of the noise made by the tall trees blowing in the wind outside. Perhaps they wanted to send him away or tell him that his presence there was out of place. She was thinking while looking at him intently, as if to judge his mettle.

"What would you do if you wanted to find someone and you didn't know if he was alive or dead?"

"The gendarmes –" Antoine began.

"No. You have to be related. I'm not."

"Well then, a notary."

"No. People like that have no imagination."

Antoine shrugged his shoulders.

"The newspapers," he said, "a notice in the paper."

"I'm looking for a man. Can you see me writing: *Contact Mme Dupin, Domaine de Pontradieu*? I already have a bad reputation . . ."

"I could look for a man," Antoine said, "without anyone raising objections."

"Would you do it?"

She was about to say, "for me", but stopped herself. He showed her straight away that he had understood her perfectly.

"Why not?" he said. "I loved Patrice. He never spoke to me about you. But that's because he wouldn't do that when he was alive."

She got up and turned her back to him as she walked towards the writing desk. She walked in such a way as to be sure that he would not take his eyes off her the whole time as she crossed the carpet, went past the fireplace and moved between the table lamp with the green shade and the armchair where he was sitting. When she sat down on the chair in front of the desk, it was done with all the supple grace Patrice had taught her. (She used to collapse on to a seat without thinking how she looked.) She more or less knew already what she was going to ask of Antoine, and that Patrice's memory would not be enough for him to do it. He would need some passion to make him act. Her body swaying in front of him would give him something to think about that night. It seemed the best way to keep his attention.

She quickly wrote three or four lines on a sheet of white paper, then walked towards him.

"There!" she said.

He read it. Their eyes met.

"You're entrusting me with a secret," he said.

She nodded, then got to her feet. She didn't give him her hand. The two of them knew enough about life to reduce their dealings with people to the bare essentials.

Nevertheless, while she was taking him to the door she said:

"You loved Patrice, didn't you? I've had his body brought here to a chapel I've had specially built. Would you like to see it?"

She took down a key from a board near the door and they went out together. It was an ideal night to visit the dead, bright and serene. The thin crescent moon cut into black diamonds by the lacy branches of the trees, stood out against the unusually clear sky.

They went into the chapel. Two graves had been sealed with stones engraved in gilt. Rose shone the beam of her torch from one to the other.

"I saw Charmaine once," Antoine said. "I was very young. She was in mourning."

"They loved each other," Rose said.

"And . . . who are the two open graves intended for?"

"Mine," Rose said.

"And the other?"

"That's the man I'm looking for. He's probably dead. Patrice was the only friend he had in the world."

They stood there for several minutes, lost in their separate thoughts. Antoine could hardly breathe. He could feel all the curves of Rose's body against him, even though there was room for a third person between them.

Even when it was snowing, Auphanie Brunel usually woke up in the morning when the bus driver, who also delivered the post, threw the bundle of newspapers against the front of the café.

She would then pull on her flannelette dressing gown and go downstairs muttering to herself as she opened the shutters. Then she would stoke the stove, put more wood on the embers and light the spirit heater under the percolator. While she was waiting she would comb her long hair, still grumbling, as she walked among the marble-topped tables in the empty room. When the percolator began to whistle she poured her first cup of coffee. She brought it to a table, sat down, spread out the newspaper, lit a small cigar with her flint lighter and became totally absorbed in reading the news.

The first of us to lift the latch usually did not arrive before eight o'clock, as that was the time it took for Auphanie to know what was going on all over the world. Anyone who was bold enough to appear before the ritual was complete would meet with a very chilly reception. We all knew it, and unless someone was seriously short of tobacco, which justified taking any risk, we respected our supplier's whim.

She even read the stock market reports; the words Penaroya, Standard Oil, Suez Capital fascinated her. She read the commodity price list to know the state of world poverty, and finally, regretfully, reached the name of the printer and publisher. The coffee, the newspaper and the cigarillo calmed her down.

On that particular day, she did not finish reading. She was up to the fourth column of the classified advertisements when these words leaped out at her:

A considerable reward will be paid to anyone who can provide information about one Séraphin Monge, who has not returned home for three years. Write to the newspaper office, which will forward correspondence.

Auphanie let out a cry. The bitter lines around her mouth had deepened since she knew that Séraphin's tortured body had no grave, but was stuck up there with nothing but broken beeches for a coffin. Auphanie's beliefs were those of simple people: the living should be in houses and the dead in the cemetery. She couldn't help thinking that he may have been carried away by the earth, like pebbles in a river, and that when she went looking for mushrooms, she could well be walking over his body. She had never forgotten the compassion she felt for him from the very beginning, nor did she forget the shy desire that had made her go into the stranger's bedroom to let him know that they were both alone, that it was a hard world and there was no need to be so proud. She could see him when his face still had the flesh she had so much wanted to stroke.

She would rail against us on lotto night and at Christmas, when she had drunk a little to much.

"Aren't you ashamed! Leaving a Christian in unhallowed ground? Aren't you ashamed of depriving him of a grave? How is it you don't see him every night in your dreams? You're a bunch of cowards, all of you!"

It had occurred to us that we could have made a bargain with her: "One night with you for putting Séraphin in the cemetery!" To be bold enough to make such a proposal, we would need to have been more certain that nothing would get back to our wives and also be less afraid of the terrain up there. We'd seen that earth in action. It was all right for the moment, but how long would that last?

Rosans, the mayor, had lectured Auphanie several times on the subject.

"Be reasonable! You know how poor the commune is. The bridge is rotten and we can't even rebuild it. We'd need ten men to find this Séraphin in the place where he's buried! Where would I find ten workmen? Where would I find the money to pay them? Especially up there. Everyone remembers how it happened. No-one wants to be buried alive."

"But there's no more movement!"

"No, but you know, with that sort of thing ... It could start to move again without warning. And then how would I look, eh? Being responsible for that! And besides, my dear Auphanie, no-one has claimed him. No-one has bothered to find out if he's alive or dead! Not once! In three years! No-one has missed him, alive or dead, for three years! So, who would pay us to do it?"

"I would!" Auphanie said. "I'll pay everything: the cost of rescuing him, the box and the burial!"

But Rosans was right. There was nobody in Les Fosses-Gleizières who would go and pull Séraphin out of the earth that enclosed him.

So on the morning when she read the notice, Auphanie rushed to the counter, scattering things right and left to find pen and ink. It was such a long time since she had used it last that the violet ink had lost its colour, and she had to look for another bottle in the storeroom. As it had been just as long since she had written a single word, she stood there for almost half an hour without moving. The first person to arrive found her there chewing the end of her pen like a schoolgirl working out a problem.

In the end she managed the few lines she had to write. The bus taking the mail down again to Barcelonnette after collecting it at Sauze could be heard wheezing its way up the Enchastrayes rise. She would have to catch it at the crossing, in the hairpin bend, if she wanted her letter to go that day. Two minutes before the vehicle appeared she was already waving her arms wildly at the still invisible driver. After she had given him the envelope, she stood there for some time watching the bus negotiate the turns on its way down towards the valley. She felt it was sending some kind of hope.

Rose had not left the house and was watching constantly since Antoine gave her the cryptic letter he had fetched from the newspaper office. It said:

Sir/Madam,

I think I know where to find this Séraphin Monge you are looking for. He arrived here about three years ago and that is the time you say he disappeared. If you want me to tell you more about it, give me some more information about who you are and if you are related.

Widow Auphanie Brunel
Tobacconist
Village of Les Fosses-Gleizières
Via Enchastrayes
(Basses-Alpes)

Rose had replied immediately, including a money order for expenses, saying that if Auphanie would come to her, she would send a car for her. But Auphanie didn't want anyone to bother with special arrangements. She would arrive one afternoon at the Peyruis-Les Mées station, and it was quite enough for someone to come and meet her as she didn't know the area. She also said that she wouldn't stay because she had a business to run, and that she would leave immediately afterwards by the Briançon train that came through in the evening, so that she would only need to be taken back to the station.

Antoine dropped her at the front steps saying he would come back later. Rose was already holding the door wide open. Hope seemed to flow into the house on a gust of wind from the tall trees outside.

"Come in quickly!" she said.

Auphanie had dressed in her modest best, with a new hat that had only been worn perhaps three times in five years. When she saw Rose she exclaimed:

"My goodness! How young you are!"

"I look young," Rose said. "Do come in."

She felt almost joyful as she closed the door behind Auphanie, who unfortunately had had the time to do a great deal of thinking since she set out that morning, including three hours in the waiting-room on Veynes station. Whatever effect it might have on those listening, she had resolved to tell them the truth immediately.

"You know," she said, "I'm not sure what you're expecting to hear, but I can't leave you any hope. He's dead, that's certain. I should have told you so in my letter, but I didn't think of it."

"When?"

"Very soon after he arrived. Perhaps a month later."

Rose, who was leading Auphanie towards the fireplace, felt her legs give way and sank into an armchair.

"Oh dear!" Auphanie exclaimed. "I'm sorry! Is he your brother?"

"No," Rose replied. "As far as you're concerned, he's been dead for a long time. For me, it's just happened. One always keeps hoping . . ."

"Was he your husband?" Auphanie asked gently.

She was twenty years older than Rose. She looked at the young woman hunched in the chair staring into space, her fingers twisting a handkerchief which was never put to use, for here as at the cemetery, she could not produce a single tear. There are people like that, who simply cannot cry. Auphanie, feeling a rush of sympathy, had dared place her hand in its floss-silk glove over Rose's tightly clasped fingers.

"No," Rose said, "he wasn't my husband. Did he suffer?"

"It would surprise me if he didn't. He was buried alive, you know . . . He had time to know he was going to die."

She took Rose's hands in both her own, then told her about Séraphin's life in the forest: the solitude; the food she brought him.

"What did he say to you?" Rose asked.

"Nothing. He wouldn't have said more than a few dozen words the whole time he was with us. And even then it was only to answer questions. He never spoke first."

"But what about here? Where he came from? Us? Didn't he ever say anything about that?"

"Never! Why, if he had spoken of this place, I'd have come long ago to explain the situation! But no! Not a word! Never! Nothing about a place or a person! Do you know what I really thought deep inside? I thought he came from nowhere, that he belonged nowhere! Do you know what I thought every day as I was preparing the food I took him? That he actually wanted to die, that he was looking for death!"

She no longer saw Rose. She was up there again, when the mountain and its trees began to slide down towards us. She imitated the way little waves rose in the earth, something no man had ever seen with his own eyes. Her hands described the strange trembling that suddenly began in the trees whose leaves rustled continuously in the branches day and night, even when there was no wind. She told of paths disappearing as the mud advanced, of the sudden absence of birds from the entire mountain, and the lone man calmly and steadily cutting down the beech trees.

"But what had you done to him here?" Auphanie asked, "for him to want to die rather than come back to you? For him to try so hard to forget you?"

"He wouldn't have said more than a few dozen words to us either," Rose said bitterly. "We tried again and again to convince him . . . He could never believe us, never hold his head high."

Auphanie spread out her arms in a gesture of helplessness.

"We couldn't get him out. They didn't want to get him out, even when the mud stopped flowing. They were too scared that it would start again. It's no use counting on them. They wouldn't dig in Polycarpe's wood for all the money in the world."

"Don't you worry," Rose said. "I'll go and look for him. I'll dig him out."

"How marvellous! If you knew the nights I've spent imagining it, saying to myself . . . Please excuse me if I'm being indiscreet, but . . . Perhaps you've had some experience of life too. Was he . . . your lover?"

"No," Rose said.

She had blushed to the roots of her hair as she looked away.

"Look, we're both women," Auphanie said. "We can tell each other anything. I'm a lot older than you and yet I wanted him. If he'd been willing . . ."

"That's our misfortune," Rose said. "He didn't want me either."

"Why," Auphanie said. "You're so beautiful you'd make a saint sell his soul to the devil!"

"Why indeed?" sighed Rose. "Do *you* know why?"

They stayed there in front of the hearth until nightfall, swapping women's secrets. The spell was only broken by Antoine sounding the horn on his van.

"Good heavens! It's time!" Auphanie exclaimed.

She quickly picked up her bag, her shawl and her hat, and made for the door. She had already finished there. She had done her duty. She was happy. That rich woman would release Séraphin from his bed of clay and bury him in holy ground. He would no longer be up there on those nights when everything rattled in the house where she lived alone, as if reproaching her for something. She would be able to sleep easy at last. Rose could hardly keep up with her to open the door.

Auphanie was about to go down the ten steps when she turned around.

"Now that I come to think of it," she said. "Didn't someone from around here come looking for him?"

"Not that I know of," Rose said, quite surprised. "What did this someone look like?"

"Um, I don't really know! It was the day before Séraphin met his death. Someone arrived, in the evening. He didn't make a very good impression on us. I think he was dark. But it was night-time and the lighting inside isn't good. But what he looked like . . . what his name was . . . Heavens above! I can't remember."

She shut the car door and away she went. In her thoughts she was already in the Briançon express, anxious that she might miss it. Without turning around she gave a little wave to Rose, who was standing in the middle of the drive.

The arrival and departure of that woman took only a moment in Rose's life, and neither she nor Rose could know that she had brought fate with her and, even though it was invisible, she had left it behind her in the armchair like some object one has forgotten.

The very next day Rose put on her best clothes so as to impress Maître Bellaffaire, with whom she had requested an appointment.

Now," she told him, "since he's dead, his bones must still be there. I want them to be dug up and brought here. I shall put them in my chapel."

"Oh, dear oh dear oh dear oh dear!" exclaimed Maître Bellaffaire, taking his head in his hands.

"Right!" said Rose. "Say no more. Whether you think that Séraphin should be buried here or there, you are going to bring up every possible obstacle to make me give up, but as I won't give up, let's leave it at that! But as for my bearer stocks, you can . . ."

"But I'm only thinking of your best interest!"

"No! To put it quite simply, in your notary's heart, you find it unacceptable because *you* wouldn't do it, and you only approve of what you do yourself!"

"Not at all! Let me say again that I'm thinking of your best interest. All told it will cost you a fortune, and it will take you two years at the very least to get the necessary authorizations."

"Be sure of one thing: that is, I'm ready to use all my wealth to satisfy this whim. Do you understand me? All of it!"

"For a box of bones!" the notary lamented, completely flabbergasted.

"Certainly! Do you find it unusual for a person to treat someone she has loved with respect?"

"Exactly!" Maître Bellaffaire exclaimed with his hand across his heart. "No-one does that! And what's more, you'll face enormous difficulties! He was neither your husband nor your . . ."

He stopped, breathing hard. Their eyes met.

"Brother . . ." The notary had some difficulty finishing his sentence.

Rose realized that she had no right to this box of bones and that her insistence was becoming more and more suspect. What would be going on in the head of a notary obliged to marry young and someone suitable, that is some plain girl from a rich family but with no hint of love? What would he be thinking when confronted with an alluring widow who stirred his imagination? Rose faced the facts: Maître Bellaffaire was jealous of Séraphin's bones. He was capable, if necessary, of legally consigning them to the depths of some junior clerk of court's office, where they would moulder for 300 years. Rose was terror-stricken and beat a hasty retreat.

"I'm sorry," she said, "you're right. And the stocks will of course stay as they are. Forget everything I said. You know . . . since Patrice's death I haven't been myself at all."

"What a pity!" said Maître Bellaffaire with a sigh.

She refrained from asking him what he meant by that. She was still upset and breathless when Antoine arrived as arranged.

"You're the only one I can turn to. Who should I see?"

If Rose had been an ordinary woman, perhaps Antoine may not even have heard her pathetic appeal. He was still isolated, perhaps permanently, in the tower of silence he had built around himself for the last two years, all his senses deliberately dulled to offer the least possible access. But Rose cast herself at him with all the weight of her irrational view of things.

"I have a favour to ask of you," she said. "What I want you to do is illegal," she added.

She talked to him passionately for ten minutes about Séraphin's bones, which had to be brought back here.

"I know you think I'm mad. I come from an ordinary background – the daughter of a miller who died in dreadful circumstances! And yet what I'm asking you is a real lady's favour! I'm asking you to fulfil a whim and I don't even know you! You can tell me that you're only my employee and that it's not your kind of work! But who can I ask to do it? Patrice must have spoken to you about me, I'm sure. You were good companions. You must know much more about me than I know about you."

"I never heard anything!" he protested. "Patrice had too much respect for you to talk about you to an employee."

"Then you sensed who I am through him!"

Now she risked a gesture dictated purely by the circumstances, something she had absolutely no desire to do. She took hold of his hands.

"She's sending me to find her lover," Antoine thought bitterly. "She doesn't even know I exist. She doesn't even see me!"

It was only when he thought about it later that he had to admit what she wanted him to bring back to her were simply the remains of a poor unfortunate man. But for the moment the hands she was squeezing around his wrists forced him to speak to hide his confusion.

"I'll have to go on a Sunday," he said. "And will you give me permission to pay the workers overtime? From what you've said, I'll need at least ten . . . And that's if they'll agree to come! Everyone's put off by death, you know! And on Sunday, what's more!"

"Give them whatever they ask!" Rose said vehemently. "And you . . ."

He had the impression she was going to take a step further towards him, so he took one step back.

"No," he said. "Don't promise anything. You'll regret it later. I don't want you to have any regrets. I'll bring your Séraphin back to you."

He turned away, about to leave.

"I make no conditions!" he murmured.

Auphanie Brunel was right: the ground had stopped sliding. Of course the gap by the old trees on the moraine, where the ground had split open, had not been filled in. It was still there like a witness, but the nasty blue colour of the vein of clay that had come away from the rock had now dried out. Coltsfoot was spreading over it, a sure sign that the ground had stabilized. Wherever the earth among Polycarpe's beeches had first swelled up then cracked open, the sun and rain had smoothed over the surface where the blue buried clay had appeared. It had faded so much that it was now the same colour as the earth.

The fallen trees had not straightened up again, but the earth on those that had been up-ended had dropped off the roots, revealing their ivory bareness as they slowly became dead wood. They were stuck there in the depths of the sick forest, like octopi standing on their tentacles and frozen in that position forever. The criss-crossed trunks had stopped their clashing noise of battle. Last spring some of the trees that had become entangled sprouted fresh green shoots on the edges of the cracks in their bark. They were so enmeshed that it was impossible to know to which of these swaying combatants they belonged. In the end, there was a large number of trees still standing, although some were at an angle, sighing and moaning in the wind as if nothing had ever happened.

Oh, we certainly didn't go to have a close look at them! We just held our breath as we noted the fact that the forces of nature were sleeping once more. Even though there were so many enticing golden Caesar's mushrooms there in the autumn, they were left to rot in the ground; we wouldn't go up there to pick them. The same applied to game: grouse could flap about in the beech brush in October, promising a good catch of plump birds, but they were left undisturbed by any hunter. We still feared the worst, and besides, there was that dead body between us and the earth. Its presence did us no harm, but the thought of it sometimes gave us sleepless nights.

We are people with an ingrained sense of duty and order: a dead man not in his rightful place in the cemetery inevitably called to us with the voice he had when he was alive. What is more, when we wanted to situate a place with a few topographical landmarks, instead of "Polycarpe's Wood" we would say "the Dead Man's Wood". Moreover, it's the name given to that chaotic area on the new land register of the commune, although it no longer looks much like a wood, a place or anything specific at all.

Quite a few of us, individually, would have been willing to go back to the wood to look for the mortal remains left there without a grave, but there were the women to consider. The moment the subject of the wood came up, they would hit the roof. And so we desisted.

At that time, the geologist who had left us so little hope three years previously came back. We recognized him with his haversack on his back and his iron tipped cane tapping on the road. That day we were straggling down to the fair at Barcelonnette, coats thrown over one shoulder, some guiding cart mules, others on bicycles, open jackets flying in the wind.

"Do you come from up there?" he asked us.

As our paths crossed, he stared at us with that curious look we sometimes see on our fellow humans' faces. That look they have which seems to say: "Well! Fancy that! He's still with us? I thought he died long ago!"

This reaction can usually be justified between contemporaries by human nature's faith in its own immortality, equalled only by its scepticism regarding that of others. Unfortunately our geologist had scientific reasons to be surprised.

You'd have thought he had swallowed a ramrod, he was walking so stiffly.

It was because he had come back from Erebus, he told us. We had no idea where Erebus was, if it was a bird or if we should know about it. From there, he told us, he in any case had a wonderful high view over the ecumene, as if he hadn't been on it but was looking at it from a balcony.

He told us that he had never forgotten us, and that our land with its epiphenomenon of local erosion had stayed with him as he travelled 15,000 kilometres away. There, when Erebus shot a column of steam into the air, it fell back on its slopes in blocks of ice weighing several tons, with the noise you would expect. He, meanwhile, was well out of the way in an artificial cave, covered in gauges with oscillating needles. During the long quiet periods, he calculated how much longer our area would survive.

He had done all the necessary calculations after he had left us all in a state of anxiety three years ago. At least that's what he told us in the evening at Auphanie's.

"I can't understand it . . . " he said.

He couldn't get over it. He frowned trying to work it out. He looked at us suspiciously with that schoolmaster's gaze typical of all those who know what they are talking about, and which means:

"Could it be that in my absence one of you has opened Pandora's box?"

He arrived, we won't say full of joy, but at least full of enthusiasm at the prospect of verifying his splendid theory and contemplating the extent of the disaster that he had so rightly predicted.

"It's amazing that it has stopped," he said. "Normally, by this time . . ."

He had that annoyed look of someone on whom reality has played a nasty trick.

"In short, you're surprised to see us still here?"

"Positively. Positively. What's more, I won't pretend that I didn't come to . . ."

"Our funeral perhaps?"

He explained that he expected our epiphenomenon of local erosion to be the end of us, or to disperse us at the very least. By crowding around him looking so rosy-cheeked and full of hope, we were ruining his masterpiece. He would have taken his torch and gone up to Dead Man's Wood there and then to redo his calculations and try to discover why the phenomenon did not conform to his measurements, all checked and correct.

"By the way," he said, "why do you call it Dead Man's Wood? It used to be Polycarpe's Wood?"

We told him what had happened. He spent all the next day wandering around the trees that had been knocked down like skittles. He felt them. He checked the fact that the crevasse had dried out. He picked up handfuls of the blue clay which had then been so slippery and heavy, and which had since crumbled into dust blown up by the wind. He gave resentful kicks at the burst mounds of earth under the trees, which still held the shape of small waves on the sea. When he came down again, his bearing looked a little less straight and confident.

"Nevertheless," he said, "keep an eye on it. I haven't said my last word on the matter. It will start again. It's inevitable. I don't know why it has stopped. It will start to come down again. That's certain."

High up on our embankment on the banks of the river where the water had changed colour many years before and had never regained its former clarity, we watched him disappear down the road as we bade him farewell with much mocking comment and waving of hands. We were wrong.

Later, one evening at about seven o'clock, a truck entered the square and stopped in front of the church. Auphanie had told us what she had done. Since then we had all been trying to make sense of such a strange thing. Who were these people coming from outside to give us a lesson or two in Christian morality?

"It's because you won't do it!" Auphanie said, telling us off. "Because you're frightened!"

We had questioned Rosans the mayor, but his reply was evasive.

"They've made a large donation to mend the church roof and a similar one for the schools fund."

Nonetheless, we still went and nosed around these men from outside. The driver wore a tie under his blue overalls, a white collar and polished shoes, which he later changed for boots. We liked the look of him.

Rosans was shaking his hand. We hung about the truck, clearing our throats. The tallest of us glanced over the side panel. Some badly dressed men we didn't like the look of were sleeping under the tarpaulin. You could make out gravediggers' tools sticking out under and around them in the gloom.

"We could have provided the labour," Rosans said. "It's the off-season for several men here."

"No doubt," Antoine said, "but they would have had too much soul-searching. Those men are Spaniards. They've been hungry for about ten years. They don't bother with soul-searching!"

"You don't know these parts."

"No," Antoine said, "I don't know your region but I know life. The people around here know that there has been a landslip. That it took a man's life, nearly two. They'd just push at the earth with the tips of their shovels, their minds elsewhere and their ears straining. The ones I'm bringing are being paid for the bones they find. The one who digs up the most will earn the most. And there's a special bonus for the skull."

"You've thought of everything," Rosans said with a sigh.

"After all," Antoine said, "they're only bones! And we're going to give them a decent burial. If we do it legally, it will take three years. They'll put us off indefinitely with everything they want for the enquiry. I ask you! Three-year-old bones! And when they finally decide to give them to us, they won't know where to find them!"

"Oh!" Rosans said. "That's why I'm turning a blind eye!"

Antoine raised his hand to his inside pocket.

"Do you want more?"

"No," Rosans said. "That's not the question."

He was surreptitiously observing our long faces. He was afraid that he wouldn't be equal to the situation, that we would think him too weak. That wasn't it. We all felt strangely, inexplicably uneasy. We're not soft-hearted people. We had the odd burst of tenderness, but on the whole, when others see us, they give up almost immediately any hope of moving us. However, without actually expressing the thought to each other, it seemed to betray the memory of the man. If he had chosen to arrive among us with only the clothes he stood up in, he must have had very good reasons for doing so.

Now that he could no longer defend himself, we were allowing him to be taken away from us and our consciences were troubled.

And so, on the following day, when the sinister-looking workers straggled up into the woods, those of us who didn't have much to do roamed around the edges of Dead Man's Wood. Oh! At a good distance away, for we hadn't forgotten what that spot on the mountain could do, and the geologist's words were still on our minds.

Auphanie, who was guiding her group, didn't hesitate to rush into the suspect area of the woods. It no longer moved; it was no longer soft underfoot. You no longer sank up to your knees in the clay as we had seen happen for years. But you had to push through the bushes, for all the shade plants had grown again. They formed an unaccustomed green layer between the wrecked trees. There were also huge tree trunks that had fallen over the path, either lying across each other or horizontal like enormously long dead bodies. The mounds, which formerly looked like freshly dug graves, had now subsided under the combined effect of the snow, rain and wind. The underwood looked so much as it always did that, if you hadn't seen the phenomenon, you would have wondered what strange force could have uprooted these ancient trees, pushed 200-year-old tree trunks into battle with each other, and by what bizarre whim of fate many were left standing almost upright.

It took Auphanie a long time in all the debris of that petrified battle to find the faded garter she had knotted where a branch forked from the trunk. Now it was more like a blackish bracelet with the bark swollen around it. But when she untied it and showed it to Antoine, she saw that the bright pink of the elastic on the under side had resisted the effects of time.

"That's it!" she exclaimed. "He's under there! Down there! Under these tentacle roots. At the time I couldn't get any closer. It was streaming down! Without making any noise. I felt as if a big animal was moving under me! That it was walking!"

She could hardly believe it as she stamped her foot on the earth that was now dry and stable.

"If you'd seen it!" she said. "No-one can know if they haven't seen it! Not even them, standing there like statues wide-eyed with fear!"

She pointed straight at us, for of course we had gathered in a group on the big outcrop of karstic rock that was like a raft in the middle of the forest.

Antoine had lined up his men and they were already working away on the light soil, but they proceeded methodically, digging the trench down a metre and throwing the soil to the side as they went. At ten o'clock they were already up to their hips and were hidden from us by the heap of earth they had raised behind them. It was almost midday when we heard them call out. One of them had raised his hand and shouted, and they gathered in a circle around him. At that moment nothing could hold us back. That's when we also went up and joined the circle.

Someone crouching at the bottom of the trench was digging with his bare hands around a shrivelled boot. You could smell the sweat of the workmen as they quietly urged each other on. They were as tense and careful as if they had just uncovered a living person.

The one they called Antoine had run over to the truck. He brought back a large white sheet that rippled as he spread it on top of the grass. They uncovered a second shoe. The first was already crumbling on contact with the air. They dug to a depth of two metres to get all the remains, which had been broken in two by the cataclysm. The head had gone down deepest into the earth as if the skeleton had wanted to bury itself in it to shield itself from the sky or life or people. When we leaned over the hole and saw him in that position, we all had the impression that the man wanted to avoid us while he was alive and found, as he was dying, that he had not fled far enough. We felt that he had wanted to abscond even further away, into that solid abyss, to escape, to escape from us, to break away from us, never to be found again. But the earth had solidified around him, keeping him within our reach as a fish is caught in a net. He was there at our mercy while they gently and carefully placed each of his bones, each of his limbs, around the hoops of his ribs on to the white sheet, which looked so out of place under these trees.

Auphanie had secretly told the priest at Enchastrayes what was going to happen. At about three o'clock we saw him suddenly emerge from the short cut through the woods. He looked white and unreal, dwarfed in all his lace by the twenty-metre high beech trees, the monstrance with its tall cross on top held by an old strap across his shoulder. His altar boy followed on behind.

They had just laid the skull on the sheet above the shoulders, which had always seemed to us as broad as a horse-collar, an impression borne out by the thickness of the clavicles. Antoine was reverently removing the plugs of earth from the eye sockets with a penknife. He flicked out the mud around the jawbones. The teeth, still intact, had solidly bitten into the clay.

The priest began mumbling a prayer to himself while the altar boy rang his little bell. You could hear the swish as all our hats were taken off at the same time. We stood there crossing ourselves and observing a strict silence.

The altar boy was digging at the soft earth like a mule with the tip of his hobnail shoes. He had that sulky look of someone to whom everything looks highly dubious. Normally he never saw the dead, invisible behind the walls of their coffins. It was the first time he had come face to face with one and in its final state. He found it huge and solemn. He couldn't wait to leave that ground. It didn't seem very solid to him and he knew its previous history. He was off as soon as he had received the holy-water basin from the priest, running as fast as his schoolboy's legs would carry him with his cassock tucked up, down the short cut and back to his house and his village, where the ground didn't move and the dead travelled only in boxes. For quite some time we could hear the jingling of the religious articles for the mass being bounced around as he fled.

We, on the other hand, stayed where we were, crowded around the skeleton as we did around Auphanie's stove. We pointed out aspects of it to each other as we would have done with a fine horse. Our workers' solidarity was expressed in cries of admiration. Our funeral oration was addressed directly to the horizontal remains of the giant we were remembering in the flesh.

"What a man that was! Do you remember how strong he was?"

A lot of dead leaves had fallen over the sheet and the bones. They were doing their work, which is to bury, as conscientiously as if the body had been left to them. We stood there solemn and unmoving, watching them fall.

"It's a pity," one of us said, "that you didn't find the hands. They were really something, those hands . . ."

Antoine shrugged his shoulders. It was autumn and night was falling. He had told off his exhausted workmen, instructing them to bring him the missing hands. But what are two hands among the tangle of all those trees, most of which were sunk up to ten metres in clay?

Auphanie arrived on the scene out of breath and waving her arms. She had been watching for hours at the dyke. She had come now to warn Antoine that two gendarmes on bicycles were zigzagging around the Déffends bends just before the bridge. If the gendarmes from the valley stuck their noses in these irregular proceedings they would be asking questions for three days, and the first thing they would do would be to confiscate the bones.

There was no more time to look for the hands.

"Wait!" Auphanie cried. "One last time!"

She lay down on the white shroud with its hand-embroidered monogram: GD. Gaspard Dupin. It was in the sheets of this family that the baby, sole survivor of a murder Dupin had wanted to commit, would finally rest in peace. We stood around Auphanie, surprised, silent and serious. Auphanie began reaching out her hands to take hold of the skull, but didn't dare do so in front of all of us, and got up looking distressed.

Two workmen arrived with a big jute sack. Antoine folded up the four corners of the shroud. The bones knocked together with a sound like pieces of broken china. Antoine knotted the shroud over them as he would have done with a bale of hay. Two workers held the sack. Antoine packed the shroud in it and put it on his shoulder. Auphanie had said:

"A sack will do! If the gendarmes happen to stop you, they won't pay any attention to a sack, but a coffin . . ."

All the workers had already piled into the back of the truck. They couldn't be seen now in the dim light and they kept very quiet. Antoine opened the door. He put the sack down at his feet. With a wave of his hand in our direction, he got up behind the wheel. The truck drove off, rocking and jolting into the evening mist. Soon it was nothing more than a red dot on the long straight road far below.

We were now alone in that empty space. We all came down the mountain slowly and thoughtfully, as if from a funeral. Someone said (we never knew who it was because of the dark):

"Perhaps we shouldn't have . . ."

No-one responded to these hesitant words, but several of us turned around as we walked to look at the mountain breathing through the evening wind in its trees. We dared not say it, we hardly dared think it, but we all had the strange impression that we'd been robbed.

Yet everything was silent above us: the mountain, the forests and the echoing beds of old glaciers. The only subdued babble came from the waters of the river, but we had heard it since birth and its noise was the same as silence to us. Besides, has anyone ever heard a mountain speak?

We are alone on earth and have only each other. Nothing; nobody warns us if we are doing good or evil. And who could have known what awaited us poor things?

Ever since the previous day, Rose had started at the least sound. She cursed the big trees in the park that caught the slightest breeze, like sails on a ship. As soon as a gust of wind from the mountain reached them, they began to moan in unison, hopeful that this new squall would be the one that would let them get under way, far from the park which they were not sure they really liked.

When this great wail arose, Rose strained desperately to hear, as it dominated every other sound. That same morning she had dressed up and gone to the hairdresser. Enough time had elapsed since she had become a widow for her to wear half-mourning, which suited her to perfection. When she saw herself in Charmaine's mirrors, she smiled with satisfaction.

It was past nine o'clock and the wind had subsided for a moment, when the hand on the knocker suddenly struck three times.

Rose ran across the drawing room and down the hall, as though happiness was standing on the doorstep. She fought with the big key in the lock. She had never been able to manage its temperamental ways and always had to use force to get the bolt to move.

Antoine was standing on the step with the jute sack containing the folded shroud on his shoulder.

"You said come at any time, but if you prefer . . ."

She opened the door wide to let him in.

"Come in!" she said, and it was almost an order. "Come!"

She led him towards the dining room, abandoning the drawing room with its draughts and oppressive memories. It was the beginning of autumn and she installed herself in front of the fire. She pointed in front of her at the table with eight highly polished walnut chairs at their appointed places as though eight people always sat there.

"Put it down here!" she said.

"There? On the table?"

"Yes. On the table. Why not?"

He did what she asked, and for the first time Rose heard the sound of Séraphin's bones knocking together in the bottom of the sack. This time she had to admit that he was really dead. All the effort she had made to forget Auphanie's words was in vain.

Nothing had changed in that room since the day when Séraphin Monge, very much alive, had entered it. Rose had come to Pontradieu as though it were a museum. Despite Patrice's repeated entreaties to make the house her own, she had never changed her mind.

"You know," she had said to him one day, "I don't really belong here. I'm just passing through."

And so she had left everything as it was. Even the large portrait by Denis Valvéranne of Gaspard Dupin looking severe, apoplectic and vaguely threatening stayed hanging on the wall. Rose even continued to water regularly the lush tradescantia plant hanging from the ceiling in its green china pot. She moved deferentially among all these ugly things, never complaining about them, and since Patrice's death she looked after them with the same dedication as she would a tomb.

By asking Antoine to put Séraphin's remains on the table, she felt she was bringing back a guest to join the dead she loved. She loved them all as a group, having forgotten how much suffering they, as individuals, had brought into her life.

"Are you having guests?" Antoine asked.

"No. Why?"

"You're dressed as though you were expecting some."

They were both staring at the jute sack so out of place on the dining table and already shedding fibres on the polished wood.

"You wanted him to see you looking beautiful," Antoine said softly.

"How did you know that?"

"We always have illusions when it comes to the dead," he said. "It's all very well to know that . . . I once put on a tie for a dead woman. At least . . . one that she liked."

"And I've put on this dress. It's the first time I've worn it."

"And now you want to be alone with him."

"Yes. I want to be alone with him. But don't leave so soon. I must thank you first."

"You don't owe me anything at all. I did it in your time. I'm your employee."

"Don't be so humble, or I'll start to think you're as hypocritical as the others. You're not my employee. I'm a woman, you're a man, we're free and alone and no-one knows that we're together. Do you need a drink to make up your mind?"

Antoine shook his head without replying. She sighed.

"You'll never dare to do it," she said. "You'll never dare to lay a hand on me if I don't offer myself to you first. But make no mistake! I've no desire to do it. I only want to give you a gift that means something to you."

"It means nothing," Antoine said. "Since you don't want it."

"Many men wouldn't be so particular."

"Don't you believe it. No man would touch you with your lover between you."

He nodded in the direction of the sack full of bones.

"My lover! He never was!"

"That's even worse. He'll always live in your imagination."

"Don't complicate matters," Rose said. "Think of your own pleasure, that's all."

"You say that word as if you didn't know what it was."

"I don't. But perhaps with you . . ."

He noticed then that she had undressed in the darkness of the room while she was speaking, no doubt to move things along so that there was no going back. She was now lying naked on the sofa in front of the cold fireplace. Perhaps she thought he could bring her pleasure. Perhaps she had decided to give in to temptation. But her own nature would not obey her.

"Put your clothes on again," Antoine said. "Thank you. You did what you could . . . But I can find women who do take pleasure in it. Why should I struggle with someone who doesn't? I can't stand virgins and it's not in my heart to be a teacher."

He turned away from her, began to leave, then changed his mind.

"I'm sorry," he said, "it was too late in the day. I wasn't able to get the hands."

Rose was alone at last with her sack of bones. Her conscience was clear. She had offered Antoine what he had no doubt dreamed of for a long time. What man has not kept alive the hope of one day sleeping with his boss's widow? She had, of course, said all the right words to dissuade him from taking advantage of the situation. She had chosen them carefully. With these words she had built a wall around her body. After that she had been able to show herself naked with an easy mind. She could even have tempted him a good deal more. She had got just what she wanted: Séraphin's remains in return for a generous offer she had made unacceptable. And yet this victory left her feeling a deep resentment against Antoine. Who was he to refuse her?

She was cold and naked in front of the freezing, empty fireplace.

Séraphin's remains lying on the walnut table were part of the silence.

"Alone," she thought, "alone at Pontradieu with my dead and the wind in the trees. All the same . . . Who would have predicted that when I was Rose Sépulcre dabbling her feet in the Lauzon and dreaming perhaps of some butcher's boy? Who would have thought that the only person I would ever love would be a dead man?"

Standing in front of the large dim mirror in the drawing room, she ran her hands over her full hips and her breasts made to be a man's delight. She saw reflected the portrait of Gaspard Dupin, immortalized in paint. His grim look judged her without pity or affection.

For weeks Rose told no-one and jealously kept the sack of bones within arm's reach. She had hidden it in the wedding chest after taking out her trousseau which would never be used now. Indeed, there were enough sheets at Pontradieu to provide shrouds for twenty generations of dead. As soon as he became rich, Gaspard Dupin had ordered his deaf wife to fill three wardrobes with them. Rose had taken out a new linen sheet with its huge monogram and spread it in the middle of the drawing room in front of the fire. She could not take her eyes off the pile of muddy bones. A kind of palette stuck out from the heap, two hands across in width and something like a baker's paddle. These earth-coloured remains had once been a man with his eyes, his penis and his soul, within and without, true or false, his soul gone who knows where, wandering or non-existent, in any case out of reach.

Rose decided at last to make the gesture she had never been able or ever dared to make when Séraphin was alive: she stroked his face. Well . . . what remained of it. She took off all her clothes in front of the full-length mirror in her bedroom and nestled the skull in the hollow of her shoulder, which it filled entirely. It was the skull of a young man. All his teeth were intact. Rose looked at it full on without trembling, lifted it up to the exact height he was when alive. She put her lips to the nasal cartilage. A strong smell of the clay in which it had been lying still rose from it. She spoke to it tenderly in the silence of the large rooms, in front of Charmaine's bed where the perfume that impregnated her dresses and furs filtered out through the wardrobe doors and lingered in the air.

Rose had been doubly jealous of Charmaine, because of Séraphin and also because of Patrice. But now she was completely at peace, and her love extended equally to the three of them without distinction.

"I'll never have mercy on any man again!" she thought.

She tried to make up her mind for some time whether she would entrust her secret to Marie. Was it pride that finally won out, as if having his bones meant that she was the one Séraphin had chosen? One Monday when Marie came to show the child to Rose, his godmother, she led her with great secrecy to her bedroom, her finger to her lips. She pointed to the wedding chest.

"Do you know what's inside?"

"Good Lord!" Marie put both hands over her mouth. "You did it!" she exclaimed.

"I told you I would!"

"The proper place for a dead man is in the ground!" Marie said sternly. "It's sacrilege to keep him with you."

Rose lowered her head.

"I've had so little!" she said.

"You'll have even less with a dead man!"

Rose swiftly raised the lid of the chest.

"No!" Marie cried.

She took a large step backwards and leaned against the back of an armchair.

"No! To me he's still alive. If I see his bones, his face will disappear forever. I'll only ever see him dead! Rose, I beg you! Close the chest! The shock . . . I could lose the baby. I'm pregnant."

"Again!" Rose exclaimed.

"Well, yes. That's the way it is . . ." Marie said contritely.

"*My* belly will never carry another man's child," Rose said.

"It would do you good. You'll end up neurotic."

Marie turned her back on her. Rose annoyed her today. The child she was carrying also annoyed her. It was beginning to move.

"A pity!" Rose said. "If you saw his skull you would love it. He is even better looking than when he had his smooth skin and his eyes. Do you remember Séraphin's eyes, Marie?"

"Yes. I remember. But seeing the place where they used to be empty –"

Rose sighed.

"And his hands? she said. "It's a pity that they didn't find his hands."

"What did you say?"

"No. They didn't find his hands."

"Show me!" Marie said impetuously.

She marched over to the chest and opened it herself.

"What's got into you?" Rose asked. "A moment ago you didn't want to see him."

"Show me!" Marie said once more.

Rose took the monogrammed sheet out of the chest. The bones rattled as she brought them out. She spread the sheet on the carpet. Marie looked

146

at the remains of the man she had loved. She knelt down, daring to touch the relics, to sort them and put them here and there.

"Good Lord!" she said. "It's true! His hands are missing!"

"I told you so! Antoine couldn't get them. He told me that it was late, night was falling and there were gendarmes –"

"The whole mystery was in his hands," Marie whispered.

"What mystery?"

"I told you. They had no lines. They were completely smooth. Like a baby's. What am I saying! A baby already has lines."

"You can't have seen properly. You told me you had been delirious, that you had been at death's door."

"I tell you that there were no lines on his hands! Even if I was delirious, I couldn't have made that up!"

"Anyway, he doesn't have them now –"

"Bury him!" Marie said. "The dead are not meant to console the living. Even if one has loved them."

She gazed at Séraphin's bones with something approaching terror.

VI

WHEN WINTER HIT HARD, CÉLESTAT SETTLED ON TO A HEAP OF FLOUR sacks and did no more than give advice. He had never completely recovered after making himself ill trying to bring Marie to her senses. His pneumonia, as Dr Jouve diagnosed it for lack of anything more specific, tended to catch up with him at the first frosts and the after-effects lingered on for a dangerously long time, sometimes until the middle of spring.

"He hardly does anything any more!" everyone said.

This observation of laziness that we had never before seen in such an active man sounded ominous even as we said it. When he passed by our chairs, lined up in front of our doors so that we could see the world go by, our conversations embroidered with tales and commentaries on the sad or happy fate of others would suddenly fade away like bouquets of flowers deprived of water. They ceased like the twittering of birds when the eclipse of the sun spreads its cold darkness over the earth and everything huddles in fear in the unnatural gloom.

Célestat must have been aware of the icy silence that fell as he passed. The fact that he still kept on smoking in spite of strong objections from both the doctor and Clorinde indicated that he had noticed it. He smoked furtively, apparently without pleasure, as if he were saying sorry for having to keep on killing himself. He walked down the street past our houses on his way to the bakehouse, where he still went out of habit, in spite of everything. He made a token gesture of help with the breadmaking, then sat down on the empty sacks. Tibère would say to him:

"Rest, Pépé! You've done enough!"

For now he was a *pépé*, a grandpa. Marie's first son, a stocky little lad with strong arms and thighs, would toddle to the bakehouse calling for "Pépé". He wanted to smoke Célestat's cigarette butt, and when his grandfather gently refused to hand it over, he would kick him angrily in the shins. Tibère was not allowed to come down hard on him; Marie had made that clear once and for all. And so Célestat tried to reason with the lad. He excused him. He understood him. He'd brought it on himself more or less for wanting to live on through him, and if he was now having to push the child outside, life itself was to blame and no-one else.

As the two-year-old child stared straight at him with a malicious look in his eye, there was a whole sad philosophy concentrated in the resigned smile Célestat gave him. There were also spectacular reconciliations with the kid who, like all nasty natures big and small, was capable of the most manipulative shows of affection, throwing his arms around his neck and offering big affectionate hugs. But even these did not take Célestat's mind off its main preoccupation.

When he was sitting on his sacks in front of the oven, his gaze rarely left the corner where the secret he shared with this son-in-law was buried. Then he would look pensively at Tibère. The young man was like an ox. He didn't engage in soul-searching, or at least didn't seem to. As long as he could have his Marie during the siesta and fall asleep exhausted against her body, the world could go on for better or for worse. He didn't care. Célestat secretly envied this person who did nothing but work, sleep and see to Marie. How old could he be? Twenty-five, twenty-eight? Célestat did know, but couldn't remember. At twenty-eight Célestat was already full of remorse at having almost become a murderer one September evening, a long time ago. At that age he already had two long lines extending from the edge of his nostrils to the corners of his mouth. He was already on his guard and it made him old before his time. His secret weighed heavily on him, but even more so the idea that he hadn't had the presence of mind to tell Séraphin that the Monges' gold meant as little to him as it did to Séraphin himself. The fact that the gold was lying there underground was proof of that. It would stay there forever since, strangely enough, Tibère didn't seem keen on it either.

149

Sometimes sitting crouched on his sacks with his idle hands dangling between his legs, Célestat questioned his son-in-law in that toneless voice of his:

"Now come on Tibère, tell me."

"Yes, Pépé."

"Tell me what happened. How you managed to kill Séraphin. After all, he was twice as strong as you."

Tibère always replied patiently, never getting angry.

"I tell you I didn't kill him. He was already dead."

Célestat didn't insist. He just nodded his head. Sometimes he went home and lay down beside Clorinde, who grumbled as she made room for him in the long-since loveless bed. Sometimes he sighed and said to her:

"I won't last much longer."

She replied with the serenity of those who sleep well and have a clear conscience.

"You're imagining it. Go to sleep."

But he didn't sleep. He kept on imagining. One night he said,

"If I hadn't been so opposed to it . . . He'd have made a fine baker."

"What are you mumbling about? What were you opposed to?"

"Séraphin. He'd have married Marie."

With that Clorinde woke up completely and sat bolt upright with fear.

"For heaven's sake! Not that! Zorme's son!"

"All the same, he saved Marie!"

"Yes. And do you think that's natural, eh? Come on! Go to sleep. Stop talking nonsense."

Célestat sighed. The only people he came into contact with obviously all had clear consciences. He would get nowhere with them. At that time he started to use a stick when he walked to the bakehouse, and people started to use the word "poor" when they saw him pass by.

"Poor Célestat, he's really just a shadow of his former self. He was supposed to be over his pneumonia, but . . ."

In the end, it was common knowledge that Célestat had cancer. When it was finally confirmed, we had detected it so much earlier that God hasn't forgiven us for almost willing the cancer to grow.

But how could God punish the multitude that shares His own essence. We prophesy like the trees, like the wind. We are one of the elements of the mystery. It's not by chance that in the beginning was the word. We are the word. We blend into one single word. We are interchangeable and certainly mortal, but so like each other intertwined in the garland of the generations. Armed with the same hostilities, clinging to the same superstitions, suspicious and quick to take offence but also capable of the same enthusiasms, we share the same imperturbable stupidity. We condemn to death although we carry death within us. The sentence is first pronounced silently, deep within us, then one of us will express it and spread the word. Then individuals, events and fate itself have no other option than to give in and conform to it. When the thing finally happens, we had all said it would. Célestat must have felt the weight of our verdict upon him, and that there was no way that he would not have cancer. And so he had it.

"They've taken him to Marseilles. He's been X-rayed. Dr Jouve says that his days are numbered."

"It certainly seemed to me that it must be cancer . . ." Tricanote said. She couldn't help feeling pleased with her powers of perception.

Célestat had thought he lived only for his descendants and that his own fate was of little importance to him. That was a theory made by a man in good health. Now Marie's first boy was nearly two and the second had just been born. (A boy weighing 4 kilos 200 grams like the first.) They had just celebrated the baptism with a profusion of sugared almonds distributed all round. Célestat had even drunk a few mouthfuls of sparkling wine – not with any pleasure! – and lit a second cigarette for the day. The doctor said, "Let him do whatever gives him pleasure!"

Around him stood Clorinde in moiré, Marie in a floral print, Tibère in a soft felt hat. Tricanote was holding the baby while Marie had her arm affectionately around the Marquise de Pescaïré. Looking at them all, Célestat felt that his wishes had been granted and that the only thing left for him to do was to let them coddle him. It was like a picture that some passer-by notices briefly in the jumble of a second-hand dealer's shop. He had the feeling that Clorinde, Marie and all the others were unconsciously acting as though he were no longer there. He had believed in the warmth of family affection, but now there was only his fear to keep him company. No-one could share that fear with him or see the same thing as he. Humankind was withdrawing from him. He found it harder and harder to discern, as though he were becoming gradually enclosed in an oyster shell and everyone else was in the open air.

When autumn had passed, Tibère helped him for the last time to go hunting from a hide in the Ganagobie woods. For the last time he heard the sound of our indescribable wind in the ocean of pines. But already he could no longer catch the smell of the dew rising through the thyme and the everlastings growing in the patches of undergrowth. It was the smell of the morning when he was a sure-footed young man with a spring in his step and an infallible eye. The only smell in the whole world that remained with him now came from the thick taste in his mouth every time he moved his tongue.

Nothing worked any more; he just had to suffer a man's death with decency. He couldn't simply sink his nose deep into the grass like so many rabbits he had shot, bleed to death and see the world no more. On that day he realized he wouldn't even taste the aroma of the bird as it roasted, and that for him there was no point in killing it.

The word "kill" made him quiver inside every time it came into his mind, and often he could not stop himself from saying it aloud.

"Tibère," he said again on that day. It was perhaps the hundredth time he had repeated it since the night when his apprentice came back to the bakehouse trailing a smell like the bowels of the earth.

"Tibère," he said sternly, "swear to me on the heads of your children that you didn't kill him."

This is what lanky Larrigue, who was usually a man of few words, told us. Quite by chance he had been passing behind the wall of the hide.

"Unfortunately," he said, "I couldn't hear the reply. A gun fired and a thrush fell out of the almond tree."

We all took him to task.

"You could at least have waited, stupid! There was no fire in the spot where you were hiding! You don't usually catch much anyway! You could have told us more!"

"No I couldn't! I already had three cages of decoy birds on my back and they were making a devil of a row!"

"You could have covered them!"

"I didn't think of that," he said contritely.

Alas, we all knew that lanky Larrigue was none too bright. But that one sentence was enough for the suspicion of a secret, which we already sensed, to lodge instantly in our minds. Apart from the sound of gold coins falling, which Chabassut had heard two years earlier, we had no idea what that secret was, but we felt that it must be of such an order that even cancer could not explain why our baker had changed so much in recent times.

As for Célestat himself, the nagging truth was bursting desperately to come out of him like pus from a carbuncle, like something that should be said, that was useful, something that wouldn't ruin everything in its wake, as it usually did. "If I got better, I'd be really sorry I'd said it!"

But he was as bloated with that truth as a wineskin with wind. He walked along the Esplanade des Évêques leaning on his cane with his mouth moving as if he were talking to himself. Not a sound passed his lips – we had watched him closely enough to know that – be we felt that one day he would say some fatal words and that we, regrettably, would not be there to hear them.

The parish priest kept hovering around the possible act of contrition with such eager anticipation that it was almost sinful. That was what kept him standing in front of Clorinde's counter, bread under his arm, for much longer than he had to. He didn't make any positive mention of it, but he did slip a few hints into his sermons. Since the announcement that Célestat had no hope of surviving, they all relied on the safeguard of confession. The priest could talk of little else with the pious ladies of the parish, especially the Marquise de Pescaïré, who took it upon herself one morning to speak of it with Clorinde.

"You know, Clorinde, Célestat's a Christian after all. Don't you think that . . . ?"

On Christmas morning Clorinde said to Célestat, who was already white as a sheet:

"You should make your confession. It never did any harm."

"Am I as bad as that?"

"No. The doctor said you still have some years ahead of you, but I can see that there's something stopping you from sleeping."

"What's stopping me from sleeping?"

"Your conscience. You talk in your sleep."

"What would you know about my conscience?"

They had never had so much pillow talk before.

These exhortations never got results. "If I still have years ahead of me," Célestat took heart, "I have plenty of time. We'll see."

On the Promenade des Évêques where you couldn't avoid people, the priest would suddenly loom up in pitiless black in front of the poor devil, who was already scared to death and weighed only 38 kilos. He gave him a deliberate smile, the only one he ever gave, in order to reassure him. "You haven't a hope!" Célestat thought, but he felt weak at the knees for the rest of the day.

In the end he was bedridden. People asked how he was. Clorinde's hand, with fingers spread, made a gesture from right to left as she shook her head.

"He's talking nonsense . . ." she would say.

"What sort of nonsense?"

"Things of the other world. I don't know. I've got better things to do than pay any attention to it!"

We weren't satisfied. We murmured between ourselves, disappointed and angry. But if Célestat had time, he was the only one who believed it. He weighed no more than 35 kilos now and we all knew, from so many examples of it, that this was the final limit reached by those with a cancer that starves them to death.

"What a lot of fuss," the primary school teacher said, "for the death of a simple man like a baker!"

"He has a secret! Do you think that's nothing, a man with a secret! And what's more," Tricanote said to him sharply, "why should a baker be less important than the Emperor of China?"

The teacher readily agreed, but we had just one fear, which we expressed with great disappointment.

"You'll see! One of these days Célestat will slip away without his wife or daughter even noticing, they're never still!"

The Dormeur house at that time was filled with new life. Marie's second son had just been born. The house was full of his wailing to be fed every two hours. You could hear the jealous elder boy yelling as far away as the Place des Feignants. With his infallible instinct he could already see half his inheritance and his mother's love disappearing before his eyes. He kicked everything in sight: even his grandmother's shins, those of the customers who smiled at him in vain. The house echoed with Marie calling Clorinde to come and help her with something. Even Charitonne whom they had kept finally, contributed to the happy din by chirping all day long as she carried the nappies to the clothes line.

With all this noisy coming and going as the household went about its daily work, there was little space for the silence of a dying man, either in the house (it was just as well that he was in bed and no longer in the way of those who were healthy) or in the hearts of his dear ones, who were too caught up in the hurly-burly of life.

Célestat had got to the stage of trying to trick death, to bargain with it: "I still have this amount of time left . . ." No-one had told him that he now weighed only thirty-five kilos. If today it took as much effort to raise a glass of lemonade – the only food he could take – as he formerly used to knead fifty kilos of bread dough, he put it down entirely to his weakness. In actual fact, the glass weighed as much as his hand, almost as much as his arm. Indeed, one gives oneself months, weeks, days to live, never just one hour.

One morning when he was not feeling too bad (he had just smiled at Clorinde who brought back his urinal), he heard some strange sounds within him. He had the not particularly painful feeling of matter dissolving inside him, like mooring ropes being unwound and falling into the water. He called out to Marie with the commanding tone of voice he used when she was late and the deliveries had to be made straight away.

Marie had almost finished breast-feeding the baby. She dropped everything and arrived at her father's bedside with her bodice still open. He watched as she approached. Nothing, not even death, at that moment when he saw his daughter for the last time, could stop him thinking that she was a fine young woman, equipped to deal with life's battles and capable of surviving any suffering. He was proud of having forged such a tool. "She can withstand anything!" he said to himself.

He wanted to tell her in one word, in one huge swallow the story of all the murdered people who stood like milestones, like crosses, along his life's path. In a split second, he would have set down the lot before Marie like a horrible picture. But there you are: he had no more time to paint it. He had only enough to say:

"It's Tibère! He killed him! Dig at the corner of the oven! Dig! Dig!"

He thought he had caught her hand with his usual grip, while Marie only felt something on her skin akin to the flutter of a cigarette paper. She broke away and rushed out to the landing.

"Ma! Come quickly! He's delirious!"

Clorinde gripped the banister and charged up the stairs two at a time to the top. She ran towards the bed. Célestat's mouth was shaped like an O. He was dead.

What with her own grief and doing what was necessary to comfort Clorinde, as well as feeding the baby and delivering the bread, Marie scarcely had the time in the days that followed to think of her father's last words, which she put down to delirium anyway.

It was also the time when she began to feel really well again after the birth, a time when, after the first child, she realized that she was most eager for sex and when she felt it most strongly. She would even hunt Tibère down in the bakehouse. They made love on the piles of empty flour sacks. One night she almost cried out "Séraphin!" She had bitten her lips so hard to stop the cry that they were swollen for three days afterwards.

One week after the death of her husband, Clorinde had taken up the reins again, serving in the shop, doing the cooking and keeping an eye on the elder boy, still a holy terror. He was wildly jealous of the wailing baby and refused even to go over to the cradle. One day when they wanted to force him to look at his brother, he kicked the crib in such a rage that he nearly tipped it over. On that day he got what was coming to him. Marie gave him such a hiding that he yelled with pain for an hour afterwards. Henceforth he took it as a warning and was much slyer in showing his disapproval. Clorinde had her work cut out with him.

"*Bé vaï*," said the women who came to the shop, "it serves him right, but what a godsend for you! It helps take your mind off your great misfortune!"

Clorinde had no need of such distractions. She had resigned herself to the worst the moment the word "cancer" had been mentioned. And then Célestat had declined so slowly that she had the impression he was just like her: a fruit that had gone to seed and would just rot slowly. Being a widow didn't change much. In the first place, except when he was ill, Célestat had spent nearly every night at the bakehouse and slept alone in their bed during the day. Love rarely lasts longer than the age of thirty with such lowly people. Célestat hadn't touched his wife after Marie's birth and the caesarian that had put an end to Clorinde's fertility. She didn't blame him for it. In her opinion, as she told her women customers, they were two trees that had borne their fruit. They had had their share of both misfortune and peace (which constitutes happiness for the poor). Dying after that was nothing to worry about. Nonetheless, she dutifully went to the cemetery every morning before opening the shop, but it was mainly to earn people's good opinion.

She passed widows standing by a grave as though rooted to the spot and inconsolable at not having thrown themselves in it at the funeral. Not she: she grumbled as she tidied around the marble headstone, weeding the grass, staking up the chrysanthemums drooping with rain. She went home holding her back.

We watched the family going about their lives, even spied on them shamelessly, knowing what we knew: that Célestat had a secret and we needed to find out whether he had taken it to the grave or not.

At one time we thought that fate had decided to leave the Dormeurs alone and that it would turn its attentions to those of us who had been living peaceful lives for far too long. But no, it had not finished with them.

If Célestat had been able to hold his tongue until the end, perhaps fate might have chosen someone else to persecute; but he couldn't. Yet he hadn't said very much, and both his body and voice had become so weak and insignificant that Marie had not attached any importance to his words. But when truth will out, nothing stands in its way or limits the treachery of its ways and means. It's like those who have been dead for a thousand years, whom we all imagine resting peacefully six feet under, and whose green-tinged bones rise to the surface the first time the pick hits the ground. That is why, forewarned by such experience, we have continued for so long to place such enormous slabs of stone over them. But stone slabs weigh nothing over the lightness of truth. Their thickness and density are just like a sieve to truth. Perhaps it may even escape, from the dust and decay of the dead, invisible, impatient and laden with all the misery that virtue can bring.

What made Marie think of Célestat's words? Was it his invisible spirit departing, travelling by moonlight down the switch-back road dotted with chapels which he had travelled so often during his lifetime, enjoying the fresh smell of the pines, talking happily to whoever he met as he rolled his cigarette? And on that night as he went back home, where he was already forgotten, did he see, could he see Lurs down there, the mountain over which the Great Bear seemed to lie fully stretched? Or was it only cosmic restlessness that brought up from Marie's memory the forgotten moment she needed to remember?

Whatever the reason, she dreamed of her father. It was on a Sunday night, the only good night's sleep she had, a night when her head was nestled between Tibère's arm and chest as he breathed heavily in his sleep; a night when she pressed her big belly against her husband's, which was as flat and tight as a drum. For, in spite of all those exhortations from Clorinde, who threw her arms in the air, Marie was pregnant again for the third time in four years.

It was in that state that Marie dreamed of her father on his deathbed. It was an awful dream: Célestat had Séraphin's face. He was saying: "Tibère killed him! Dig at the right corner of the oven! Dig! Dig!"

Marie sat bolt upright in a second, fully awake and completely lucid. This disturbed Tibère, who groaned and rose up like a mountain, taking the pillow with him as he turned over, then fell asleep again with a big peaceful sigh. He never knew that his fate was sealed in the stillness of that night, in the nearness of an ordinary couple who enjoyed being alive.

Marie sat there listening to the night, listening to her heart, which seemed to beat outside her body. The child in her womb, also suddenly awoken from its sleep, gave her a furious kick in the stomach.

"Tibère killed him! Dig at the right corner of the oven!"

It was as though a thundering voice had said these words outside in the street and they still echoed in the air. She was gasping for breath. She was on the point of giving Tibère a vigorous shake to wake him and tell him straight out about her nightmare. After all they were husband and wife and they should share everything, everything that is except what went on inside her while she was making love with him.

She was on the point of . . . But she was a child of her race whose finest virtue was keeping silent. The moonlight coming through the window eliminated all the mysterious shadows from the bedroom, but its brightness was no more reassuring than the dark. Marie shivered in that light. The silence was so complete that you could hear the water flowing in the fountain in the Place des Feignants. Marie knew that the silence had not fallen at that precise moment and that there was really no voice saying the words she had heard in her dream. Lurs was quite devoid of any presence, real or imaginary. Everything was peaceful, calm and deserted.

Marie got up, nevertheless, and went to the window to make sure that the silence was as she expected. Her nightdress flapped like a tulip around her big belly and buttocks, but the night breeze reached her skin and gave her goose flesh. She turned around towards Tibère who was lying flat on his stomach, naked to the waist. She opened her mouth to call to him, not to tell him about her nightmare but simply for company. She changed her mind. The man worked six nights a week and he had a right to sleep on the seventh. That should be sacred for everyone. She then went back to bed. "I'm not thinking straight," she thought, "the baby's upsetting me."

She huddled on her side close to the bedside table, pulling all the blankets over her. Tibère was left with only a triangle covering his behind. She turned her pillow over and over again, and finally fell asleep.

On sunny Sunday afternoons in Lurs, apart from the echoes of a game of *boules* being played under the chestnut trees, it was as quiet as it is at night. The streets and paths were deserted. We were all in our properties, working just as we did during the week, which was our best way of amusing ourselves.

Tricanote, who was keeping her goats in the ruins of the château, was the only one who heard Marie cry out.

Six months heavily pregnant, Marie disappeared one Sunday afternoon when everything was quiet, when her two children and her husband were sleeping, and when her mother was polishing the pans on the Roberval scales. All Tricanote heard was that great cry she told us about and the door of the truck slamming shut. The *boules* players saw it charging down the road towards Peyruis in a cloud of dust.

She still wasn't back by nightfall, or by the next morning. The Dormeur household resounded with squawks of protest. The little ones wanted their mother. Tibère, white as a sheet, was incapable of uttering a word. Clorinde wrung her hands.

"She's always off somewhere! The slightest thing and she's off! But now, with two little children! With her big belly! For heaven's sake Marie! You'll be the death of your poor mother!"

Rose was startled. For the umpteenth time she was reading the passionate correspondence between Patrice and Charmaine when he was at the front and her husband was still alive. She had been about to throw these papers in the fire countless times since she discovered them in Charmaine's chiffonier, then could not bring herself to do it at the last minute. The faded ink, now quite white, tracing the words that spoke so subtly of love and eroticism, had often almost made Rose feel an excitement she had not known before. She hastily gathered up the letters and stuffed them back in their shoebox.

The sound of the door knocker echoed through Pontradieu.

"Who would bang on the door like that?" Rose wondered.

She was annoyed as she flung the door open impatiently, ready to upbraid whoever was there.

"Good Lord!"

She closed her mouth immediately as her hand flew up across it. She stepped back, horrified at the sight of Marie whose huge frame took up the whole doorway. Marie with her inscrutable face and the ten years she seemed to have aged in one hour now looked like her mother, Clorinde Dormeur.

"Good Lord!" Rose said once more.

Marie walked past her without a word and sank on to a sofa, holding her belly in both hands.

"Good Lord!" Rose said. "What's the matter? You're not going to lose the baby, I hope?"

"No, no! Don't worry! That's something else. Don't you worry, he's stuck fast! Unfortunately!" she added.

She took a white handkerchief from her handbag and dabbed her eyes. They were quite dry, but her lips were trembling and her brow was damp with perspiration. She was panting like someone who has just knocked into something and can't get her breath back.

"Marie! I'm really worried! Tell me what's wrong."

"No! I can't! He's the father of my children."

"What has Tibère done to you?"

"I can't tell you. Can I sleep here tonight?"

"Yes, of course. But . . . And what about the little ones?"

Marie waved her hand as though she didn't care.

"My mother's there, and my godmother, and Tricanote . . . That's enough to spoil them. Have you got something strong?"

She lowered her eyes but kept watching her friend coming and going to get what she wanted. Rose was crouching on the carpet in front of the sideboard where she was looking for the liqueurs.

"You did tell me, didn't you," Marie asked quietly, "that your Antoine hadn't found Séraphin's hands?"

"Yes. Why do you ask?"

Rose was surprised as she walked back towards Marie and looked at her intently as she poured her a glass of Arquebuse. Marie took the glass from her and drank it in one gulp. She sat there stiffly holding her solid breasts as she choked, then coughed violently. Rose knelt down in front of her.

"Marie! Tell me what the matter is!"

"Not for all the money in the world!"

Marie looked away. She watched the evening sky growing dark among the trees through the big windows of Pontradieu. Good Lord! Was it only yesterday that everything was so good as they all sat around the table in the peace of the back room behind the shop?"

"Do you remember when Charmaine died?" she said. "Do you remember that night when I broke your housekeeper's gun in two when she wanted to kill Séraphin? You weren't there of course, but I've told you about it so many times . . ."

"Why are you thinking of that?"

"I had strength of character then! But I still have some, don't you worry! I won't give in! I won't give in!"

She hit her knees with her fists which, in spite of her present size, were no bigger today than when she was eighteen and still thought that Séraphin would marry her.

"I'm going to make you some soup," Rose said. "You can sleep in Patrice's studio. It's the pleasantest room in the house and you won't have to climb the stairs. You must eat and you must sleep. Tomorrow . . ."

"Tomorrow everything will be just as fresh in my mind as it is today."

"Tomorrow you'll tell me all about it."

"No! Never! I haven't anything more to say to anyone. Ever!"

"All right!" Rose said. "You won't tell me anything."

"Don't tell the others I'm here."

"No. Don't worry about it."

But there was the truck just left there in the middle of the driveway. The Marquise de la Pescaïré arrived at seven in the morning. Old people get up early. She had hired a taxi. Rose, who was upset by all that had happened, had only just managed to get off to sleep. She had got up three times during the night and gone to the studio. When she opened the door quietly, she had seen Marie fast asleep across the bed, looking huge under the red eiderdown. Each time she had felt like getting in close beside her and making her spit out her secret by any means in her power. "What a strange feeling it must be," she thought, "to feel the body of a pregnant woman against you. Husbands are the only ones who have that privilege . . ." But she hadn't dared to do it, and went back to her cold bed. It was the first time in their lives that these two passionate women had slept alone under the same roof. Marie, who was exhausted and in a deep sleep, seemed to accept the situation with perfect tranquillity; Rose had to make an effort to feel no regret.

The Marquise de Pescaïré fell to her knees at the bedside where her goddaughter was weeping bitterly.

"Marie! What's got into you? I knew you would be here. You must come home! The children are crying all the time. Your mother has palpitations! And your husband! Have you thought of your husband?"

"Oh! Don't talk to me about him!" Marie cried.

Her tears dried up instantly on her cheeks. She was suddenly up on her feet again, scrabbling around for her clothes, dressing in fits and starts.

"I don't want to have anything more to do with him! Ever!" she cried. "Never again! I'll come back, but I'll sleep at your place!"

"No, please!" the Marquise begged her.

"Yes! Or I'll stay here!"

The taxi with Marie inside stayed in the Place des Boules until the return of the old Marquise, who had gone to parley with the family.

"Yes!" said Clorinde.

"Yes!" said Tibère. "Whatever she wants!"

"Good Lord!" exclaimed Clorinde. "Whatever she wants, provided she takes care of her children!"

"I'll take care of my children! I'll take care of everything! But I don't want to see any more of Tibère! I don't want to eat opposite him! I don't want to sleep in the same bedroom!"

"Leave her be!" Clorinde said to Tibère. "She'll get over it. It's her condition that makes her act this way. She'll get over it. Just wait a while. And while you're waiting, don't cross her!"

"I don't want to cross her," Tibère agreed. "She's my wife. She's my mistress. She's the apple of my eye. No. Heaven forbid. I don't want to cross her."

He was sent up into the loft above the bakehouse to sleep, the same place he occupied before he was married. Clorinde brought him his dinner, just as she used to. His children came and made a fuss of him.

But at night ... At night in the bakehouse, he was alone with his reflections. He thought back over anything he should reproach himself with. He couldn't find anything. He kept seeing Marie with her arms tight around his neck as she half choked him during her orgasm.

"What's the matter with her?" he wondered aloud.

He was such a simple and peaceable man that he had forgotten all about what he had buried under the corner of the oven. Since then, broken cages Célestat had used for carrying his decoys had been stacked up on that very spot for lack of space. And that was on top of an old boiler full of coke, which they were always going to give to the needy for their fires.

"What did I do to her?" he would say to himself with his arms hanging limply at his sides.

One day as he was sitting there, he happened to look down at the dirt floor near the boiler and noticed that the outline of the bottom could be seen in the softer earth, not far from the precise spot where it always stood. Then he also saw that the two decoy cages – one was more battered than the other – had been moved and put back in the wrong order. From that moment he was paralysed with fear. He couldn't bring himself to dig and check whether his secret had been uncovered. He preferred doubt to certainty. He preferred anything to the truth.

He had never been in Marie's presence since the day she insisted upon legal separation. Sometimes on Sunday nights, when he should have been sleeping, all his senses cried out for Marie. Then he would quell his fear and his humility and whisper at the door of the girl's bedroom, which had also been his. He hoped that she was listening and missed him. He was counting on the urgent need she must be feeling, she who was never more eager to make love than when she was pregnant. But he scratched at the door in vain and, having accomplished nothing at all, fell asleep in the end on the rough mattress in the draughty loft. When he awoke in the morning, he was chilled to the bone. The door was always closed, always locked, inpregnable. He would press his ear to it. Marie was asleep and breathing deeply. He went away, feeling quite alone in the world.

One night, however, when he had just climbed the steep stairs like an old man, hitting each step, the door at which he had so often begged to be let in, was suddenly jerked open.

"Come in!" Marie said.

She liked lamps set very low. They were made of sculpted glass in pink or green, portraying señoritas with Andalusian combs in their hair and playing castanets. Tibère had never seen the room lit any other way. Marie even used to berate him if he ever lit the ceiling lamp, which threw a stark light on to the whitewashed walls. On that night, however, he thought that the bulb must have been changed to make the light from the ceiling even more blinding.

"Come in!" Marie said again. "What are you waiting for?"

He went in. There on the white counterpane pulled up tightly over the one pillow in the middle of the bed Tibère immediately saw Séraphin's hands, now reduced to skeletons, just as he had cut them off from the body he couldn't save, as it had already been sucked down into the clay. It was the only time in his life that he had had to think really quickly. Séraphin's hands were like a drowning man's: clutching, beckoning. Tibère had seized them with all the strength of despair and had cut them off with his razor-sharp knife to bring back proof, because Célestat had said to him: "If you don't find Séraphin, don't bother to come back. Keep everything, but don't come back." Now, he was anxious to come back to claim Marie and this was the only expedient he could find to prove that he had done everything in his power to give back the box of coins, and that it wasn't his fault if he had failed.

"Murderer!" Marie hissed at him. "This is the last you'll see of me!"

Tibère's legs had given way under him and he fell to his knees. His nose was on a level with the cloth soiled with brown spots, but it was still in as good condition as when it had been woven long ago from rough hemp in some poor farm around Lodève. He stared at it. On it, spread out flat and intact, just as he had carefully placed them, were the remains of what had been the hands of Séraphin Monge stuck to the hemp with every bone in its right place. How could that man's hands, which had been so powerful and firm, be reduced to this fine tracery of fragile bone?

Beside the cloth was the open sugar box, and in the stark light from the ceiling the gold coins were glistening so much that they formed a mirror surface bright enough to make you turn your eyes away. Marie was standing on the other side of the bed, fully dressed. She had got even bigger in the month since he saw her last.

"Since you've been so keen on knowing the truth of the situation, as you put it," she said, "well, there it is! Take a good look at it, if you dare!"

"Marie, I didn't kill him! It was the earth that swallowed him up! He was already dead when I cut off his hands. I told your father that he was already dead!"

"What about the gold? Don't tell me that my father gave you all that gold for nothing. He couldn't stand Séraphin. He had something against him, I don't know why. He was only sorry at the end. He told me everything!"

"No! He couldn't have told you everything, otherwise you wouldn't be here persecuting me! The gold was neither his nor mine. It was yours! Séraphin gave it to him for you! Your father didn't want to keep it. That's why he sent me to give it back to him."

Marie shook her head.

"You killed him!" she said, without raising her voice. "You must have done it. It was all too convenient for you. With him alive I would never have married you. But you haven't killed him in me. He's there! And there!"

She touched her left breast then spread her hand over her belly.

"He's there!" she cried. "And you can't do anything about it! I was thinking of Séraphin when he was conceived! I was thinking of him when they were all conceived!"

"Marie! You must believe me! I'm a good man. Haven't you ever noticed that? How could I do something like that?"

"I don't believe you! No-one will believe you! A good man wouldn't cut anyone's hands off. Do you know what you must do now?"

"You want me to fetch the gendarmes?"

"No. That's not what I want!"

She had moved around the bed and covered the bones again, gently and compassionately folding over the corners of the cloth. She walked towards Tibère with a menacing look in her eyes. They were as cold as porcelain as she stared him full in the face. There were no memories of the past, no mercy in that look. She almost pushed him outside with her heavy belly.

"You know what you have to do now!" she said.

She had driven him back into the corridor. She slammed the door on him with a bang. He stood there disheartened for a few moments. He could hear her weeping bitterly behind the door.

"Marie! You must believe me! I didn't kill him! I swear it on the heads of our children! He was already dead!"

That closed door was so like Marie's stubborn brow. He was like the frantic fly hitting the window pane, not understanding anything of what is going on inside. He banged on it every night from then on.

Marie covered her ears and turned over heavily towards the wall. In her pitch-black bedroom three doors down, Clorinde wrung her hands in despair. Sometimes their father's groans woke the children who began to cry and call out. Marie tapped loudly on the wall.

"Have you finished? Go to sleep or I'll get up!"

They were too scared not to obey, just as Tibère obeyed, went away from the door, down the stairs and back to his mattress again. He was one of those numerous people who feel remorse for something they have done only after they have been found out. Until then, they feel in the deep recesses of their soul, that while it is between them and their conscience, they are bolstered by it and sleep easy.

He had accepted the truth of the matter very well until then, but since Marie had flung it in his face, he couldn't get Séraphin's hands out of his mind. "And who knows," he wondered, "whether he was really as dead as that after all?" His fingers had immediately been covered in the blood that gushed out. He kept seeing that blood. Soon he no longer dared to go scrabbling at Marie's door or beg her in whispers, for he was no longer so sure that he hadn't killed Séraphin.

As for us, we felt that misfortune was once again bearing down on the family that had already been so sorely afflicted. We were aware that Marie had shut Tibère out of their bedroom, and we highly disapproved of her, women included. In the beginning, we had been surprised and scandalized to learn that this couple was at it so much, especially as we were not. Consequently, when Marie cut her lawfully-wedded husband off from what she had a duty to provide, our surprise turned to worry and alarm. We knew that he was a man who couldn't do without his wife, and we feared that sooner or later his mood would affect the quality of our bread.

To do him justice, we had to admit that he slipped up only once. On one morning only his bread tasted like what you could buy with no great enthusiasm anywhere else but here. But that didn't reassure us, for seen from behind, he reminded us more and more of Célestat, when he first began to suffer from cancer. Such a fine figure of a man! So strong, so straight! And he always had a kind word for everyone. A man who could have been so happy. You could see it in a sudden light in his eye when he forgot to be sad. Ah! During all that time we spent judging her, we didn't spare Marie in our private conversations.

One night Tibère killed himself at the fountain.

One of us who was leaving on his bicycle to do his shift at the Saint Auban factory saw him coming out of the bakehouse with his two buckets and his rifle across his shoulder. Poor Tibère's head must have been in such turmoil that scarcely two minutes before he died, he didn't know whether he was going to fill his buckets and go back to knead the dough or use them in some way to blow his brains out. He must have made up his mind at the last minute, while the containers were overflowing under the jet of water. He put them down on the ground. The trigger guard had broken off Célestat's gun a long time ago. The hair trigger was free. It could easily be hooked on to the handle of one of the buckets, which is what Tibère did. Then he put the barrel of the gun under his chin and pulled with both hands. The heavy bucket with its twelve litres of water resisted, but not the trigger, which went off.

There were twenty or thirty of us that night who immediately jumped out of bed in our nightshirts and ran to the fountain. Marie, who was fully dressed, joined us almost at the same time. She had Tibère's body brought into the conjugal bedroom from which he had been banished for weeks. Her calmness didn't even surprise us. We didn't know what her secret was, but we knew she had one.

We found the dough in the trough, already salted and ready to be worked. Marie said she had already done it with her mother when she was fifteen. Her father had dislocated his shoulder and if we wanted to help him . . . We were shocked, and protested.

"In your condition! Think of the baby! Think of your own grief. Don't think of us!"

Our disapproval had changed in an instant to boundless admiration for her strength of character, which only grew in the days that followed. We voluntarily went without bread, as no-one had the nerve to get some delivered from Peyruis. In actual fact, we only missed two batches: on the day of the tragedy and the day of the funeral, out of respect.

Marie had taken charge of things so well that she had put an advertisement for an employee baker in the paper a week earlier. One arrived on the day of the funeral. The majority found this initiative quite disturbing, but there were several of us who praised her without reservation and were very pleased about it.

"I felt Tibère was deteriorating," she said. "He badly needed to take a rest."

She still had about three weeks to go before the baby was due, but she took charge of the funeral nonetheless. Her belly commanded respect. It's not often that a widow in full mourning and heavily pregnant accompanies her husband to his last resting-place.

About 200 of us were ready to form a chain to carry her to her bedroom if need be. But no. The baby came into the world on the due date. And it was he, the poor innocent child, who paid the price for everyone.

VII

WHEN TIBÈRE AND MARIE'S LAST CHILD WAS BORN, HE WAS BLIND. He weighed four kilos 100 g, almost as much as his brothers. He wailed when he was born like every other child in the world. He even yelled, but he didn't cry. He couldn't cry. Dr Jouve said that his tear glands were blocked or more or less atrophied. He said that the eye needs to be constantly irrigated and without that continuous lubrication, it cannot see. At least that is what we gathered from these explanations, poor distant witnesses that we were, never receiving news that hadn't been distorted or transformed by those who had only heard it in passing in the first place.

"It's the shock she had when Tibère killed himself!" moaned Clorinde.

Tricanote nodded her head.

"And yet," she said, "she showed real strength of character under the circumstances! If something like that had happened to me . . . God forbid!"

"Exactly!" Clorinde replied. "She controlled herself! The poor little thing's so sensitive!"

In fact the poor little thing had seized her destiny and claimed to be in control of it. Her three children were her symbol, her security and her shield. We didn't say, we had never said "Tibère's sons"; we always said "Marie's sons". After Tibère's parents from Lodève had been kissed goodbye at the funeral, all they could expect henceforth was to go away and be forgotten. They were sent one New Year's card from the whole family to say that the children were well and they sent a kiss to their grandpa and grandma who unfortunately lived so far away.

As soon as it was certain that the youngest was blind, Marie spared nothing for his treatment. She had him looked at by all sorts of specialists. She went to Marseilles, to Lyon, even as far as Paris. Every time the verdict handed down was the same, as pitiless as it was imprecise (for science never ventures to make assertions without adverbs): it was *probably* a natural malformation. Dr Jouve grumbled:

"She could have spared herself all that expense! I told her, 'He has atrophied lachrymal glands!' It's rare, but it exists."

"Well then, he'll see through music!" Marie said.

She employed a music teacher from Manosque who was also blind and had a special method.

"Right!" she said. "I'll come and fetch you three times a week and give you your train fare back. I want this poor little fellow to develop a love of music. It's all he'll have in life!"

We watched her battling with life, getting used to what she couldn't change and making the best of it. She had silenced us all by hiring a baker on the spot between Tibère's death and his funeral.

Marie was an unusual woman who never felt guilt or regret. It seemed as if the fact of having been robbed of Séraphin, like being robbed of an inheritance, gave her rights in everything: morality, propriety, hypocrisy. She never made any mystery of visiting the worker she hired in his garret. She saw it as necessary for her physical health.

He was a sturdy fellow with broad shoulders whose hair grew very low on his brow. We realized straight away that she had dazzled him even though the first time he saw her she was close to giving birth. But this young baker entered the house only at Easter and Christmas. He never had a napkin ring. Nor did he ever have a nickname, for Marie changed it sometimes when he gave signs of wanting to dominate her.

We all knew that she had inherited Célestat's secret and that Tibère Saille, who hadn't made old bones, was implicated in it. We also knew that if we wanted to share in it, we would have to keep Marie under constant observation.

However, a woman with a secret had never seemed so serene. She had acquired a domineering gaze that made us lower our eyes, even though we were usually in the habit of holding our own on that score.

"My goodness, how she's changed!" people said.

She hadn't changed. Her nature had crystallized. Everything about her had hardened: her feelings, her breasts, her bottom. Instead of crushing her, the misfortunes fate had dealt her seemed to have tempered her character. Instead of spoiling her looks, her three pregnancies had made her more beautiful. She was glowing with youth, health and vigour. We just wondered why her mouth tightened and her eyes narrowed when she looked at us. Then we remembered that she was keeping a secret, and that seemed explanation enough.

As soon as she was on her feet again after the birth and had put her affairs in order, Marie began making deliveries again in the truck. Clorinde hadn't stopped serving behind the counter. For thirty years she had worn navy dresses with white spots. From the time she became a widow, the white spots were on a black background. It was the only change she allowed herself to make. She was still irredeemably ugly, but now had an unhappy look that never left her. In the afternoon, when the customers had emptied the bread baskets, she would sit in front of the door on a low chair. She kept an eye on the children who were playing or fighting. In the early months, she also kept her ears open for wails coming from the first floor where the blind baby might be hungry or need something.

Sometimes Tricanote or the Marquise de Pescaïré or some other person would come and sit on other chairs that were always vacant. Our common fate invariably inspired groans and never cries of joy.

"Oh! Heaven help us!"

"Oh! God Almighty!"

We strained our ears behind half-closed shutters in summer, but to no avail. We never heard anything but these lamentations repeated over and over again and punctuated with sighs, to which the more Christian Marquise would sometimes add:

"May divine mercy forgive us our sins."

We were no further forward. And yet we knew for sure that these three women, by tacit agreement, were putting much more into their moaning and wailing than mere complaints, and that when their three heads were together, they didn't even need words to communicate silently on so many subjects we were keen to know about.

"Where do you think she's gone this time?"

"Oh, to Rose's place. What do you expect? They're hand in glove those two since . . ."

"Since when exactly?" Tricanote asked.

"You know."

That was at least one thing we'd found out: when Marie took a long time with her deliveries, she was making a detour to Pontradieu to see Rose Sépulcre.

When Rose had rushed to Marie's side on the day of the tragedy to render the same service she had received from her friend, Marie said to her quietly:

"Don't try to console me. I'll explain later."

Marie wasted no time. She went to Pontradieu immediately after Tibère's funeral and the birth of the blind baby soon after that. Rose saw her appear one afternoon, carrying a parcel tied with string. She put it down on the table.

"What is it?" Rose asked.

Marie didn't reply. She untied the string around the parcel and pulled back the paper.

"Sit down!" she said.

Rose did as she was told.

"Look!" Rose said.

Before Rose's eyes she unfolded the hemp cloth she had dug up from its hiding place in the bakehouse. Rose cried out with horror and sat bolt upright.

"Why are you showing me that? Why have you brought me that?"

"They're Séraphin's hands," Marie said.

"Good Lord!" Rose whispered. "Are you sure?"

"My father told me on his deathbed."

"And you believed him?"

"No. Not straight away. I thought he was delirious. It was afterwards, when I thought about it. He said to me, 'Dig at the right-hand corner of the oven.' That's what I did. Do you remember the day I arrived here so upset?"

"Yes, I remember. I remember you said to me, 'I can't tell you anything! He's the father of my children!'"

"Right. That was the reason."

"And you bore all that without saying anything to anyone? Without saying anything to me?"

"Yes. But I told him. I even said to him that there was only one thing left for him to do."

"And did he do it?"

"Yes. Not immediately, but he did it in the end."

"Good Lord!" she said again. "How you must have suffered!"

Marie gave a slight shrug of her shoulders.

"Not as much as all that. That's what's so strange. I wouldn't say it to anyone else but you, but I hardly suffer at all, hardly ever. As you can see, I've been able to put all my affairs in order. I've never stopped looking after the children. Everyone admires me, but I don't find anything to admire in what I do. It's not even an effort for me to do it."

She was silent for a moment.

"I must be thick-skinned," she added.

Rose looked at her intently. It's true that she had the rosy cheeks of a happy woman. She was, of course, dressed in black, in the severe baker's apron that made her look thinner and older. She had pulled her hair back into a big bun, as it was long and thick.

She said to Rose:

"At last I can wear mourning as much as I like. You see, Rose, I think I used up all my store of suffering when Séraphin left us. Now that I know he's dead, nothing can hurt me any more."

"What about your son who's blind?"

"Oh! Of course . . . and even there, I sometimes wonder. When I knew his father was a murderer, I'd have had an abortion if I'd still had time. Oh, I pet him as much as the others, but . . . I have to make an effort to make it seem natural."

She glanced furtively at Rose.

"Sometimes . . ." she said, "I have the impression that he didn't come from me."

174

The two women looked deep into each other's eyes. Rose was also in mourning, but on her the close-fitting black habit looked somehow indecent and guilty. "She can't help looking attractive in spite of herself," Marie thought. She squeezed Rose's hands in hers, but a trace of jealous wariness still crept into her affection and her need of the other woman.

"Rose, tell me the truth now. Have you buried Séraphin's bones yet?"

Rose looked away and shook her head.

"I've put them away in a little antique chest Patrice used to store his paints and brushes."

"And you take it out and look at them sometimes?"

"Yes," Rose said.

"And sometimes you might even kiss them! Please tell me it's not true?"

"It *is* true, I tell you!" Rose exclaimed in a defiant tone.

Marie suddenly pushed her friend's hands away.

"You're mad!" she said. "Dead people's bones are meant to be buried in holy ground, not to be played with! Has your famous chapel been consecrated yet?"

"Yes, the parish priest came when I had the bodies moved here."

"Well, now you must put these hands with the remains of the body and bury them properly."

"Yes," Rose murmured, sounding contrite. "I've been promising myself to do it for ages."

Marie was satisfied. She went back to Lurs feeling much relieved. "At last," she thought, "they won't be so close to each other. In the same room! In the same bedroom! Come on, you're just as silly as she is!" She mentally reproached herself. "You've seen your father die. You've seen your husband die. What feelings can they still stir up in the living? So what can a bag of bones do?"

She hurried into the house. The blind baby was crying with hunger. She gave him the breast, cuddled him and talked to him. The Marquise de Pescaïré, Tricanote, Clorinde, everyone smiled contentedly.

"That's our Marie!" we said, as if she'd been there all the time, while she was actually at Pontradieu jealously guarding Séraphin's remains. We thought it was touching to watch this new friendship between two women rivals.

"They've both suffered the same fate," we said. "Both their husbands blew their brains out. The poor things."

And it was true that the fact of having suffered a similar fate had sealed a special friendship between the two women. They couldn't get enough of each other's company.

"You know," Marie said, "while I refused to believe that Séraphin was dead, I didn't really like you."

"While you didn't believe I loved Patrice?"

"I believed it as long as you did."

"You know, it's strange," Rose said. "It's because I was afraid of his face, because I couldn't bear to look at it any more that Patrice finally killed himself. But now I no longer see it disfigured. I see it looking perfect, in fact I can't even imagine what it was like then. You probably won't understand this, but I see him just as I saw him in the beginning, when you couldn't understand how anyone could love such a horrible face."

"I still wonder how you managed it. Um, at night when he . . . Um, when he made love to you . . . Oh no! I just can't imagine it!"

"I didn't feel anything in his arms, if that's what you want to know. And yet I was sure I loved him in the beginning."

"Never? Didn't you ever wonder why?"

"I was waiting for it to happen."

"I experienced it the very first time," Marie said proudly.

She stopped short, then turned her head away. She was about to tell Rose more than she intended. She changed her train of thought.

"And I knew much earlier than that, since I was a child, that I'd feel it straight away."

"Not me," Rose said shaking her head. "I made poor Patrice's life a misery with all that. All he wanted was for me to come! If you knew how he caressed me!"

"Well, fancy that!" Marie sighed. "Fancy that! You poor thing, you haven't even got that! Well what do you do to forget that time passes, then you die?"

"I never forget it," Rose said.

Marie couldn't say anything, she felt so dismayed.

"And yet . . ." Rose continued.

She was twisting her hands and wondering if she really should put herself at Marie's mercy by giving up her last secret.

"And yet?" Marie asked pricking up her ears.

"And yet, when I dream, I manage to . . ."

"You manage to what?" Marie asked, squeezing her hands.

"What do you call it?"

"What?"

"You know, when a woman . . ."

"Yes," Marie said. "I've read the word in a book, but I've forgotten it. Anyway, what it means is the best thing in the world. Perhaps the only thing there is."

"Well," Rose said, "I feel it in my dreams."

"With whom?"

Marie had instinctively withdrawn her hands from Rose's. She stiffened.

"With Séraphin," Rose confessed in a whisper. "With him, when I dream I . . ."

"You come!" Marie shrieked. "You're crazy! Making love with a dead man when there are so many live ones!"

Rose realized immediately that Marie still loved Séraphin, even though he was dead. She was happy to give her the impression that she could imagine him alive and making love to her at will in a dream. She never admitted to her that it had only happened once, when Patrice was still alive, and that all her calling to him and wringing her hands had no effect: he had never visited her again.

Marie instantly felt strangely jealous of Rose, who had been able to know Séraphin in the flesh, even though it was in dreams. She could not imagine him completely as he was and, in the confusion of orgasm, even this imperfect image would slip away from her so that she couldn't have her fill of it to the end. It was Tibère, very much alive, whose neck she clung to with all the strength of her strong arms; Tibère, who put his hand, which she bit lustily, over her mouth to stop her from crying out so much; or else, since Tibère had killed himself, it was the baker, who had no name, but who pinned Marie to the rudimentary bed with all the strength in his back. Once Séraphin was dead, he had no flesh to fit the shape of her body inside or out, in spite of his surprising presence in her memory. She felt it wasn't fair that Rose could meet him in her dreams.

During the whole time that the passionate friendship lasted between these two highly-strung women, they never really lowered their guard.

"As far as I'm concerned," Marie said. "I need more than dreams. They all know it up there in Lurs. They all take it as read. Not that they haven't tried to make me conform. But in the end it was I who made them give in. They've never been able to make me hang my head, men or women. God forbid! They're wild animals! If you take your eyes off them for an instant, they'll tear you to pieces. In short, I've taken a workman as strong as Tibère. Men are all the same in bed ... More or less ... I'm very adaptable, and I do my share, but that's all there is to it. It's just hello, goodbye and each one back to his own place! I feel as though I'm still eighteen and nothing has happened to me!"

She grasped her friend's hands again.

"How good life would have been, Rose, if nothing had happened to us!"

"I'm alone too," Rose said. "Did you forget that? The only difference is that I live here."

With a wide sweep of her arm, she indicated all of Pontradieu surrounding her from the trees outside overlooking the park to the silent swans on the pool and the farm extending as far as the banks of the Durance. It had weighed so heavily on her heart and soul that now she was enshrined in the property and was completely one with it.

She took Marie by the hand, leading her out on to the fragrant box walk she had had extended as far as the tomb.

"I did what you wanted," she said. "Now they're all there together."

The tomb was a cheerful place in sun or shadow, set off by the slender, graceful form of four young cypresses rising to a point at the top like candle flames. The two women stood in front of it with their arms around each other's waists, talking of their dead. Rose had had a plaque set above the black wrought iron door. The inscription read:

Charmaine Dupin
Patrice Dupin
Séraphin Monge

They loved each other in life; they are united in death.

She had left a blank space under the last name. Her name would be inscribed there when the time came.

Marie felt a pang at the thought that she was excluded from that quartet, that she was an intruder among them, but she felt such peace in this place that she came back there constantly, rushing off to Pontradieu as much for the tomb as for Rose.

Winter, summer, autumn, spring, whenever it was fine, the two passionate friends would sit among the fresh golden grass at the foot of the mound on which the tomb had been constructed. There they would talk endlessly about their wasted lives and their painful memories. They wondered how they had ever been those radiant, indomitable girls who thought that the world had stopped at their eighteenth birthday, and that love was there for all.

They gave a rueful laugh at their silly ideas.

"At least you have your children," Rose would say.

"That's true," Marie replied. "I have my children."

She expressed this obvious truth with no great conviction, then went on to say:

"But children, you know . . . Men are the ones who want to reproduce themselves. Most of the time we women do it to please them, because we love them. But when we don't love the man then children are more of a chore than anything else. At least that's how I see it. But you look as if you miss it? You're still young. Wouldn't you like to have one or two kids? They'd fill your life. You're rich . . . You've spoken to me about someone called Antoine . . ."

"I'm used to being free, rather like you and your bed."

Out of the corner of her eye, she noticed that her friend looked slightly plump in her black dress, and automatically – at least that is what she thought – smoothed her skirt over her decidedly flat stomach.

"No thank you," she said. "I haven't the vocation for it."

This is the way they spent their time at the tomb whose echoes were full of so many idle words. There was a long, wide gravel walk leading up to it where the children could play in safety under their mother's watchful eyes. Marie would pack them all into the truck, and as soon as she arrived let them loose in this open space where even the blind boy could come to little harm. Rose sometimes criticized her for giving him so much freedom.

"Well," Marie would say, "he has to get used to the world as it is. He'll have to get scratches, twisted ankles and skinned knees, like any other child! I know, but that's the way it is. He must think he's normal! Anyway, his brothers keep an eye on him."

One day when the blind boy had just turned four, Marie arrived at Pontradieu as usual with her whole brood. Ange, the eldest, who was nearly eight, had become resigned to his brothers' existence and even liked them in his own way, that is to say he always organized games so that he could win something. They were strong, stocky lads with big thighs, big calves and big heads, at least the two eldest were; Ismaël, though just as strong, had a much slimmer build. The three of them would engage in some serious rough and tumble, the blind boy by no means the least of them. Ange had an inventive mind. He organized his brothers into playing blind man's buff, and of course it was the blind boy who had to play the blind man. Marie stepped in firmly to forbid this mockery. But it was Ismaël himself who stamped his foot and wanted to be allowed to play.

He would go alone and unaided to the Place des Feignants without walking close to the walls, finding his way just from the sound of the fountain. He took great pleasure in identifying his brothers, their friends and also the girls who stood around them by feeling their faces. Especially in the case of the girls, as soon as he felt their skin within reach of his fingers, his hands became very gentle. They only skimmed over cheeks and eyebrows, but he could identify the girls without thinking.

On that day at Pontradieu, his two brothers, Ange and Bertrand, the second son, had moved away from him down the gravel walk, exchanging their jerseys. They had kept a fair distance between him and them, as they usually did. It was Bertrand who told the story again twenty years later as he continued to do all his life to groups who became more and more sceptical as the century progressed.

"Don't forget that my brother Ismaël was blind. But that made no difference. He recognized us faster and more easily than us when we were blindfolded, and we had two eyes. We tried to look taller by standing on empty tins, or smaller by crouching down, and sometimes we smoothed our hair with soap, but it was no use; we could never catch him out. Even when we were in the town square in Lurs and an adult came and stood in the middle for a joke, Ismaël would go around him without touching him. He came straight to us with his hands out in front of him and was never put off by any obstacle. Remember that: *Never!* It was useless to move out of the way or try to escape by crawling away from him; he would catch up with us, intercept us; you might even say he detected us! He tried to explain it by saying that it was as if he were iron filings and we and all the children of Lurs had been magnetized. That's to help you realize that he *never* missed his mark.

"Now on that day at Pontradieu, his brother Ange and I were alone. The gravel walk was wide and we were sure of what would happen because it *always* happened like that. We were sure that Ismaël would sniff the wind and invariably come towards one or other of us. I can remember it as though it were yesterday. My mother and Rose Sépulcre were sitting in the grass. They were knitting and chatting, paying no attention to us.

"I saw my brother Ismaël raise his eyes heavenward with an instinctive gesture I've never noticed in anyone who can see. What's more, afterwards he never made that gesture again. He began to walk, but unusually tense and stiff, unusually quickly. It was not his normal walk. He was like a robot, moving jerkily, mechanically. That's it! Mechanically!" Bertrand Saille, the second son, would say twenty, thirty, fifty years later. "And then," he said, "I

181

saw immediately that for once he wasn't coming towards either my brother or me. He was walking towards something between us. I thought first that he was going towards our mother, and for that reason I didn't try to catch up with him or call to him. When I realized, it was too late. He was scarcely three metres away from the tomb and heading straight for it. It was as if for him – as for us and the children of Lurs – the tomb was like a magnet. I've already told you about this tomb. It was a kind of high, narrow chapel in very bad taste: high gothic style with a turret at each corner, all marble and wrought iron. Even the three steps leading up to the door were marble. My brother Ismaël went towards these three steps . . . and that's where he fell."

That's where he fell. He had tripped on the first step. He fell full length, hitting his forehead on the edge of the top step leading to the front door.

"Ismaël!" Bertrand shouted.

Suddenly torn from their melancholy musings or sad secrets, Marie and Rose rushed to the chapel. Without thinking of seeing to the blind boy first, Marie grabbed the two oldest and slapped them soundly in turn. But it was done in a flash. In those days Marie was as swift as lightning. She rushed towards her third son but Rose had already lifted him to his feet again. She was crouching in front of him, full of soothing words and caresses, and holding him up by his armpits.

The blind boy had a bump on his forehead that was bleeding and the skin was peeled right off his knees, which were beginning to ooze blood. His mouth was wide open as he let out a long loud wail which made his strong little chest expand and collapse. The older two, who were also yelling from the sting of the slaps their mother had given them, ran up nevertheless to see what had happened, as they were worried about their brother.

"I remember it!" Bernard related. "His nose was running down all over his lips, but my mother didn't think of wiping his face, which she did almost automatically for each of us."

"He's crying!" the eldest said, trying to stifle back his own sobs.

"Of course he's crying, you stupid boy! Do you think he liked falling down? He could have split his skull open! He could have . . ."

Marie stopped short and roughly turned the boy towards her.

"He's crying? What nonsense are you talking?"

She held Ismaël at arm's length in front of her. Then she saw that enormous tears were gushing from the child's clear eyes – eyes you could never imagine not being able to see – and were rolling down his chubby cheeks and over his snotty lips.

"Rose!" Marie yelled. "He's crying!"

"Good Lord!" Rose exclaimed.

"Now, I don't know," Bertrand related, "if my mother and Rose fell to their knees instinctively or if it was to look more closely at Ismaël. In any case, that's how I remember them – on their knees in the gravel, which must have pressed into their skin, but they didn't feel it.

"Then this amazing thing happened. Ismaël escaped from my mother and Rose, rushed towards me looking on from afar, grabbed me by my belt and began to kick my shins, crying and yelling all the while. My mother had warned me: I had to put up with anything from him, I must never raise my hand to him, and if I did, she said I'd be really sorry. I was certainly not going to retaliate. He was hurting me, but it was sheer astonishment, much more than my mother's threats, that stopped me in my tracks. Then he suddenly let go. He began to turn his head, looking all around him, then rushed over to a big stone from the Durance that was lying on the path among the other smaller ones. He picked it up and threw it at the door with all his might. He shouted. I remember that he shouted, 'That'll teach you!'"

At this moment in the story there was always someone who would interrupt him:

"That'll teach you what? And who is 'you'? What does all this mean?"

Bertrand would nod his head wearily. As far as he was concerned, it was obvious: all children are vindictive and attack the things that have hurt them because, like adults, they are reluctant to blame their own stupidity. That is the explanation he gave before taking up the story again.

"Unfortunately, the stone hit the window, in spite of all the wrought iron lattice protecting it. The artist had designed a whole black fireworks display in iron, but nothing saved the window. The stone made a hole and crazed the glass around it. You can go and see it for yourselves. It happened more than fifty years ago and the pane of glass has never been replaced! It's still crazed. The hole made by the stone my brother threw at it is still there!"

"Good Lord, Rose! He's crying!" Marie kept saying.

It was perhaps the fifth time she had said the same thing. Normally she would have put Ismaël, blind or not, under her arm and given him something to yell about. Not this time. The two astonished women were still kneeling on the gravel, feeling no pain and unable to get up. And the child was coming towards them with a baleful look in his eye, as he was still angry. He was gathering together all the saliva in his mouth. He looked as though he was about to spit at his mother, but decided against it. A four-year-old already knows how far he can go.

"Marie!" Rose murmured. "Do you realize? Your little boy . . . he can see . . ."

"What are you talking about?" Marie said.

"He can see, I tell you! Look! Look at the way he's staring at me. He has a nasty look in his eye. Have you ever seen a blind person with a nasty look in their eye?"

"It's true!" Marie whispered.

She staggered to her feet. She dared not look hard at Ismaël. Rose was holding him although she was not steady on her feet either. They stood there beneath the trembling cypresses, rambling, stammering disjointed phrases. Astonished and unable to believe what they were seeing, they watched the child walk confidently over the ground. His eyes were scarcely surprised at the daylight, let alone dazzled after four years in the dark. He just glared at it with that same nasty look. It was Rose and Marie who couldn't see straight any more, so overcome by an obvious fact they dared not even mention to each other.

The memory of that moment in the minds of the two women was always clothed in a kind of haze that blurred the outlines of people and things, the quality of the light and even the consciousness of time elapsing, as if reality had deliberately wanted to preserve a mysterious dream-like atmosphere.

"It's not possible!" Marie whispered. "It's a . . ."

Rose quickly put her hand over Marie's mouth.

"Never say that aloud, Marie. Never! They won't believe you, which

184

wouldn't matter, but they wouldn't be happy until Ismaël was blind again so that they could feel reassured. They'll do anything to prove they're right!"

"Who are 'they'?"

"People! Men! Who knows? Anyone would think that you don't know them!" Rose added with a shiver. She was looking at the tomb with a strange look on her face.

"Above all, never mention the place where this happened. They can't even understand why I removed my dead from the cemetery."

Marie shrugged her broad shoulders.

"You're talking nonsense," she said. "There's a natural explanation. My little boy regained his sight naturally. Dr Jouve will have no trouble explaining it to me."

"Come," Rose said gently. "Let's go and fix him up. He has skinned knees and a big bump on his forehead."

One on each side, holding the boy's hands as he calmed down, the two friends moved on down the box path towards the house. The two older boys, silent and slow under the weight of the event, followed timidly behind, heads bowed. A light wind blew behind them in the young cypresses around the tomb.

The opulently ugly drawing room with the Venetian glass chandeliers welcomed them all like a haven. As soon as they had attended to Ismaël's wounds – he began to yell again for a short time when the arnica touched his scratches – the two women collapsed on a divan, exhausted.

"I'm afraid," Marie murmured.

"You're afraid because your child can see?"

Rose got up and went to the sideboard, which she managed to open rather clumsily. Her hands were trembling. She felt a strange tingling between her shoulder blades, and the small of her back was cold.

"I shouldn't be surprised," she said. "When all's said and done, I'm afraid too."

"I should be wild with joy . . ." Marie said.

Rose sank down beside her with the bottle of brandy she had brought back with her, the sugar basin and those ridiculous little glasses that hadn't been used since her wedding day. She filled them and handed one to Marie. They drank together in one gulp. Rose filled them again.

"I want some," whined the eldest child.

"No!" Marie said.

"Just a little bit on a lump of sugar!" Rose said.

She dipped two lumps of sugar in her own glass and gave them to the two older boys. After all the drama, the youngest one had fallen asleep sucking his thumb with his nose in the cushions. A canon would not have woken him.

"Here you are!" Rose said. "Here's the key to the summerhouse. Go and play with Patrice's alarm clocks."

"They'll wreck everything."

"Go and play!" Rose ordered.

She watched the two older boys clatter down the stone steps of the main staircase leading up to the house.

"What does it matter if they break everything?" Rose said. "We must talk."

She pulled Marie towards her and took her hands.

"No-one must know about it," she said, "or they'll think we're mad."

But in spite of appearances, one is never entirely alone in this wretched part of the country. That's why with us, truth, like oil, always comes to the surface, even though at first everyone agrees not to talk about it.

Don't forget that we were all closely watching these two families singled out by fate. And so we found out, as people always do when they really want to.

As it happened, there was an old woman further off in a field of rye picking wild salad greens. There was a shepherd with his flock feeding among the carpet of purslane growing in an old vineyard. There was a postman carrying the mail to Les Pourcelles, who had taken a short cut through the poplar grove in Pontradieu. He was slow, as he used a cane because of rheumatism, which often comes with the job. It kept him awake at night and worried him a lot during the day, because he was not full-time and feared he might be dispensed with by the powers that be. Most important of all, there was Floréal Lucrèce, Rose Sépulcre's tenant farmer. He was very close and could

186

have been seen, had it not been for a screen of smoke rising from the swathe of stubble he was burn-beating not far away.

Everyone reported that they had distinctly heard the sound of the child's body when he fell, the cries of surprise and alarm from the two women, the yells of the two frightened older children. Floréal decided to go as quickly as possible to the spot where the cries had come from, but when he reached the avenue in front of the tomb, all he saw was a family calmly making its way back to the château holding the children by the hand.

"Good Lord!" Marie wondered. "What will I tell my mother?"

When she arrived back at Lurs and parked the truck, she opened the door of the shop with Ismaël in her arms, as he hadn't woken during the whole journey. He was sleeping with the dummy firmly fixed in his mouth. Although he had turned four, he made a terrible fuss if anyone forgot it. The older boys were dazed by the fresh air, the undeserved slap they had been given, and the extraordinary happening they had witnessed. They didn't say a word and were sent to bed straight after supper. Marie had managed to get past her mother by hiding the toddler's swollen face and bruised forehead.

When they were alone and the dishes had been done, Marie said to Clorinde.

"Ma . . . I don't know how to tell you this . . ."

"Good Lord!" Clorinde exclaimed. "Don't tell me you're expecting again!"

"No!" Marie protested. "No! Don't worry. I'm taking precautions."

Marie was surprised. Clorinde had never given her any hint that she knew about her daughter's escapades at night in the hired baker's garret. Marie lowered her glance.

"No," she said, "that's not it. It's Ismaël! Now don't make a fuss. He can see."

"Oï! What are you talking about? Who can see?"

"Ismaël. He isn't blind any more. He can see."

"Good Lord!" Clorinde exclaimed.

She nearly knocked the chair down in her haste as she rushed towards the stairs. Marie barred the way.

"What are you doing?"

"I want to see him! I want him to see me!"

"Tomorrow," Marie said. "He's asleep."

"Good Lord!" Clorinde said again, clasping her hands. "He can see! How can that be? When did you notice it?"

"He fell."

"Fell? Good Lord! He didn't hurt himself, did he?"

"Yes. He has a big lump on his forehead and two skinned knees. Don't worry, it's nothing. Rose put some arnica on them. It's when he got up that we noticed he could see."

"Good Lord!" Clorinde could hardly speak.

Marie had turned away from her and was ferreting about among the suppliers' bills in one of the sideboard drawers. There, enclosed within the covers of an old diary held together with an elastic band, were all the opinions and prescriptions of the medical specialists Marie had consulted since Ismaël's birth. She brought over this improvised folder and slapped it down on the table.

"The thing is," she said softly, "that he shouldn't be able to see."

She fell on to a chair. She thought of the indomitable Marie she had always been. Today she felt weak; all her strength had left her. She hadn't been with the baker for a week because of her dates, and had promised to go that evening. She didn't feel like it. She didn't feel like anything. The half-formed thoughts whirling around in her mind as a result of the miraculous event had paralysed her with fear. She was filled with holy terror.

Next morning, however, there was a positively glowing grandmother standing behind the Roberval scales. Tricanote and the Marquise de Pescaïré protected her from our curiosity like a human wall, for we had all heard about it very late the previous evening.

The delivery man who picked up the mail from one side of the Durance to the other had told it to the postmistress. The old woman gathering the wild salad had not been able to resist the pleasure of spreading the word. When she heard the cries that afternoon, she had come to see what was happening. Hidden behind the smoke from the burning stubble, she had come up near the chapel with her ears pricked. She had heard almost everything she needed to hear.

Now, as she was going home with her apron full of greens, she was overtaken by the delivery man in his bus, which rattled like a set of saucepans that had come off their hooks. He stopped to give her a lift – without charging her, of course – as the driver was bored all alone with his sacks in his dreadful old rattletrap. She gave him the news as a way of thanking him.

"You know a woman in Lurs with a blind boy?"

"*Pardi*! That'd be Marie Dormeur."

"*Hé bé* – well now – you can tell everyone that now her boy, her little boy can see!"

It took less than half a day for Dr Jouve to drop everything and part the bead curtain at the bakery door.

"Clorinde! Is Marie there?"

"She's making the deliveries," Clorinde said cantankerously.

She couldn't bear the way Dr Jouve, in all the thirty years she'd known him, had never greeted anyone properly.

"Right! When she comes in, tell her to call in and see me."

He went off without saying goodbye, then changed his mind. His long horse-face reappeared through the bead curtain.

"With the boy, of course."

"No, no Marie! You're mistaken. Don't tell me that this child can see like you or I! He may be able to make out a kind of hazy white light that is his form of daylight, but for everything else, he guides himself instinctively. Being blind from birth is not the same as being blinded by accident, you know. The other senses develop and become much sharper to make up for the one that is missing . . ."

Dr Jouve had just examined Ismaël as best he could, as the child was as slippery as an eel and kicked out when no-one was looking. The doctor's opinion was unshaken.

"In addition," he said, "there's all of this!"

He pointed to the certificates from the distinguished ophthalmologists who had made the diagnosis, and which Marie had thrust at him.

189

Marie looked contrite as she said, "You asked me to come, so I came . . ."

It was late in the afternoon. Slanting rays of sunlight flooded into the doctor's green consulting room. For the last few minutes he had been trying to shoo away a blinding light that hit his face and obstinately pursued him like an unwelcome fly.

It was the child Ismaël. Using a round mirror taken from his mother's handbag, he skilfully caught the refection of the sun and disrespectfully aimed it at Dr Jouve's long face. Marie watched with a wry smile as the doctor tried vainly to get rid of the reflection. She said quietly:

"Do you really think, Doctor, that he'd be able to give you a *gari-baou-baou* if he couldn't see?

"What's a *gari-baou-baou*?"

"You know very well! That! The children's trick he's playing on you now: dazzling you with the mirror he took from me! Stop it now Ismaël, or I'll smack you!" she shouted at the boy.

Dr Jouve said nothing for a full minute as he stared at the kid, who returned his stare.

"No," he said reluctantly, "he couldn't."

The flat of his hand landed forcefully on the packet of certificates which proved beyond doubt that the child Ismaël Saille was, and should remain, incurably blind.

"Either they're all asses," he said, "or . . ."

"Or . . . ?" she asked.

"Come now, Marie. Where were you when it happened?"

Marie shrugged her shoulders.

"What has the place got to do with it? He was playing, he fell, that's all there is to it."

While no-one was paying attention to him, the boy had gone over to the armchair where the doctor's neutered cat was sleeping. It was a ginger male that must have weighed five or six kilos. He wanted to pick it up and pat it. The tomcat was not happy and clawed him. The child began to yell.

"See what you've done!" Marie said. "You should have left it alone!"

Dr Jouve crouched down in front of the boy and stroked his hair. Tears of rage and pain were streaming down Ismaël's face.

"The strangest of all," the doctor said pensively, "is not so much that he can see, as that he can cry."

"Should I bring him back to you?" Marie asked.

The doctor shrugged.

"Well," he said. "Why would you bring him back? He can see, he can see! What more can I do?"

He licked his thumb and began looking for something among the specialists' certificates scattered on the desk in front of him. He didn't find it.

"But by the way," he said, "the first time I sent you to the specialist, I wrote you a letter . . ."

"I must have destroyed it," Marie said, "or else it's been lost."

That was not true. Before leaving the house, she had taken it from the bundle of letters and had put it back in the sideboard drawer. Now she congratulated herself on her foresight.

"*Parbleu*," she thought, "he used the word 'incurable'. He would really like to take that letter back! Too bad. We all have to face up to our own responsibilities."

Dragging her reluctant, complaining son behind her, she set out with the impressive series of attestations proving that Ismaël should have been permanently blind firmly tucked under her arm. Dr Jouve accompanied her to the door and stood on the doorstep reluctantly watching her depart.

"Why won't she tell me where it happened? 'He fell, that's all there is to it.' That's nothing new. I know where he fell! That's the first thing the old woman told the delivery man: 'It happened in the park at Pontradieu, in front of the tomb that crazy Rose Sépulcre had built there.' Why does Marie want to hide it?"

He watched her go up the steep main street in Lurs, while the kid skilfully kicked at all the pebbles in the road, as if to mock him.

He eventually turned, opened the waiting room door and went inside. At this late hour it was now empty. He went upstairs towards his office stroking his goatee beard. He suddenly struck his open right hand against his left fist.

"And yet he's blind!" he cried.

His wife ran to the kitchen door looking alarmed.

191

"Have you started talking to yourself now?"

"There's reason enough," grumbled Dr Jouve.

Marie had not been to Pontradieu for a week. During that week Rose was still stunned and could think of nothing but what had just happened. One evening a woman arrived at the property all splattered with earth. Actually, her quite acceptable clothes and polished shoes were only stained here and there with splashes of mud. It was Rose who later remembered her appearing like that because this woman was the messenger from a region where the state of the terrain was of the utmost importance, and all the inhabitants were tainted with it through and through.

"Do you recognize me?" the woman asked.

"Of course!" Rose said. "Come in. Sit down."

Auphanie also smelled of the earth that had splashed her. She was so conscious of it that she had rubbed herself over with the *eau de rose* that had been sitting unopened on her chest of drawers for nigh on twenty years.

"I'll dirty all your furniture!" she said apologetically.

"Dirty it?" said Rose, somewhat surprised. "Not at all! You're quite clean."

"Oh," Auphanie said. "I look it, but . . ."

She sat on the edge of her seat, clutching her handbag on her knees. She looked Rose squarely in the face, perhaps so that Rose could read in her periwinkle blue eyes all the misfortune that had befallen everyone up there in the Fosses-Gleizières valley on the banks of the waters that flow into the Champanastays.

"You can't imagine," she said, "how long I hesitated before coming here."

"Calm yourself, please," Rose said. "Tell me about it."

She had realized immediately that the person facing her, with their knees touching, was extremely upset. She held out her hands to make things easier for her, and Auphanie clung on to them like someone drowning. Rose felt the roughness of fingers used to being in washing up water all day, the type of fingers which usually don't give those who own them time to think.

"Everything's going!" Auphanie said. "The wave of mud is dragging everything with it. Yesterday it hit the wall of the cemetery. Those who can afford it have started moving their dead to Enchastrayes. The other night we heard a terrible noise. It was the trunk of one of Polycarpe's beech trees crashing through the wall of the communal wash-house. The men can't use the urinal any more: it's thigh-deep in clay. The gate to the school playground won't close: one of the side pillars was knocked down and took half the iron grille gate with it. The wind pushes it at night and it creaks like a weathercock turning this way and that. And another thing! The front of my café. It's hanging over the edge! One of these days it'll tumble down to the river. The men come around the back way to get a drink. I don't feel at home there any more! It's like living in the street! The Martels, the richest people in the district, have only half their barn left! The church steeple has a crack you can see the sunrise through! Don't you think that's enough?"

She stopped speaking, quite out of breath. Even sitting in the dim drawing room with the chandeliers gently swaying in the draught, she could still see her own countryside slipping and sliding away.

"Don't you think that's enough?" she said again.

She was now gripping Rose's hands like a vice.

"The geologist was right: it wasn't normal for it to stop! He didn't believe it! He looked at us as if we were playing a trick on him – as if we had hidden the key to a door! Now he's back. Now he's jubilant, telling us, 'I told you so!'"

"That's not very kind!" Rose said calmly.

"He's a scientist!" Auphanie said, as if that explained everything.

"Well then?" Rose asked. "What can we do about it?"

"Give him back to us."

She turned her head away as she said these words almost in a whisper.

"Give who back to you?"

"Séraphin. While he was up there and his remains were in the mud, he was the bone that stuck in the Leviathan's throat. The earth had stopped trying to swallow us up; the earth dared not move any further! We all realized it, you know, hardly a week after we gave him back to you. Straight away it started to crack again. Straight away, there it was on the move. We should have known that if he was so determined to die up there with us, he must have had his reasons!"

Rose had to force herself to laugh, but she managed it.

"My dear woman!" she said. "My dear woman!"

She had pulled her hands away, struggling to hide her agitation, and now she was slapping her thighs and laughing loudly.

"Come now. Surely you're not silly enough to believe that?"

"I don't believe it," Auphanie said. "I can imagine it. The others don't believe it either. They refuse to believe it. But I can see in their eyes that they still hope in spite of themselves, in spite of what reason tells them. But what difference does it make whether we believe it or not, if it's real."

"It's not real," Rose said.

Auphanie took her hands again but didn't feel the instinctive withdrawal that Rose could not suppress. Auphanie was thinking of just one thing. When she told the people who frequented her café what she intended to do, they urged her: "And above all, make sure you tell the lady that we're in great need, that nothing does any good: neither engineers, nor bridges, nor barricades. Nothing! Tell her that our only hope is in things we can't talk about."

At that moment Rose began to shake her head in denial and kept on doing it right to the end.

"You people are rich," Auphanie said humbly. "Your land is solid, you have fields that are quite flat and will never move. What difference would a few bones more or less make to you?"

"No," Rose said. "Here they are and here they stay. This is where he came from."

She felt no compunction in delivering Auphanie out to be swallowed up by the October night. "I should have got the farmer to take her to the station," she thought. "Oh well! She'll have to manage on her own!"

Her knees were trembling. Later in the evening, when Antoine came for her orders and to report on the day's work as he always did, she replied distractedly, walking up and down wringing her hands. When she finally straightened up to say goodbye to him, he felt for the first time that she needed him and that she was going to tell him to stay.

194

But he had the strength of character not to let her see it. She called to him:

"Antoine!"

"Yes, madame."

"Would you mind making a detour to Lurs and telling Marie that I need to see her?"

"Yes, madame. I'll do it now."

No, she didn't need him. She gave him an absent-minded "thank you". He heard the sound made by the wooden bar as she pushed it into its slot to secure the door. This was the first time it had ever been lowered since Pontradieu was built. She even wanted to shut the three bolts, but only one would move as the others had never been used, even when Gaspard Dupin had lived there in fear. They were encrusted with rust and solidified grease.

Rose had never been afraid of the dark or death, even on the day when she had discovered that her father had been crushed beneath the grinding stones of his olive-oil mill. But on this night she was freezing cold from head to foot. She went to the wardrobe, took out her fur coat and put it on as if she were going on a trip, then paced up and down the darkened drawing room. All alone again, she felt the full weight of the silence she thought she liked so much. The wind made no sound even in the tall plane trees, where it always blew through the branches.

"I must be mad," she thought. "I don't know where I am any more!"

Suddenly the light from a headlamp shone through the upper window. Rose stood still. It was past ten o'clock. Who could be coming at this hour? It didn't matter. Anything was better than this solitude, this silence. She heard the knocker being struck by an impatient hand. Rose hurried to unbar the door.

"Are you barricading yourself in now?"

It was Marie.

"It's you? I wasn't expecting you until tomorrow."

"I know. I was at my godmother's. It was my mother who made me think something was wrong. She said, 'Someone came from Rose, a good-looking man. He asked if you could go and see her tomorrow. And then, just as he was about to leave, he came back towards the counter and said, 'She can do as she likes, but I think it would be better if she went this evening.'"

"But I didn't tell him anything!" Rose exclaimed.

"Well then, maybe you don't need to say anything to him."

Rose collapsed into an armchair.

"Listen to me! I have shivers all down my spine. Listen to me!" she whispered, clasping her friend's hands.

And then she reported everything the woman who smelled of mud had told her.

Auphanie went out into the night alone and walked along slowly, feeling the full weight of Rose's refusal.

"What will I say to the others?" she wondered.

She arrived at the Peyruis-Les Mées station well before the train was due. She saw a local woman sitting in the shelter with a basket of tomme cheeses by her side. She was an elderly woman from Lurs, taking a present to her granddaughter in Digne who had just given birth under difficult circumstances. Auphanie sat down next to her. She was feeling depressed, and so she talked. Otherwise, how would we have known?

The old woman listened, nodding her head, not particularly interested but full of sympathy for anyone who was alone. However, when she mentioned Séraphin's name, the woman from Lurs turned towards Auphanie and didn't take her eyes off her from then on. She was hearing answers to questions we had all been asking each other for some time.

The train whistled in the distance. The two travellers got up quickly, worried that they wouldn't have time to get in. The old woman took hold of Auphanie's arm.

"Well now!" she said, and these were her first words. "Well now! You did say that you've just come from Rose Sépulcre's house, didn't you?"

"Yes, from Pontradieu."

"Well, well! I must tell you this! There's someone from here – a boy – who was blind till now, or so it seemed, and now he can see like you or me! And do you know where it happened? That was at Rose Sépulcre's too!"

"Who is it?"

"Oh, just someone!" the old woman said evasively.

The train drew to a halt in front of them. The two women wanted to be alone to think over what they had just heard. They both opened a door to a third-class compartment at a good distance from each other. Before getting in, the old woman called out to Auphanie:

"Perhaps it wasn't a good idea to let that Séraphin go!"

How could we have found out? We were consumed by anxious curiosity. There wasn't one of us who didn't crouch in front of little Ismaël and suddenly move our hands back and forth in front of his face to see if he blinked.

It was difficult to catch him alone as his mother hardly let him out of her sight, watching him like milk heating on the stove. It was even more difficult to get him away from his two brothers whom we thought little St John "Golden Mouths"[3], incapable of speaking anything but the truth because they were young and supposedly innocent. But Marie had taught them well. They either said nothing or swore at us. We just knew that their mother was behind it, so we tried questioning Marie herself.

"Come on Marie! Don't tell us that! It's hardly possible for something like that to happen! It's incredible!"

Marie would shrug her shoulders and take no notice, shielding her children from our relentless interrogation.

Clorinde was in a continual state of anxiety. Seeing us all so worked up, thin Mme Jouve the doctor's wife had no hesitation in predicting the worst to the baker's wife. It was well meant.

"My husband is adamant: unfortunately this improvement can only be temporary."

Clorinde was tight-lipped, but burst out once the customers had moved away.

"You skinny scarecrow! You shouldn't say anything! And I can't say anything because of business!"

Business had nothing to do with it really. Clorinde had soundly rebuked

---

3 St John Chrysostom: the name Chrysostom meaning "Golden Mouth".

clients for much less than that. It was Marie who had told her firmly:

"Don't say anything! Keep mum! She's just fishing for information!"

I may be a ruin, but can't the stones themselves tell what they know about this story? So many people come here alone. They walk over us unsteadily, making our foundations and their broken beams echo in the silence. And don't they come here precisely because they hope we'll speak to them?

The only thing still intact from the farm that I used to be is the big wash trough, the *bugadière*. You can see it from here through the rubble of my walls, with its white knot-holed planks still in their slots. I can remember. I can still see the last time the last woman piled all her winter sheets behind these planks to do her washing.

We would whisper to each other on the wind at night, from one ruin to another, firstly the story of the man who knocked down his house. Listen to me! I've seen them all. They choose my broken walls when they need to talk privately or to love in silence, because I'm some distance away from the village, at the end of the Promenade des Evêques. Quite a few children have been conceived here, among my stones on the beds of nettles that block the entries to my crumbling cellars. They are so thick and soft that if you are passionate enough, you don't even feel them under you.

I witnessed Rose's excitement when she was in seventh heaven thinking that with Patrice she had found the man of her dreams. I heard Marie's despairing sighs as she called to Séraphin in all the improbable places she thought he might be hiding. I often saw the melancholy young baker with the fine black eyes sobbing within my walls because Marie didn't love him.

Never in all my ruin's existence did I think that something so altogether different could happen to Lurs. It was the postman who gave me the first hint. One evening I heard the sound of his familiar tread as he walked over me. He had been having an affaire for more than forty years with Thérésa Curnier, who was twenty years older than he. As they were both married, they had found it convenient to meet here in my ruins among the box bushes that grew thickly and over three metres tall. If they were discovered, they could leave separately and make their escape in any direction. In the beginning, when they were twenty and forty, they were scarcely visible, as they were passionately in love. Now he was more than sixty and Thérésa was almost eighty. They were widowed, and now it was more friendship than anything else, at least I suppose it was. Besides, they had stopped coming a long time ago. I had almost forgotten them.

That night, they arrived in a hurry. They spoke so softly that at one stage I thought they might be dead and that they were ghosts tottering from one stone to another. What's more, they were wearing black and made no sound. But they were speaking to each other and I saw their faces in the light until the moon hid behind the clouds. Usually, when ghosts visited me in search of their past, I could never make out their features.

They had come up to what was left of my old tiled *potager*, and had sat down close together on the bench in the corner of the hearth, which was still standing. I saw that they were holding hands. The old woman had put down the black straw basket she used for carrying her cheeses. She always had it with her. The postman asked:

"Why did you call me?"

"Because I can't stand it! I can't keep it to myself any longer! I can't tell anyone! The other evening when I was waiting for the train a woman told me a weird story!"

The old woman spoke like a sink overflowing with water, and so quickly that the postman had to stop her and ask her to go over it again.

"It doesn't make sense!" he said. "Try and explain it a bit better."

"I can't! The woman herself didn't explain it any better! It seems that Séraphin Monge was buried in her village, and since then they say that the earth stopped sliding."

The old man shook his head.

"You're mistaken. Séraphin Monge is buried over there in Pontradieu. I should know. I pass it every day. His name's on the door of the chapel."

"Exactly! The woman told me she'd come to fetch him back, and Rose Sépulcre refused!"

"And a good thing too!" the postman exclaimed. "That would be the last straw! What about us then?"

"What do you mean, 'us'?"

"You must know what happened to Marie Dormeur's boy? The one who was blind and who can see now?"

"He fell," the old woman said. "But do you know exactly where he fell?"

"I certainly do. I saw it. I heard people shouting and went up there. Not really close, mind you. If they'd seen me, they might have asked me to do something and I didn't have the time. But I certainly saw what happened, and straight away I said to myself that it wasn't natural, that there was something peculiar going on!"

"Go on with you! You're talking nonsense!"

"And what about you? Aren't you talking nonsense when you tell me that Séraphin, already dead as he was, stopped the earth from sliding down?"

"It's not the same! *I* didn't make it up. Someone told me!"

"Yes, but I saw it! I saw the boy get up, pick up a big stone and throw it at the chapel window. I *saw* it! And that's not all. I went back the next day – it was Sunday – and sat down on the same spot where the boy fell. I was thinking, 'What have you got to lose if it doesn't do you any good?' I fell asleep there in the sun. It was very fine and warm. And then – now listen to me Thérésa – I got up, picked up my sack, and forgot my cane! It must be there still!"

"*Voï!*" Thérésa exclaimed.

"Yes, indeed! I'm not using my cane! I can walk like a young man. Haven't you noticed that I'm not using my cane?"

"No."

"That just goes to show how much attention you pay to me!"

"Anyway, *qué sien qué siégué ora pro nobis*! Let's not say anything about it. Let's keep it to ourselves. No-one must know about it. They'd lock us up!"

Off they went, filled with fear. Then they parted and I never saw them again.

My part in this story was over in a flash, the primary school teacher wrote in an exercise book. I spent six months in Lurs as a supply teacher. The colleague I replaced had broken his pelvis when he fell from the roof of his house, which he wanted to repair himself.

Now that I have retired, I try to forget it. I try to believe that between

November, when I arrived, and March when my poor head couldn't bear it any longer, nothing else happened in Lurs other than six months of almost constant school-teaching boredom, as usual. And yet now, from a great height and a great distance, I feel I must write these words that no-one will read in a school exercise book. They will fill only a few pages.

I am not making judgments; I am not making comments; I am only reporting the facts as they happened in my presence. I had a pupil. He was ugly and he was dirty. As well as that, on his very plain face was a strawberry mark with bristles that stood out like badger hairs. His father was a pork butcher. Every time the kid inadvertently went through the shop instead of down the corridor, the customers would put off their purchases until later.

Dare I relate the rest like some lecher shamelessly describing his escapades?

I remember, it was after Christmas. Even at the end of the holidays the effects of those feast-days were often still being felt and there were always a lot of absentees. As it happens, on that day the children were all there. As this group of youngsters gazed straight at me with those clear eyes of inveterate liars that I know so well, there was a kind of tremor of happiness in the room. I was calling the roll and the boy with the badger bristles was missing. No, he wasn't missing! He was sitting in his usual place, but with a charming face like all the others. It was perfectly smooth. I was so stunned by it that I said the very last thing I should have, "Have you had an operation?" At that, the whole class began to scream with laughter and stamp their feet, going out of control, which they do so well. I slammed the lid of my desk and shouted, "The whole class will do 100 lines!" That calmed them down immediately. A hundred lines is a serious matter, if you don't forget to ask for them.

A boy raised his hand to appeal against such an unjust punishment. Another called out from the back of the class.

"Sir, he hasn't had an operation! He went to Séraphin's tomb!"

He was a boy with a round head and glasses who was going to enter the seminary. Moreover, he already had the earnestness and oiliness of the country priest. As it was raining at break time, I managed to corner him in the covered part of the playground.

"What's all this story about Séraphin?"

He explained to me that somewhere on the other side of the Durance there was a tomb where a person called Séraphin was buried. He had been a child martyr. And he had heard tell that the little boy from the bakery had regained his sight after falling in front of the tomb. Also, on a certain night, the pork butcher's son had crept out and gone there. When he came back he got the hiding of his life, but his lupus had disappeared. At the end of the story he added:

"Of course, Sir, *I* didn't believe any of it. I'm not as naïve as that."

I was foolishly about to reply, "Oh, really? And how do you explain the disappearance of that mark?" Luckily I noticed the gleam in his eye behind his glasses. The little bastard saw me coming. My love of reason would give him an advantage over me. I stopped myself just in time.

But staying silent did not make the fact disappear. As I walked up and down the rows giving dictation, I was irresistibly drawn towards the child with the lupus. It was something quite different from lupus, but the pupils called it that, and I unconsciously went along with them. I couldn't take my eyes off him. Once, like St Thomas – would you believe it! – I allowed myself to stroke his face in the hope that it was all an optical illusion. That made them all chortle, whereupon they all held up their innocent cheeks to make me ashamed of my favouritism.

All I could see in that class was the pork butcher's son. He didn't take his eyes off me, smiling sweetly all the while. He was literally forcing his cheeky face on me as a denial of my convictions. (Have I mentioned that I was a Marxist?)

The fact is that one day I couldn't take it any longer and I left. Oh, it was not something I did light-heartedly or without a struggle, but the whole basis of my beliefs collapsed in the light of those anomalies. Perhaps I was weak-minded, but from that moment I became convinced that the world is a splendid abomination: splendid if you do nothing more than look at it, an abomination as soon as you think of the nasty tricks you are compelled to witness. It was then I came knocking on the door of the Carthusians. Perhaps I was drawn to the place where they live in silence. They set little store by the confused story I told them. I even have the impression that they smiled to themselves. I've been serving them since then. I'm no more of a believer, but I have less time to think about it. Through solitude and physical labour I have managed to convince myself that I was the victim of an illusion, and that back there in Lurs, the pork butcher's son still had his horrible strawberry mark and the ineffable existed only in the darkness of faith.

"Don't ever imagine that Lurs gratefully accepted these wonders," Maître Bellafaire the notary said to the archivist when he was almost ninety. "Quite the contrary! We were sure that the apparent benefits were just one more proof of the curse that hung over us. And is there any worse spell laid on a village than to be a mockery to other villages? So you can imagine how tight-lipped we all were about our secret, and determined that it wouldn't get out.

"Alas! The truth is like oil: it always comes to the surface. If we had been as cautious as we claimed, we'd have gone about our business as usual. Until that time, the masses said by our priest scarcely attracted more than forty worshippers, and they were women, mostly past the first flush of youth and beauty, who had nothing to offer up to the Lord but sacrifices costing them very little. I went anyway, as a notary can't afford to be seen as an unbeliever, which would cast doubt on his integrity.

"But what happened? Suddenly under the vaulted ceiling all greasy with the dirt of ages, there were eighty, a hundred of us. Propped against the third pillar on the left, there's a statue of Christ preaching with a strange expression on his face. This wooden Christ all dressed in red looks to me as if he can't believe his eyes. There are even a dozen men standing somewhat anxiously behind the door – ordinary men, I'll grant you, but men all the same! – where formerly you would scarcely see two or three town worthies, and even they looked uneasy.

"Nonetheless, it goes without saying that if it was to be something quite extraordinary, divine intervention through Séraphin's bones did not operate every time and was always an exception. We notaries, who witness countless injustices in this world, could feel with some reason, that it would not be available to everyone in heaven either.

"I speak from experience," sighed the ninety-year-old Maître Bellaffaire. "My son was born with a pronounced curvature of the spine, and at his present age of sixty plus he is still a hunchback, and everything leads me to believe that he'll still have that disability when he dies. And yet, God knows how many times when he was in his teens his mother and I took him secretly at night to Séraphin's tomb. God knows that there was no lack of prayers to the Lord as we knelt on the gravel, sometimes for a good part of the night!

"And yet ... If the legend has survived, it's because of the holy cries of surprise from those close to the privileged few who were cured. For of course the whole family united around the one who was saved and, even if their antecedents were blatant atheists, they would then wallow in religion with all the lack of restraint of the newly converted. They suppressed the feeling of revolt in those who, having always been good Christians and received nothing, submitted with some bitterness to the law of divine injustice."

These are the words of the ninety-year-old Maître Bellaffaire. Although he was shaky and used a walking stick, he was mentally alert right to the end.

For a long time, for as long as he could, the parish priest at Lurs closed his eyes and ears to the rumours that came his way. He indignantly tore down the hideous ex-voto that had been stuck up on one of the Romanesque pillars in the church – the one behind the Christ in the red robes, to be precise. It showed the hairy flaw that afflicted the pork butcher's son, but three times as large and, in one corner, his face as it was now all rosy and smiling, photographed for the Forcalquier fair on Palm Sunday. He had quietly put the small picture up himself when he thought no-one was there, but a pious woman of irreproachable virtue, who had come to change the flowers on the Virgin's altar, heard the sound of the hammer knocking in the nail. She thought she should not keep it to herself, especially as the picture consisted of a naïve but recognizable painting of the chapel with its marble turrets in the park at Pontradieu, set against a background of rather nightmarish mists.

The faith professed by the priest, who was born in Molines-en-Queyras, was vague and very much of this world. He lived and moved among all kinds of doubt with his eyes fixed firmly on Rome and its encyclicals. He had been handed over to the power of the Church as a timid youth from the seminary onwards, and if he conceived of heaven behind the Church, it was always abstracted and symbolic, like a secondary manifestation of some essential phenomenon. "This would have to happen to me!" he groaned.

That is what he said when the priest of Peyruis, who came from the same region as himself, sometimes came to visit. They both had solid, square foreheads made to resist the onslaughts of both intelligence and superstition. The priest of Peyruis was very old, and would pat the younger man's hand reassuringly:

"Leave them alone! Don't let them get any hold over you! They'll forget about it. False beliefs bring their own punishment!"

But every Sunday and even during the week the flood of worshippers kept growing in the church at Lurs. The feet of the faithful tramping over the old flagstones sounded like an obedient flock.

"You'd think they were suddenly taking shelter in the church as if it were raining outside! I'm sure they've added another saint to the list of martyrs," the horrified priest thought, "and they don't much care whether we recognize him or not!"

What finally made him suspicious was the fact that, in spite of the crowd, he never had any more confessions – a dozen in all – than he had when the sanctuary was two-thirds empty. He tried to find out from the children in the catechism class, but to no avail. The fear of getting their ears boxed could plainly be seen in their eyes. You felt they had been well schooled by their mothers. Everything went on under the seal of silence.

The disbelieving priest sometimes crouched down in front of Ismaël and stared deep into his clear eyes, as Dr Jouve often found himself doing, and for the same reasons. The child returned these inquisitorial stares without batting an eyelid. The priest then tried to intimidate the older brothers.

"Bertrand! When and where did you brother see daylight for the first time?"

"I don't know, Monsieur le Curé."

"And if he insists," Marie had said, "you tell him that your brother was never blind. It's a family secret and no business of his."

"But Maman, it's not true! It's a sin to tell a lie!"

"And the smack you'll get! That's not a sin I suppose?"

Marie was not the only one to lecture her children. The pork butcher's wife had also threatened to make her son's smooth cheek red again when he had whined at her that he dared not lie to Monsieur le Curé.

"You stupid boy! The truth! They'll burn you at the stake if you tell them! It wouldn't be the first time. And it wouldn't be the last either!"

And so, not only did our people mistrust Dr Jouve, who represented science, or the school teacher, the touchy upholder of free thought, but we also distrusted the Church and all her threatened fear and trembling.

If our priest had looked at us more closely when we were packed in the pews in front of him, he would have understood that we had good reasons for huddling under the protective arches of his church. It wasn't wild hope so much as ancient terror that made us tremble. We reacted like startled rabbits to anything unexpected. We raised our eyes to the roof at every ring of the little bell. Every time the big bell rang in the steeple, our mouths opened, but the silent cry was never uttered. We weren't much affected by "suffered under Pontius Pilate", but we all remembered the trumpets of Jericho.

Séraphin's intercession, however enigmatic, was a simple sign compared with the mystical Signs, but we didn't see anything good in it. It opened up a whole frightening perspective which included everything to which we had hitherto either paid lip service or professed only through expediency. That included the Resurrection, the immortality of the soul, and Hell. Consequently, our fervour did not radiate the confidence of true believers. As the appearance of white caps among the dead leaves in the forest indicates the existence of a large population of mushrooms, in the light of that small sign which had chosen us as witnesses, we imagined that all the rest could be true, could await us, reach us, strike us down. And so, given the way we had lived our lives until then, and the way our parents and our ancestors had lived theirs, we foresaw an eternity of God's wrath rather than His eternal love in store for us.

Therefore, far from delighting in it, we restrained with all our might our inclination to believe in the miracle. We laughed at ourselves openly when we gathered together, if we were out hunting or playing *boules*. But when the lampman's little daughter came down with typhoid fever, that didn't stop us from secretly carrying her to Séraphin's tomb one night. Of course we carried her back dead as a doornail, but what did that prove? Séraphin was still only a novice at intercession, we thought. Our Lord must often send him packing.

And so, if our priest had taken the trouble to look into our souls, he would have found a pitiful mixture of holy terror and fear of ridicule. He would have had compassion for us. But he was a man who preferred to suppress the facts within himself. He didn't take this sudden distortion in the logic of things very seriously and he thought that all in all his colleague from Peyruis was right: all he had to do was to scorn these alarming signs, as he had been doing for the last ten years with the rheumatism that attacked him in various parts of his body and sometimes twisted it like a grapevine.

That is to say, until the day a car pulled up at the presbytery. It was shiny and looked so magnificent that all Lurs trooped out to see it. A woman in black got out wearing elbow-length gloves, but a dress that was transparent against the light. This strange messenger silently handed the priest a sealed note. It was a brief message, four lines long, salutations included. It summoned him to the bishop's palace in two days' time. The parish priest of Lurs trembled as he folded it up again. To him, the curtness of the note did not bode well.

VIII

WHEN MONSIGNOR GODIOT, THE BISHOP OF DIGNE, HEARD ABOUT
Séraphin Monge for the first time, he was reading the works of
Oecolampadius in one of his gardens.

They were called gardens, although they were very small, but the fact that
they were set out in terraces and boasted some fine trees permitted the use of
this luxuriant plural. There was also a large wisteria that hung softly over the
150 yards of an Italian pergola. Bees buzzed undisturbed among the bunches
of flowers, between the leaves and the blue sky. It was an ideal ambulatory
and Mgr Godiot liked being there.

This prelate was over six feet tall and weighed sixteen stone. The few
photos there are of him show a large head with the small narrow eyes
of a Dauphinois peasant and a jutting chin. The total effect, however,
is not without a certain grandeur and finesse. The sash emphasizing his
ecclesiastical plumpness – a sign of his chastity – heightens the calm power
of this important person who, thirty years after his death, looks ready to
come out of his frame to absolve you with a full understanding of what is
involved.

And yet, Mgr Godiot had the wide, long feet of the non-dreamer. No
prelate had a soul less likely to know turmoil. He was a man who liked
working in his study, which he rarely left except for confirmations. Canon
law, customary law, common law held no secrets for him. He would spend
ten hours a day shut away in the austere study of the Church Fathers. His
faith had been robust until now. Ploughing the Gospels as a peasant ploughs

his land, he possessed an inexhaustible source of replies to hurl at anyone who dared argue. The very sight of his person, apparently so simple, gave a sudden feeling of certainty to anyone whose faith was wavering.

One particular day he had received a haggard priest who had rushed there from a region deep in the mountains, where the only road had recently fallen down to the river in an avalanche. This priest had just confessed to him that man and nature had combined to destroy him, and he had lost his faith along the way, as one loses a wallet.

"I order you to stop thinking!" the bishop told him. "Your place is to act, not to think. Your hands should be cracked and painful in winter! Be cold! Be hungry! See unhappy people! Go wherever death is! But not silent death. It deprives man of any regret. You want death that God has prepared a long time in advance. One that gives plenty of notice. Learn from those who are dying. Only one atheist in ten holds out against death. You'll see the others fall at Christ's feet like flies! Do you want to be like them, poor wretched man, you who should know better? Do you want to be like them at the hour of your death?"

He sometimes thought of that priest as the bees buzzed overhead in the wisteria. Life had some delightful traps to lure one to its vanities. Didn't he himself love this mauve light, these busy bees and so many other things as well?

Mgr Godiot had been a worldly man in his youth. He still retained the outer appearance of one. Grace had touched him through excess, but one aspect of his worldliness that still remained was his taste for risk-taking. He liked to keep the ambiguities of his soul alive, to wrestle with the demon instead of keeping it prudently at arm's length.

He was aided in this exercise by the Baroness Ramberti who was descended from a quartermaster sergeant ennobled by Napoleon during the Empire for his commercial talents.

Patronesses are usually very respectable. This one wasn't. Her age – forty – her perfume, her daring dresses, her cheeky hats with their elegant feathers, her opulent wealth, her wild generosity, everything about her suggested repressed love, hard won. His Grace preferred not to know if, perchance, she may have been divorced.

He imagined himself to be playing the temptation game with her and winning every time. He received her more than was wise, more than was reasonable. There were always so many unfortunates to be helped and she was always so resourceful and ready to help. And when their conversation sometimes strayed to the beauty of the woods in autumn and the regret of vanishing youth, how could the devil creep into such innocent talk?

When a heavy silence revealed their underlying agitation – and these were the times he liked best, as he could pit himself against temptation – she would sometimes say to him:

"Aren't you worried? Don't you feel afraid?"

He would say to her then:

"Believe me, my dear, it's much better for our peace of mind if people are reassured by imagining the worst about us, than if they think we are as ordinary as they. Our situation would become untenable if, on the other hand, they knew we were engaged in nothing more than charitable works."

However, it was when she got up and he escorted her out that everything began to falter between them as they walked towards the door close together and in step. It was then that he could see the short hair on the back of her neck revealed to his gaze like a prelude to other secret curls. She left a hint of perfume behind her although she never put any on before her visit. It still remained in her clothes and around her, all the more nostalgic as it came from a distance, from a party, an invitation, a social gathering perhaps a week or a month ago. As it evaporated it mingled with, and finally became, her own smell.

Every time he took his leave of her a phrase crystallized in his mind, a veritable diamond waved in front of him by the devil in person: "To take a woman in his arms." After such a battle, what a sudden, wonderful feeling of peace to hold her against his heart at last, to have that indescribable image, that indescribable contact nestling against his shoulder and looking at him with those golden brown eyes.

The inscrutable nuns who showed visitors into the bishop's study were not at all worried. They saw His Grace's idyllic mortification of the flesh as something done for form alone. Indeed they knew for certain that the

Baroness Ramberti was a *femme barrée*. This rare physical disability which blocked the door of her senses made her unfit for copulation and no doubt also for fornication, or so the sisters hoped.

On this particular day, Mgr Godiot was sitting under the pergola reading Oecolampadius. This austere writer, who had prudently been put on the Index, made him reflect, with some affection, that by allowing him to cultivate his regrets with the Baroness Ramberti, the Catholic Church had made the pleasantest heaven possible, the most sympathetic to the human condition and ultimately the most welcoming.

This is what he was thinking when his meditations were interrupted by a stream of Piedmontese curses coming from the street down below the retaining wall. He leaned over the railing to find out what was causing all the noise.

There were two tiny workmen, perhaps twelve years old, who were wielding shovels taller than they were around a mound of mortar, which they both had been mixing. But one of them had just dropped his shovel and was dancing around a heap of gravel, shaking his hand and swearing with pain.

"What's wrong?" shouted his companion.

"It's my whitlow! I hit it against the shovel! That hurts, y'know!"

"You're soft! How many times have I said that you only have to go and pray at Séraphin's tomb? He'll get rid of your whitlow!"

"You're getting on my nerves with all your talk of Séraphin. If you think I'm going to believe all these . . ."

"Don't believe it then!" the other boy cried. "Go on sick leave then! The boss will replace you. I've had enough of doing all the work for a cripple!"

"If I stop work, my mother won't feed me. The people at home count on my pay."

"Then go and see Séraphin, *accidente!*"

"All right! I'll go on Sunday. But don't say anything to my mother. She's a strict believer. She'd slap my face."

"I won't say anything. I'll lend you my bike to get there."

They set to work again in silence, as they needed their breath to vigorously mix in the gravel. Mgr Godiot watched them from above. With their skinny arms, their twisted legs, their thin bodies and, above all, the inevitable fate that could already be seen on their ugly faces, they were old before their time but already perfectly aware of what the future held in store for them.

His Grace sighed as he shut the volume of Oecolampadius, which he found futile and which, incidentally, he never opened again from that day. He had suddenly wilted at the sight of those wretched tiny brats, just wisps of straw, just links in the chain, unknowingly suffering the humble misery of mankind.

He felt such pity and compassion that he had hardly registered what the two Piedmontese had said to each other before becoming absorbed in their work.

They reminded him the following week, when Mgr Godiot came to meditate once more in his garden. There they were again, both of them shouting and swearing, full of energy. They handled their shovels well, no doubt wanting their boss to be satisfied with their work.

"I see your whitlow's been cured, hasn't it?"

"It doesn't hurt any more."

"There you are! I told you all you had to do was to go to Séraphin's tomb. He's worse than St Rita! You see," the kid added shrewdly, "he's younger."

For nights on end, these few sentences from two insignificant people insidiously invaded His Grace's sleepless hours, much more than they should. They even managed for a time to supplant the image of the Baroness, who had left for Ferrara to see to an inheritance.

Sometimes, when his assistant bishop, the vicar general, brought him a sheaf of work which he put down on the desk, His Grace hesitated asking a question of him. He was a worldly priest with a mind as sharp as his body was thin, intelligent, but narrow-minded. He was as quick as a cat and would appear suddenly before His Grace out of nowhere. He would simply appear; he could emerge anywhere, unexpected, unpredictable.

Thank Heaven that the sisters on duty hated him and, as far as ecclesiastical cunning is concerned, he was no match for these nuns whose bleach-burned hands had been in the pus and blood of hospitals around the world for more than thirty years. This had given them extraordinarily quick minds. For example, they always had major tasks to do in His Grace's waiting room when he was receiving the Baroness Ramberti. The auxiliary bishop assistant could give them all the filthy looks he liked, they simply shook their heads under their veils and took no notice.

Mgr Godiot thought that the man was there to observe him, to give him marks which he measured against a standard in some corner of his memory. And he did this without any particular authority, without having received an order from anyone, for no particular purpose other than the pleasure of seeing come true what he desired with all his heart: that his superior in the hierarchy was not his superior in nobility of soul.

"He's waiting for me to slip up so that he can triumph over me," His Grace thought. "There's no advantage in it for him; it's simply for his personal edification."

He had the archbishop's ear, and could well have arranged for his assistant to be promoted to higher functions and consequently moved from Digne, but he declined to do so. Quite the opposite: he was fascinated by this person and acted according to the book. He still kept a place for him in his prayers, however, as he thought that such tenacity could only be explained by some hidden suffering in his soul.

And yet, when he heard the nonsensical conversation between the two young workers beneath his walls, Mgr Godiot thought that his assistant was sometimes a great nuisance. Time and time again he was about to tell him about the astonishing thing he had heard, but decided against it. Perhaps it was because he saw an encouraging gleam in Mgr Beckx' eye, a gleam that invited him to confide in his assistant with all confidence.

"If any irregularity crops up in my diocese," the bishop thought, "he'll hold it against me and judge me. Let's keep it quiet."

Yet he was worried by a strange foreboding, which he vainly tried to get out of his mind: the idea that there was some major occurrence that he should know about immediately and which he could not talk about to anyone either in the hierarchy or among his flock.

It was when he received the Baroness Ramberti the following week that he realized she could be something other than an instrument of charity or temptation incarnate.

"You are intelligent," he said. "Your position in society means that you meet a lot of people, hear a lot."

"Oh! Oh!" the Baroness said, at a loss for words.

This was the first time in the five years they had known each other that Mgr Godiot had complimented her directly on her mind. She made no other comment than these two startled exclamations, but waited to hear what was coming next.

The bishop had got out of his chair and was walking up and down in his soft shoes. His weight made no sound on the parquet floor. He twice passed the closed door of his study, and could thus tell from the clattering of buckets and the clacking of sandals that the sisters were on guard duty. Nevertheless, he did not speak straight away, convinced that as soon as he opened his mouth, ridicule would fill the atmosphere around him like wildfire.

"I beg Your Grace not to beat about the bush like this!" the Baroness remarked, growing impatient.

"It's not easy . . ." His Grace said.

For a moment, a fleeting moment, she thought that he was about to tell her of his love, as he was so brazenly staring her in the face, and it was the first time for many years that they had not seen each other for a week. She prepared herself, she was ready, to tell him the truth in all honesty.

His Grace gave a deep sigh and said, "Do you know a place called Séraphin's tomb?"

"No!" the Baroness replied, taken completely unawares.

"Well, then, get to know it. Find out what you can and report it to me. Use the utmost discretion!"

"You do me an injustice!" the Baroness exclaimed. "For my part – I can't speak for you – nobody even knows I know you, except at functions. As far as the ladies on my committee are concerned, I see the auxiliary bishop. Moreover, most of the time I only deal with the temporal service, and in any case, I only ever mention the secretary."

"You're an amazing woman of the world," His Grace said. "It's a pleasure to pray for you."

When he saw her arriving the following Wednesday, he noticed that she hardly dared sit on the edge of her chair and, unusually for her, kept her knees pressed together. There were no feathers in her unfashionable hat. She looked penitent, like a schoolgirl caught breaking the rules.

"Summon the parish priest in Lurs," she said. "It falls within his province, not mine."

"But what else have you found out?"

"No. Don't ask me anything, I beg you. I wouldn't dare speak to you face to face."

"But what is it about?"

She shrugged her shoulders and looked away.

"Superstition," she said.

He thought about her reply for a few seconds.

"It's just what I feared," he said. "I did the right thing turning to you. You are very level-headed."

He congratulated himself on not having said anything to his assistant, who would have laughed the whole thing to scorn.

"I don't even understand why you wanted to find out about all this nonsense!" the Baroness exclaimed, a little vexed.

Several replies came to the bishop's mind at the same time. He refrained from expressing them. Instead, he took a piece of paper from his writing case and said to the Baroness as his pen scratched over the page:

"For several reasons, I do not want anything of this strange notion of mine to be recorded. Do you understand me?"

"Perfectly!" the Baroness replied, with a hint of mockery.

She felt a strange sense of well-being sitting there in front of His Grace. The words they said to each other on any occasion came together so harmoniously that surely their souls must also be in unison. When their minds met it was like the ring of pure crystal. If it hadn't been out of the question, she wondered, how could their flesh not also be partners?

His Grace's pen swept majestically through the arabesques of his signature. He waved the sheet of paper in the air to dry the ink quickly.

"Give this letter in person to the incumbent at Lurs," he said. "Can you go there today?"

"I can go there immediately," the Baroness said.

"You're as good as a sister! I'm extremely grateful to you."

"Why do you have so much unhealthy curiosity about this business? What do you have to gain?"

"I have everything to lose . . . But I'm putting myself at your mercy here: do you think I have the right to ignore a single sign, if by chance God has sent one to us?"

From Lurs to Digne, changing trains at Saint-Auban, was almost a two-hour journey. Monsieur Isnard, the parish priest of Lurs, trembled every mile of the way. In those days, when a country priest was summoned by the bishop, it was never for anything pleasant. The hardest thing for him was not knowing what they would blame him for. He had examined his conscience over and over again since the day he heard the beep of a car horn in front of the presbytery. A woman in black gloves and a cloud of crêpe-de-Chine handed him the envelope from Mgr Godiot with a minimum of words. He had found nothing to reproach himself with, and yet wild suppositions about the sanctions that would rain down on his head had fuelled his imagination. He thought that they would no doubt cut his salary, and he would have to help with the harvest next year to make ends meet, and that this year once again he would not be able to replace his old green-tinged soutane.

He stopped in his tracks on the footpath well before the boulevard. A terrifying thought had struck him. They were going to transfer him! Lurs with its 330 souls was already dull enough, but there were certainly other Christian deserts in the Basses-Alpes where a guilty priest could be sent to starve.

"They're going to appoint me to Saint-Symphorien!" Monsieur Isnard thought, "or to Le Brusquet or La Bréole! To Chavaille or Draix! No. To Aurent! Or maybe to Sigoyer!"

All the places where there were not fifty souls to save, where thieves short of money wouldn't have got 300 francs fleecing everyone.

He vainly tried to look more presentable when he was standing in front of the green door, which had never opened to him since he left the seminary. Meetings with bishops usually took place amid the ceremonial pomp, or in the rustic meadows of wayside chapels.

He was shaking as he handed his letter to the nun who admitted him. She had the busy look of an examiner who has other things beside that to do. She started and adjusted her glasses to see better.

"But," she protested, "this paper doesn't have the Bishop's letterhead!"

"I don't know . . ." Monsieur Isnard said, feeling embarrassed.

He was going to explain, in all innocence and in his own defence, who had delivered it to him. Divine mercy spared him this blunder, as the nun added almost immediately:

"However, it is certainly His Grace's signature and I recognize the paper."

Nevertheless, she didn't give up straight away, barring the door with her plump, voluminous body. She looked pained, doubtful and suspicious. Seeing her standing there like that, Monsieur Isnard was convinced that she knew all about the bishop's grievances and that the whole diocese must already be quivering at the dreadful revelation.

In fact, the sister was thinking very quickly about the motives that could make His Grace summon a priest privately. It was clear that the primary reason was to bypass his assistant, as everything went through his hands and he screened everything. But what was his purpose? That would have to be clarified later. For the moment, the prelate's unexpressed wish had to be obeyed and this priest sent to him right away, before the auxiliary bishop could poke his nose into the business. He must have been listening there behind his study door, which was always half-open. It was too late. Thin as a whip and long as a wet week, Mgr Beckx, the auxiliary bishop of Digne was already hastening down the stairs, his sharp eyes gleaming behind his pince-nez.

Father Isnard was even more afraid of the auxiliary bishop than he was of the bishop himself, for he had only ever seen him in his superior's shadow and his power to terrify the poor country priest came from that very self-effacement.

"What is it?" the man in black asked the sister, who turned towards him.

Sensing some windfall, he stretched out his neck towards the rustic priest who smelled of fresh grass. The sister give him the letter to read, but without letting go of it herself.

"In his own hand"! Mgr Beckx murmured. "What an honour!"

He thought that the sister would never let go of the letter and, as it was too menial a function for his rank, would never let him take the priest from Lurs to the bishop himself. That would have been the only way to coerce Monsignor either into telling him why he had personally summoned Father Isnard or into knowingly lying to him.

"Ah! Monsieur Isnard!" he said brightly. "Since you are here, I can give you some details about His Grace's visit for the confirmation. It will save me having to write and you having to reply."

He took charge of the priest, laying a friendly hand on his shoulder and led him around the vestibule, talking quietly in the confidential tone of the confessional. He couldn't keep him long. The sister knew what needed to be said in these kinds of unimportant talks with country priests. She was already beginning to fidget impatiently.

"I'll hand him back to you now!" Mgr Beckx cried with a saccharine smile.

Monsieur Isnard followed in the nun's rapid steps towards the bishop's study, just as he had once walked towards his director's door with the lowest mark in the whole seminary for having confused the two St Augustines. Now as then, his legs felt like jelly.

When the door swung back, he found himself looking at the huge prelate who was standing, leaning on his desk and watching him approach.

"All the affliction of the Church is concentrated in this priest's humility and terror," His Grace thought, full of pity. "And yet we've come to this: filling our most faithful servants with fear, when they should know our love as they know the love of Christ!"

"Calm yourself," he said gently. "I'm not blaming you for anything."

He pointed to the chair where the Baroness Ramberti normally sat. Father Isnard made trembling gestures of denial and deferential refusal.

"Sit down, I tell you!" the bishop ordered.

He sat down squarely in his own armchair. When the priest had finally settled, he gazed at him thoughtfully and at length, wondering if it was faith or poverty that had inspired the vocation of this man with the face as lined as an old apple. He gave him all the time needed for his fear to subside. When he saw that the priest had calmed down, he asked him:

"Well now tell me, what do you know about Séraphin's tomb?"

It was the only thing Monsieur Isnard had not expected. It didn't seem possible that a prelate would ask about that dreadful local story, concern himself with it or take it seriously. He looked at the bishop's high forehead, as he dared not look him in the eye. So, they had asked him to travel for four hours to talk about Séraphin's tomb? He didn't know what tone to take: guilt or embarrassed laughter. Furtively, he tried to read the bishop's expression. His superior's face was cold and serious, without a shadow of scepticism.

"Well? Did something happen with this tomb?"

"Yes, Your Grace. A blind boy fell there. When he got up, he could see."

Monsignor Godiot nodded his head several times.

"Right," he said. "Tell me everything you know. Leave nothing out. Take your time. I want to know everything."

Blushing and nervous, the parish priest of Lurs related what he had understood from what everyone was obviously trying to hide from him. He saw the brow of the man sitting opposite him growing darker by the minute. The bishop, incidentally, was not looking at him. He was gazing through the window at the restlessness of the plane trees as the wind silently tangled their leaves. This was a moment out of time. The priest's stumbling words were muffled when they reached his ears.

"'The shadows of faith'," he mused. "Where the devil did I read that?"

He recalled the whole quotation:

"'The answer is not to look for that connection, not to judge anything, but to simply stay in the shadows of faith. Following the rule of the blessed John of the Cross, I want to go beyond everything without judging it and stay in the obscurity of pure faith. The obscurity of faith and obedience to the Gospels will never lead you astray.'"

The priest from Lurs fell silent. When he was about to begin describing the episode of the ex-voto and the pork butcher's son, his courage failed him. He sat there opening and shutting his mouth for several seconds, but not a sound came forth.

Monsignor Godiot rose to his feet and stood with his back to him. On the wall behind him was a map of the Basses-Alpes where each parish was marked with a cross. The bishop was holding a flexible cane and, as he spoke, this unusual ruler moved menacingly over the map of the lower alpine region. It was made up of mountains and forbidding valleys, where nests of people clung like eagles' nests on to the hot, waterless folds, and places without stones were less profuse there than the piles of stones that had been dragged out of them. It also had livid gashes around the blue lines of the rivers that zigzagged like lightning from one parish across to another, where the cemeteries were scrupulously represented leaning over and balancing precariously over the void, just as they did on the dismal hills in reality.

The capricious cane wandered from one parish to another, sometimes lingering on one of them as if the bishop was hesitating over the final destination where Father Isnard would be sent to languish if he failed to do what was asked of him. And then the bishop said:

"Take care, my friend. I want an exact account of the facts as they have come to your notice, without adding or omitting anything. I will be the one to make judgments."

With a heavy heart the priest then told him about the ex-voto, of the strawberry mark that disappeared from the pork butcher's son. He said that when the village primary teacher saw the cure he left without warning, without even locking his door, without correcting the homework to be handed back the following day. The word went around that he had become a Carthusian monk.

"Good!" the bishop said. "At least there's one beneficial result!"

He was being sarcastic. Whatever the sudden revelations prompting him to bid the world and its pomp goodbye, he thought, a good primary teacher will never be anything but a worthless monk. His soul would never be wretched enough nor his mind become sufficiently lost. He could never bring himself to sink deeply enough in the shadows of faith.

"I've told you everything I know," stammered the exhausted priest.

"And it's no small matter!" Mgr Godiot sighed. "I might add for your guidance that under the same conditions a Piedmontese manual worker I know was cured of a whitlow!"

"Heavens!" exclaimed the parish priest. "Scandal has erupted even here!"

"It won't be a scandal," the bishop groaned. "It will be worse. We will make ourselves look ridiculous."

"I hope Your Grace will do me the kindness of believing that I don't believe in this nonsense. It's not the first time that the people have been taken in by an illusion . . ."

"Whether we believe it or not, we must find out everything we can about this strange affair and, if need be, condemn it in full knowledge of the facts."

"I've spoken about it to the incumbent at Peyruis," Father Isnard said timidly.

"Monsieur Trotabas?"

"Yes, Your Grace. He thinks we should let time do its work. He says that the people of Lurs will forget."

"Abbé Trotabas is a great fool," the bishop muttered. "Bringing it to light is the only way of silencing such talk. Otherwise the thing will go underground like my workman's whitlow, spread like wildfire and strike us down!"

"My church is full to bursting every Sunday," Isnard said sheepishly.

"Good Lord! There's nothing like the false promises of illusion to incite them to prayer! Now then, Isnard. Can you see a way of getting your two parishioners to come here? What were their names again?"

He looked down at the few notes he had hastily written:

"Marie Saille and . . ."

"Rose Sépulcre."

"You told me Rose Dupin."

"Yes. I'm sorry. Although she is a widow, we only ever call her by her maiden name."

"Do you think you can send them to me?"

"I'll try, Your Grace. But may I tell them the real reason?"

"No! Definitely not, if they are as you describe them. Tell them anything you like. I gather Mme Dupin is rich? Talk to them about charitable works. Tell them I need them for some committee or other. I don't know. You'll find something."

He had already begun to accompany his visitor to the door.

"One other thing," he said. "Has Mgr Beckx seen you? Has he asked you any questions?"

"He asked me if I knew why you wanted to see me."

"And what did you tell him?"

"The truth. That I didn't know."

"Well done! That's just what you should have said."

The bishop placed his hand, which was as big as a battledore but always as smooth and slippery as if he had just powdered it with talc, on the scrawny priest's drooping shoulder as he prepared to leave.

"Look as hangdog as you can when you walk through my waiting room," he said. "Don't accept anything if the sisters offer you something to eat. You're no match for them. Anything you say would take you further than you intended. Humbly thank them, refuse and go quickly. They'll think that my reprimand has taken your appetite away. Go back to Lurs reassured: say nothing. Nothing will happen to you."

His Grace's words sounded hollow, they tolled the knell. There was no possible protection on this earth for a poor little country priest caught between the will of the Church and the opposing will of God.

In the days that followed, the auxiliary bishop sat up and begged like a performing dog for His Grace, trying to find out what was going on with the parish priest of Lurs. His Grace observed him through half-closed eyes as he virtually rolled on the ground, almost at the end of his tether, berating the sisters, castigating the Episcopal Council when it met, but the bishop told him nothing.

"If I gave in," he thought, "he would never more be able to look at me without smiling."

The parish priest of Lurs walked back from the station, arriving at the presbytery at about nine o'clock. He passed the open shutters of his flock who were eating their supper. At the corner of the Rue aux Herbes he took special interest in the Dormeur family, the bakers. There were five of them around the table in the room behind the shop. Marie's three sons had their backs turned to the window. At fourteen, twelve, and ten, which were their ages at that time, they were already solid lads too broad for the backs of their chairs: their elbows touched and jostled with every mouthful they cut. You could hear the cutlery solidly hitting the china with the confidence of people who know they are in their rightful place.

Clorinde with the deeply lined face ate almost apologetically, wiping her lips after every mouthful as if she were not in her own home. Next to her was Marie, definitely in charge of everything. Monsieur Isnard standing in the shadows looked at Marie who was in the full light of the ceiling lamp. As she didn't know anyone was watching her, she was not on her guard and therefore completely natural, without the affectation of a smile or even a pleasant expression. This round dimpled face, well scrubbed with Marseilles soap and without a hint of make-up or anything else, remained the same for more than 30 years, without a line or wrinkle. But the face she showed the world was a mask: fixed, impenetrable, stubborn, suspicious and pitiless.

"Good heavens!" Father Isnard thought. "She was so lively, so light-hearted, so naïve when she came for her first communion. So that's what life has done to her."

And indeed, he had never really looked at his parishioner Marie since those far-off days, not even when he had married her, not even when she became a widow. Until the day when he saw her there in charge of her family at supper, he had never taken any notice of her, no more than of any other of his female parishioners. He had seen the people of the parish so often in his normal day-to-day dealings with them that in Father Isnard's mind they had all merged into one vague flock.

"Whatever Mgr Godiot might think," he reflected, "it won't be easy to get her to agree to anything."

He noticed other well-lit windows behind which the peaceful villagers of Lurs celebrated the evening meal. In the pork butcher's house, where there were only three of them, it was the boy with the strawberry mark who was sitting under the light and facing the window. In spite of his calling, Monsieur Isnard had been one of those who couldn't repress a start whenever he suddenly came across the lad when he still had the brown hairy stain. Now he couldn't stop looking at his new delight-ful face.

He was thinking as he walked unsteadily over the sharp uneven paving stones, as we all do, that these extraordinary happenings in Lurs were a serious puzzle and a very unfortunate occurrence for an ignorant country priest. The fact that Mgr Godiot wanted to know about it seemed a more than possible threat to his peace of mind.

The part of the street which narrowed just before the church was the darkest in Lurs. The scanty street lamps, set far apart, respected the dim light of the sanctuary. Monsieur Isnard was surprised that he didn't have to feel his way against the walls as usual to avoid stumbling. He looked upwards and saw that the modest rose window above the door, scarcely bigger than a bull's-eye, was glowing as though it were Christmas Eve. Monsieur Isnard was intrigued. He went up the four steps and pressed down the latch, for in those days the church was open night and day. The door opened reluctantly as usual with the loud creaking sound the priest knew well. He went down the two slippery steps on the other side. As he approached the altar to genuflect, he noticed the statue of Christ. There were strange gleams of light dancing on the red robe. He only half concentrated on a short prayer and then got up, astonished at what he saw. The candle-holders contained their usual blobs of tallow twisted in hideous, baroque shapes. All the candle rings were empty. An unopened packet in thick blue paper was lying under the money box, proving that no-one had lit a candle to any of the saints for quite some time. And yet the church was bathed in a dim flickering glow that seemed to beat like a heart of light right up to the points of the arches, where it even brought some of the azure blue ceiling to life.

Father Isnard turned towards the darkest side chapel, usually the one with the font almost hidden at the back. The brightness came from that wall, to which a large heavy picture on jute backing had been relegated. It had been mouldering in the sacristy for some time. It was one of those bad reproductions that the monks of St Sulpice used to turn out in their workshop to earn their keep during the nineteenth century, flooding all the poor churches in France with them. It showed St Anne being taken up to heaven by two angels with large wings. When the sun at the summer solstice sometimes lit her face with its huge eyes raised up to the parted heavens, this saint of high lineage made the incumbent of Lurs feel distinctly uneasy. Despite the profound depths of her faith, it always seemed to him that the saint's ecstasy was very much of this world.

On this evening, the bad painting was lit up even more indecently than on its annual summer solstice showing. Six tall, fat swan-white candles were burning without smoke or smell on the flagstone floor between the wall and the font. They didn't come from the stock continuously provided through the pious generosity of the Marquise de Pescaïré. They were no modest candles; in fact their stately splendour bespoke blatant ostentation. They would burn for four days and nights before expiring.

"Those candles cost three francs each!" the parish priest of Lurs murmured apprehensively.

He wondered who in Lurs could spend 18 francs at one time to devote them to St Anne. And above all he wondered what exorbitant prayer the immaculate whiteness of these candles could possibly be hiding.

He was still full of these thoughts when he went to bed. During the night he had an inspiration, which came from his instinctive mistrust of any unusual ideas that might now be filling the heads of his parishioners. He could see the large painting near the burning candles. St Anne? The adoration of the blessed mother of the Virgin was not a Provençal custom. No-one had ever asked for the intercession of this St Anne taken up to heaven by seraphim. Séraphin! The priest sat bolt upright in bed, horrified at the thought.

"They're burning candles to Séraphin! That's the last straw! And in my church!"

He leapt out of bed in holy terror. He pulled on his soutane over his bare skin and rushed over to the church. The candles were scarcely any shorter and were burning straight and true. Kicking wildly, he knocked them all over and stamped out their flames with his heel. The total darkness brought him to his senses, but he was shaking with anger and feeling guilty that he had not been able to control himself in his own church. Confidently feeling his way to the altar, for it wasn't the first time he'd made his way there in the dark, he was about to kneel down and make an act of contrition for his troubled state of mind. It was then he thought that a woman's perfume, such as he had never smelled before, was floating above and around the smoke from the candles. He realized that someone was there in the dark, someone he hadn't noticed when he arrived in a rage.

"Who's there?" he asked.

"Someone who asks you by what right you judge piety by your own limited understanding?"

It was a calm, deliberate woman's voice, which apparently didn't belong to anyone local. Nevertheless, he tried to guess who was hiding in the shadows.

"Is that you, Eudoxie? Is it you, Philomène? Is it you, Aglaé?"

"No," said the stranger. "Why try to find out? All souls are equal. Why did you knock over my candles?"

"There are proper places for them," the priest said. "You should have used those. And besides, your candles are ostentatious. They radiate the sin of pride."

"Their size corresponds to the magnitude of what I am asking."

"Whom are you asking?"

"Don't try to trick me. Whoever the intermediary, one always asks the Lord."

"The only authorized intercessors are the saints in the list of martyrs."

"It seems to me that St Anne . . ."

"St Anne is not the one to whom you're burning candles."

"You have unusual intuition," the voice said, "for a country priest. But you're right. I was praying to the more beautiful of the two angels."

"The most beautiful angel," the priest said, "is . . . But who are you?"

"A parishioner who asks to be heard in confession."

"Well, that's different! Wait until I turn on the lights. You won't find the door of the confessional on your own."

"I'm there already," the woman said.

Then, in the silence of the church, a voice began to whisper and went on for a long time. She said:

"Yes, I went to Séraphin's tomb and I will tell you why, even if you don't want to know."

When the priest left the sanctuary, night was well advanced and the stars above the village rooftops were no longer in the same place. He studied them carefully as he slowly walked along the street, as if they could give him an answer, a logical explanation, to what he had just heard.

"Rose! Rose! Do you know what's happened?"

Marie had pulled up the truck at Pontradieu in a cloud of dust. She had slammed the door and raced up the steps.

"What?" Rose asked apprehensively. "Good Lord! What's happened to us now?"

Marie collapsed into an armchair, her well-developed chest held tightly by her crossed arms. Every time Marie encountered Rose after her son had regained his sight, every time she looked deep into her eyes, she saw the same uncontrollable anxiety her friend constantly felt. They huddled together out of fear and reasoned with each other endlessly. Until the event that had turned their lives upside-down, they had been only feeble, luke-warm Christians. Actually, apart from the automatic reflexes inherited in their genes and acquired in their youth, which forbade eating meat on Good Friday, made them go to midnight mass or make the sign of the cross when a funeral went by, they hadn't thought much about the mysteries of faith. Any more than the rest of us.

Now they went to morning mass with eyes timidly downcast like fervent churchgoers. You couldn't say that their newly acquired fervour brought them peace of mind or made them any happier. In fact they were filled with dread as they confessed their faith; it was fear that drove them more often to the church door, especially Marie, who until then had made love without giving it a second thought. Now she did it feeling all the while that the roof of the attic where she joined her lover was going to fall down on her head.

"Do you want me to tell you, Rose? I would rather my child was still blind!"

"Good Lord! That's a terrible thing to say!"

"And all the rest of it! Don't you think that's horrible too? We used to live in a stable world where there were the living and the dead. Now we don't know where we are! The others, who can't see further than the ends of their noses, make the best of it. They take advantage of their good luck. Look at the pork butcher's wife. Since her son's face has cleared up, she's as happy as can be! Do you think she ever says to herself, *if that's the case*, she might well be held accountable somewhere for the two abortions she's had?"

"What do you mean, accountable?"

"Of course, Rose! Just think about it for a moment. If all that is true, if my boy owes his sight to Séraphin's intervention *elsewhere*, then *all the rest* must be true too! Everything we've never believed in, or believed in half-heartedly. That means we will be accountable for everything!"

"My coldness with Patrice," Rose said, "I may look as though I'm not responsible for it . . . My icy coldness . . ."

Marie clapped her hand to her mouth:

"Good Lord! And Tibère! He begged me to believe him for so long! His words had such a ring of truth! And what if it were true that he hadn't killed Séraphin?"

"My sister Marcelle who I don't like . . ." Rose murmured.

Marie gripped her arm.

"My lovers!" she exclaimed. "Have you thought of my lovers? Of what might happen to me?"

"Ah! Is that what you're afraid of?"

"Yes," Marie confessed, almost in a whisper. "I'm afraid that Séraphin is nothing and behind him is God! If that's the case, we're lost!"

These sombre thoughts dimmed her love and, feeling vaguely resentful, she let her eyes stray in the direction of the tomb, which she could just make out in the distance.

"And if there is a God," she said, "there'll be a hell of a lot we have to give up!"

This was the state of mind of the two poor distracted women who faced each other once again on that summer day at Pontradieu when Marie had just arrived and rushed up to Rose in great agitation. Rose looked at her apprehensively.

"Do you know what's happened? The bishop wants to see us!"

"The bishop!"

"Monsignor Godiot!" Marie gasped, quite out of breath. "The priest just told me. With the child . . ." she added.

Rose took hold of her hands.

"Marie, we mustn't go! He'll worm it all out of us. Those people are so much cleverer than we are."

"Oh!" Marie said, "he didn't put it like that. The priest had been told what to say, and it came from high up! It seems they need us for good works!"

"My foot!" Rose said. "You did say that you have to bring your son, didn't you?"

"That's what he wanted."

"Let's not go!" Rose said. "They can't make us. Everyone will laugh at us if he manages to make us talk. And he will!"

But deep inside Marie's need to challenge fate had been growing stronger with the passing of time.

"There's no reason for us to be the only ones lying awake at night with anxiety. Even a bishop must know sin!"

"My poor girl!" Marie said. "Do you really think those people can feel that kind of anxiety?"

"They're men, aren't they?" Marie said. "You don't know them, but I do, and they're all the same. I'll tell the bishop the truth. Since he wants the lot, I'll give it to him!"

His Grace was sitting in his study biting his nails. He had been anxious for months, ever since he had seen those two women and lifted the ten-year-old boy up on to his desk to get a closer look at him, and the bishop didn't like anxiety.

He could see the two women now. Although completely different, they were like sisters, but always ready to help each other out, watching the other's inscrutable face so that, if necessary, they would tell the same lies; they also told the truth together, but sounding so false and hesitating that one didn't know what to make of it.

Only in wartime, in men who faced death together, had the bishop encountered this meeting of souls, deep to the point of osmosis. The strength of their feeling for each other had its roots in permanent, unrelenting fear.

229

"That's what it is," Monsignor Godiot thought. "It's fear, but more like terror. They're afraid of me, of course, but they're ten times more afraid of what has happened to them."

Yet they were strong women, no doubt about that, and both toughened by life. No doubt they had more plans in the back of their minds than they realized themselves. He could tell that one of them usually took pains to make herself up, but on that day she had put on almost nothing, for the sake of decorum. But even like that she had the beauty of a Persian miniature His Grace had admired in certain coquettes when he mixed in society. The other one had vigorously washed her face with Marseilles soap and the bloom of her beauty came from her complexion. While the Persian miniature modestly lowered her eyes beneath their long lashes, the other woman calmly and steadily held the bishop's gaze.

In the beginning she kept her child between her legs with her arms across him. Monsignor Godiot almost had to drag him from her to sit him up on the desk. He then crouched down to the child's height to look into his clear eyes where a kind of impudent mockery seemed to dance in golden glints. When he had looked in silence for long enough, His Grace had given the boy back to his mother with a pat on the cheek. He had no experience of children, who had always intimidated him and made him feel ill at ease. He could barely look them in the face. To him they were a disturbing puzzle: in each one of them a life was taking shape for which they were not yet accountable.

But how did this one take what had happened to him? Did he think it was chance? A blow that had released some blockage inside his eyes? He didn't seem any more devious than most children when they are on their guard with adults. But there was not the slightest trace of any kind of mystical transfiguration. If he had been singled out by a particular grace, it had had no effect whatever on the salvation of his soul. This child had no sense at all of being blessed. He just took things as they came.

When he had had enough of this irritating mystery, His Grace turned towards the two women who were anxiously holding each other's hands. At first he thought he should treat the matter with scorn.

"You say he couldn't see. How do you know?"

Marie got up, nervously rummaged about in the bag she had brought with her, and drew out an untidy bundle of papers. After genuflecting awkwardly, she came up to the bishop with arm outstretched and handed them to him. He began to read.

"But what is all this?" he said after a moment or two.

"The certificates that prove my boy was blind."

"What do you mean? These are hand-written pages."

"Yes. I wrote them."

Marie lowered her eyes for the first time. She suddenly realized that she was up against quite formidable forces with her intelligence, which she knew was limited, as her only weapon. She added, as though making a confession:

"I copied them. But I've got the real ones in a drawer at home."

"You mean the originals?"

"Yes, that's it," Marie said quickly. "The originals."

"Ah!" His Grace said.

He began to see this full-bodied, sensual woman in a new light. He could not help feeling a kind of admiration and respect for her. Indeed, there was no denying that while he made them wait a respectable time in the room outside under the watchful eye of the two nuns, and having sent the auxiliary bishop on a mission, the thought had briefly occurred to him that if he happened to see proof of the child's blindness at birth, he would only need to destroy it and everything would go back to normal.

He was full of admiration for Marie because this thought had come to him suddenly, and he had hardly given it time to appear before he squashed it. Now to have enough time to copy all the certificates – there were ten accompanied by numerous letters – Marie would have had to start thinking three days ago about this bishop she didn't know. So, she had anticipated that thought by more than 48 hours, a sudden thought immediately suppressed, which she shouldn't have even suspected.

He noticed that Marie had one dimple close to the corner of her mouth which gave this part of her face the hint of a passing smile, while all her other features were motionless and controlled. She was sitting with her back to the window, against a background of branches silently tossed by the wind. It was at the end of a summer that had been half halted by two or three storms. His Grace kept listening for a sound above that of the wind, which would bring everyone to attention and make him join his hands.

"Thank you for coming in spite of your nervousness," he said. "And please stop trembling in my presence! Is that what they taught you in your Christian childhood?" he added sadly. "To be afraid of your pastor?"

"If we are afraid, Your Grace, it's not because of you. It's because of our ignorance."

His Grace considered the Persian miniature who had just spoken. She was also on her guard and, if need be, was capable of seeing through him.

"And do stop holding each other by the hand as if you were lost in the woods! Tell me everything," he added after pausing for a moment, "without adding anything or leaving anything out, as if these things had happened to someone else, not you."

He remained undecided for some time after this interview about how much he should believe of the two women's story. However, they were the only witnesses. The wife of the pork butcher in Lurs had let it be known that she would never come, either with her son or without him: she was too afraid that once the secret was out, divine mercy would become incensed and restore things that should never have changed to their previous state. At least that is a résumé of what the parish priest had written to the bishop in a roundabout way. As for the two Piedmontese workmen, one of whom had been cured of his whitlow, they had told barefaced lies without batting an eyelid right to the end, genuflecting all the while. If scandal came, they would not be the bearers of it.

"Perhaps I won't have time to prevent it," His Grace thought anxiously.

There was a knock at the door and the sister who was always bustling about entered without waiting for permission.

"Baroness Ramberti is outside and asks to see you."

This announcement startled him. Had he forgotten her? He was in the habit of taking some time to prepare himself for their meetings. It was not to give any finishing touches to his person, which was of little importance to him. No, it was to steel his soul against its first instinctive reaction, and the first reaction to the Baroness was to hold out his arms to her. He hadn't seen her for such a long time: since the day he had charged her with the secret mission of going to the parish priest of Lurs and asking him to come and see his bishop.

For some unknown reason he had heard nothing of her since then. Mgr Beckx, who didn't like to see his bishop enjoying serenity for too long, grumbled about her desertion. He had unfinished charitable and vocational business which had been on his books for some time, and Mgr Beckx insisted that they be concluded. Mgr Godiot finally gave in and sent a note to the Baroness, thinking that she wouldn't reply as she was in Ferrara again. That was not the case. There she was without any warning. She had slipped past the sister before she had had time to open the door wide for her.

His Grace's mind had been elsewhere, concentrating on the picture of the two trembling women from Lurs whom he had kept in his sight without being able to work out whether they were lying or telling the truth. As a result, His Grace had not been able to think of the Baroness since the last time he saw her.

Nevertheless, he noticed straight away that there was a subtle change in his visitor, in her whole person. He paid no attention to it at first, although it made him uneasy. She was still the same dangerously beautiful woman, always in daring hats worn with such elegance and confidence that no-one thought of making a comment or laughing. But her face had lost something. It no longer radiated that impertinent assurance so typical of her, and the vivacious sparkle in her eyes had gone out. An unexpected reticence had also muted the tone of her voice. Everything about her seemed to anticipate something she feared. Even her quick-wittedness seemed to have received a warning shot: with her almost instinctive sense of mischief, she had slipped under the sister's guard at the entrance, but now she stood against the door paralysed, not daring to go in.

She usually walked quickly across the room and bent to kiss the opal ring His Grace held out to her without thinking. Today she clutched her green leather handbag to her like a shield. Even at that distance the bishop thought he could almost see the heart beating in this woman who had suddenly become so strange.

233

"You summoned me," she said. "I have obeyed your command."

He noticed with regret that she lowered her eyes, that he could no longer have those visual fencing matches with her from which he always claimed to escape unscathed. He suddenly missed them enormously.

He was also still standing there tall and solid, fingering his pectoral cross. The hair around his tonsure was golden and the sunlight streaming in the window from the setting sun made the figure of the bishop look like a timeless portrait.

"Which means that if I hadn't summoned you, you wouldn't have come?"

"No," she said. "I wouldn't have come."

He gazed at her in silence as she obstinately kept her head down and her handbag clamped to her chest.

"Very well!" he said. "Sit down and let us get to work."

Instead of going to her usual armchair opposite the bishop, she chose a chair standing alone against the wall and sat there.

"How can I hear you so far away!" His Grace complained.

"I must, I'm afraid. I'll speak clearly."

He made a gesture of resignation. For more than an hour they looked at sad cases and talked about charity: of how difficult it was to carry it out effectively and choose between deserving cases, which they had to do, but it was sometimes heartbreaking. They also took a certain number of urgent decisions. When they had finished, the Baroness Ramberti snapped her handbag shut.

"Excuse me, Your Grace," she said quickly, "but I cannot come and kiss your ring."

He was about to reply, "You've not usually shown me such coldness," but he felt he should not say those words of reproach. He merely said the following:

"You're leaving us already?"

He stood up to accompany her to the door and open it for her. Not for anything in the world would he have deprived himself of this ritual, which always gave him a delightful little thrill. He caught up with her in three strides. He thought later that man's soul cannot be forever on its guard, for before noticing that Baroness Ramberti was not wearing make-up or perfume, he suddenly felt the woman's body pressed against him. As she held him he could feel the weight of her breasts and the beating of her heart. He almost closed his arms around her, instinctively, but the thought of how dishonourable and ridiculous the situation would appear a minute later if he didn't take control, suddenly made his pride come to the fore. He did not escape, however, the humiliation of seeing himself for the rest of his days as he was in that moment: in retreat, roughly pulling that delightful body away from him, making a rampart of his desk between himself and the Baroness, who hid her face in her hands.

"What has got into you?" he said, but in a very restrained voice.

The fact that he had chosen his words carefully did not spare him from feelings of guilt. He had detected the change in her as soon as she came in, if only from the greater sense of agitation he had felt at the sight of her. Seeing her, he had suddenly ceased to delight in the free and easy, bantering, slightly superior manner he always had in her presence. He immediately thought – and should have acted on it – that she presented a new danger and he ran the risk of no longer being able to control the urge that drew him to her.

Now she was standing far from him, slim, supple, with full hips, judging from the perfect gentle curve of her flat stomach, and still wearing that hat, which for the first time did look rather ridiculous. Her face, blushing with embarrassment, had the pleading look of someone dying of thirst at a fountain that refuses to give water. She may well have held out her arms again towards an elusive quarry.

"What has got into you?" His Grace repeated gently.

Her reply came from the other end of the study, where she was leaning against the door.

"Until now I was not a real woman. Until now I only looked like a woman, and what's more I hardly knew I was one . . . I was hardly aware of it. Then you asked me to do something for you: you sent me to see the parish priest in Lurs."

"What do you mean: I wasn't a woman?"

"I was blocked, a *femme barrée*! Do you know what that means?"

"No . . ." the bishop said, taken aback.

235

"Of course," the Baroness replied, "Mme Récamier never interested you. Well then, I'll tell you. A blocked woman is a woman who can't have sexual relations because of a natural abnormality. Even if she really wants it," she added. "There's a . . . natural obstacle between her and . . ."

"Good Lord!" the bishop exclaimed, almost under his breath.

He suddenly felt vaguely bitter at the idea that for so many years the temptation he thought he had overcome was nothing but an illusion, and that if he was unaware of this defect on a conscious level, he had always known it in his flesh. His so-called resistance was therefore nothing at all. There was no doubt that she was telling the truth, because if he had put himself out of reach of the Baroness today, it was his pride, perhaps his vanity reacting to the ridiculous sacrilege of such a dishonourable couple. Even now, standing so far away from her, he had difficulty restraining the impulse that threatened to propel him towards her.

They looked at each other face to face, but almost twenty feet apart, the unspoken admission burning there between them but keeping them apart.

"But what has happened? Have you had an operation?"

She hid her face in her hands as a hard, painful laugh shook her like a sob.

"An operation!"

She raised her head and looked straight at him again.

"I went to Séraphin's tomb!" She almost shouted at him.

"What?"

She crossed the room and leaned on the desk in a confronting manner, but without taking her eyes off the bishop opposite her.

"Yes. For days and nights until he answered my prayer! I burned obscenely large candles to him! If you have any doubts, just ask your parish priest in Lurs. I made my confession to him. And I also asked Dr Jouve to examine me. Ask him his opinion!"

"You confessed to the priest in Lurs! You told him everything you told me?"

"Yes. And a lot more besides!"

"You actually engaged in this childish behaviour! You!"

"Six days and six nights! And with the greatest fervour, if you must know!

But don't think that being singled out like that brings me any joy? On the contrary, it fills me with horror! I've been living in a state of unspeakable anxiety ever since. But I love you! I owe thanks to the Lord for having delivered me! I love you in the flesh! As a man, and not as a priest! Is that clear enough?"

She was literally crying out her love, but although her mouth was wide open her voice was so low that the sounds could hardly come out.

"But surely you're a Christian?"

"Yes! But not to that extent! I would be content to be a sinner because, Your Grace, there's a chance that this short life may be the only ray of light that exists for us, the only one granted to us for eternity. Don't you feel that everything is unsure. War is coming!"

"Ah! Is that what you're counting on? But war is a mere incident. And if you want to know what I really think, war only represents the deadly futility that could help damn our souls if, using it and the prospect of its dreadful pitfalls as an excuse, we became such poor creatures, so worn down by its horrors that our only defence against despair was to join our miserable flesh. That is the main danger. War itself can only end our earthly lives!"

"Do you dare tell me in plain words that you don't desire me?"

"I confess to you that I do," the bishop said softly. "I'm only a man, a wretched man. Yes, I fear I might give way. Just as I'm certain of meeting death with serenity, I also stumble, I falter faced with the temptation of your adorable body, your adorable mouth, your adorable mind. I'm telling you all this because today is the last time we shall see each other. From now on send me Mlle Imbert in your place!"

"Mlle Imbert!" the Baroness sneered. "You won't be able to forget me. I'm quite sure of that. You'll writhe in pain in your lonely bishop's bed! You'll call to me in vain!"

"Is that what you wish for me? Suffering?"

"Whatever form it takes, it will never be anywhere near as great as mine. Your pride will be enough to overcome it."

"I've told you that I love you. Isn't that humble enough for you?"

"You must be very sure of the immortality of your soul if you dare to bargain with me like this."

"But Madame, I *am* sure of it!" the prelate replied simply.

She was about to make a stinging retort, but he didn't give her the time.

"And also of yours," he added gently.

At that moment a belatedly perturbed nun flung open the door of the study without warning. She saw the majestic figure of His Grace behind the desk and the Baroness Ramberti standing a suitable distance away, looking stiff and formal. The quick-witted nun saw that a reassuring hostility existed between these two people and immediately gauged how deep it was. What she could not know was that love, all the more magnificent because it was impossible, burned between them among the flames of Hell.

Neither the bishop nor Dr Jouve would ever forget that date, normally peaceful and unremarkable in the natural progression of days and seasons. Misery ruled over men but not over nature. It was one of those early autumns we sometimes have in these parts. A light powdering of snow had fallen the previous night, capping the Tête de l'Estrop only to disappear at sunrise. In the Chavaille valley a single maple tree among all the green trees had suddenly and inexplicably begun to turn flame red.

Grumbling and angry with himself, Dr Jouve slammed the door of his car and looked at the bland façade of the building in front of him. He had been annoyed with himself for the last three days for having accepted the interview, during which he intended to be as supercilious as he could. At that point he was not even sure whether he would knock at the door and turn back, but he nevertheless found himself walking in the right direction. He raised the knocker. After he had knocked, he found himself taking off his hat in an automatic gesture of politeness. He immediately punished himself for it by angrily banging the hat back on his head with his fist. When the nun opened the door, he did not greet her, so as to avoid calling her sister.

He simply announced himself by saying, "I am Dr Jouve."

This nun had put bedpans under the withered buttocks of more than a thousand old men scarcely any older than this one and certainly just as bad-tempered. She did not reply, but turned around and preceded him to the study door. She knocked and His Grace called out, "Come in." The sister stood back and, as he passed her, the doctor had enough time to see that her inscrutable face was every bit as forbidding as his own.

"Monsieur," Dr Jouve said, "permit me not to kiss your ring, as I do not share your convictions."

"I did not intend to offer it to you. As for the rest, every man is free to choose his own form of suffering."

"What do you mean?"

"That if you prefer to suffer as an atheist rather than as a Christian, you have the right to do so."

"But I don't suffer, whatever you may think!"

The prelate shrugged his shoulders.

"Come now!" he said. "No doubt you replied without thinking. Well . . . I didn't ask you to come for a consultation to convert you. Did I ask you to sit down?"

"We haven't had the time!" Dr Jouve retorted as he took a seat, his cane across his knees, his pince-nez firmly fixed on his nose, and a bold, questioning look in his eye.

"This man is in good health, clear-headed and sensible," the bishop thought. "He'll give straightforward answers. He's somewhat lacking in kindness and good will, but . . ."

"Anyway, thank you for having answered my call," he said.

"Oh! You wrote 'for a consultation'. I'm a doctor. If you wish to consult me, here I am!"

"I am bound by the secret of the confessional," the bishop said out of the blue. "And you are obliged to keep professional confidentiality."

Dr Jouve nodded.

"We are men who deal in secrets," he agreed.

"I've called you here," the bishop said, "to talk with you about . . . about the Séraphin mystery."

Dr Jouve leaped to his feet as though he had been stung.

"You're not going to tell me that *you* also believe all this nonsense? You haven't had me come all this way to discuss that?"

"Yes," the bishop said.

"It's incredible! Allow me to take my leave. I have patients waiting."

"Will you have me believe that your thoughts frighten you?"

Dr Jouve instantly sat down again.

"If that's a challenge," he said, "my patients can wait!"

The bishop shook his head.

"I'm not challenging you. I'm just a poor mortal, and so are you. I want the truth and you should want it too."

"There's a hoax as big as a house behind it all! Do you expect me to waste my time on that?"

"As big as a tomb!" the bishop sighed. "And that's why we should expose it together."

"I'd be surprised," snapped the doctor, "if the Church doesn't try to take all the credit in this case as usual."

"You're mistaken! The Church detests hoaxes, if only to avoid the sarcasm of men like you."

"Well then, if that's the case, what do you want of me?"

"You had plenty of time to examine the Saille boy. In your opinion, was he blind at birth."

Dr Jouve began to chew the end of his moustache. He got up, went to the window and gazed at the plane trees tossing in the wind. After all . . . wasn't everything ultimately unreal? This wind we know so well, the sun rising in the east, the depths of the sky, the return of the seasons, the birth of a child or the love between two people, everything which seems to us firmly fixed in an intangible logic doesn't stand up for five minutes if we analyse it, simply because it's only one kind of logic among many others that our particular capacity for knowledge cannot conceive. What does it prove after all if these inexplicable cures occurred at a place called Pontradieu or anywhere else for that matter? What good could that do us?

"I could take refuge in professional confidentiality," argued Dr Jouve, who preferred not to answer with a simple yes or no.

"Come now! It's not a crime to be blind. And besides, the Saille boy can see now. So? Was he blind or not?"

"He was," Dr Jouve admitted.

He kept silently cursing all the certificates and prescriptions the dreaded

Marie kept in the drawer of the Henri II sideboard, with the balls of string and reels of cotton, under the savings bank books.

"That's one fact we have established: he was blind."

"Oh no! Don't think it's as simple as that! I'm the only one in Lurs at the moment who has the courage to assert that the Saille child was blind! For now they're all in league, claiming that he could see just a little, that he could see shapes! Our good Clorinde even claims that he could come down the steep stairs from the loft by himself and go around the open trapdoor to the cellar! How do I know what they're capable of inventing? There's not one, including Tricanote, who won't confirm that one day he went straight to the stake where the goat was tethered in the middle of his father's field, and untied her!"

"It seems to me you should help them in this task."

"Why should I help them? I'm a man of truth. It's a fact that the Saille child was blind at birth. There's no doubt about it. What is not admissible, is the fact that now he can see!"

"I'm not asking you to tell me how that can be possible."

"Precisely, it's not."

"But it's so."

"Yes, it's so."

"Well now, in your opinion was this blindness incurable?"

"It was."

"His mother and her friend claim he fell. Isn't it possible that somehow something was unblocked as a result of the injury? Something was suddenly reactivated? I've heard that a jolt sometimes . . ."

"I'm not knowledgeable enough to give you an answer to that. And, of course, I wasn't there. The two women are the ones who related the incident. Just think how incredible the thing is. Countless precautions are taken after a cataract operation to make sure the patient doesn't suddenly see daylight again. Now here's one, and blind at that, who had the light shine straight in his face! Instead of screaming in pain, he blithely starts throwing stones and breaking windows! What really happened? We'll never know. But the hypothesis of a concussion that could have caused the cure is just as improbable as that of divine intervention."

"No!" replied the Bishop of Digne.

He got up and slowly began to circle around his desk and the doctor, who was still seated.

"No," he said once again. "The Church has only admitted exceptions with the greatest reluctance. Many of us baulk at the greatest of them all. It must be openly admitted that we are ashamed, not of Christ's death, but of His resurrection! If you only knew, so many Christians, in the presence of another Christian, cannot confess without blushing: 'Suffered under Pontius Pilate, was crucified, dead and buried; on the third day he rose again from the dead.' I've even seen priests – God forgive me! – who falter when they mention this article of faith and can hardly look me in the eye!"

"Why are you confessing these abominations to me, when you know I'm an atheist?"

"Because you're a doubting Thomas. If you had been able to touch the living Christ after examining his dead body, you too would have confessed the faith."

"Undoubtedly," Dr Jouve sighed.

"On the other hand," His Grace complained, "here are my good Christians, ready to kneel down before a little heap of bones, all that was left of a very ordinary man, and ready to believe that these miserable remains can do anything! You must admit, it's distressing!"

As he launched into this diatribe, Mgr Godiot was a striking picture of episcopal indignation at its most intense. Dr Jouve quoted, with a slight sneer:

"*There is still no salt on the tail of the absolute!*"

He had read this statement a very long time ago in some book whose author and title had escaped him for ever.

"Ah! That's right, blame it on the obscurity of faith," His Grace cried. "It's easy: 'The answer is not to look for that connection, not to judge anything, but to simply stay in the shadows of faith.'"

"Fénelon, spiritual letters . . ." Dr Jouve muttered.

The prelate stopped in his tracks.

"How do you know that?" he exclaimed.

The country doctor shrugged his shoulders.

"I too tried to believe," he said, "in the past and in vain."

"So that you still have some respect for matters of faith?"

"Let's say . . ."

"And you wouldn't like to see it reduced to some pitiful remnants of superstition?"

"No doubt. If I have good reasons not to believe in Christ, I have better ones to positively refute country legends that circulate for centuries, which can never be completely eradicated. Do you think I'd be happy if your moral teaching was trampled underfoot and ended in ridicule?"

His Grace seized his deep armchair and lifted it as if it were light as a feather. He walked over and put it down beside the doctor. The chairs had originally been opposite each other, suggesting a court. By changing the seating the bishop wanted to indicate that they were both perfectly equal, and hoped Dr Jouve would take his gesture as such. When they came to tidy up next morning, the two nuns were astounded by this strange rearrangement of the furniture, which they hastened to rectify.

Seated in this unaccustomed position, the bishop's bulk and height looked as if it were about to engulf the thin body of Dr Jouve.

"I didn't ask you to come here to speak to you only about the blind boy who can see or even about the pork butcher's son and his strawberry mark."

"That reminds me! They also stubbornly claim that the child never had a lupus, and all their customers back up their testimony with that barefaced lie!"

"There is someone, however," His Grace confided, "whose testimony I would consider irrefutable."

"Someone . . . whom I know?"

His Grace nodded his head.

"Someone who has consulted you."

Until then Dr Jouve had accepted the confidential contact between his thin person and the bishop, but at those words he gave a sudden start and moved away from his companion. He turned to look at him more closely.

"This is as far as I'll go regarding confidentiality," he said.

"Yet you did admit that we are, each in our own sphere, men who deal in secrets."

"Exactly! It would never occur to me to start questioning you about the secrecy of the confessional."

His Grace carried on regardless with a sweeping gesture that deliberately brushed aside this slight obstacle.

"It concerns a woman," he said. "An intelligent, clear-headed woman, a woman of some worth . . ."

He described her to Dr Jouve with a melancholy warmth of which he was not even aware. The doctor, who was observing him closely, stopped him at that point, perhaps to spare the bishop's modesty.

"A very beautiful woman," he said gently. "A woman who could inspire a great painter. She said to me, 'There's no need for me to tell you my name, as I'll never see you again.'"

He got up now and walked to the window to massage a cramp that sometimes attacked him.

"She said to me," he continued, 'examine me carefully. Someone may want to know what you have discovered. Tell him.'"

He slapped his forehead and pointed at the prelate.

"Was that you?"

His Grace nodded.

"If you confirm what she told me, I'll believe you. I had complete confidence in her."

"I found nothing at all. No particular indication of any kind. She was perfectly healthy, perfectly normal."

"She was a *femme barrée*," the bishop said, almost in a whisper. "She admitted it to me herself. I don't know what it is, but you must know."

"Blocked? I can assure you that she wasn't!"

"She wasn't any longer. She was the one who urged me to consult you to prove her statements. It's the only testimony I believe."

"Her statements? What statements?"

"That she went to Séraphin's tomb, prayed night and day and lit candles in the church at Lurs. I questioned the parish priest and he has confirmed both. She made her confession to him."

"She wasn't blocked," the doctor said gravely. "I gather that is what you wanted to know?"

His Grace said nothing but indicated that was the case. They were now both on their feet and the doctor was already walking towards the door. The bishop was on his right. He had lost his natural stateliness, his smooth manner and his faultless urbanity. He seemed to have aged ten years in a few minutes, which gave him the appearance of an unhappy man. Dr Jouve would willingly have patted him on the shoulder to comfort him, had His Grace not been much taller than he.

"Let time take its course!" he said. "People forget their saints, the true as well as the false, just as they forget their benefactors, their torturers and exploiters, and those who kick up the dust in front of them in the hope of making themselves unforgettable. One fine day they're all reduced to nothing more than an excuse for feasting, dressing up and fornicating. People confuse them and make cheap religious pictures of them. One fine day the people of Lurs won't even remember this tinpot Séraphin. Then they'll be quite happy to cling to the essential vagueness of your dogma on heaven. You people have the best of it with your cure for death!"

The bishop was probably going to answer him, but at that moment the whining of the newly installed siren was heard all over the town. The two men in the study stopped and stood there almost at attention. If there was a fire, it would sound three times. Otherwise . . .

It sounded for a quarter of an hour at regular intervals, catching its breath while the sound slowly died and disappeared into the wind, then starting up again at full volume with solemn modulations as if the person in charge took pleasure in making it proclaim catastrophe.

When it was quiet, and there was a lull in the wind, the alarm bell from a neighbouring village took over from the siren. From Courbons, Les Sieyès, Champtercier, or as far as Le Chaffaut perhaps. We didn't know. An alarm is intended to be heard from far away and they were all sounding at once.

"War . . ." the doctor said quietly. "We were expecting it, weren't we?"

"Yes," the bishop said.

He crossed himself slowly and solemnly.

"Excuse this show of religion," he said. "I was a stretcher-bearer in 1914."

245

"And I was cutting off legs – legs which were sometimes only holding on by a few threads of flesh. And when I say legs, it's out of respect."

The bishop was not listening to him. Baroness Ramberti had made it known throughout Digne that she would leave with the Red Cross vans on the first day. He was thinking that he would never see her again. The two men stood there unusually still as if the spring that made them move was now completely released. They gazed at the windows until the daylight faded and was replaced by their own clear images in the glass. Night fell, a dense dark night, a night from the beginning of time. Without the reassuring light from its street lamps, Digne descended into war. Everyone was stunned; nothing moved; there was no sound. There was only the soughing of the wind in the branches of the big plane trees to echo these portents of the unhappiness to come, as if they were the only ones to understand what had just happened to the people.

IX

WHEN THE ALARM WENT OFF IN LURS ON THAT DAY, 3 SEPTEMBER AT about seven o'clock in the evening, we were all busy hoeing in our vineyards and olive groves. The grass had grown thickly. The vines and the tree roots needed weeding before the harvest to make the picking easier.

At the call of that bell, so similar to the happy peals at a baptism, we all stopped digging the earth at the same time and put down our tools. We suddenly looked as if we were gathering our thoughts to listen to the angelus, a custom that had not been observed by anyone for a long time.

All those who were in the village, especially the women mixing the salad for the evening meal, rushed to their doorsteps as they would for an earthquake. They stood there stock-still, heads up, all eyes turned towards the steeple.

We, the men, were already old. We'd been in the '14–'18 war. We weren't worried for ourselves anymore: it was for our children. Memories of Verdun came flooding back, Verdun which we thought we'd forgotten in twenty years of happiness. Which of us, I ask you, wasn't tempted to shoot off three fingers of our child's right hand, in a hunting accident? You know how sensitive those triggers are, and hunters are careless, aren't they? Of course, no-one risked it. At that time the Republic still had execution squads.

Yet we kept thinking of the war memorial with its 58 names. War had become bigger and better since then, and the obelisk wouldn't be high enough for twice as many names. It would have to be extended.

We watched our sons, our sons-in-law and our nephews going down the road back to the village on foot, horse-drawn carts, or riding their bicycles. They would go straight to the drawer in the bedside table, take out their military service book and look up the section on mobilization to find out when they would be leaving. We wondered which of them this time would have their names on the roll of honour.

I remember. I was counting the green olives on a little tree I had grafted myself, four years earlier, when I was more than seventy. That was also on 3 September. My father always used to say, "When you see an olive when it's time to harvest the corn, you'll see ten when it's time to harvest the olives." It was nearly time to pick the grapes, but I had already counted something like fifty on a young branch.

Now on that day when the sirens rang, if I'd decided not to leave my farm for the next five years and live in the wooden cabin I'd built there – I was a widower; if I'd made do with the 500 kilos or so of potatoes, fifty kilos of beans, thirty marrow and twenty measures of olives my property provided; if the clear water of my well had been enough to quench my thirst, then I would never have known that the war had begun or that it had ended. No foreign soldier ever trod over my land or came near my cabin, for there is a vast world for soldiers to fight in. They think they take over the entire earth, but when they've left, leaving devastation behind them, some tenacious reed they thought they had crushed will always rise up again. They can comb the world with their expert eyes seeking out what might have escaped them, but there are always humble people lying low in cabins tucked away in the olive groves, quietly waiting until the warriors have finally slain each other.

We had always thought that the end of the world would be like an explosion of fireworks which would blow us all away at the same time and hurl us into the depths. We would be instantly consumed by the fire from heaven, then immediately consoled by everyone dying together. We were going to find out and remember all our lives that it's quite the opposite: it never ends and not everyone perishes. But until then, how peaceful it was!

Nothing happened at first, apart from the absence of the young men and the fact that the old men and the women had to do the work to keep the family property going. At first there was the fear of seeing the gendarmes ride up to a house to deliver the bad news, but we soon noticed that, with the exception of someone here or there – maybe three or four for the whole region – there were no casualties. We couldn't believe it: we observed this war which killed so few people with some suspicion and from a considerable distance.

However, time passes for everyone – even for wars – with the exception for those little people on the sidelines, whom fate fortunately forgets. They are passed over for one purpose only: so that someone can bear witness through the centuries to the horrible tricks destiny plays. They never change, living peacefully from father to son, from mother to daughter. Of course they also die, but it's not noticeable. From generation to generation they live quiet, unremarkable lives that we envy, lives in which nothing seems to happen.

If they are photographed in front of a fountain – mother, daughter, grand-daughter, twenty or forty years apart, and whatever may have happened far from this fountain – they look so exactly like each other, discounting a few details of dress, that you are sure they must also be strangely similar inside. These are people who pray to God perhaps ten times a century, but it's enough to believe in Him and lead a peaceful life. These were the uncomplicated kind of people who made up the greater part of the population of Lurs at the time, and we were proud of this humble existence, this anonymity.

The fighting seemed over in no time: we heard about the battle, we heard about the defeat. We were annihilated; we got to our feet again. We didn't stop going about our work for a moment. We were the exemplary, calm folk who remain unmoved by everything.

We weren't young, but we weren't old men and women either. Our crowd consisted of those who are already otherworldly in certain things, but who also shamelessly cling to life for all sorts of little tastes and little pleasures.

Loud voices shouted down at us from all parts of the country, however, that the nation had been humiliated and that it was our fault. We listened to them gravely, hanging our heads in penance, but we knew deep inside that nothing disappears as quickly as the humiliation of nations. They are all humiliated, or have been, at some time or other. The survivors of a single war in their whole lifetime will always live long enough to see their country take no notice of having been nonetheless greatly humiliated. As if humiliation was as unimportant a thing for nations as it was for people. Under these conditions and given these sacrilegious thoughts, our obvious happiness was hardly surprising.

There was naturally some worry about the prisoners, but they wrote to us. The son was over in Westphalia, Bavaria or Prussia. Every morning he harnessed the team to work in the fields growing crops for the victor, who relished his victory and was well entrenched in Bolshevik *raspoutitsa*. The farmer's wife wasn't too nasty to him. The old men appreciated hard work and shared their margarine with him. When it rained for a month, he learned German, which could come in quite handy in the future. He wrote: "I grin and bear it. I hope that the property is not being affected too much."

Fine! He was alive! We could eat and drink with an easy mind. We would take a sly look at the monument to the fallen when we passed, knowing that our child's name would never be there. Our consciences were clear on that score, in fact no-one could outdo us: all our prisoners had their parcel every week and sometimes two on high days and holidays.

We spent days in the sun on the rampart wall drinking in the extraordinary peace that reigned over the whole area, from Lure to le Mourre de Chanier, from the Tête de l'Estrop to the rock wall at Mirabeau, vainly trying to get some idea or catch some echo of the atrocities being perpetrated elsewhere. But it was impossible to imagine in our silent contentment.

The old people said, "Séraphin's watching! Séraphin's over there! We've nothing to fear!" These very old people could no longer control their thoughts and rashly let these sacrilegious words escape their lips. In actual fact, we didn't know who or what was watching. As usual, we were simply happy, and the war with its tragedy and horror existed for only a few. Some who had no prisoner in the family experienced sudden feelings of pleasure and well-being, such as we had never seen them enjoy during the whole peacetime period. This was because time had stopped. The final line of our destinies would not be drawn before the end of this enigmatic, unforeseeable time we called the end of the war. Between our lives as they were today and that indefinite time in the future, the days had ceased to pass; they stagnated. The war had frozen time.

Hunger was our diversion. There was a period when we had to think about food first and foremost, if only for the prisoner's parcel. We had to think about where to find it, get to it before others did, and how to accumulate it. And we weren't the last to clear the Burle grocery's whole reserve of sugar, salt and pepper. Neither chocolate, eau des Carmes, Fernet-Branca, paregoric elixir, nor syrup of the Alps (high in sugar and for medicinal use) escaped our hoarding instinct once unleashed. Ten years later at the back of our cellars we found mummified bottles of glycerophosphate, which we'd bought by the box-load from pharmacies in Forcalquier and Manosque.

We made preserves from whatever we could find, for example Cossack jam. This entailed boiling thirty to forty kilos of fruit for ten days in the large pot used for the pigs, obviously without sugar, until it reduced by eighty per cent. After that, it was put into jars. The whole family took turns tending the fire that had to be kept going day and night. Those who had the most money bought a goat. Smartly dressed in white collar and felt hat, they would take a stately walk at nightfall to let it feed along the hedgerows. We saw clerks of the court raising pigs themselves. We began to hoard wine in our cellars, not even offering any to others when it had turned sour, as if there was ever any chance of it running out.

We spent sleepless nights worrying whether the mice might get into the flour, or weevil into the dried beans. Our worries used to be about worthy subjects, now they were petty and mean. We no longer thought about our eternal salvation; we stopped fearing death. Provided that our provisions were stored away behind solid locks, protected by traps and rat poison, everything was all right.

Then the war, surprised at having failed to attack us full on, suddenly assumed aberrant forms, the better to make us die from its effects anyway.

Marie watched anxiously as her children grew and the war dragged on. Ange was seventeen. He already had black down on his upper lip, which would grow into a moustache in less than a year. Bertrand couldn't keep his eyes off Aglaé's thighs. She had a bad reputation in the village, and on Saturday she would deliberately walk past the lad swaying her hips when he got off the bus from Manosque, where he went to high school.

"Try to behave yourself!" Marie said to her. "I don't want you leading him astray."

"And what about you?" replied the girl in question. "Do you behave, eh?"

Yes, she did behave herself. She had to. The strapping young man who had been her outlet had gone off on the second day. He was a prisoner in Swabia. Marie sent him parcels and kind words. He complained in the cards he sent that they weren't more amorous. Marie replied quite logically, "What's the use, since you're more than 1,000 kilometres away?"

The only person she had been able to find to replace him was a tired fifty-year-old. What's more, his bread wasn't good. Marie had to go and help him at night. It didn't help her very much. She had had to put the truck up on blocks and go back to the three-wheel bike to make deliveries. With this routine, however, she had lost three kilos and looked five years younger. She also worked in the garden, as we all did, but in her case she was trying to wear herself out, which she found difficult. She had to do all this work with the nagging sensation of unfulfilled desire, which many women between twenty and sixty felt more or less keenly at that time. In addition to that, she kept a constant eye on the subtle changes taking place in her children.

Ange, the eldest, had teamed up at boarding school with sons of notaries, who dressed like boy scouts and sang at fairs the Vichy song inspired by Marshal Pétain, *Maréchal nous voilà!* He had become infatuated with the willowy, blonde daughter of a chemist, whose older student brother wore a black armband with a cabalistic sign on his raincoat and a beret with a badge. Ange also left a newspaper called *L'Action française* lying around in the room behind the shop. Marie tore it up in front of him and threw it in the fire without saying a word. One day he came back from high school also wearing the Basque beret stuck on the side of his head, but without the badge, plus some sort of shoulder belt across his chest. He announced that Stéphanie – that was the blonde girl's name – had promised to marry him when the Germans won the war.

Bertrand, the other boy, was perhaps more worrying. He spent half the night and the days when he was not at school with his ear against the wireless set. All the neighbours knew that in the Dormeurs' house they listened to London, "Les Français parlent aux Français". Men on bicycles from the neighbouring factory at Saint Auban would suddenly appear, furtively raise the bead curtain, and without saying *bonjour* simply ask,

"Is Bertrand there?"

If he was at home, Bertrand who was usually so reluctant to obey, would come running.

Marie was at a loss to know what to do. She went to Pontradieu, knelt before the tomb where Ismaël had banged his head on the marble step. At the same time she had a frightened feeling that Séraphin's power, strong enough to give Ismaël back his sight or remove the lupus from the face of the butcher's son, could only offer paltry protection against the immensity of war. She then went to pray at the church as well.

"Dear God! Please don't let my children be caught up in the war."

Rose said to her,

"But Marie, I don't understand you. It's quite normal for your boys to want to be patriotic!"

She replied,

"You're the last person who should find that normal! Remember Patrice. If his face had been whole, you'd have had an orgasm with him!"

She stopped short.

"Oh, I'm sorry! I don't know what I'm saying any more!"

She flung herself into her friend's arms. She beat her forehead with her two fists.

"Really! It's so damned stupid! There are at least thirty million French people who couldn't care less! Look! In Lurs alone! How many of them are just waiting quietly for it all to finish? Must my children be among the few tens of thousands who will lose their lives in it? Well they haven't a hope against me! I haven't raised them for seventeen years for that!"

At night in the room behind the shop, she brought all her intelligence to bear trying to convince them. She spoke quietly, for she had to proceed warily.

"Now both sides are fighting for the worst reasons; tomorrow they'll make peace for equally bad reasons, and you, you'll be dead! You'll be among the unfashionable dead, like those of 1914. People will laugh at the reasons that wound you up. Oh, they'll celebrate you! They'll sing of your glory! But they couldn't care less about glory! When they get you to kill, when they order you to kill, it's to get rid of one of those obstacles that separate them from their ignoble aims. And these aims are the same for every motherland or fatherland!"

She angrily cut the slices of bread they wanted.

"The clever ones don't listen to them! The clever ones always come out of it! Just look at Maître Bellaffaire. Does he send his son to get himself killed? Not likely!"

"He's a hunchback!" replied the two schoolboys in unison.

It was true. He was a hunchback. It was not a good example. The whole basis of her reasoning could fall down since it stumbled over this small example. Marie, much deflated, realized that her average intelligence was not equal to the theories propounded by the old men who were indoctrinating her sons.

These old men didn't die in the 1914 war, but that wasn't enough for them; others had to die in this one. Using these old men, the motherland recruited young men to make up the enormous deficit of war dead contracted with other nations. They combed the country, preaching the cause of one side or the other, armed with the same unanswerable argument: "You see, if we want to keep our seat in the concert of nations, we must win! We must fight! If not, France will become a third-rate country!"

This is what her children retorted to Marie, who didn't understand why, after all, France couldn't have been a third-rate nation if this would keep all her sons alive. But she understood very well that the more the war dragged on, the more it was likely to increase her children's enthusiasm for it.

She was desperate to find a solution, so one Monday night when her workman had a day off, Marie took the rusty spade with the worm-eaten handle that had been gathering dust and spider webs in the shed next to the bakehouse, among a lot of other discarded tools. It was the same spade that Célestat had used to bury the Monges' gold; the same one that he and Tibère had taken to bury Séraphin's hands; this was also the one that Marie had grabbed after her father's death to discover that macabre secret.

It was with some reluctance, because she found it so horrible, that she unearthed for a second time the fortune that she thought she could forget until she died. She remembered all too clearly the day she had stood behind the bed in the starkly-lit room and allowed Tibère to come in order to confront him with what she thought was the proof of his crime. Besides, hadn't he fallen on his knees beside the skeleton of those severed hands and all that gold? And hadn't he killed himself to escape those visions?

A heavy silence reigned in Lurs that night. It was late and the night was very dark. All the farms and villages were little nests of buildings lost in shadow. Marie found her way in total darkness, knowing every inch of those streets, houses, nooks and crannies. Donkeys sniffed under doors as she went past. She had fished out from the back of her wardrobe the only pair of gloves she had ever owned: the white floss-silk ones she had worn at her wedding. With these gloves she burrowed in the earth and, still wearing them, brought back the heavy box of ill-gotten gold she found so repellent.

She bolted the door after her. The entrance to the bakery was the only way into the Dormeurs' house and the shutters were never closed. There was only a set of tubular copper chimes above the door, which tinkled when anyone came in or went out.

Marie took no notice of it, nor did she take any precautions going up the stairs carrying her load. Clorinde was snoring in her bedroom with her mouth open and her arms crossed. Going to bed at nine o'clock and getting up at six, she had always slept like that, with her door wide open, unconcerned about whoever might see her or whatever might happen. Marie didn't slacken her pace going past the door even though the parquet floor creaked and groaned atrociously. She went up the stairs to the second floor where rooms had been made in the attic after the birth of her children.

She opened one of the two doors with no more care than before, and turned on the light. The bulb in the ceiling had been painted with methylene blue. Her two children looked blue as they lay there on the bed. It was summer and they had thrown off their bedclothes. They slept naked, flat on their backs with erections from some vague erotic dream, no doubt.

"Gosh!" Marie said. "Wouldn't it be a sin to deprive women of that? And they want to get themselves killed! Stupid kids!"

She looked at them quite unemotionally, objectively. Both on their backs and a metre apart, they slept with their mouths open like Clorinde, but without a sound. There was eighteen months difference between them. They had both been conceived in the wild transports of their mother, clinging for dear life to a love she had never known. She looked down at them with their long muscles strangely blue and their chubby faces strangely relaxed and expressionless in sleep.

"Little bastards!" she said under her breath, but there was a kind of pride in her voice.

They were lying almost a metre away from each other, yet although they were not conscious of it, the right hand of one of them was tightly clasped in the left hand of the other. They always slept like this as children: they went to sleep separated, lying back to back and on their sides, but an hour later they would be found on their backs, still quite far from each other but with their hands joined.

Marie had found this strange behaviour worrying and slightly indecent, so when the eldest was ten she had had another bedroom built to separate them. But it was a waste of time as they would later be found in the same bed, still separate, and sometimes half out of bed if it was too small to allow that separation, yet still with hands tightly clasped, as if they feared they might lose one another.

It was very strange that these two, given their profound differences, never let each other go. Otherwise, they didn't really communicate. Conversations between the two of them were limited to monosyllables, exclamations or insults. They often fought, sulked for weeks when they never spoke to each other, but apart from the time when they were at boarding school, they never slept in separate beds, and even during their worst quarrels they could still be found with their hands linked.

Even though, from their earliest childhood, they had always rushed to the other's aid when one was attacked, they never shared anything and kept any present strictly for themselves if they thought the other not entitled to it. In much the same way, they were very keen on money, and Marie had no illusions about their morality or their selflessness. That is why she had dug up the sugar box from the corner of the oven.

"Little bastards!" she said again through clenched teeth. "If I knew they were lucky enough to escape getting killed, they could become leaders. They've got the makings of it, the recklessness and the appalling selfishness. But I can't take the risk!"

On the round table at the foot of the bed was one of those Moroccan beaten copper trays that Célestat had won in the lottery at a fair. It was the first prize, and it was huge.

Marie raised the box high in both hands, turned it over and opened it. A shower of gold rained down on the copper tray making a fearful clatter.

"There's not one man in a thousand," she thought with her country-woman's good sense, "who wouldn't wake up at that noise. And if my sons withstand it, so much the better for them!"

But they didn't withstand it. They squirmed about like worms, struggling against being woken so suddenly. Their hands had separated. They must have been fast asleep until that moment.

"Just like my mother!" Marie thought. "Even a shower of gold would have no effect on her!"

To stop them from sinking back into oblivion, she scooped up a pile of coins from the box and let them cascade down on top of the others on the table. This made the boys sit up at last, rubbing their eyes with their fists, yawning and opening and shutting their mouths.

"What babies!" she said scornfully.

They suddenly realized it was their mother who was looking at them. They still couldn't work out whether they loved her or only feared her. They were surprised to see her standing there fully dressed, with her heavy bun of blonde hair, her arched eyebrows, her full lips which often came out with such stinging words, those dazzling white teeth and sarcastic smile. They also became aware that they were naked and had erections. They leaped up in panic and struggled with each other for the sheet to cover themselves.

"No need to carry on!" Marie said calmly. "It's quite natural at your age. And don't forget that I washed your bottoms for years. Come here!"

They obeyed, tangled in the sheet they were still holding.

"What's that?" she asked.

"Gold!" they chorused.

They had never touched any before, but they were eyeing the fortune greedily. The heap of louis had woken them up better than a cold shower.

"Good!" Marie exclaimed. "You've recognized it straight away! Yes, it's gold. I don't know where it came from. Possibly, almost certainly it's ill-gotten gains, but in the meantime, it's mine! I don't know how much is there. I've never counted it."

She had a sudden inspiration.

"You know your godmother's property?"

"Pontradieu?"

"Yes, Pontradieu. Well, there's enough there to buy it."

"Including the big pond?" Ange said.

"Including the vines?" Bertrand said.

"Including the vines, the pond, the farm and the 200 hectares and the 1000 olive trees!"

She wasn't really sure of what she was proposing: the pile of money seemed so paltry compared to the glorious property that Pontradieu represented to her. But she thought she needed to make them dream of something huge. It was her last defence against the war.

They reached out their hands towards the golden profusion of money that took on a strange glow in the bluish light.

"Touch them!" Marie cooed invitingly. "But be careful not to scratch the coins, or they'll lose some of their value."

"Why are you waking us in the middle of the night to show us that?" Ange asked.

"Because I've been thinking. You two do like money. It's nothing to be ashamed of, it's not a fault, but as soon as anyone gives you ten francs, you hide it away so that you can go and gaze at it, and it's the devil's own job to get you to spend it."

"Just say it outright, we're mean!"

"No!" Marie said with a false smile, "you're just careful with your money. Now, don't give me that aggrieved look. You'll have to start taking a good look at yourselves if you want to live!"

"And what about you? Do you take a good look at yourself?"

"Indeed I do!" she said. "Don't ever doubt it. Not only do I take a good look at myself, but I actually find myself quite beautiful!"

She had a sudden desire to pull them to her and hold them tight, as she had that day when they were very small, the day their father died, and say to them, "Oh! My poor children! If you knew what life was like!" And to burst into tears. But it was neither the time nor the place, and she controlled herself as usual.

"There now!" she said. "If you promise me, faithfully, not to take part in the war, on either side, when it's all over I'll share this gold between you in two equal parts, so no-one will be jealous!"

"What about Ismaël?" Bertrand objected.

"Oh! Ismaël's not like you. Money doesn't interest him. The only thing that matters to him is his piano!"

"He's not a real man!"

"Be quiet! He's not fifteen yet."

She watched them as they ran their fingers through the louis. They had plunged their hands into the small fortune as if they wanted to wash them in it. But in the end they both regretfully removed their fingers from the pile of gold at the same time, and both shook their heads.

"No," Bertrand said. "You're asking too great a sacrifice. What about France? Have you thought about France?"

"You are my France!" Marie replied. "I couldn't care less about the other! There are quite enough people to deal with it. They don't need you."

They continued to shake their heads like stubborn mules, even though they could not take their eyes off the gleaming pile of gold and all it represented. Marie felt helpless as she realized the power of what was holding them back. She was frightened to see how the old men and their ideas were, for a time, able to modify the basic character of their victims – for a time, just enough for them to be killed, one way or another.

"Even gold!" Marie thought, quite disheartened. "Even gold can't do anything against it!"

"I have principles!" Ange said, his voice choking.

"I have principles too!" Bertrand said. "And I piss on yours, fascist!"

"Bolshevik!"

As often happened, they were about to come to blows.

"Go on two minutes more like that," Marie warned, "and I'll slap you both so hard you won't forget it in a hurry!"

Then she calmly put the coins back into the sugar box, smoothing them out so that they would all fit in.

"In any event, rest assured of one thing," she said in a restrained voice, "as long as I'm alive and you are not yet twenty-one, the war won't come near you and, above all, you won't go near the war! Now you can go back to bed!"

She left them, carrying the useless box that she was going to bury again at the foot of the oven. Her whole body was trembling. She felt desperate, at a complete loss as to what to do. And on top of all that, she needed to make love.

"Séraphin!" she moaned.

She thought she had seen him in the shape of her virile, sleeping sons. The deep distress she felt at having failed in her attempt did not stop her also feeling the keen physical longing of her desperately useless body as badly as toothache.

The long winding street in Lurs had seen so much war and peace come and go without leaving any trace behind between the stones on the road; the walls of the ancient houses had seen so many Dormeurs live and die through the centuries. The whole of her birthplace seemed to breathe calm and resignation.

Outside in the street, the night was amazingly gentle, as if the war with all its noise only existed in Marie's head.

Next morning, however, she was boiling with indignation when she went to see Rose to share her dismay.

"Can you believe it? Even gold won't change their minds! What on earth's got into them?"

"Their country," Rose said timidly.

"Yes? But, can you imagine, they each have their own! According to whichever brainwashing propagandist they follow! And as they're not the same . . . !"

She got up, too agitated to stay seated for long.

"No, no! It's unthinkable! It would happen to me. The eldest isn't even eighteen! They still have two years with nothing to worry about. And in two years the war will be over! But no! They want to go and get killed right now."

"Calm yourself, Marie. Not everyone dies in a war."

"No, not everyone, but all the fools do! All those with principles. Principles!" she went on. "Principles!"

She clapped her hands together and raised them to the heavens in a gesture of utter frustration. She sat down again quite worn out with worry. Rose, sitting opposite her, saw how much she suffered from having sons.

"Don't lose confidence," she whispered to Marie. "Séraphin won't abandon you. Remember Ismaël!"

"Thank goodness I have him!" Marie groaned. "Thank goodness he's only 15."

"I've never asked you," Rose said, "but ... why did you call him Ismaël?"

"Because he's an orphan. And also, remember, he was handicapped at birth. So it seemed right."

"Who was Ismaël exactly?"

"Well now! I think he was a slave, or something like that."

"In any case, he was a Jew," Rose said.

"I suppose so. I've only known Jews existed since the newspapers started insulting them. Before that I'd never heard a thing about them."

"Me neither," Rose confessed. "All I know is that Judas was a Jew."

"Jesus too . . ." Rose said thoughtfully. "Speaking of Jews, now that I come to think of it, one came to the bakery the other day."

"A Jew, in Lurs?"

"Yes. I was helping my mother stick bread coupons into the record book. It was about three o'clock in the afternoon. Someone raised the curtain and said, 'Good afternoon ladies. You wouldn't be able to sell me a bit of bread, would you? I haven't any food tickets and I haven't had anything to eat since yesterday.' My mother replied, 'My dear man, if we gave bread to everyone without coupons, we'd be in a pretty pickle! They'd have closed us down

261

in no time!' 'Ah well,' he said, 'I'm sorry to have troubled you.' He was just about to leave when he suddenly stopped with the curtain still raised in his hand. 'Who's playing the piano like that?' It was Ismaël practising in his bedroom. You know he plays for at least four hours a day! Our heads ring with it! I told him, 'It's my son.' 'Your son? How old is he?' 'Nearly fifteen.' 'But where did he learn to play?' 'Oh, you know, here and there. He's been learning music since he was three or four. He even had a teacher in Manosque, but with the war you know . . .' 'Could I just go and see him?' He didn't even wait for me to say yes. He went straight into the back room and up the stairs towards the sound, quite quickly for his age. I could see that he had completely forgotten he'd come to ask for bread, even though he must have needed it . . ."

Marie stopped for a moment to catch her breath. She had been a little breathless of late because of her sons and not being able to make love.

"They came down together, Ismaël and he," she continued after a moment. "In the meantime my mother, who can't stand seeing anyone in need as you know, had gone rummaging around in the storeroom and come out with half a loaf of dry bread and some hard cheese in a paper bag. 'Oh well,' she said to me, 'I can hardly let the poor old man leave with nothing.' As I said, they came down together. The old man had his hand on the boy's shoulder. 'Ma! This gentleman's a pianist!' Ismaël was looking at him as though he were the Messiah. 'Oh!' the man said. 'In a very modest way! I used to give lessons in Paris.' That's when he told us he was a Jew, that he had fled and that he didn't even have a ration card, and hardly any money. He'd thought he would be all right in Digne, but it wasn't possible, even there. So he left on foot with only one suitcase. It was there at his feet – a leather case that weighed hardly anything at all. 'I had to leave everything behind,' he said. 'There was no time.'"

"Heavens!" Rose sighed. "What misery there is on the roads at the moment!"

"To cut a long story short," Rose continued, "my mother and I told him the place wasn't safe, and that the road down below was full of Germans, who passed through all the time with tanks and trucks, and that they sometimes even came here wanting bread with coupons they'd got from heaven knows where! He shook his head. 'You can see them coming,' he said. 'Now, about this mountain behind you . . .' 'Lure?' 'I don't know what it's called, but I would think a man could hide there safely.' 'I'm sure that . . .' 'I'll give your son lessons!'

"'Oh, yes, Ma! He'll give me lessons! I need them. I know I'll never get there on my own!'

"My dear Rose, if you were in my shoes, what would you have done?"

"My dear Marie, exactly what you did!"

"Mind you, there was one thing I wasn't happy about: he told me that my piano was tinny. *Qué sien qué siégué* – anyway – he's up there at my godmother's, hidden in the Phare du Soleil. The piano has been taken up there and Ismaël goes every day. If you knew how happy he is! And the man, the Jew, well, he's just as happy. He said to me, 'Since I've known your son, I'm no longer afraid. I can be of some use at last!' But now it's our turn to be afraid! If anyone knew that we were sheltering a Jew in my godmother's house . . . Can you imagine? She's nearly 90! I'd hate anything to happen to her."

She stood up once again. Would she have the nerve to come out with what else she had to say? She walked up and down in the drawing room at Pontradieu, which had known such sumptuous gatherings in the past. Heavens! Had so many years gone by since peacetime? She took a deep breath.

"And then there's Ange," she said. "How long can we be sure of not letting anything slip out when he's there? He's at home every Thursday and for the holidays. If ever he denounced a Jew, he'd be shot. That's for sure!"

Then she added between clenched teeth.

"Who knows? Perhaps I'd see to it myself!"

"You're talking nonsense! Do you really think he'd do that?"

"He would," Marie said gloomily. "Those are his principles. When someone refuses a heap of money out of principle, he's capable of anything."

Now it was Rose's turn to get out of her chair and walk up and down on the carpet.

"Perhaps there's a way," she said at last. "Have I ever shown you the cellars here at Pontradieu?"

"No!" Marie said, surprised at the question.

"Come with me!" Rose said.

She took her friend by the hand and led her into the main hall. She took a big key from the board, which also held those of the tomb and the arbour, where poor Charmaine had waited for Séraphin one night under the Virginia creeper. There, too, were the keys to the paddock, long since destroyed on Rose's orders, where the savage dogs had been kept. The whole history of Pontradieu was written on that board in the symbols of those keys, hanging there for so long but scarcely rusted, some with no locks to fit. Still holding Marie by the hand, Rose walked up to the panelled wall.

"It really is a rich man's house," Marie thought. "In all the time I've been coming here, I never knew there was an opening in the wall."

The door was cut the same size as the walnut panel and fitted in perfectly with a bevelled edge, so that there was no break in the carved scroll at the top and bottom, and the joins were lost in the mouldings. The hinges themselves were invisible. The lock was on the other side of the door frame, the keyhole hidden by a wooden cover of the same walnut colour. There was no handle. When Rose put in the key, it turned silently in the lock and the door quietly slid open without having to be pushed.

"It really is a rich man's house," Marie said to herself again, full of admiration. "It must be a great consolation to be a widow in a place like this."

As soon as the door opened a strong, warm tannin smell rose from the depths and now hung in the air about the two women. It was smooth and somehow reassuring. Rose turned on the switch. A dim light shone down a damp staircase, where each step was a single block of stone. Rose went down in front of Marie, almost on tiptoe, as though she were entering a church. From the very first day when Patrice had shown it to her, she had never entered the place without a feeling of respect. She was more captivated by these rows of racks filled with dark bottles and lit by small dull-red lights than by the chandeliers, Charmaine's grand piano, or the library.

"Look!" she said. "Here it is!"

She had led Marie on a winding path between pillars, barrels and metal racks with written labels indicating their contents. The vaulted ceiling abutted a wall with a storage unit and rows of bottles set into it.

"Wait till you see this!" Rose whispered.

She stood on tiptoe then felt about with her left hand. The wall bristled with saltpetre. She did this for quite a long time. Patrice had revealed Pontradieu's secret to her only once, as the thing itself had no great importance at the time, and she hadn't paid much attention to exactly what he was doing.

Marie, who was watching her with great curiosity, suddenly heard the rattling of bottles bumping against each other. Rose had stepped back.

"Look!" she said in a hushed voice.

The storage unit was very slowly sliding along the ground to the right, where it disappeared into the wall with the crystalline sound of glasses clinking.

The two women stood somewhat fearfully in front of the empty space. Then they hesitantly moved forward into the passage that had opened up before them. It immediately led into a Romanesque vault built of large stones. The atmosphere was as solemn as a crypt. Here there was no smell. Here the complete stillness of the air carried no echo. They could hardly hear their footsteps advancing. The rounded flagstones on the floor shone as though they had been washed the day before.

"Its shape is almost like the inside of a baker's oven!" Marie said admiringly.

"The temperature is the same summer or winter," Rose said. "Patrice used to say that this place is completely isothermal."

It was an imposing room with walls reinforced at regular intervals by pillars topped with strangely carved capitals illustrating biblical stories. The stone was scarcely worn. The room was dimly lit by two small basement windows encircled by the twisting tails of two snakes carved from a single piece of stone. Looking through them at ground level, one could see the maples, the pond, and the swans gliding over the water by the fountain. The strange, unnatural light in the place still evoked the deep plots that must have been hatched there in times gone by.

A shadowy outline surrounding a large, lighter section of flagstones on the otherwise dark floor, suggested that a huge object must have stood there. It looked as if these shapes came from an earlier period than the construction of the vault, and the sun and rain had slowly built up the mark around the stones which were sheltered from the weather by the mysterious mass that stood on them at that time.

Marie pointed to them. There was a light area in the shape of a large perfect circle, cut by four equidistant crenellations, but she dared not put her foot on it.

"What is it?" Marie asked.

Rose shrugged her shoulders.

"Goodness!" she said, "Patrice didn't tell me anything about it. You see Pontradieu was built on the ruins of a former convent. With the same stones," she added. "Well, you know, with convents . . ."

She was whispering. She moved forward very hesitantly, with Marie breathing hard at her heels. They both looked overawed, as though they were in a church.

"A convent?" Marie murmured. "Are you sure?"

Her eyes hadn't left the trace of the enormous object on the ground, indicated only by the great expanse of the lighter stones. She was wary and on the alert, like a frightened rabbit.

"Brr!" she said with a shiver. "This place gives me goose pimples!"

"Me too!" Rose said.

They clung together filled with a vague apprehension. Almost without thinking, Rose placed little kisses on the milky-white skin of Marie's neck.

They had stopped in front of a huge fireplace on one side of the vault, rounded at the top like a seashell. The side of the mantel rested against a low *potager* nicely lined with big red glazed tiles. A strange instrument with claw feet used for heating stood on the tiles. Deep cracks scarred its surface, revealing the stark white fireproof lining. It looked at though it might have exploded long ago. It had been cold for ages. A kind of copper still eaten with verdigris sat in pride of place above it.

"It's an alchemist's athanor," Rose said.

"A what?"

"An athanor. Patrice told me."

"And what's an athanor?"

"Heavens! I don't really know. Patrice didn't tell me anything more. He shrugged his shoulders as he said the word."

Marie stared at this skeleton of a hearth, the pupils in her shrewd blue eyes reduced to pin-points.

"Perhaps he was mistaken," she said.

She felt a slight breath of air about her body. She could never say what it reminded her of, but an idea suddenly came into her mind. At first she thought it was mad, but it took root quickly and deeply. The more she struggled against it, the more it encircled and bound her, dazzling her with its obvious logic.

"The war will never come looking for them here!" she exclaimed.

"What do you mean?"

"My children! If I shut them up here, the war will never reach them!"

Rose shook her head.

"There are times when I wonder if you're not a bit mad!"

"Why? Because I don't want my sons to go to war?"

She took Rose's hands between her own.

"Will you help me?"

"You know very well that I always do whatever you want."

She put her arm around her friend's waist and led her out of the strange place. Marie had got over her fears and now saw it as an impenetrable refuge.

"But Marie," Rose continued gently as they went up the stairs, "are you seriously thinking of shutting your sons up in here?"

"Yes," Marie replied firmly.

"Do you realize that they'll hate you for it? That they'll never forgive you?"

Marie stopped in the middle of the step and gripped the handrail. Rose heard her nostrils quiver like a horse about to take an obstacle. She nodded in agreement with what Rose had just said.

"Never! Do you think I haven't turned it over in my mind? I think of it every night. I say to myself, 'If you manage to stop them from going to war, they'll never forgive you!'"

"You won't be able to bear it. You're their mother!"

"I will bear it," Marie said. "I didn't have them for myself but for them. They must stay alive. Even in spite of themselves. Haven't you noticed how desperately France needs casualties at the moment? They won't stop getting people killed until they reach the 1914 numbers on the monument!"

"You sound like Antoine."

"Antoine?"

"Antoine. My overseer. One of Patrice's friends. I don't know what I'd do without him."

"Is he your lover?"

"No," Rose said. "Not even he. I'd have to want it, and you know that's not what I want."

"A pity," Marie replied. "You'll wither away."

"Come on Saturday," Rose said. "He'll be here then. You can talk to him. He's a man you can trust completely."

Marie put her hand over her mouth as she exclaimed,

"Good heavens! What about the Jew! I'd forgotten him completely with all this!"

"Bring him," Rose said. "I'll do what I can."

"You know what you're risking if he were found here?"

"You know what I'm risking if I keep your sons?"

"Rose!" Marie said, giving her a hug. "I'd never forgive myself if anything happened to you because of me!"

"Nothing will happen, Marie. You keep forgetting the most important thing."

"What?" Marie asked.

She stood back from her friend and looked into her eyes.

"Séraphin . . ." Rose whispered. "You keep forgetting. You forget he's watching over us."

Marie turned her head away. All her solid good sense made her shy away from considering the implication of what Rose had said. She wanted to forget; she didn't want to believe. The beneficent aspect of Séraphin's protection, such as Rose imagined it, was a much more frightening threat hanging over Marie's life, taking everything into account, than all the wars in the world.

"Bring your Jew along," Rose said once again. "He'll be safe here. The farmer listens to London on the wireless and no-one ever comes near us."

"We can hardly have him marching along the highways and byways," Marie pointed out. "Is it possible to get across the ford?"

"He must have been travelling for some time. The water has risen during the storms."

"Too bad! He'll just have to get the bottom of his trousers a bit wet."

It's more than fifteen kilometres from Lurs to Pontradieu by the bridge at Les Mées or the one at Oraison, but if you know the ford over the Durance, at low water it's only a bare hour's walk.

And so, one fine night Marie took a lantern and accompanied the Jew to Pontradieu via the ford. He was a small scrawny man who hardly weighed fifty kilos and wore glasses. He was as delightfully enthusiastic about things as a teenager, and besides, Ismaël never left his side. They talked together for hours. German phrases would suddenly come out of his mouth, spoken with such fervour that Marie became quite alarmed.

"Why are you speaking German," she asked him, "since they want to exterminate your race?"

"Unfortunately yes, Madame. I can't help it if these people have provided the most beautiful music in the world."

"They're a country of slaves," Marie retorted. "I hope they all die in Russia. They despise us because we don't like war, while they should despise themselves for liking it so much."

"I'm afraid judgments about races and peoples are more complex and need to be qualified," the Jew said quietly.

"Well, I'm not complex," Marie said. "I hope they all die in Russia. I'd never go to Germany, even if I was forced to. I'd rather kill myself! They only had to stay out of our country. It's a good thing if the Americans flatten them with bombs. And you more than anyone should be ashamed to speak their language!"

"But Madame, I'm only showing your son the titles of the works he's playing. Beethoven, Schumann, Mozart! I can't help it if they spoke German."

"Don't worry," Ismaël said to his friend. "My mother is immovable! Especially when she has decided not to understand!"

On the night she took the Jew to Pontradieu, Marie was in a very good mood as she crossed the ford carrying his light suitcase. They paddled through the water, stumbling on the large pebbles. Ismaël kept a tight hold on his friend's hand and sometimes supported him under the armpits when the bottom was too slippery. They arrived at Pontradieu at about three o'clock in the morning.

Rose was waiting for them. She hadn't seen Ismaël for a long time. She couldn't bridge the gap in her memory separating the four-year-old blind boy she had lifted up from the steps of the tomb and the adolescent who was taller than her, standing there as if changed into a pillar of salt by her presence. He must have gone through many stages and shed a lot of skins to finally emerge shining and new at the threshold of manhood. Even his eyes seemed new. Rose remembered him as a lad with a lot of reddish hair; now he had a curved forehead and his hair was black and unruly. He had been a pink, chubby-cheeked boy and he now had the gaunt, hollow cheeks of an adult in turmoil.

When she gave him her hand to shake she had the impression that for some unknown reason he would never give it back to her. Marie always dressed him in black velvet and white shirts with wide, open collars. This was her idea of how a pianist should look. Almost without knowing it, she had slowly come to prefer him to the two others, to believe that he was more her son, and to find consolation in him.

Ismaël had not let go of Rose's hand because he had just caught sight of Charmaine's piano in the dim light at the back of the drawing room. Rose had had it brought there as an ornamental piece of furniture and had placed a large vase on it filled with flowers which she constantly renewed. That evening Ismaël had eyes for nothing but Rose and the piano. As it was three in the morning and everyone was speaking very quietly, he dared not open the lid and sit down, but he stroked it like a cat. Rose watched the way his hands slid over the polished wood, which reflected them.

"You may come and play as often as you wish," she said.

"What!" Marie said. "Are you being formal with him now?"

"Oh!" Rose exclaimed. "I'm sorry! I see him so rarely and he's changed such a lot."

How could she tell her that there was nothing in common between Marie's little son and the young man standing before her, and that the profound mystery she sensed in this new person was at least as intense as the one she had witnessed the day he regained his sight?

"He'll come three times a week," Marie said. "If that's all right with you," she added. "He can't do without his teacher any more."

"That's overstating it a little," the Jew said.

"No," Marie replied. "I'm as ignorant about music as I am about everything else, but I do realize that your lessons are worth much more than the board and lodging we give you."

She walked around Charmaine's piano, inspecting it suspiciously. Perhaps it was because of it that Séraphin had seemed to prefer this rich man's daughter, with all her make-up, to her.

"He'll never want to play on his own piano again!" she complained.

"Madame," the Jew said, "your son is worthy of instruments of this calibre and even much better ones. You mustn't hold it against him."

"Maman!" Ismaël exclaimed. "You know that . . ."

He threw his arms around Marie's neck. He still retained some childlike gestures, which he did not actually possess as a child. This spontaneity rather offended Rose. It forced her to go back down a track she thought had vanished between herself and Ismaël. It forced her to take account of the fact that the child in him was still quite close.

Marie quickly and firmly removed him.

"That's enough!" she said. "I know: yours is nicer because I gave it to you! Although you didn't say anything when your teacher told me that it was tinny!"

She laughed in spite of herself. Ismaël laughed, so did Rose, and the Jew himself joined in. It was past three o'clock in the morning and they were laughing happily, light-heartedly at Pontradieu, as if the war did not exist, as if men were not hunting down others.

And yet the war was drawing closer to us as summer approached. Its waves washed closer and closer to Lurs and our peaceful lives. It would suddenly appear somewhere around us in muffled calls and discreet whistles. Sometimes through open windows we could briefly catch the blaring words from wirelesses badly tuned to the French broadcast on the BBC: "*Ici Londres. Les Français parlent aux Français.*" Old men would come knocking on the shutters of young men's houses, "Get going! 'They' are coming this way!"

The news we got was sometimes true, sometimes false. And night after night at first, then both day and night, we had the incessant droning noise above us, drilling through our skulls. It was the carpet of planes going over the Alps. They flew at 4000 metres altitude and we couldn't see them, ever, but that didn't stop us from automatically scanning the sky. Their din blocked out all other sounds for miles around. Sometimes when we were on the rampart or in our still shamefully soft beds – as if by some divine plan time had passed us by – we thought we could hear the carpet of bombs which would eventually fall from the carpet of planes, even though we knew it was impossible. We were well aware that the noise originating 300 or 400 kilometres away corresponded exactly with the image of people with their bodies ripped open in dark streets, crushed under rubble or with their flesh splashed live like a star over soft beds like ours.

We said to each other, "They must be getting the worst of it!" thinking of our enemies. But these comments between husbands and wives were never made with any joy or triumph. Not everyone could have the luck to be defeated first, we said.

Occasionally the song of the frogs was interrupted by a salvo of shots in the distance. It was three or four rebels who had joined the maquis, who were badly advised by old men too impatient to see them do battle. They had foolishly got caught in some dead-end and were shot on the spot without any other form of trial.

We sometimes heard a single shot much closer to home. Early next morning on the side of some minor road, someone would find the body of a well-dressed, prosperous and highly respected person of note, whose funeral we dared not attend as the funeral oration always ended in a deafening silence. The death notice always appeared with the words: *lâchement assassiné* – killed by cowards.

That was our own war. We hardly had to worry about it provided we were poor and had no passions or principles.

But this was not Marie's case: she lived in a state of anxiety. Ange, the eldest, would be eighteen in two months and could do what he liked, in other words he could join the Legion of volunteers against Bolshevism. He talked of nothing else. As for Bertrand, already two or three workers from the factory who carried briefcases like notaries had come in a delegation to tell him off, "Well, what are you waiting for?" Marie had received them with some very sharp words. They had threatened her, "You be careful, Marie. From now on, all those who aren't with us are against us!"

It was then she made her move.

"Are you quite sure?" Rose asked.

"Yes," Marie said. "I don't want my sons' lives to be sacrificed for the country's future."

"This is Antoine Maujac," Rose told Marie that evening. "You can tell him anything."

Marie stood there unable to say anything. Luckily he came to her aid.

"I think as you do about the war. You want to hide your sons?"

"Yes," Marie replied, "but they don't want to."

She stared at this tall, slim man with the sad, thin face, who never said an unnecessary word. "Oh," she thought. "To be able to rely on somebody!"

They dined together: Rose, Antoine, the Jew and Marie, who had brought a bag of millet biscuits to supplement the fare. She had a private word to Rose in the bathroom.

"Rose! Will you swear to me that he's not your lover?"

"No," Rose said. "I don't need to swear on that account."

"All right! Too bad!"

"What do you mean: too bad?"

"Oh!" Marie replied. "Too bad all round! Propriety, morality, Hell, everything! I want him!"

"Well! You certainly don't waste any time, do you?" Rose said in tones of admiration.

Marie belonged to no-one, but she surrendered to Antoine on the spot, without thinking, almost without breathing. She amazed him with her sexual frenzy. He loved her, but she told him,

"It's not you I love! You mustn't believe that. It's love itself. I've only loved one man in my life and I never made love with him!"

"Séraphin?" Antoine asked.

"How did you know that?"

"Rose . . ." he said.

"I know. She loved him too, but he didn't love her. I'm the one he loved! Madly," she added, blushing slightly.

"I've seen his bones," Antoine said pensively. "I weighed them in my hands."

"And yet," Marie whispered, "if you only knew . . . Was he a man?"

"Marie, have you ever seen anyone who wasn't a man fill a whole sack with his bones?"

"Have you ever seen a sack of bones restore sight to someone who was blind?"

"Let's make love, Marie, and talk no more of that, or we'll have a quarrel."

She filled his mouth with her tongue to stop him from saying anything further. She gave in like a coward. She wanted to be faithful to Séraphin but she didn't want to lose her lover either.

Within a month, Antoine Maujac had done marvels with the crypt at Pontradieu. Using wooden partitions, he set up a comfortable studio flat with a double bed, reading lamps, books, records and a carpet. He brought in a wireless set and camouflaged the antenna.

"Two!" Marie said, "You need two sets! They each listen to their own nonsense!"

Antoine nodded his head, fearing the worst.

"They'll tear each other to pieces, just the two of them alone together."

"No. One night I'll bring you here while they're sleeping. They don't share the same ideas but they hold each other by the hand when they're sleeping."

"They'll knock you out and get away when you bring them their food."

Marie drew herself up to her full height.

"I'm their mother!" she declared. "I'll knock their blocks off if they dare raise their hands to me! They're sure of that, believe me!"

Antoine was fired with enthusiasm by this woman with the angry eyes who literally wrung his neck when she climaxed in his arms. He worked with a will, assisted by the Jew, who worshipped Marie.

When everything was in place Marie secretly packed two suitcases. She sent them to Pontradieu by the bus, now fitted with a gas-generator, which made deliveries when it could. Then one day she announced to her two eldest,

"We're having supper at your godmother's this evening. Make yourselves look a bit respectable."

"At godmother's? But there are loads of roadblocks on the bridges!"

"Don't worry about that. The water level is down. We'll go over by the ford. It'll be dark by nine o'clock."

"I'd advise you to eat in your room," Rose said to the Jew. "It's best if the eldest boy doesn't see you."

"But since you're going to lock him up . . ."

"Do *you* think it will work? Before a fortnight's out, they'll charge right over her when she brings them their food!"

She had already asked Marie,

"How will you go about shutting them in?"

"I'll drug their food. With some valerian. Or else . . . Perhaps we should open one or two of your bottles."

"Do you think they like wine?"

"I don't know, but they'll like yours."

And indeed, they were drunk as lords when they were brought down to the crypt, not without some difficulty. Marie, Rose, Antoine and the Jew had a terrible time getting them down the stairs to the cellar. When they got there, the boys were so captivated by the wine they had tasted that they kept reaching out their hands towards all the bottles in the racks.

"My bullyboys!" Marie said. "We'll give you some Saint Estèphe 1921!"

When they were finally laid on the bed that Rose had made up with her own monogrammed sheets, Marie stood looking at them for some time.

"Leave me with them," she said.

"Alone?"

"Yes. Surely you don't imagine that I'd leave them like that? They'll sleep now, and tomorrow I'll explain everything to them."

"I'll stay with you," Antoine said.

"No. This is a mother's work. If you stay, we'll make love. I'll watch over them as I used to do when they were sick. I owe this night to them. Don't think it gives me any joy to deprive them of their freedom."

He was the last to leave. He took her hands and looked deep into her eyes.

"I admire you, Marie," he said.

At first the two boys were so stunned that they resigned themselves to the situation, but Marie had their curses ringing in her ears by the time she left Pontradieu the next evening. After three hours of discussion, she had definitely not won the battle of words. Her arguments in favour of life and love did not sound strong: life to be preserved so that they could know its pleasures and experience love. They talked of the motherland, of ideals. They were only words they had learned and repeated, but the principles they put forward trumpeted their eternal worth so loudly that Marie could only shrink before them with shame for her selfishness.

"We'll escape!" they promised. "We'll never see you again! You're not our mother any more!"

Marie went to the tomb and knelt down. She wrung her hands in despair.

"I'm alone, Séraphin! All alone. I may look strong, but I feel as weak inside as I did when I was four years old and didn't know if what I was doing was right or wrong."

The cypresses around the chapel, which were beginning to grow tall, murmured their consolation above Marie's head, but there was no reply on this earth for those trying to find out where to look for the good, and whether it was better than the bad.

The following day she proclaimed the following story loud and long,

"They made me sweat blood! Two strapping lads like that are too much for a woman on her own. I've sent them to boarding school at the Timon-David

Brothers' College at La Viste in Marseilles. They'll find out what discipline is really like there!"

"But they'll soon be back for the holidays," the neighbouring women pointed out smarmily.

"No. At the Timon-David College they keep the difficult ones for the whole year! They're not unhappy. There's a big meadow behind the establishment and they're helping with the hay."

"You're too hard on your youngsters!" Clorinde moaned.

"No!" Marie replied. "They're too hard on me!"

She lived in a state of anxiety. She filled flour sacks with provisions and at three o'clock in the morning she carried them on her shoulder all the way to Pontradieu by way of the ford. She also had to find another crossing, as the Germans were not the only ones tracking down young men.

The chief recruiter who had been hanging around Bertrand had come in through the bead curtain three times.

"Bertrand's still not here?"

"I told you that I sent him to the Timon-David Brothers."

"Right! But if your next allocation of flour is confiscated, you'll only have yourself to blame!"

"I make you 100 kilos of free bread a week. Isn't that enough?"

"From flour we provide for you!"

"What of it? How about the baker? Do you pay the baker, eh?"

"Anyway, Bertrand wanted to come with us, and you're the one preventing him! We'll remember that!"

She had to evade their traps, change her routine, take the provisions in small quantities to her godmother at the Phare du Soleil, then pick it up later. She lost five kilos in weight.

"Your bottom's getting thin!" Antoine lamented on the rare occasions when they could meet in a thicket by the side of Ganagobie. They made love on a bed of pine needles beneath the singing branches of the peaceful pine forest. For two or three hours they could believe it was peacetime.

The men of the maquis, however, were not the greatest danger Marie had to face. One day she saw a young girl on a white bicycle coming up the steep road to Lurs from the chapel. She found the hill hard going and had to finish the last part on foot, pushing the bike.

Marie watched her approaching the bakery with a strange feeling of apprehension. And yet there was nothing disturbing about her. With her pleated skirt, lace gloves and little cape, she looked like a film star. She had beautiful blue eyes and a fair complexion. She was delicately dabbing her brow under her blonde hair. She said "Bonjour madame" politely and asked if she could come in. Marie held back the bead curtain for her.

"I'm Stéphanie Aumusse," she announced.

"I know," Marie said.

Ange had described her in such loving detail that she had recognized her immediately.

"My father has made enquiries," Stéphanie said still dabbing her temples. "Your two sons are not enrolled at the Timon-David de la Viste college. I don't care about the younger one, but Ange is one of us. He must do his duty. You cannot and must not prevent him."

"Heavens! I certainly did the right thing!" Marie thought. "And he'd be better off dying in the war than marrying this leech!" She stared at this girl so fair her flesh was almost translucent, but who held her gaze. How could someone look the rosy picture of a poppy in a field of corn and yet be so hideous on the inside?

"If you don't want to find yourself in serious trouble," Stéphanie said, "you'd do well to tell me where he is before . . ."

"Before what?" Marie said haughtily.

"We can make you tell us where they are."

The girl was no longer looking at Marie as she said these words; her eyes were vacantly turned towards the Post Office calendar. She had taken of her gloves and was slapping one against the other as she spoke.

"You know," Marie said, without raising her voice either, "there are tougher ones than you to be found under bramble bushes these days."

They silently sized each other up for at least a minute, the bright-eyed young girl and Marie, who already had a few silver threads in her thick head of hair. Marie noticed Stéphanie's slender neck. "If I put my hands around it," she thought, "not a soul in the world could help her. I'd shut her up in five seconds flat!"

"Think it over," the young visitor said. "Think of all the means at our disposal. I'll come back in a week and I shall expect Ange to be here."

She put her gloves on again and said with a smile while straightening her hat,

"Do you know that you might be my mother-in-law?"

She turned on her heels, then lightly and gracefully got on her bike. Marie ran to the ramparts to watch her departing.

That same evening, a distraught Marie spoke to Antoine about the meeting.

"Hold on!" he said. "Don't worry! I'll warn the person who needs to be contacted and say what needs to be said."

Marie immediately sprang out of his arms as though she had been stung.

"What? You? You're involved with those people?"

"Let me explain. There are several different groups."

"And you're part of one?"

"Yes," Antoine admitted hanging his head. "That's one of the reasons why I can't see you often. I'm in charge of a transmitter, parachuting weapons, and well . . . Like everyone else . . ."

"You're risking your life," Marie said.

"No more than anyone else."

"You! You dodged the war in 1914! And now, when no-one has asked anything of you, you decide to join the fight!"

"It's not the same this time," Antoine said seriously. "Despite the language, our lightness and their heaviness, despite the brainwashing, there was not such a great difference between the French and the Germans in 1914. We killed each other, for nothing really, but we could still respect one another. Not this time. They have blood on their hands; their leaders are madmen. Oh! I'll admit it's the bankers who lead our side. But at least we can get something out of them! But madmen? What can you discuss with madmen? They must be destroyed, that's all there is to it!"

"But if you're one of them, how can you accept me hiding my sons away?"

"Because I love you."

He was stroking her hands to calm her down, as he would have done with a frightened animal, but to no avail; she was staring at him, full of mistrust. He was no longer her friend. They didn't make love that evening. The war had come between them. It even invaded the humble carpet of pine needles in the forest by Ganagobie, even though the breeze still sang softly through the trees as if people did not even exist.

Antoine only knew Marie well up to the waist. He didn't know what she hid up above in her head. If he had, he would not have triumphantly shown her, less than a week later, the death notice cut out of the regional newspaper: ". . . have the sad duty to announce the death of Mademoiselle Stéphanie Aumusse, *lâchement assassinée.*"

For the girl with the blonde hair and fair skin did not live to see the end of summer. At the June solstice she was discovered in a channel near Savels with her neck broken. Her father the chemist lived to an advanced age. Accused of collaboration, deprived of citizenship rights and living in a two-roomed flat, he had all the time in the world to think about the dead girl, who had also been heroic but never had her name on any monument.

Marie buried her face in her hands.

"Good heavens!" she said. "I'm the one who ordered this atrocity!"

"No!" Antoine said. "I didn't have time to speak to anyone about it. She had other denunciations on her conscience."

He wanted to take her in his arms to calm her.

"Leave me alone!" Marie cried. "Don't touch me! I suddenly feel I'm getting old!"

And yet this chain of events and all the care she had taken would not have been enough to save Marie's sons from themselves had it not been for love.

By the end of three days clinging to the bars of the basement window, Ange and Bertrand were already beginning to develop the convict spirit. The small window was large enough to slip through feet first, then raise the arms high to get the shoulders out; anyway, if they placed themselves diagonally . . . anyway it was worth a try.

"You hold me up and push me," Bertrand said, "and once I'm outside, I'll pull you out."

"Yes," Ange said, "but first we have to saw the bars."

It was not so long ago that they were reading comics in which sawing through prison bars was child's play. They gripped those that Antoine had installed. They were hand-forged and rough, twice as thick as the boys' thumbs. As a precaution Marie had given them the tin forks and silver knives used for weddings. They were rounded and blunt, as they had never been sharpened. The boys were beginning to wonder what they could use to make files. They had also thought of overpowering Marie when she brought their meals, but a mixture of respect, love and fear still held them back. Prison hadn't hardened them enough.

Not being great readers or record lovers, they spent most of their time dreaming of their escape, kneeling side by side on the bed, clinging to the bars on the window.

It so happened that the hot summer arrived early that year. The temperature was quite bearable in the crypt, but outside it was becoming very humid. The leaves on the plane trees hung down like still, green, doleful bats. The great pond was like a mirror on which the swans drifted with their heads under their wings.

One afternoon when the air was so hot and heavy that they had even forgotten the war and their sad plight, the boys were dozing, a newspaper over their faces to keep away the flies, and their hands joined as usual. Then they heard a jumble of words in the distance threaded with the sound of laughter coming closer, bursting out just in front of their window, together with hurried footsteps scattering the gravel.

"Jeanne!" cried a shrill voice. "Are you coming or aren't you?"

"I'm coming!"

The boys leaped up at the same time and pressed their faces to the bars. They saw two girls in black smocks holding each other by the hand and talking about the pond. They had their backs turned to the window.

"It must be cold!"

"Just a dip."

"You know we're not allowed to!"

"Too bad! It's too hot! The lady won't eat us! She's never said anything to us."

"The lady, no. But what about papa?"

"They're both in the fields. Make up your mind, Rirette."

Then something incredible happened right in front of the teenage boys. They had never seen anything like it in their lives. The two girls raised their arms and began to undo the top of their smocks, which buttoned behind. At the fourth button a wiggle of the shoulders freed the top of their bodies, then the whole torso. They were wearing little girls' cotton knickers. They were unbuttoned with the same graceful gesture and slid down to their ankles.

"Gosh!" said the boys, holding their breath.

When they first saw them, they thought they were very young girls, but now that they were naked the boys could see that they were their age.

The vision didn't last long. They held their noses and jumped into the pool. They came up to the surface again letting out loud, piercing cries.

"You're mad getting me to swim in this icy water!"

"Move yourself! Hey! Let's swim after the swans!"

The birds stood up to them, looking threatening, extending their necks and ruffling their feathers. The girls squealed madly then dived with their legs out of the water and their bottoms bobbing before they sank down and two plump faces reappeared. Sometimes one of them managed to grab on to a swan. She put her arms around its neck while it tried to escape with a great beating of wings. Sometimes they managed to squeeze the strong neck of a fleeing bird between their small, high breasts. The swans would unfold their enormous wings and for a moment pull the girls' naked bodies with their buttocks tensed right out of the water. Then they let go. Then the angry swans would chase them, pecking at their shoulders, and the air would be filled with the hissing of the birds and the squealing of the naiads.

In the course of their whole lives, Marie's sons rarely received a gift as rich and rare as this delightful vision through their prison window during that horrible summer.

They came at the same time each day. Each day they got out of their smocks with the same movements and plunged into the pool to take on the swans. The birds gave them no quarter. It became rarer and rarer for the two girls to succeed in imprisoning the long swans' necks between their firm breasts. When one of them managed to do it, the boys could see that their eyes were shut and there was a little smile of secret bliss on their faces.

"Shall we call out to them?" Ange said.

"No! Don't do that! We'll never see them again!"

They fell asleep with a painful erection from knowing desire and not being able to satisfy it. They lived only for that time between three and five in the afternoon, when the two playful, squealing girls appeared and jumped into the water together. The boys were warned of their arrival a good half-hour in advance by the trumpeting swans that suddenly became agitated and beat the surface of the water with their wings as a warning.

But the two girls were not afraid of them. They pretended to shriek with terror but still threw themselves into this bizarre confrontation with the huge birds. The lightest of the swans must have weighed a good fifteen kilos. The two boys in their hidden room could hear the strange panting of the two naiads in the course of the battle.

The swans would sometimes make a sudden dive underneath them, lift them up and toss them over. Their legs would part and their little feet thrashed the air. Their behinds were pert and pink. For the two prisoners, it was pure intoxication. Suddenly the girls had enough and, pursued by the swans pecking at their buttocks, they swam to the edge and jumped up on to the wide marble rim where Gaspard Dupin had taken his last walk. They were as firm and lithe as fish, anointed by the sun and gleaming in the summer heat. Their eyes, their baby faces with their bonny round cheeks, were hidden by the strands of their hair. When they walked briskly towards their clothes, right in front of the boys at their ground-level window, the lads could see the tight curls on their plump pubis and their hermetically sealed genitals.

Bertrand and Ange hardly spoke to each other and no longer fought. At night, when their hands automatically moved to join, as they had done all their lives, they quickly withdrew them as though they had touched red-hot iron.

"What arses they've got!"

"Oh, yes!" Bertrand fervently agreed.

Their cocks throbbed against their stomachs. They no longer even bothered to turn on the wireless. Their principles had faded away, their condemnation of their mother had disappeared. Eternity could yawn before them provided that every day between three and five, the two daughters of the farmer at Pontradieu came and did naked battle with the swans. What could the war offer compared with such joys?

One morning the two boys woke later than usual because the sun had not risen. They rushed to the window before even thinking of making their coffee on the little stove Antoine had installed. They could see the sky through the opening. They saw the poplars and the aspens, their leaves blown by the east wind. Further away towards Lurs and the Durance, the black clouds on the horizon hung heavily over the invisible hills. The storm broke at about two o'clock, and the rain flooded down. Occasionally it seemed to pause for a quarter of an hour, then it started up again. The two boys clung to the bars, full of dismay. They kept their eyes on the pool and the wide space in front of it, the playground of their joyful nymphs. The happy swans spread their wings and surrendered to the pouring rain, which deloused them. The tips of their tails quivered with pleasure. They noisily trumpeted their feeling of well-being, quite indifferent to the lightning that sometimes rent the air around them and bounced off the marble rim in blinding flashes.

When evening fell, you could hear the Durance flowing swiftly over the full width of its bed, making the ford give way. Then there was only the one growling sound made up of the rushing water and the planes 4000 metres up where the sky was clear. The thunder had ceased and the rain was merely heavy.

"They won't come any more," Bertrand said miserably.

They collapsed on their bed, worn out from having anxiously waited for a whole day during which they hadn't given a single thought to having something to eat, despite their normally huge appetites.

And, just as if the storm had the power to make reality disappear like a dream, and the naked girls with their shrill laughter had never existed, when the two dejected boys were on the point of falling asleep, their hands sought and gripped each other for consolation.

X

WHEN ISMAËL SAT DOWN AT THE PIANO, ROSE WOULD STOP WHATEVER she was doing, tiptoe in silently and settle into some armchair hidden by a curtain in the window recess so that she would not be seen.

He would play for hours, in another world, lost in the contemplation of a mystery that continually filled him with wonder and became his real world. When he sometimes stumbled over a difficult passage that he had not yet mastered because he had not thought about it first – no doubt because of his youth – he would crack the joints of his fingers with anger. He would repeat it once, ten times until he had thought it through and it flowed naturally.

"Don't get excited!" the Jew always told him. "Keep thinking of your tempo! The tempo, that's the most important thing. Don't forget that no-one has yet found Mozart's true tempo!"

Rose listened religiously, with hands clasped, leaning forward without moving.

Sometimes a droning sound would suddenly come up over the horizon above the château, rolling on, buzzing like a swarm of angry bees. It would soon absorb the music and eventually silence it altogether. The music disappeared humbly, slowly becoming inaudible. Then Ismaël resigned himself and stopped playing. He waited with head down for it to finish. The Jew hunched on the divan listened to the noise with his eyes raised to the ceiling.

"The wrath of God!" he said.

It passed us by; it was for others over there beyond the mountains. Death at that distance made no noise. It was more like a statistic, losing its meaning and no longer touching the heart.

Here everything was peaceful. Ismaël had often glimpsed Rose's shadow as she discreetly hid herself in the dark corners of the drawing room to listen. It was no doubt during these hours that he acquired something of what he had been lacking until then, and what took him ten years to recapture calmly later so that he could communicate it to those who listened to him. The Jew knew that Rose was there without seeing her, simply from Ismaël's playing, which became radiant or richly sombre. The adolescent boy was confessing his love through his fingers. He never knew nor ever asked whether Rose sometimes had tears in her eyes as she listened to him on those days, for they had so little time and the silence between them was consumed with activity.

At about midday on the day of the story that so distressed his brothers, Ismaël arrived at Pontradieu via the ford, as he usually did three times a week on Marie's orders. The water level was low. It hadn't rained in the whole of the Durance basin for months, but on that day the sky was black and rumbling from one side of the valley to the other. You couldn't make out the outline of a single cloud as they flowed in one single stream across the sky.

Ismaël always felt a secret joy whenever he arrived in that park. He knew he would have Rose as an audience, and the feeling was like coming back home of an evening. He took the sighing of the trees that greeted him as a friendly blessing. The chandeliers were lit in the drawing room as if evening had already closed in. Rose's fleeting shadow sometimes appeared behind the windows as she went about one task or another.

Ismaël stood for some time at a distance watching the spectacle of the château beneath the looming storm. One of its corners had a fissure like a gash, inflicted a long time ago by a bolt of lightning. Later in his life, on stormy evenings, Ismaël would light a candle on the corner of his piano, in memory of that day. He would then turn out the lights and ask people to talk very quietly. He would see again the park at Pontradieu and the gash at the corner of the château. He would see Rose's shadow passing back and forth behind the big casement windows.

If the person with whom he briefly shared his life asked him on those occasions,

"What are you thinking about?"

He would reply, "Nothing."

"Tell me the truth. Are you afraid of storms?"

"No, I like them."

He would ask to be left alone. Then he would play by candlelight. He always played the same thing. He was playing for himself alone. And for the dark. For on that day at Pontradieu, either he had chosen inner solitude or it had been imposed on him.

Destiny's warnings must be loud and clear, so the storm took some time to gather over Pontradieu and the valley. A dull rumbling could be heard for hours. Nevertheless, it didn't prevent the carpet of planes rolling out above it and even drowning it out three times during the course of the day. They sounded heavy and angry as they passed over from west to east, but almost light-hearted when they came back, at least that's what the lighter droning of their engines clearly suggested.

The Jew was sitting hunched in his armchair. He was listening. He was listening to the storm and to the planes. He was listening to Ismaël playing the *Appassionata*, whenever the noise outside permitted, and thinking that, ignorant as she was about music, even Rose could not fail to understand the declaration Ismaël was making to her through his playing.

It suddenly began to rain with the alarming noise of a deluge that kept rising in a crescendo but never reached its climax. At about six o'clock, the roaring of the Durance added to the threatening noises outside.

"You won't be able to get back across the ford," the Jew said.

"I won't be able to get back across the ford . . ." Ismaël thought, his heart pounding.

He looked around the room for Rose, who was standing in front of a window, pretending to watch the rain falling. Her right hand was placed against the curtain. As she was standing with her back to him, Ismaël took the opportunity to admire her to his heart's content. At thirty-eight Rose was in full bloom like a dahlia and at the height of her beauty. She was enough to send a fifteen-year-old boy into a state of panic.

"You won't be able to cross the ford," the Jew said once again. "Madame Rose, he'll have to stay here."

"Yes," Rose said. "He'll stay. There are plenty of bedrooms here."

She drew the curtains at four windows, one after the other. Ismaël had stopped playing. This was the time when he usually went back to Lurs over the ford, happily climbing up to the village, completely forgetting the war. His surly mother would greet him with some rather rough token of affection, and his grandmother, who always smelled of bread, kissed him with endless lamentations of "my poor boy".

Now that night had fallen, it was difficult to make out which of the sounds from outside came from the storm, the droning of the squadrons or the rumbling of the Durance whose waters were rising higher and higher. All one could do was listen anxiously.

"I need a drink!" Rose said.

She got up from her chair and went to the cabinet where she kept the liquor.

"What with this storm and the war, I must have a drink! You don't drink, do you?"

"Never," the Jew said. "Only water, as you know."

He had just finished speaking when the electricity was cut off. The three of them found themselves in total darkness. One minute, two minutes went by as they waited in silence. Outside the walls of Pontradieu that evening the world was a hostile place, but inside, Ismaël was filled with the expectation of happiness.

Rose, who was standing in front of the cabinet when the room was plunged into darkness, remained there hardly daring to breathe. "Heavens!" she thought. "He won't be able to play any more! I must find him a candlestick. I wanted him to play for me all night! I'm so much alone! I shouldn't be left alone like that!"

Hearing Ismaël playing on Charmaine's piano had become her whole life in just a few days. When he arrived and knocked at the door, the Jew would say,

"Well now, there's your boyfriend."

"Oh! How can you say that? I'm old enough to be his mother."

"Exactly," the Jew replied.

This conversation never went any further, because Rose would immediately stand up. She hurried away and flung open the door, just as she used to do for Patrice before she saw him as he really was. She had to stop herself from bobbing a comic maid's curtsey to Ismaël as she also used to do for Patrice. She didn't give a name to this rush of feeling; at most she imagined that the music consoled her for being the poor creature she was. But when he sat at the piano for hours, she did nothing but listen to him. She never said a word or complimented him on his playing. She felt too humble to say anything.

"Love needs a helping hand," the Jew thought with a sigh. He also longed for someone to hold his hand on such a night, and yet he made his way to the staircase through the streaks of lightning that lit up the intricate wrought iron banister. He crept away to his room and quietly shut the door.

"Ismaël," Rose said.

She had put everything she dared not admit to herself into that call, perhaps because she could only see the youth in bursts of lightning.

"I'm here, Madame," he said.

Like Rose he had noticed that the old Jew's chair was empty. He stood up and made his way towards her almost like a robot, stumbling against the divan.

"Stay there!" Rose said. "There must be a lamp here somewhere. I would like . . . Well, I would like . . . Could you continue playing?"

Ten seconds went by while she swallowed before adding,

" . . . for me."

It seemed to him that she was a long way off as she explained,

"It calms me when you play."

Violent claps of thunder now rent the air around Pontradieu. When they crashed, the continual growl of the Durance and the droning of the planes passing overhead could no longer be heard. The lightning streaked through the darkness in the drawing room time and time again. Rose had just discovered a kerosene lamp on a desk and placed it on the piano.

Ismaël once again found himself walking towards Rose. He had no control over it; all he could feel was a quivering deep inside and a dryness in his mouth, as though he had been terrified by something. Walking towards Rose was an action. Now he was well aware that the reason he could sometimes make his fingers produce wonderful sounds in music was because he was not cut out to be a man of action. Action filled his heart with panic, even if that act would bring happiness. He was never more relieved than when he had failed in doing something. Each time he gave up, he brought the bitter fruit of his failure to the piano. For him it was always a catalyst in his search for perfection.

And so that night he held his arms out in front of him in the wild hope that they would meet nothing but empty space, and therefore nothing new would happen to him. He did indeed encounter nothing but empty space, to his great relief. But then the perfume of mock-orange wafted through the darkness. It grew in profusion in the park, where Rose brushed against it so often that its perfume pervaded her. Here in the darkness it found a place in Ismaël's heart, where it would dwell for years to come.

"Don't light the lamp!" he asked her.

They spoke softly as if they were not alone, as if there were a secret they shared and no-one else could hear, and, as if the storm wanted to help them, for a time there were no more flashes of lightning. They were surrounded by total darkness with only the perfume of mock-orange to guide Ismaël to Rose.

"Are you afraid of the storm?" he whispered.

She replied just as quietly.

"Not usually, but tonight I am."

"Can I do anything for you?"

"Yes," she said.

He felt Rose timidly place her hand on his forearm. She had found him in spite of the blackness and, since he had made the effort to come to her, she found it quite natural to reward him with that touch.

"I love you, Madame," Ismaël said.

Naturally he meant "I want you", but at that age the border between the two is still uncertain. It was Rose who put it right.

"It should be very simple," she said.

Rose cried out for the first time in her life on that stormy night, because what overwhelmed her was as gripping and heart-rending as a burst of pain. She had felt this sensation only once when she dreamed that she was making love with Séraphin. But when she cried out then, it was from the depths of despair, not with open, spontaneous pleasure. In that cry of joy, which was the same as pain, she escaped from twenty years of silence and came to life at last. It was only afterwards, when she went over it in her mind, that she thought about Ismaël being only fifteen. With her he had satisfied shameful puerile or bizarre desires that he must have had since childhood, but she joyfully accepted these delightful displays of depravity. She had dreamed of them herself for such a long time. In the realm of eroticism they were identical, and complete novices. And besides, it was not true that he was only fifteen. When he sat down at the piano, she found he was as old as time.

The storm accompanied their lovemaking throughout the night. The flashes of lightning allowed Ismaël to gaze at Rose's body to his heart's content. He never tired of exploring it. The most beautiful night of his life was spent in the crash of thunder, the deadly noise of planes, the sudden crack of gunfire in the distance, and the sad, muted roar of the Durance.

At about five o'clock in the morning, they were awoken by an impatient hammering on the front door. Voices with the local accent were shouting outside,

"Madame Dupin! Madame Dupin!"

They were sleeping in each other's arms on the bed where Rose had always been alone since Patrice's death. They slept together as though they had been doing it for ever.

Rose jumped out of bed, grabbed a dressing gown and ran to the door as if obeying an order, completely forgetting the Jew in her haste and confusion. She remembered him when she was in the vestibule listening to the knocks shaking the door, wondering anxiously who it could be and uncertain what to do. All the worst things happened at night in those fearful times. Was it the military police? The Gestapo? These infamous names had suddenly been heard among us, we who had never asked anything of anyone.

"But they wouldn't shout my name," she thought. It could also be one of the wandering groups of badly armed resistance fighters sent by false rumours to skirmishes they were bound to lose, thinking they were the hunters when in reality they were the hunted. Rose opened the door wide. They were two gendarmes in shiny capes streaming with rain.

"Be careful!" they warned her. "There are raids going on. If you are hiding any Jews in the house, Madame Dupin, send them up into the mountains!"

With rare exceptions, the entire gendarmerie had been among the first to turn a blind eye and to help when they reasonably could.

"Now?" Rose asked.

"No. We think it's planned for tomorrow. Otherwise we wouldn't have been able to warn you."

Ismaël, who was sitting on the bed, watched her lit up by lightning as she came back into the room. She threw herself into his arms, newly fresh and alluring.

"The gendarmes," she whispered. "They woke us up. So much the better!"

"Why? For my brothers?"

"No. Because of the Jew. There are going to be some raids."

Ismaël jumped out of bed. Rose caught him by the arm.

"They said it would be tomorrow," she said.

"I must go and join them!" Ismaël exclaimed.

He had just thought that if one can make love at fifteen, one can probably also carry a gun, and that if anything happened to the Jew he would never forgive himself. He thought that he was there to defend him, that he didn't have the right to continue blithely playing the piano. Although it was a scarcely audible lament coming from the depths of his unconscious, he was also thinking that he had just experienced the ultimate happiness, and that from that moment, repetition would only dull it. He had to stay on that peak. These are things that you tell yourself when you are fifteen and have had your fill of something wonderful.

"I'm going!" he said.

"But where are you going?" Rose said with alarm.

"Where I must!"

He dressed without haste, then put on his shoes. He stood in front of Rose, who was trembling all over.

"Tell my mother . . . No, wait! She wouldn't understand. I'll write her a note."

He sat down at the writing desk where Charmaine had written to her husband during the first war: "My love, this nightmare will end!" Pieces of furniture cannot respond to the sad whispers of the people who use them. They can only creak sometimes at night in memory of them.

"There you are!" Ismaël said. "You can read it. Give it to Marie."

"But what about me?" Rose protested.

"I love you. I'll never forget you!"

He realized that if he took her in his arms he would stay. And so he fled. She heard him open the door and bang it shut behind him. There was no going back. Rose just sat there in a state of utter confusion, feeling the same distress as when she had been unable to stop Patrice burning his paintings. She stood up. As the silk folds of her négligée slithered across her stomach, she felt the sensation she had longed for but never thought she would ever know: the desire to make love again.

She went and knocked loudly on the door of the Jew's bedroom.

"Wake up! Get dressed! They're coming. I'll have to hide you!"

He was there in a trice. He must have gone to bed fully dressed. He came to the door with his braces down and the rest of his clothes bundled up under his arm. His eyes were still watery with sleep behind his glasses.

Rose and Marie had agreed they would only send the Jew into the crypt as an absolute last resort, because of Ange the fascist.

"Are they here?" the Jew asked, trembling violently.

"No. But they could come at any time. The gendarmes have just warned me. I'm sorry," she said, "I'm very upset!"

With that she burst into tears and, as she used to do when she had been scolded as a little girl, she leaned her head on her arm, with her forehead against the wall. "He chose the war rather than me!" she thought bitterly.

They spent the rest of the night fully clothed in the drawing room, watching and listening, he overcome with anxiety and she with despair. The storm had ended at last. The Durance still rumbled, but you could only hear it occasionally because the squadrons of planes seemed to be continuously humming overhead. They seemed to be flying lower and lower, confident now of being able to destroy everything without fear of retaliation, in a last surge of anger and vengeance.

When Rose awoke, freezing cold after an hour's heavy sleep troubled by nightmares, she saw that it was day and she drew the curtains open.

It was a day of deep mourning on the ground and great joy in the clear sky. It was cold on the plain, with mists masking the foliage on the battalions of poplars. The swans, whose plumage had been soiled by the heavy rain, were looking bad-tempered as they began to swim, having also spent a bad night.

The misty plain seemed like a ghost's shroud, and above it on the distant horizon rose the Tête de l'Estrop. The light from the rising sun streamed over a light covering of snow that would not last the day. A bell tolled from the other side of the river, taking advantage of a break in the din to ring in the first mass of the day. It came from high up, in the Ganagobie priory, where three or four monks lived cut off from the world.

Rose gave a despairing sigh.

"I have to get some air. I go up to the tomb to pray every morning."

"I'll come with you," the Jew said.

"No!" Rose exclaimed. "What if they arrive during that time?"

"No, no!" the Jew replied. "I'm not going to stay here alone. I'm nervous too, you know! By the way, where's Ismaël?"

"That's why I'm crying!" Rose said. "He's gone."

"Gone? Where has he gone? Has he gone home?"

"No. To join the maquis! He left a note for his mother. He said he had no choice."

"He'll ruin his hands!" the Jew groaned. "He hasn't the right to do that! He's not meant to kill!"

"Good Lord!" Rose exclaimed.

A very old memory had just flashed into her mind and rekindled her pain. She remembered as if it were yesterday how she had held Séraphin at gunpoint to stop him from killing his own father, Zorme, whose gun she was aiming at his chest. She remembered that he had calmly moved the barrel aside saying: "Father or not . . ." And then he had walked over to the bed where Zorme had fortunately just died. Heavens! How young she was then! She loved Patrice, who had remained outside the house, but he had never made her tremble with that mysterious sensation, more intense than cold or fear, that came over her as she faced Séraphin and filled her with happiness.

The old Jew's words had revived this feeling from twenty years ago, for when she was standing beside Zorme, who had found release at last, and Séraphin, who was breathing so heavily, she had said: "You see. You weren't meant to kill!"

"What's wrong?" the Jew asked.

"I've just remembered something . . ." Rose murmured. "Come!"

The park was waking to the warmth of the new day, with cheeky blackbirds calling here and there, splashing about in the dripping trees. The summer light shining on the swirls of vanishing mists and lighting up the valley as far as the Tête de l'Estrop was an invitation to set out and explore. Not a plane was to be heard in the sky. Nature in all its freshness had never been in such contrast with mankind: it was so indecently joyful in the face of their grief.

Rose and her companion walked along the paths to the tomb, surrounded by the strong smell of wet box bushes. Full of tender sorrow, she had just confided in the Jew about her love for Ismaël.

"Do you think he loves me?"

"More than he'll ever love anyone."

"You're right in reminding me that he won't love only me!"

"In the course of our lives," the Jew said, "we unfortunately have to suffer the vagaries of time. I don't know if it has ever struck you, but one always confuses them with the vagaries of love."

Rose grabbed his arm and pulled him back behind some box bushes clipped into a crescent. She had just heard the sound of an engine in the drive.

"Get down!" she told him.

A large black mass sped past them and the box bushes, which showered them with drops of rain water. Rose's face was quite wet. If they had gone a step further, they would have walked right into one of those dark cars they had heard so much about. The very sight of them filled people with terror, like a nightmare. This time it had come for them.

"Let's get back quickly!" the Jew said. "Hide me in the crypt!"

Panic-stricken and unable to think straight, he had already begun to run back. Rose hung on to his arm.

"You're mad!" she cried. "They're already on the terrace. They'll knock on the door, open it, and inspect everything. We'll fall right into their hands!"

"Well then, let's get away!"

"Where? The bridges are guarded. There are barricades with metal spikes at all the crossroads manned by Feldgraus[4] armed to the teeth! You wouldn't get as far as a kilometre with your gaiters, your glasses and your hat!"

"What shall we do?" groaned the Jew.

"Come with me!" Rose said.

She seized his hand.

"Come! Don't be afraid. He will save you!"

"Who?"

"The person I'm taking you to."

He wanted to break away from her. The woman was dangerously out of her mind. It was time to escape on his own. She held on to his hand with all her might.

"You'll have to drag me away!" she said. "I won't let go of you! You're like a startled hare. You'll do the first thing that comes into your head and they'll catch you in no time!"

She was dragging him along almost by force, around the summerhouse thickly covered with wisteria, and finally into the long stretch of tall reeds

4 Term often used by the French for German soldiers, referring to their grey-green uniforms. [Tr.]

intersected by a path. She came out between the poplars in front of the tomb, separated from it by the empty forecourt.

"Run!" she said.

The tops of the four cypresses were swaying gently against the brilliant sky, washed clean by the storms of the previous night. She pushed the Jew in front of her as hard as she could.

"Go in quickly!"

She tried to shut him in. He tried to escape from her and to open the heavy door, which was hard to move. But Rose was stronger than he was. She had pressed herself against the door and was pushing her companion's hands back inside.

"Stay there! It's your only chance!"

"My only chance? Shut up here like a rat in a trap! You're mad! Who will protect me?"

Rose pointed to the floor and the oblong surrounded by marble, where she had buried Séraphin's bones.

"He will!" she said. "He will pray for you."

"You're completely out of your mind!"

Rose shook her head.

"You have no choice! Kneel down and pray with him!"

"Pray? We need seven to pray!"

"Well today you'll have to do it alone."

"And besides, I'll be damned if I've ever prayed! It's . . . ages since I've been Jewish! I could have gone to my death not ever thinking of it, not even remembering it. I despise Jews as much as other men, or I like them as much, if you prefer it that way! What's the difference?"

"Be quiet! They're coming!"

No. No-one was coming. Rose was imagining where the henchmen were going and what they were doing in the house. They would take their time, considering everything, neglecting nothing, like hunting dogs. They would take everything out of drawers and wardrobes simply for their own destructive pleasure, as they disliked any evidence of happiness. They must have discovered unmade beds, including her own, where perhaps they were sniffing out nostalgic traces of the smell of love.

It was only at ten or eleven o'clock, when the planes had started their racket again, that they heard the deliberate footsteps of two people on the gravel. The morning was still as beautiful as it had been when Rose left the house. Even the blackbirds were still boldly chirping in the wisteria. Beyond the walls of the tomb, the wind could be heard blowing through the cypresses around it whenever there was a break in the flights of planes passing overhead.

"Stop your teeth from chattering," Rose whispered. "You have to help too. You must have faith in him."

She had managed to make him kneel. They had joined their hands over the gravestone covering the mortal remains of Séraphin Monge.

"This is childish!" the Jew whispered. "You'll see!"

Rose squeezed his fingers even harder. The sound of the measured tread crushing the gravel blocked out all other thoughts. They were approaching. Then they stopped.

Rose, hiding in the shadows, looked through the cracked window pane and the wrought iron bouquet protecting it. In the bright sunlight she made out two huge silhouettes in bulky black raincoats, their hands hidden deep in their pockets. These clothes were meant to intimidate, but above them were the unprepossessing heads of ordinary, insignificant men with slack features. (This very ordinariness would be their salvation, as they escaped being caught when they were later hunted down for retribution.)

Before the war these men had always looked at themselves in the mirror and despaired over their lack of importance, and then suddenly it was suggested that they should rig themselves out in black and leather and put on huge, noisy boots. They realized that in that disguise, with both hands tucked into their belts, they could strike fear into mothers who knelt before them. But they were really only puppets under their jaunty berets, only blank oval faces (distinguishing marks: none), which had found in others a reason and a will to exist.

Rose was looking at two examples of the type for the first time in her life. They were very close, scarcely three metres away. She was panic-stricken. She thought that they were in an almost hopeless situation, that she had made a criminal mistake in leading the poor man into that dead-end. She cursed her superstition. She cursed Ismaël regaining his sight, which was probably due to natural causes, but which had led her to make the unpardonable mistake of leaving the Jew alone and defenceless in the presence of these torturers.

However, the steps of both men stopped at the same time. The two henchmen looked at the door to the tomb with the crazed glass window pane.

"Open it!" a voice said. "What are you waiting for?"

"No. A Jew wouldn't take refuge in a Christian tomb. If you want to look stupid, open it yourself! You'd have to be a complete idiot to hide in a place with no way out. And I've never met a Jew who was one."

"One what?"

"An idiot."

They stood there close together in silence, strangely contemplative, hearing the sound of the breeze in the four cypresses, as if for the first time. Rose felt herself shrinking with every minute that passed. She was shivering so much that she had to hold on to her pearl necklace with both hands to keep it still as the shudders ran through her.

"Come on!" the voice said. "The birds have flown. Those bloody gendarmes must have warned them. They knew it was in the air. We'll have to shoot a pair or two if we still have time . . ."

Their heavy steps were hesitant at first, but the sound of gravel crunching under their boots receded, faded, and finally disappeared. Rose and the Jew stared wide-eyed at each other, expecting them to return. The sweat on the old man's face gleamed in the shadows. They suddenly heard the sound of an engine starting off at full throttle only a few paces from their hiding place. It also receded, faded and finally disappeared. Then, all that wafted over the silence was the breeze murmuring in the cypresses, a blackbird whistling in the mock-orange and then, approaching from the distance and slowly taking possession of the sky, a new carpet of planes advanced like the leitmotiv of the war.

Rose and the old man stayed there straining their ears for more than an hour, still on their knees, still trembling, not daring to move. Rose was the first to get up.

"No!" cried the Jew. "Don't go out! It can't be true."

But she went out regardless. As the door of the tomb was always kept well oiled, it made no noise when she pulled it towards her. She stood for a long time in the full sunlight looking at the sky; she couldn't get enough of that warm light. The old man eventually joined her.

"It can't be true!" he said again. "It can't be true!"

He leaned against Rose's shoulder. She noticed that he was weeping, and she took hold of his hand. Then the reality of her life suddenly took possession of her again. "This evening I'll be alone again as always," she thought. "But now I know, unfortunately, what it's like not to be."

The old man was standing directly in front of her trying to catch her eye as she sadly turned her head away.

"Why?" he asked. "Why didn't they look for us? Why didn't they come in? They could have!"

"Why indeed!" Rose sighed. "Believe me, if I knew the answer to that question, I'd never worry about another thing in this world!"

Our village of Les Fosses-Gleizières, where Séraphin Monge came to die, was made up of three hamlets built in a zigzag because of the meandering river. Our steeple had a fissure, so that when the sun set it looked as if it was pierced with gleaming arrows like a painting of St Sebastian. Our café had a large oblong split across its threshold at ground level, and our terraced gardens were leaning closer and closer to the sheer drop of the mountainside. If we no longer believed in anything up there in our village, we certainly had good reasons for thinking that way.

On a moonlit night, a large section of our mountain shone like the skinned muscles of some giant bull. It was funnel-shaped with widely flaring sides, and it seemed to teem with life in the light of the moon. This was the impression created by the intricate network of rivulets running down it, making the site of the land-slip a constant threat. The phenomenon that had caused it was now perfectly visible, although only in skeleton form. All that remained of the Dead Man's Wood, the place where Séraphin had been buried alive, was a bare black slope.

Retaining walls, reinforcements and traps to catch falling material, which had cost so much money and effort, were now pushed up or driven on to the heaving earth. It looked as though it had solidified, but it still kept rising and sinking like the sea we had heard so much about but never seen.

From a distance, our countryside looked like a burst belly. The sight of our fields, our hamlets and our forests with their slit belly offended the cheery villages down below opposite us. Perhaps they even blamed us a little for having so much ugliness on show and being unable to do anything about it. Human bodies can be buried, but those left by nature are forever exposed to the open air.

The slide had attacked the cemetery and split it in two. It had not been possible to pull out the rotting coffins for lack of funds, and so they remained down there in the depths, linking the two sides of the fissure. Before all this happened, our visits to the cemetery on All Saints' Day were full of decorum, and the graves with their traditionally decorated zinc roofs were widely admired. Chance visitors on All Saints' Days are now greeted by the disorderly spectacle of the fissure slashed from one side of our cemetery to the other. There was sometimes a full metre gap between the "to my husband" and "sadly missed", and down below, the bier of the beloved could be seen at a strange, almost upright angle, beginning its dive towards the bowels of the earth, or else pushing up its gravestone like a ram as though called to the Last Judgment, which had already begun. Do you think that gave us any joy?

The war, when it arrived in the Alps in 1940, took prisoners from us and burned our tall hay barns leaving only black walls. It left us with only the strength to survive. Taking care of the dead would not come until later.

We thought that the mountain could have spared us, at least for the duration of the war, so that we didn't have to take everything on the chin in one mighty blow. Then it would have seemed fair. But no. By continuing down its own path, this phenomenon of local erosion proved to us that we were dealing with two distinctly different things. The war was an argument between men and not reason enough for the earth to stop carrying out its eternal work.

The Jewish geologist came back to our region out of necessity. After predicting what would happen and being so surprised that the phenomenon had given us such a long respite, he could hardly believe his eyes. He was open-mouthed in admiration at the work of nature. He said to us over and over again that he never thought he would live long enough to see here, in this little corner of the earth, the direct demonstration of the power of God, in whom he firmly believed. He was so overjoyed he forgot he was Jewish.

When his race began to be persecuted, he had immediately thought of us at Les Fosses-Gleizières. To him it seemed like a blessed place where the only disaster came from nature, and where he thought it unlikely that fate would add the horrors of war to what had already happened. In that he was mistaken, of course.

The first thing he did was to ask Auphanie for advice about being a wanted man and how he should react. The room at the café where we all used to congregate was now at the edge of the precipice and had long ago been declared unsafe. The two leafy elders, the last remaining trees of that height, by the walk where we used to play *boules*, had long ago been pulled into the water. They had half taken root in the mud and, lying in the bed of the Champanastay, they flowered feebly in spring with half their foliage, the other half being buried in the mud.

Auphanie now ran her café in the old coach house where travellers on foot and on horseback used to stay a century ago. You reached it around the back of the house, and in winter when snow blocked the door of the coach house, you had to get to the upstairs level through Auphanie's bedroom, which we crossed quickly, looking neither to left nor to right.

It gave her no pleasure to see the ill-omened geologist turn up again. Although she knew it was unreasonable, she couldn't help thinking that if he had held his tongue perhaps nothing would have happened. She had to make an effort not to berate him with words like:

"So what? You didn't see the calamities coming for your race, did you? And they hit you full in the face. That'll teach you to be so precise about ours!"

And yet this man whose name we had forgotten became Auphanie Brunel's last lover. Neither of them went into it with any joy. She resented his predictions as if they had been orders given to nature. For her part, at forty-five-plus her fine figure was beginning to turn pear-shaped. But for both of them, everything seemed to be cracking under unbearable pressure: shutters, doors, furniture, parcels, and sometimes some hidden hollows outside in the mountain. It frightened them and forced them into each other's arms out of sheer desperation.

We were so much under the spell of our own tragedy that we were probably the only locality in the mountains that managed to forget the war. Our hearing had become more acute and our sleep much lighter. We used to sleep heavily because we worked hard during the day, but now a mere whisper would drag us up from the depths, alert and breathing hard, with our elbows buried in the pillow or under our wives' generous bosoms. We weren't thinking of the planes, even if they were flying low over the mountains; we weren't thinking of the Gestapo, even if a column of trucks was climbing up the winding roads around Vars down below opposite us, looking for some maquis group in the glaciers. No. We were thinking, "It's up there . . . just now. A cracking noise. It's near the Bonnabels. It must be the last corner of the barn roof that's finally fallen down."

There was another family who were even higher and more exposed on the edge of our chasm than the Bonnabels. Their name was Austremoine, a strange name in these parts. Every autumn they lost more land and more money. The earth flowed away at the rate of a hectare per year.

They were a family noted for taking their children out of school at the age of nine to teach them milking. As a result, from father to son their foreheads became lower and lower, their moronic thinking more and more obvious, and lines of envy and greed more and more deeply etched.

As misfortune would have it, the cataclysm chose their side, attacking their plots of land and consuming large chunks of it. It could have come towards us, who have Christian resignation and are ready and prepared to undergo the trials it may please God to burden us with on this earth. But no. The cataclysm was linked to another misfortune that would strike people far from here who had no connection with us, and it needed the credulous, irrational Austremoines to help carry it out.

There were no women left in the Austremoine family. Consequently, apart from potatoes which they boiled and milk which they drank plain, they ate only game and meat. Their mother was dead. She was a bad housekeeper, but at least while she was alive she did keep house. Whenever the three sons saw a woman, they would make a wide detour for fear of being looked at. If someone a little way off waved to them to ask them something, they would scuttle off like rabbits, holding each other back by the belt so that they wouldn't be the last to flee. For some time now these primitive creatures had been turning an idea over in their slow minds.

"Say what you like," the eldest asserted, "but as long as he was here, it didn't move any more. We had no worries. Whatever the priest says, they won't shift me from thinking that there was holiness beneath it all."

"No-one disagrees with you," the second said, "not even the mayor, and he's a free thinker."

The youngest, who was a head taller than both of them, never said anything. He just kept nodding his head in agreement, without forming an opinion or making a decision of his own. He had long ago delegated the tasks of thinking and deciding to them.

At the very mention of the free-thinking mayor, the eldest spat scornfully on to the stone floor.

"All his land is safe. You'd think he was controlling the whole thing. For a while it looked as though his field of rye at Pyéchabert was going. But then, oh no. It came our way, and ours copped it! Say what you like, while Séraphin was in our land . . ."

They went over and over that question in their minds as they sat in front of their hearth full of the ashes of a whole winter's fires. It was cleared out every spring. Sometimes one of them said "Listen!" and they strained their ears. It was a live spruce tree cracking somewhere in the distance as it was pulled into the chasm by the movement of the land-slip.

Their old father, a man with age and experience, agreed with them.

"You're right. He'll have to be brought back here. If it didn't do any good, it wouldn't do any harm."

They took a whole season to work out how to put their brilliant idea into practice.

One evening after he had been thinking about it for some time, the eldest Austremoine said,

"We should take advantage of it."

"Advantage of what?" the second son asked.

"Of all the confusion. Don't you hear the planes? Don't you hear the gunshots from all over the mountains? Don't you see what's happening. They put on armbands, dig out the box of old guns in the stable, then off they go."

The youngest, who never opened his mouth, stopped nodding his head. He raised his hand and said,

"And they get themselves shot!"

The eldest shook his head.

"If we can't stop the ground slipping we'll have nothing left, and then we won't need anyone else to blow our heads off."

"You don't even know where he is."

"Yes, as a matter of fact I do! When they came and took him away about twenty or so years ago, I was there. I looked at the owner's nameplate under the steering wheel of the van. The address was there too. All we'd have to do is go and look. We'd find it in the end."

"The place? Do you know where it is?"

"No. I've never been there, but there's a map of the whole region at Auphanie's. We only have to go and look. It should be marked on it."

Off they went. Auphanie did indeed have a big school map of the Basses-Alpes, which was brought to her from an even more deprived village than ours about twenty years ago when their school closed. It used to be pinned up in a prominent place in her café. Since she moved, it had been stuck up against the arch in the coach house where it was impossible to knock in a nail. With its green patches denoting forest, blue lines for rivers, its white mountains and its names of villages, this depiction of our corner of the world inspired Auphanie's dreams of travel. It meant as much to her as the Post Office calendars, which she collected. She was none too pleased to see the Austremoine brothers put their dirty fingers all over it.

Nevertheless, she had to put up with them every evening, whereas they used to come only four times a year after mass at Easter, Christmas, All Saints' Day and Rogations. Now they were always there. She had always known them as men who never said good day when they arrived or goodbye when they left, in fact they never said anything. She had always known them as men who ordered one infusion between two of them. (They had booted the youngest one out on some occasion in the past, and he had taken it as read that henceforth he wasn't wanted.) They used to drink from the same cup, one on each side. Now they ordered two hyssop teas and they talked – a lot and passionately. Sometimes they banged their fists on the marble tabletop, then stood up suddenly, knocking over their chairs. They charged over to the map, which was in a dark spot, and lit it up with their cigarette lighters. They explained something to each other by tracing a route with their big dirty fingers. They spoke at full volume, as if they were alone. Their noses glowed with sun and alcohol, for they were drinkers, but only at home to save money.

It must be said in our defence that no-one liked them or went near them. Perhaps it was because the name Austremoine was so peculiar that it made us suspicious. And they were a shifty lot, even in the way they moved. What's more they must have learned to be shifty very early in order to earn their meagre living, and no doubt that was what made them seem suspect. Although we were poor ourselves, we've never liked the poor. And besides, when they wanted to sell us a hare or haunch of venison they had poached, they drew them out of their *taillole* – the wide cloth belt wound around their waists – with a gesture that was as obscenely sly as if they had opened their flies.

Auphanie kept a close eye on them for fear they might march off with her map. One evening she distinctly heard them say the word "Pontradieu", and from then on she listened very carefully to what they were saying. She began to spy on them and soon learned what they were plotting.

One evening, the Austremoine brothers did not appear at the café. Auphanie rushed to her inkpot and quickly wrote these lines on a sheet of cross-ruled paper:

Madame, take care! From what I can make out, there are three untrustworthy characters from around here who have taken it into their heads to steal back Séraphin Monge's relics from you. You know me. You know that I too have begged you to give them back to us. But you were so kind to me both times I came to see you that I can't help liking you, and would not want any misfortune to happen to you. Take advantage of my letter. I hope it will get to you in time, despite the difficulties of the times we live in. God keep you.

Widow Auphanie Brunel

The Austremoine brothers set out on foot and side by side like plough horses, and at the same pace. It was 130 kilometres to Pontradieu, but they avoided major and minor roads, paths and tracks, choosing instead to charge through woods, gorges, rivers and fords. Whenever they saw tracks of deer going in their direction they followed them, thinking that the wildlife were as keen as they were to keep away from people. (The Boche soldiers themselves had come to like a casserole of young wild boar.) The Austremoine brothers were good poachers and used to living like wild pigs themselves. Their itinerary went in a semi-circle, rising up to the border of the Drôme then falling back to the Durance valley at the end of its trajectory. They stumbled across dead bodies, both civil and military, but didn't bother to stop as they didn't need anything. They had three good guns, which hadn't been used for four years, but they had tested them in an echoless spot in the mountains before they left.

They slept during the day, with one of them keeping watch over the other two in case their snoring attracted unwelcome attention. They did all of this almost without eating, except for some cheeses, hardened in the wind, that could be heard hitting against each other at the bottom of their game bags. The cheeses were so hard that the brothers couldn't bite into them, and had to scrape them with their teeth. In order to make heaven look mercifully on their enterprise, they made the sign of the cross and kneeled down at the foot of all the wayside crosses erected in the fervour of former times at crossroads and clearings.

They heard rifle-fire, cries of the dying, orders issued in a foreign language. They saw barns go up in flames, trucks in the distance on roads they were careful to avoid. Along the railway line from Sisteron to Veynes, which they had to cross, they found a large locomotive lying on its side against the embankment, with steam still issuing forth like an old family kettle.

That incessant hum like a swarm of angry bees made by the planes flying overhead accompanied them everywhere, both in the dense woods and the open valleys they sometimes ran through when there was no cover. The aircraft were always heard but never seen.

Nothing or no-one stopped them on their journey.

Marie rushed into Pontradieu, dripping wet up to her waist. The water in the Durance had not yet fallen to its usual level after the storm of the previous evening. The ford had narrowed enormously and she had had to grope around to find it. She was weighed down like a pack-horse. The haversack strapped to her shoulders must have weighed 15 kilos. It was full of tins, jars of jam, chickens wrapped in cloths, and two-kilo loaves of bread as solid as bricks.

"I thought I'd never get here!" she cried. "Oh, my poor boys! They must be starving!"

"Of course not," Rose said. "Would I let that happen? Aren't I here? They were fed as usual. They're acting rather strangely, though. They left half the omelette I made them for lunch."

"Be careful!" Marie warned. "I did tell you not to take food to them. One of these days they'll knock you down and that'll be the end of everything! They'll never dare to try it with me, because they know what I'd do to them! I'd rather know they went without food for a little while than see them go off to play soldiers!"

"Knock me down?" Rose said. "Never! They're as gentle as lambs. They don't even bother to mark things on the operations map. They spend all their time watching the swans swimming on the pool. They're daydreaming!"

Marie gave a start.

"They're daydreaming? Good Lord! I've never seen them daydreaming in their lives! But what's happened to you?"

"What do you mean, what's happened to me?"

"You don't look the same. Nothing here looks the same."

She looked deep into her friend's eyes.

"You look happy," she said. "You look as if . . ."

She pulled Rose to her and began to sniff at her like a hunting dog.

"You smell of love!" she exclaimed suddenly. "You absolutely reek of love!"

Rose blushed right up to her forehead.

"You should know," she said. "and it's better for me to tell you."

"For you to tell me what?"

"Ismaël . . . We were alone last night. The electricity was cut off."

"Ismaël? You're not suggesting that . . ."

"I'm not suggesting, I'm telling you! Oh, I know!" Rose added. "You can swear at me, you can hit me, you can do what you like. There's not a thing you can say that I haven't said to myself already."

Then she suddenly felt the arms of her impetuous friend Marie hug her tight, and heard a string of exclamations.

"Heavens, what joy! Heavens, I'm so happy! If only you knew! I was so afraid he'd start with the wrong person! You've made me so happy! And you. It used to upset me seeing you like that. It really did!"

She held her friend at arm's length to look at her more closely.

"Tell me. You came, didn't you? You came?"

Rose looked down.

"Oh, yes . . ." she said. "You know . . . He's extraordinary. And his music . . ."

"What joy!" Marie said again. "We should be ashamed to be so happy with everything that's happening all around us! But, well, that's life!"

"You know I love him," Rose whispered.

"Yes," Marie said. "That . . . We'll see about that! For the moment, the main thing is that you've both been initiated, you've both begun. And where is the little devil now? I'm dying to see him. It's the first time he's slept away from home."

She chuckled.

"We'll have a good laugh! I'll ask him about his first impressions. The cheeky young devil! Music! Blame the music! And at fifteen!" she exclaimed with a hint of pride in her voice.

Since Marie came in, Rose had unconsciously been crumpling Ismaël's note to his mother, which she was holding in her hand. She had steadfastly looked her friend in the eye when she confessed that she loved her fifteen-year-old son; yet she dared not look up when the moment came to hand over the few hastily written lines that would wound Marie like a knife.

"He's gone," Rose said miserably.

"Gone!" Marie bellowed. "Gone where?"

Marie opened her hand. The piece of paper had now become a shapeless mass since Rose had been mangling it in her anxiety. Marie snatched it from Rose and smoothed it out. Ismaël had written:

Maman, I can't stand by any longer while so many of my friends are being killed in the cause of freedom. I'm going to join them. Forgive me.

Marie sank on to a sofa, which creaked under her weight. She moaned and put her hands flat to her sides with the same unconscious gesture she used to make when her belly was heavy with one or other of her children. A long cry burst from her in spite of herself. It astonished her, as she had never before uttered one like it. When she was young, in Lurs, she had heard a lamentation like that from a doe that had been mortally wounded instead of killed outright by an unskilled hunter.

"Drink this!" Rose said, taking charge.

She handed her a brimming glass of fiery brandy. Marie pushed it aside.

"No!" she said, and her voice was hoarse. "Nothing can help the pain I feel ... It's agony! If he'd wanted to torture me, he couldn't have found a better way! Oh, the little bastard!"

She stood up suddenly, her face glowering.

"It's your Jew's fault!" she cried. "He must have filled Ismaël's head with tales of his people's suffering! Just you wait! I've got a few things to say to him! There's no chance of him going to the front! Would he rather send the young ones? Just you wait! Where is he?"

"In his room," Rose said. "If you knew what we went through this morning!"

"I don't care! I want to tell him just what I think!"

"Let him sleep. Please! He has nothing to do with it. Do you know what he said to me when Ismaël left? He said, 'He's mad! He'll ruin his hands!'"

"Good Lord! It's true. His hands!" Marie exclaimed.

She hammered her clenched fists against her thighs.

"But where can I find him? And what state will he be in when they hand him back to me? Have you seen Antoine? I haven't seen him for a week. He's the only one who can get him back for me."

"Antoine? He let me know that he was going away, that he'd come back, that he was needed somewhere, in short that I had to read between the lines. My dear Marie, it's the end of everything! What do you want to do?"

"Just one thing!" Marie shouted.

She got up, grabbed the haversack full of provisions and marched down to the cellar. Rose followed her timidly, drawn along in spite of herself by Marie's impotent fury punctuated with cries of anguish.

"Knifing me in the back!" she cried. "Torturing me like this! How could he do it? How could I ever have imagined it? At fifteen! Going off to die for the motherland! Silly idiot!"

She gave a determined push on the stone that opened the crypt. Looking guilty, Ange and Bertrand sprang away from the window, where they had been clutching the bars.

"There you are!" Marie said. "You're free! Your brother has seen fit to go and try his hand at the war. And he managed to get away from me! I'd hate you to be jealous! Why should I deprive you two of the experience! If you want to go, go! I'm not stopping you!"

She sat down heavily on the unmade bed. The small window was at her eye-level and she stared unthinkingly at the swans as they glided majestically over the smooth, peaceful waters of the pool. It was three o'clock on a hot afternoon. The storms had not quelled the summer heat. Further away on the horizon, the hum of another flight of planes began softly and then grew louder until it filled the air.

Marie felt devoid of all hope. She was overcome by the bitterness of her failure; it weighed down on her and aged her by ten years. After all that effort, all that argument, the war had finally won. It cast its spell over everyone. There was no use trying to fight it. Death beckoned wherever you looked. Like mosquitoes around a lamp, men rushed towards it as if they were tired of waiting for it to come to them.

"Well then?" Marie said. "What are you waiting for? The door's wide open!"

They kneeled down in front of her as she sat there biting her nails, her sign of complete despair, and something she had not done since the far-off time when she searched high and low for Séraphin. Her sons' heads were on a level with hers. They looked at her intently.

"But, Maman," Ange said hesitantly, "we don't want to go."

It was then she noticed that her two young men were looking wonderfully happy and contented, with an expression she had never seen on their faces before. For as far back as she could remember, they had looked disgruntled, tense and anxious, always watching out of the corner of their eyes for anything that might be given to someone else and not include them. She had often despaired of making happy men out of them. Although there was still something poignant in their expression, it was not the same. The look in their eyes was open and frank. It showed suffering, but of a normal healthy kind, as if they had sublimated their petty cravings and jealousies, freeing their spirits from matter at last. They were there in front of her, shyly, sweetly reaching out to stroke Marie's hands.

Suddenly a long tinkling laugh followed by the cries of two girls tickling one another filtered through the fronds of the plane trees outside in the heat. The boys immediately turned away from their mother. They jostled for room at the window. Marie was intrigued and drew closer to them. With them she witnessed the charming spectacle of the two plump pink teenage girls throwing off their clothes with gay abandon, thinking they were alone, then diving among the swans with squeals of delight. The swans, on the other hand, honked with fury to see their mirror surface so violently disrupted.

"So that's it!" Marie exclaimed, keeping her voice down. "Shame on you!"

She felt like laughing and crying all at once. Curiosity got the better of Rose, who had been following what was happening from the doorway. She had also come up to the window to see what they were looking at.

"Why, it's Lucrèce's daughters! They'll catch their death! What if their father sees them!"

Bertrand turned to Rose.

"They've been coming for a fortnight," he said. "They're too hot. They're too ..."

His voice was trembling like an old man's. Ange, with his face pressed to the bars, was uttering low moans.

"Well then? What are you waiting for?" Marie whispered. "What you're doing is sly. Love should be declared in the full light of day! Face to face! You're free. Out you go! Dive into the pool with them! They'll scream, they'll run away, but tomorrow or the day after, they'll come back. You'll see. Ange!" Marie called in a tone not to be denied.

She had put out her arm in front of them as they turned around and were about to rush out.

"You two! Keep your underpants on! I don't want to have any trouble from old Lucrèce. Later on, we'll see. And don't lay a finger on them! Otherwise ... !"

It was this extraordinary presence of mind, which everyone acknowledged, that made Marie stand out from other women.

"So, that's why they were daydreaming," Rose said pensively. "Why they weren't eating. Well, you've won. They're tied hand and foot now. That's all they can think about."

The two women watched the two lads come out on the terrace, stripped to the waist. They threw themselves straight into the water without even taking their trousers off.

"They're good-looking boys," Rose said.

"Yes," Marie said.

The girls' horrified cries never reached them. All they saw were the mouths wide open with astonishment, for a new carpet of planes came over the horizon and their din swallowed up all noise of human activity. Every day that they flew over, it seemed as if they were coming a little closer to the earth, and the throbbing of their engines became more menacing. Until then our noses were always in the air as we tried to spot them, but now we stooped as they zoomed past.

"We shouldn't," Rose said. "It's a sin when so many people are dying! But I almost wish that they'd stop, that they'd drop their bombs on us. Then I'd die knowing happiness."

She grasped her friend's hand and interlaced her fingers with Marie's. "I haven't thought of anything else since last night!"

Marie broke free and put her head in her hands.

"Oh, Ismaël!" she groaned. "You'll be the death of your poor mother!"

They made their way out of the crypt in a state of such high emotion, with such mixed feelings of elation and anxiety, that they left the door wide open behind them. The squadrons of heavy bombers had moved on towards the north. They could still be heard in the distance, ploughing through the sky. Others were returning, flying lighter and higher, sounding more like dragonflies, with a drone which was also lighter and higher: it was their victory song, their paean of revenge.

When the women reached the entrance hall they heard two knocks at the front door.

"The postman," Rose said without any great interest. "I'm not expecting anything, as usual."

She went towards the door. The two boys, soaking wet and shivering, opened it before she got there.

"Go and dry yourselves quickly," Marie said. "Tomorrow you'll wait for them fully clothed. And you'll wear your good white shirts!"

Rose put her hand into the letterbox, took out a single letter and unsealed it.

"Marie!" she exclaimed.

She held out the sheet of paper from a school exercise book on which Auphanie Brunel had written her message.

"That's all we needed!" Marie said gloomily. "Are you going to inform the gendarmes?"

"The gendarmes? They're with the maquis. Haven't you noticed what's happening around you. You can't rely on anyone these days! No," Rose said firmly. "I have my father's gun. I'll get it out. Too bad. I'll use it if I have to. I don't want anyone touching Séraphin."

"Nor do I," Marie said. "Now that you've reminded me, I also have my father's gun. We won't let them take him from us."

"No!" Rose said in full agreement. "After all, it's our lives and our past. All that counts for more than the war!"

"Yes," Marie declared. "It could have been our whole happiness."

Rose took hold of her friend's hands.

"Marie! If I should die before you, swear to me that you will never, ever, allow Séraphin's bones to be taken away from Pontradieu!"

"Never!" Marie exclaimed fiercely. "Never! You can set your mind at rest on that score."

XI

WHEN ISMAËL LEFT PONTRADIEU, TAKING THE FORD AND THE SHORT cuts across Ganagobie, the Lauzon and Sigonce, he reached the abandoned shepherd's house near the Cruis pine wood. He knew what and where it was from those old men who looked like mushroom gatherers, sidling up to young men as if to whisper strange propositions in their ears, while all they wanted was to urge them to die for freedom. They had been recruiting tirelessly for months in cafés, in factories, at games of *boules* and at clandestine dances in cellars.

Ismaël deliberately made a noise as he walked across the huge stretch of stony terrain that separated him from the camp. When he reached the edge of the beech forest he saw a dim light among the ruins, and someone stuck the barrel of a gun into his ribs.

"I'm alone," Ismaël said. "I've come to join up."

He was as happy as a king, of Olympian calm, and delightfully weary from his night with Rose and the thirty kilometres up hill and down dale he had travelled during the course of the day.

He could not tell whether it was the heights of happiness he had experienced more than the affection he felt for his teacher that had made him rush off to try and get himself killed. It was then or never. The overwhelming wave of joy that had swept over him called for death so that he would never have to face the inevitable let-down. He had held Rose in his arms all through the night while she called him "*mon amour*", and he was still intoxicated by those wonderful words. All the time he had

316

been walking, he kept smelling Rose on his hands and on his chest through the open neck of his shirt, resenting the strong odours of Lure mountain, which made it fade. Any later impressions could never be anything more than an accompaniment of unimportant themes, a string of useless moments wearing away the intensity of that supreme moment. In the mind of the fifteen-year-old boy, the height of happiness is reached only once. What did he care about the aggressive, hairy young man smelling of sweat, who was no doubt suspicious of his casual attitude and kept pushing him roughly with the point of his gun towards the dull light spilling out from the ruins like the halo around a glow worm.

He had just enough time to avoid hitting the joist as he was sent through the door and down into a cellar by the gun jabbing him in the ribs.

"What is it?" a voice barked.

"Someone who says he's come to join up."

There were two of them standing behind a hissing gas lamp on a trestle table, where there was a map spread out as well as two unimpressive firearms that looked as if they were made of cardboard.

Ismaël was naïve enough to believe that the first defenders of freedom he met would be like those heroic shouting men in the bas-relief of *La Marseillaise* around the Arc de Triomphe, which he had seen on a postcard. But no. These men were short, stout and suspicious, with piggy eyes and balding heads. They bit their nails. They looked bored.

"Where have you come from?" the older one asked.

"I'm getting away from the Germans," Ismaël said. "I want to fight."

"I want to know where you come from. Who are you?"

"My name is Ismaël. I'm a Jew."

"Did you hear that? He's a Jew."

The other man shrugged in a gesture of helplessness.

"Ah, well . . ." he replied with resignation.

"How old are you?"

"Seventeen," Ismaël lied.

Fortunately he had inherited Tibère's beard, which had darkened his cheeks for the last three months. Added to that, a sparse growth of coarse hair like pig bristle crowned his upper lip.

"Seventeen!" exclaimed the man questioning him.

"Tell him to go and take a bath," grumbled his companion. "We're not running a nursery here! And he's a Jew to boot!"

Ismaël had never seen either of the two men, nor the young one who still had the gun in his ribs, just for the pleasure of it apparently. They had Parisian accents. Fortunately they were not from around here.

"Have you ever handled a gun?"

"Never," Ismaël said.

He bit his lips so as not to add, "I'm a pianist." But he realized he was in a bad enough situation already without making it worse with this detail.

"So much the better. I don't have one to give you."

The two men walked around Ismaël, sniffing him out almost under his nose, staring at him all the while.

"A rich boy, eh?" sneered the one who had shrugged when he heard the word Jew.

Ismaël was wearing the same clothes he had on when he left Lurs two day ago: his black velvet suit and his white shirt with the soft wide cravat, which was the way Marie imagined a musician should be dressed.

"If my mother could see them putting me through this," he thought, "she'd be at them tooth and nail."

"I shouldn't take you," the man interrogating him said. "I don't like the look of you . . ."

He sighed.

"But I don't have any choice," he added.

"But what are you going to do with the brat?"

"He can still walk. Do you know anyone else around here who's still in a fit state to do much walking?"

The other man looked down. The questioner raised a greasy hand towards Ismaël's shoulder, which was higher than he was, to signify no doubt that he accepted him as one of their company. This ancient gesture has been used since the Roman Empire by recruiting sergeants throughout history when they succeed in collaring a volunteer.

"Right," the stocky man said as he drew him towards the door. "Do you know this region fairly well?"

"Very well," Ismaël said.

"This is what I want you to do. Go up to the shepherd's house at the fork in the Saint Étienne pine wood. You'll find a camp like this one. Ask the guard for Donald. Donald!" he repeated, wagging his finger. "Tell him – now memorize this carefully – tell him, 'The Samarcand rendezvous will not take place.' Can you remember that?"

"Yes," Ismaël said.

"Good. After that, come back here. I'll see what I can do with you."

He pushed him outside as roughly as the young man on guard had pushed him in. Once again Ismaël ducked. He had the feeling that they would have liked to see him hit his head. He had gone about five paces when he heard his name spoken like an order.

"Ismaël!"

He turned around.

"Yes?"

The instructor sighed. "So it's not a false name. It really is that."

He shouted to him once again.

"If the Krauts capture you, get yourself killed! You wouldn't stand up to torture and then we'd have to come and shoot you ourselves!"

"So much the better!" Ismaël said to himself.

The night sky between Cruis and Saint Étienne was dangerously bright and clear. All the cliff ridges on the Ganagobie plateau sparkled in the moonlight. A lulling wind around the Augès peaks moaned softly in the distance. You could hear it from here, where everything was still. This illusory peace was first broken by a swarm of planes droning constantly for an hour. But this time you could see the shining points of their fuselages, as you sometimes see the scales of a shoal of fish breaking the surface of the sea.

Ismaël was in a state of high excitement. He climbed up the flank of the Lure like someone possessed, even running from time to time, vainly trying to get out of breath.

The night was pierced by flashes of light in the deep woods. The crack of gunfire could be heard, and a distant, continual rumbling that Ismaël in his romantic ignorance took to be cannons. They were tanks making their way along the roads. There were also cries and calls carried by the echo.

They were cries of the dying, of suffering, or passionate curses hurled at the enemy, but the pathos of those calls was lost in the distance.

It took Ismaël only two hours to reach the shepherd's house near Saint Étienne whereas it usually took three. But once he had left Cruis, he cut straight through grassland and valleys, avoiding the usual paths.

Near the edge of a wood which hid the moon, he stumbled over an unexpected obstacle and crashed to the ground, sprawling his full length into the undergrowth. He put his hand out for support to get to his feet again when his fingers sank into something cold. It was the cheeks of a dead man. The changing light filtering through the branches made him look horribly white. The torn shirt he was wearing looked like a bloody waistcoat still shimmering in the fitful moonlight. His eyes were wide open. Next to him was the obstacle he had stumbled over: the still-warm body of a soldier in the grey-green German uniform. He must have taken longer to die.

"Thank you, Mother!" Ismaël said aloud and with feeling.

He was thanking her for having inherited her character, as these were the first dead bodies he had ever seen and he did not cry out, he was not horrified and he didn't want to run away. "I hope my own death will one day seem as unimportant to me," he thought.

He turned the German's body over. He saw a face with chubby cheeks, as white as the other man's, and of about the same age. "Not even twenty," Ismaël estimated. His eyes were also open wide with surprise. He and the Resistance man had let go of the firearms they had used to kill each other. Ismaël picked them up in turn. The German's weapon seemed more solid. He took it with him, as the two dead bodies with their strangely staring eyes had somewhat lessened his desire to die.

The house was silent. The light from a lantern flickered at a small window below the roof. Moonlight swept like a searchlight across a large open area in front of the house shaded by two plane trees. Ismaël was beginning to learn something about combat and the silence had worried him. He saw a black heap on the top of a pyramid-shaped pile of stones. As he had already seen two bodies, he knew immediately what the black heap was. He looked up. There at an open window a figure like a puppet hung limply over the sill, with its arms dangling in space.

Ismaël could hear orders being shouted beyond the house in the depths of the forest. The track through the trees crossed a strip of cleared land, and in the distance he could see something that looked like a large metal pot and made a noise like a coffee mill. It shone in the treacherous moonlight in spite of its camouflage. He flung himself flat on the ground. With his nose in a tuft of savory, he watched in fascination as the machine lumbered along. He had just learned how to crawl over the ground to save his neck. It came naturally: a hundred generations of soldiers who had crawled through all the wars were vying for the honour of teaching him.

It was clear that he wouldn't be giving his message to anyone. The Samarcand rendezvous had indeed taken place here. It was also clear that death was all around him, perhaps in the two or three shadowy forms that were silently moving along the edge of the forest track, no more than 200 or 300 metres away from him . . . At eye-level he could see a large burst of flame spreading down on the plain in the direction of Oraison and Pontradieu. A wave of anxiety gripped him.

Clinging to the earth as though he were trying to embed himself in it, Ismaël felt a dull rumbling shake the ground. Still flat on his stomach and holding his gun at arm's length, he began to retreat toward the section of young oaks, scarcely twenty years old, whose star-shaped tufts made a thick shield. He was panting now, but not from shortness of breath. A feeling he had never known before was beginning to come over him, dampening the exhilaration that the memory of Rose still inspired. It was fear.

Once he was sure of being out of immediate danger he stood up again. He zigzagged back to the post near the Cruis pine forest where his offer had been so ungraciously received. But he instinctively walked bent over, moving along like a monkey, making as little sound as possible and avoiding clearings too brightly lit by the moon. He suddenly found himself at a road. He had come too far down. He saw blue beams from headlights going around bends in the road and coming closer. He took cover, once again flat on the ground. He began to like this exercise. A Beethoven symphony he had heard on an old gramophone at college was running through his mind, which had been completely thrown off its normal course. The music had overcome his enthusiasm, now it overcame his fear. It rose irresistibly to his lips, but was inaudible to anyone but him. It gave him that feeling of eternity he needed so that he would not feel entirely alone.

He came down to the pine wood camp at Cruis from above. A strong smell of powder, burned petrol and something dirtier and more penetrating still lingered over the ruins. The pale light still flickered, but from the unaccustomed silence, the gutteral orders echoing beyond Mallefougasse, in the direction of Augès, from the sound of rapid gunshots and distant curses – perhaps the last words of a dying man – Ismaël realized that death had passed this way a short time ago. A body in German uniform lay across the doorway through which he had been pushed at the point of a gun. Ismaël stepped over it. The two short, fat men who had questioned him lay slumped over the table, face down on the map. The lamp still hissed between them. The smell of defecation, which affected Ismaël more than anything else, came from these three bodies so similar in death. "Not only do you have to die," he thought, "but you have to die in filth!"

It was an appalling thought, and he took time to reflect for a moment. He had the strange impression that the war kept receding as he approached, like the tide going out. He felt that death wandered across his path, patient and unconcerned, certain to get him in the end. In a very short time it had just missed him several times: either he had just left or not yet arrived. Not long ago he had heard the sound of boots tramping along the path where he was hiding less than 100 metres away, and then suddenly fade out, as if the mountain had engulfed them. The war was like lightning: it struck anywhere, by pure chance, with no rhyme or reason. Here it was being fought blindly, at random and hand to hand by two ghosts of armies in disarray. In all this confusion he wondered where and to whom he could be of any use.

"To report!" he thought. He needed a pretext to get going again and not stay sitting in the straw next to the now useless leaders, reflecting endlessly on them and on the blond head shining beneath the German helmet, all aggression spent. Like the first body in the grey-green uniform he had seen in the forest, this one lying across the doorway was a very young man. The victors were scraping the bottom of the barrel.

Ismaël stepped over the body and set off again. The defecation smell of the dead would always remain his memory of the war. A little way off, one of the black heaps he now had no trouble identifying was a body kneeling against the wall of a water tank. He recognized the thick, coarse hair of the young man on guard who had pushed him into the cellar early in the evening.

A strange idea came into his mind. It occurred to him that man cannot feel compassion for many corpses at one time. When there are more than two or three, his inconstant heart is inevitably drawn to what is unusual and eye-catching, and from that moment his general coldness is only moved during a solemnized group remembrance service.

He had walked so quickly through the Le Deffends woods that he had begun squelching through reeds before he realized where he was. He was about to cross the reed beds of the Lauzon, which were flooded by moonlight and stretched as far as the eye could see over the Montlaux area. He then changed direction towards the screen of trees that followed the course of the stream. He went into the water with his shoes on. This was one of several strange sensations he felt during that night, as it was something he would normally never dare to do. He smiled as he thought what his mother would have said. The treetops met overhead and provided a welcome coolness in the hot night. Ismaël knew where he was going now. He only had to reach the bridge over the stream between Montlaux and Sigonce. From there on it would take an army to flush him out.

He reached the bridge when the moon was at its highest point in the sky. The water swished softly as it spread over the huge flat stones. Ismaël went up the slope to the left through the elms and the aspens. A thick black hedge of tall briars blocked his path. He battled his way into it. He was in familiar country.

He heard a panting sound in the bushes and was conscious of the fact that he didn't even know how to fire the gun he had dragged along with him. Someone made a noise like a charging wild boar. It was one man, whose panting sounded like panic. In a ray of moonlight, Ismaël saw a thin, gawky man with shaggy hair and beard coming out of the thicket, saying,

"Stop messing around! Put your gun down! You'll shoot yourself in the thigh! Where did you ever see anyone hold a tommy-gun like that?"

He lifted up Ismaël's arm as he said it.

"Don't be afraid," he added, "we're both in the same shit!"

He was as emaciated as a mangy cat. An ugly, dirty beard, ridiculously sparse, covered his hollow cheeks. Ismaël felt ashamed of his black velvet suit and soft cravat. But this fancy-dress outfit had received the baptism of death and he hadn't even realized it. He didn't know that it was sticky with the blood of the two that had killed each other near the shepherd's house at Saint Étienne, and he had come too close to their bodies when crawling in the grass.

"I've spent six hours at the bottom of the well!" the man said, still panting.

He collapsed at Ismaël's feet near the trunk of a pear tree, not even feeling the sharp thorns at its base. He smelled of dank earth and was soaked in water with containing threads of rust, which steamed around him as it dried out in the heat of the night.

"I stayed for six hours hanging on to the rope in the well," he repeated, "with my head under the bucket. They fired at the bucket but I'd dropped into the water. They thought I was dead and didn't have time to climb down. They lobbed a grenade into the well, but it didn't go off. I'm shivering, but it's not from cold. Six hours! At the bottom of the well!" he said again, as if he were the first to think how incredible that was.

He spoke wildly.

"My name's Laviolette . . . Well . . . That'll do for now!" he said.

"Mine's Ismaël."

"Are you Jewish?"

"I intend to be. They deserve it."

"Oh!" Laviolette said. "Who deserves anything but a kick in the arse the way things are at the moment!"

"What do you mean by that?"

"I mean that the stupid bastards gave the order too soon! You see, they don't care much if we win or lose! They know it's all over, and that the Yanks are going to drive out the Krauts in less than no time! They just want as many dead bodies as possible so that they can boast about it when the day of reckoning comes. And there'll be plenty, believe you me! There are at least 1,000 Krauts in the area, with machine-guns, mortars, the lot! A thousand!

Enough to seal off all the crossroads and all the bridges, even those over streams! They were calmly coming down to get themselves surrounded by the Yanks, weren't they! And we had to go and corner them!"

He began to give a grotesque imitation of those who had given the order.

"'Come on lads, we have to go! You can't count on anyone else! Let's be responsible for our own liberation! Freedom is bought with blood and sweat!' My arse! Do you see them doing any liberating? Believe me, it'll be just like it is in ordinary wars: very few leaders die. Oh, I grant you some will get killed! You can never predict how things will work out!"

He continued speaking so volubly on this theme that Ismaël realized he probably hadn't spoken for days and that it was pouring out of him like water from a burst dam.

"You know," Ismaël said unconcerned, "at the moment I'm so happy I'd die with a smile on my face!"

"Don't worry," Laviolette said sarcastically, "you won't even have time for your mood to change. It'll happen to you very soon."

The moon had not yet set. It was leaning towards the west and becoming more and more translucent. Ismaël and Laviolette could now easily see each other's faces. Snails had started slithering up the briars around them in compact clumps.

"I'm done!" Laviolette groaned. "I've been walking for four days. I haven't had anything to eat since yesterday morning. Krauts or not, I've got to get some sleep!"

"Not here! Come with me!" Ismaël said.

He knew that between the bridge over the Lauzon and the top of the Ganagobie plateau, there was an area which was a kind of geological fracture. The earth had been squeezed up in tight folds with paths between them created by erosion. There were fifteen furrows hollowed out by water flowing down these paths between the folds. Some were fifty metres deep, others seventy, and two of them were nearly 100 metres. All of them ran parallel to the Lauzon. When you reached the top of any of them, there was Ganagobie in front of you. You felt as though you could reach out your hand and touch it. The slopes leading up to it were steep and full of nasty prickly bushes:

large hawthorns with several interlinked trunks, tall brambles falling over like weeping willows and reseeding themselves in a damp crack at the bottom of the furrows, and dog roses, both dead and alive. They formed obstacles that deterred all but the most determined. Even the wild pigs made a detour around them.

When Marie's sons were aged between eight and twelve and she despaired of controlling them, she would wear them out by dragging them from Lurs to this place and, to finish off, she made them go over the fracture field by promising them they would be at Ganagobie any minute.

"It's just behind there!" she would tell them.

Their tongues would hang out like hunting dogs and they kept quiet for three days afterwards.

"You'll kill your poor lads!" Clorinde would complain.

To which Marie would reply,

"It toughens them up!"

When he met Laviolette at the Montlaux bridge, Ismaël intended taking shelter in that tangle of brambles. Each time they went up and down a fold his companion would swear at him. At the bottom of the sixth, Laviolette collapsed against the side wall of clay covered with coltsfoot.

"I'm not going any further!"

"This is far enough," Ismaël said. "We're in the middle. If anyone wanted to find us, they'd have to come as far as we have, from one side or the other."

Laviolette didn't bother to reply. He slowly hunched over with his nose in the clay wall. Ismaël watched him sag then collapse on to the trickle of water, where he stretched out, oblivious to everything. He too lay down and thought of Rose. He soon fell asleep.

When they awoke, it was dark again. They had no idea of the time or of how many hours they had slept. Laviolette was still snoring. Ismaël shook him.

"Come on!" he said.

"If I could smoke one! Just one!" Laviolette murmured without opening his eyes. "I'm dying for a smoke! I haven't had a cigarette for four days!"

"You'll have some tonight," Ismaël said. "Come on!"

They reached the plateau after dark. Laviolette hadn't stopped ranting and raving about his present situation since he regained consciousness. He talked incessantly; horror spewed from his mouth. He had seen everything in the three weeks since he'd been parachuted in: bodies at the foot of church and cemetery walls, bodies hanging from street lights, people buried alive.

"All the result of a blunder most of the time," he said. "Through stupidity! Or misunderstanding! The opposition are thick as bricks, but if you thoughtlessly rush out and attack them, you can't complain if they shoot you! Of course," he sneered, "the most important thing is for the leaders to come out of it all right. 'To commemorate us', or so they say!"

"You talk like my mother," Ismaël said.

"Is that what your mother says? Well, she must be quite a woman!"

"Oh, yes!" Ismaël said, with great conviction.

Tears sprang to his eyes. He hadn't seen her for four days. He hadn't seen Rose for more than three. He felt the desire to go back to Pontradieu and wallow in her love as strongly as he had felt the wish to die the day before. But first he was hungry and thirsty. Without worrying about his exhausted companion, he began to run towards the spring. It flowed gently under a thick layer of maidenhair fern. He fell to his knees in the mud around the stone basin and drank greedily from the stream of water coming from the earth above it. Laviolette had sunk down panting beside him. To him the spring seemed like a miracle. They stood up out of breath and belching from having drunk so much liquid all at once.

By the light of the moon striking the cliff face, they suddenly saw a kilo loaf of bread sitting on the edge of the basin where the monks beat their washing. It was whole and intact, but hardly seemed real. Had the people from the monastery left it there for whoever may have need of it? Was it someone, perhaps now dead, who had been surprised by his pursuers and fled with no time to pick it up again?

Whatever the answer, the presence of that bread was so powerfully allegorical that the two men just looked at it for several minutes before daring to lay a hand on it. They finally shared it as fairly as they could. Strength and hope came back to them with every mouthful. They took a last drink at the maidenhair fern spring, which they were loath to leave, and set off again with their mouths full.

"Come!" Laviolette said. "It's risky, but we have to find out what's going on. Let's go up on to the cliff."

Ismaël followed obediently. From there the valley spread out under the moon looked rather like a happy scene on a Midsummer Day.

The waters of the Durance were the colour of liquid pewter as it lazily wound its way from one end of the valley to the other, oblivious of man, oblivious of the war. You could see the outline of the fields, straight as a die. You could see the tell-tale dark spots of villages, huddled in fear. Not a single light flickered in any of them. But the fires were visible all over the plain and around the perimeter of the hills. Down at La Fuste, up at Hautes-Plaines, in the distance the whole hamlet of Les Varzelles, and on the heights of Entrevennes behind Oraison. There was even a fire burning merrily on the slopes of Mondenier, but it was hard to explain given how bare the land was over there.

From the droning of the planes, there were also fires down the La Bléone pass into the mountains around Digne. The dull sound of explosions followed or preceded by bursts of fireworks could be heard coming from around Sisteron.

It was the big event of the war. The war, which had hovered around us for so long, which had leapt over us, was now amongst us. There was a continuous flow of vehicles moving down the highways and byways. You could only see them from the moonlight reflected in their windows and unlit headlights.

"It's them!" Laviolette said, his voice almost choking. "I tell you, there's at least 1000 of them! They're everywhere! It's like I told you, they were going to come down anyway! And our people had to give the order for us to go up and attack them! Now it's like a hive that's been kicked over. They're shooting at anything that moves! They're even shooting at hares! They're scared witless, like us! And they're cornered because the bridges have been blown up as far as Grenoble."

But none of that stopped the crickets from singing; nor the distant cries of pain, nor the droning of the carpet of planes, nor the noise of heavy bombing of strategic points in Sisteron or Digne. These are the crickets that would all stop at the same time over vast distances at an eclipse of the moon, or a sudden drop in temperature of two or three degrees, or the footsteps of a poacher silently walking across their dry grassland. The sound of men killing each other, however, did not seem to disturb them in the least. There was even a mad cicada clinging to the still-warm trunk of a holly-oak, mistaking the moonlight for sunlight. It was chirping softly, as a pale reflection of its triumphant daytime song. There was a smell of grass in the air, and wafts of perfume from a lone clump of lavender growing in a crack in the rock kept the two men aware of its welcome presence.

Ismaël thought that if he lived, he would always remember the smell of that lavender, so unusual in the dead of night. He tried to make out Pontradieu in the distance, everything within him straining to regain his haven. To hold Rose in his arms again and know that moment when, with trembling hands, he would slip her silk knickers over the flesh of her rounded hips. He would have had no regrets had he died while still imagining such delight.

As for Laviolette, his only company were thoughts as bitter as the lavender stalk he was chewing to take his mind off the craving for a smoke.

"Look!" he said. "From this vantage point it's easy to see what they're trying to do. The location of the fires are an indication of their plan. They've begun surrounding pockets of resistance I was ordered to join. They must be wonderfully well informed," he said bitterly. "And we'll never know who gave them that information!"

"Don't worry," Ismaël said. "We'll get out of this all right. You don't know who you're with!"

"An impetuous kid!" Laviolette sighed wearily. "And in love with death! Seventeen, my eye! You'd be fifteen at the very most."

"Come! You'll see," Ismaël said.

He slipped purposefully down to the beginning of the track that went under the holly-oaks.

"Come where?" Laviolette asked. "They're everywhere!"

"Just come! I know a place where you'll be safe."

It was on this dim, rough path full of bumps and potholes, but completely hidden under hazel trees and tangled arches of tall brambles that Ismaël told Laviolette the story of his blindness. They had begun walking with one close behind the other, but by the end there were more than five metres between the two men. So great were the older man's misgivings that he had drawn back the further they went.

"I'm a free thinker," Laviolette said, "and as such I don't believe your cock and bull story."

"You'd better pray that it's true," Ismaël said. "It's our only hope."

"What is?"

"The place where I'm taking you!"

There's an unnamed stream between the hills of Lurs and Ganagobie, crossed by two bridges: one is 2000 years old and the other hardly eighty. One overlooks the local road, the other overlooks the highway. The two fugitives walked along the riverbed under the bridges as the moon was growing pale and day was breaking. In the distance, the mountains around Barcelonnette were covered in a rosy glow, and just thinking of the word urged Ismaël on.

At that time, there was a vast marshland of bulrushes where the teal made their nests at the meeting point of the stream and the river. It came from the capricious Durance, which often changed course depending on the rise and fall of its waters. They found a deserted duck screen where a mat of teal nests made an ideal bed. The tops of the rushes closed over them. The stalks shivered in the wind and the heads knocked against each other with a strange whispering sound, then all fell silent at once. But the sounds of war continued. The planes were now diving down low over roads and bridges, no longer in formation. The two men in the rushes were aware of the ominous silence when they swept off, the furious din when they returned, followed by the rapid shooting at some invisible object, then the majestic swoop into the sky again, buzzing like joyful dragonflies, proof that they were lords of the sky.

But Laviolette and Ismaël were on the ground. Through the rushes they could see motorbikes driven by soldiers in grey-green uniforms. They heard shooting, definitely on land. They saw two bodies drift past face down in the stream beyond the reed beds, becoming snagged on the roots of a white willow that had been dead for more than thirty years. But they were too exhausted to pay much attention to anything. They slept covered in flies, their faces filthy, their mouths open. At about three o'clock in the afternoon, during a brief period when he was sleeping less heavily, Ismaël thought he heard the knell tolling in the church at Les Mées. The familiar doleful sound of the bell had so often reached Lurs when the wind was in the right direction that it did not disturb his sleep.

On the other hand, the two men started like jumping beans at the infernal noise of planes flying quite close to them and at only ten metres from the ground. They were uselessly firing at the railway track and showering it with bullets, which ploughed into the ballast.

"Let's beat it!" Laviolette said. "If the rushes catch fire we'll be roasted alive, and if their aim's bad we'll be killed by the Yanks! That'd be the ultimate absurdity!"

"The ford!" Ismaël cried. "I know it like the back of my hand!"

The water was still up to their thighs. The current was strewn with bits and pieces that were still smoking and floating rubbish that smelled of burnt debris and charred rags. A smouldering beam of wood, still hissing, sailed down the middle of the stream like a funeral barge. A sky-blue dress caught on a protruding nail billowed out like a sail. The water smelled of rotting walls and stable straw, some of which formed little islands slowly revolving in the eddies. Over the sandy bed of the wide part of the Durance, the water shimmered with small satiny spirals. As the moon had not yet risen, it was impossible to tell in the dim night light whether it was oil or blood.

There was no real shelter between the Durance and the square grove of Pontradieu rising out of the plain like a fortress. They followed the irrigation channels, bent double, sometimes running for cover under hazel trees that provided occasional dark spots where they could rest and catch their breath. The moon suddenly rose between l'Estrop and le Cheval Blanc, and from then on nothing was hidden in the valley. It was a full August moon which took no notice of men on the run. On the contrary, it made their large shadows stand out clearly on the roads.

On the Dabisse road, there were four labouring motorbikes and a vehicle making the now familiar coffee mill noise that accompanied all the alerts during the five days since Ismaël had left Pontradieu.

"There it is!" he announced.

"You're taking me right into the lion's mouth!" Laviolette said. Before them was a big field of potatoes ready for harvesting, and at the end of the 100-metre-long rows stood the park of Pontradieu, looking as black as a wall in the night.

"There it is!" Ismaël said again, his heart beating fast.

They would have to cross the field without cover, but once at the end of it, he could take Rose in his arms again. However, all Laviolette's attention was focused on the group of vehicles travelling down the road.

"They'll cut us off!" he said.

"It's cut off everywhere," Ismaël replied. "We saw it from up there. They're surrounding all the pockets of resistance. They'll drive us into their machine-guns like rabbits! There won't be any escape!"

"Let's get out of here!" Laviolette said. "That place of yours is hopeless! I'm going back up the Durance."

"They'll take pot shots at you from all the bridges! The moon won't set before six in the morning. It's as bright as day out there! They'll be able to see you standing out against the pebbles a kilometre away!"

"What else do you suggest?"

"Come with me," Ismaël said. "Trust me."

When they arrived at the other side of the field, they saw flashes of light through the trees in the park.

"Come on!" Ismaël said again.

Looking through a hole in the hedge they could see the facade of Pontradieu brightly lit up by the moon. The figures of two German soldiers stood out clearly as they hammered on the front door. From where the two fugitives were hiding, it was hard to make out their grey-green greatcoats, but they were wearing their ridiculous high caps. A shot rang out. It was one of the soldiers firing at the lock on the door.

"My God! Rose!" Ismaël groaned.

He made a move to rush off. Laviolette just managed to grab him and hold him in a solid grip.

"Are you crazy? Do you think I've done all this to end up getting killed in some chivalrous exploit of yours?"

"Stay then!" Ismaël said. "I'm going!"

"I'll knock you out if you make a move!" Laviolette growled menacingly. "These soldiers don't kill women. You'll have to learn to tell them apart. The Krauts are methodical: they allocate the work. For some it's war; for others it's butchery."

Ismaël struggled, not about to give in. He was mortally afraid for Rose.

"If we don't take shelter," Laviolette said, "they'll catch us like flies. There are at least four motorbikes. They must be combing the thickets. Where's your shelter?"

"Over there!" Ismaël said.

Through the poplars, the chapel looked almost blinding with the moonlight shining on its pink marble and casting a long, oddly-shaped shadow. To get to it they would have to cross the open forecourt where the three children used to play hide-and-seek, shrieking with delight.

"That's where I fell when I was blind," Ismaël whispered, "and when I got up I could see as well as I can see today!"

"Is that all you're proposing as protection? Listen, I have my own convictions," Laviolette whispered back. "You surely don't think I'm going to change them on the strength of nonsense like that?"

"Do as you like!" Ismaël said.

He dashed forward. An urge as irresistible as the one that had drawn him towards the tomb when he was four years old was now controlling and guiding him. He pushed open the door and found himself in the dark. Laviolette was beside him, panting. He pushed the door shut with his skinny behind and leaned against it.

"We're caught like rats in a trap!' he breathed. "But this is worth it, if only to prove to you you're a loony!"

"Lie down!" Ismaël ordered.

He had just heard the sound of a car engine approaching. The beam from a blue headlight swept over the ceiling of the tomb. Tyres crunched over the gravel path. Suddenly the dull blue light aimed at the door of the tomb changed to a bright white. Two car doors banged. The two hunted men heard the click of firearms. An order shouted by a stentorian voice rang out a few steps away and echoed in the vault like a drum. The special lights on the vehicle shone all around the walls inside the tomb. There was only a thin area left in shadow above the floor where the two men lay stretched out like corpses.

Steps approached on the gravel. They could hear the heavy animal breathing typical of men at war, who always think they are powerful but are also afraid. Anyone who has heard this inimitable panting like a bear above his head can never forget it, any more than the man doing the breathing over a nest of the enemy he has to shoot first or be shot. He wakes in the middle of the night in peacetime, thinking he can hear it, but it's the humiliating sound of his own fear and his own worthlessness that he's remembering.

Ismaël felt the preparatory tensing of muscles in Laviolette, who learned it as an obedient resistance recruit in English training camps. He heard the sling of his rifle moving, and laid a hand on Laviolette's arm, whispering,

"Don't be stupid!"

The soldiers standing in front of the tomb exchanged four sentences in German and then there was silence. A silence still dominated by the sounds of war in the distance: the carpet of planes, a convoy driving north up the road, shots being fired, the dull thud of distant explosions. The silence directly above the fugitives continued. Then the heavy breathing from the two soldiers suddenly stopped and the sound of boots on the gravel was heard once more. The tramping footsteps moved away. Ismaël and Laviolette were breathing each other's sweat. The beam from the headlights turned blue then disappeared altogether. The vault was in darkness again. It took several minutes for the two hunted men to stop shivering like frightened animals.

"Why didn't they come in?" Laviolette whispered. "They could have!"

"What do you know about what they could or couldn't do?"

"You lot are hopeless!" Laviolette groaned. "Wilfully ignorant! Ignorant!"

He banged his fist on the cold tombstone where he was lying.

"Ignorant!" he repeated angrily. "Ignorant!"

He was overcome with despair but also with exhaustion. He collapsed over the marble slabs and fell asleep. Ismaël had but one thought in his head: to go and find Rose. He tried to stand up but fell down again. The strain of five days on the run, his path strewn with bodies at every turn, had taken all the strength from his legs. He tried to reach out and push open the door, but fell down beside the still body of Laviolette.

He fell asleep immediately in spite of the cold marble, as one does at fifteen. But reality had not yet finished with him, wanting him to remain clear-headed so that it would finally teach him what life was all about.

The moon, which had risen in the La Bléone valley, was moving across the sky. Its light flooded the vast forecourt in front of the tomb and moved up across the wrought iron door, bathing it in a soft iridescence, through the glass cracked by a stone thrown by a four-year-old child years before. The moonlight stopped, and shone gently but insistently on Ismaël's face. He moaned and tossed about for some time, trying to get away from it by turning over in his sleep. But he could feel it on his back like heat from the sun. His nose was down a crack in a badly sealed tombstone, which exuded an unforgettable musty smell. It was subtle and bitter-sweet, something like the smell of a pheasant twisting in the draught of a cold cellar. This insidious mixture of mock-orange and flesh ever so slightly bruised would certainly not allow a person to sleep anywhere near it. Ismaël's eyes opened wide.

His hands with their slender fingers were spread out on the marble slab covering a grave. The moonlight shone down in such a way that Ismaël could clearly see his bones under the skin, which had shrunk slightly after four days almost without food. He wanted to take them away from the light so that he would not have to look at them. It was then that the brightness of the moon shone straight on to the tombstone and the inscription newly engraved in gold lettering:

Rose Sépulcre

1906–1944

Ismaël threw back his head and began to howl like a dog.

XII

WHEN OLD MAN AUSTREMOINE OPENED HIS EYES IN HIS GARRET, HE heard what sounded like gentle rain on the roofing stones, as he did every morning. It was actually the dew falling. It was the salvation of Le Parpaillon, La Tête de Moyse, Le Brec du Chambeyron, invisible behind the shady side of the Gleizières heights, where everything was still black. Every day in summer he awoke to this light drumming. "As long as I can hear that," he thought, "I'll know my hearing is still all right."

He got up, put on his boots and went downstairs. He had always slept half-dressed, a habit he had learned from his father. But since the land had started to slide towards his property, he fell asleep at night with his belt done up and his socks on.

When he got to the bottom step, he was surprised by the silence, before remembering that he had been alone for so many days. Usually his three unshaven sons were sitting up in a line like a string of onions on the bench behind the axe-hewn table, taciturn and eternally unsmiling. Although they were not there, he imagined them as they were every morning: each with his brawny arm firmly around his bowl of milk and chicory, for fear that someone might snatch it from him.

The cat sitting on the low chair had been on edge since the previous evening. It gave old Austremoine a reproachful look as he passed by. It was waiting by the cold hearth for the warmth it expected every day. Peasants living 1400 metres up light the fire before daybreak in August, especially when they have only the fireplace to heat liquids.

Old Austremoine leaned over the heap of ashes. He pushed some aside with the tongs to fish out a few live coals. He steadied the tripod, took down the black saucepan from under the chimney piece, and poured out some water from a demijohn that always sat on the little fire stove in the corner of the hearth. At that moment he heard the cat give a long, anxious wail. He turned to it.

"*Qué as*? What's wrong with you?" he said.

The cat didn't move. It looked like a stuffed animal, petrified, its legs stiff, its back arched almost in two and its hair standing up along its spine. Its dilated pupils expressed that terror peculiar to cats, which can make any human take fright. It was staring at the window with the dirty panes into the misty daybreak rising between the muck from the stable and the edge of the forest.

"*Qué as*?" he repeated.

But he trusted a cat more than a dog to give warning of something untoward. He followed the cat's instinct, went over to the door, raised the latch and opened it wide.

The mountain air flowed into the room, smelling of deep, dank earth. The wind often made a kind of creaking noise, but it did not drown another sound that had been heard there for some years. No matter where you were, it was impossible to trace its origin. When anyone asked them about it, the Austremoines would reply, "It's the mountain moving." Those who asked that stupid question would shake their heads while touching their foreheads.

The corner of the house extended over the slope of the hillside so that Austremoine could not see the horizon. He walked as far as the dunghill and shaded his eyes with both hands. The sun had just come half up over the steep side of La Tête de Moyse. Its slanting rays fell across half the landscape. Everything above it was bright and shiny morning; everything below was still battling with night.

At the bottom of the big field, in the fading shadows at the edge of the spruce trees, old Austremoine caught sight of his eldest son limping along, bent over under the weight of a large jute sack. He hurried down towards him. His son fell down on one knee and the sack slipped down from his shoulder.

"*Qué as?*" Austremoine repeated, as he had done to the cat.

He suddenly felt a surge of father's instinct, which more than thirty years of harsh living had driven out of him. Besides, it was the first time he had seen one of his sons brought to his knees and trembling like a tree about to be chopped down. It was also the first time he had seen one of them on his own. They normally stood close together like a wall: all dark, huge, hardened by mountain life never to feel self-pity.

Austremoine caught hold of his son around the waist.

"For God's sake don't forget that!" his son said.

Austremoine put the sack on his shoulder.

"Where are your brothers?"

"Dead," groaned the son.

His father let him fall back on to the wet grass, swarming with green-bellied beetles at daybreak. He also dropped the sack, which clinked like broken china as it hit the ground. The son groaned with pain.

"Leave me lying here if you like, but don't throw me down like that! Every bone in my body hurts!"

"Dead?" Austremoine repeated.

The son held out his arms.

"Carry me to the house!"

But the father couldn't lift such a weight. He had to drag him, with great difficulty, up to the farmhouse, the limp useless feet leaving a furrow in the wet grass. He threw him on a straw pallet in the scullery on the ground floor.

"Go and fetch the bones!" the son moaned.

"But what about your brothers?" old Austremoine asked.

"I told you. They're dead! We fell into a German ambush. I've got a bullet in my calf. I can feel it against the bone!"

"Let me see!" the father ordered.

He picked up a bottle of brandy as the son dragged himself over flat on his back, crying out with pain. His father lifted him up to remove his trousers and saw a black pustule swollen like a boil, exuding yellow pus.

"A bullet?" the father said. "That's been done by buckshot! Since when have the Germans been using buckshot? Are they that desperate?"

Young Austremoine flopped over on to his stomach with a groan. He couldn't even turn his head towards his father, his neck was so stiff. The old man poured the equivalent of two glasses of fiery brandy on his leg. The air began to smell of it. The cat jumped off its chair and disappeared outside.

"It was two women!" the son groaned. "At least I think it was two women. We'd just replaced the marble slab. Everything had gone according to plan. We'd got everything. It all happened as we were leaving. Those two bitches were watching us behind the box bushes. They shouted to us to stop. Then we fired and they fired. We laid one out cold on the spot, but not before she got Georges in her sights. He fell forward on to the gravel. We knew he was dead!"

"You idiots!" the father growled. "And I suppose you were close up side by side as usual, so that they couldn't miss you?"

"We were facing up to them!" the son moaned. "I'd taken the sack of bones from Georges. I couldn't fire with the load I was carrying. And you know Eustache ... He's so cross-eyed, he'd miss a bull. So we ran off through the woods. The other fury followed us. She knew the terrain better than we did. She kept aiming at us and we kept firing back. We hardly had anything left in our cartridge pouches, and neither did she, apparently. That's what saved us. But it's true about the Germans! We came across them at the Le Moine bridge. There were at least five of them. That's where Eustache was killed. I already had the buckshot in my leg from the beginning. By some miracle I got out of it. I haven't got the strength to tell you all about it, but ... It was a miracle! Perhaps because I was carrying the bones. The bones are there, aren't they?"

"Yes, they're here," the father said.

He shooed away the cat that had come back out of curiosity and was rubbing its back against the sack, purring.

"I'll harness up the cart and take you down to the hospital."

"No, not the hospital! The bloody Krauts are everywhere! If they find me with buckshot in my leg, they'll shoot me!"

With arms flailing, he made a great effort and managed to turn over on his back again. He crossed himself. It was his last conscious gesture. From that moment on, he repeated the same thing over and over again:

"Bury the bones where he used to be! You'll see! It'll stop! Everything will stop! You'll see what that bloody mountain does! Put Séraphin down its mouth like Jason with the Leviathan! He'll stop it flowing! It won't take any more of our land! Go quickly! Run! Go and bury Séraphin Monge!"

He lasted for a whole night. In the morning his back was arched up like a sickle. You could have crawled under his body. Only his neck and the ends of his feet were touching the bed. He looked as if he was laughing. His lips were pulled back showing all his gums and his big yellow teeth set in a silent laugh.

"I don't know how you can do it!" old Austremoine said. He had never seen the tetanus grimace before.

The son's body suddenly collapsed like a puppet, and he fell dead on the side of the bed. Old Austremoine put the sack on his shoulder and went out of the house.

He was alone. The planes had begun circling around again, flying lower and lower. Over mountains and valleys, you could see smoke rising in trails, in swirls and in patches. You could hear the noise of explosions vibrate in the calm morning air. An enormous black cloud drifting towards Italy from behind La Tête de Moyse had come between the earth and the sun.

Carrying his bag of bones, he began walking towards his destination.

It was night in Digne and a tall, bald priest was stumbling through debris left by the bombing. He was pushing one of those bicycles that the Arms and Cycle Factory of Saint-Étienne advertised in its catalogue for thirty years. A big black-painted cane basket, which the people here call a *toilette*, was firmly attached to the solid carrier. He made himself known to the guard posted there to prevent any pillaging. He said he had been summoned by His Grace the Bishop, which was not true. The parish priest scarcely knew whether he dared knock at the door of the bishop's palace in his present state: poor, muddy, and the bearer of a wildly improbable story.

Dust floated over the debris, which still suddenly collapsed from time to time, and was slowly settling over the ruins. Beams protruding from the rubble were still smoking, as were ripped mattresses and mirrored wardrobes which had spewed out all their linen, the family pride.

On that hot night, Mgr Godiot was standing at an open window in his study. He watched the moonlight weeping over the damaged city. He was listening for Digne to vent some groan of legitimate complaint at the injustice of it all. But nothing happened. The proud city maintained its silence as usual.

Mgr Godiot had lost twenty-five kilos. His ecclesiastical belly had sagged like that of a woman who had borne too many children. His flesh was drawn down towards the ground along his bones. Flabby cheeks hiding much of his mouth gave him the sad face of an old dog, and the large head, once so majestic in the fullness of his flesh, seemed to have shrunk to half its size.

This physical decline was the result of a vow. When he was with Dr Jouve and heard the warning siren ring out for the first time, he had resolved to offer up what was most important to him for the misery of the world.

"Dear Lord," he said in silent prayer, "I can't promise you great mystical fervour; it's not in my nature, and my soul is not capable of such flights. I enjoy perfect physical health and enviable mental stability. But I believe in You with all the fervour of my simple heart and my ordinary intelligence. What can I offer my God but my hunger? My unworthy mortification is, alas, purely material. I'm not an ascetic by nature."

From that time on, this hearty-eating prelate had been slowly starving. He would look sympathetically at the fat, greasy Protestant minister he sometimes met on his way to the cathedral. For his part, he ate only bread and a little milk from a goat that fed among the wild fig trees on the Bléone slopes and was very reluctantly milked by one of the nuns on duty. Sometimes when he was taking the air in his gardens where the sisters grew potatoes instead of flowers, the smell of non-existent braised beef would rise up from the street outside, especially for him.

The people of the Basses Alpes, however, did not want to see Mgr Godiot, who had been their bishop for so long, condemned to short rations. At that time our land was a network of fertile though poor farms. The hard work of their women could feed a lot of people and gifts from the peasants flooded in. It was sent on to the hospitals in large amounts, but a little was kept for the clergy.

To get around this difficulty, when war broke out Mgr Godiot made up the story that he was suffering from a bad stomach ulcer, for he hated any show of piety. He did not wish to be responsible for any vow but his own, nor to encourage anyone to follow his example.

On that night, however, Mgr Godiot had not been thinking of his empty stomach or his physical decline for some time. He was surprised at the depth of the silence around him. There was not even the sound of the planes. They seemed to be ashamed to show themselves again after having blasted Digne with a useless surplus of bombs dropped at random. Yet Mgr Godiot was also surprised that a people's suffering was not more audible. The day after tomorrow, when thirty-seven coffins would be ready for the thirty-seven bodies whose various parts would be duly identified and put together with the now limited resources available, Mgr Godiot, coped and mitred, would pronounce absolution for these needless casualties.

And among them would be the remains of the charming Baroness Ramberti, who had been in his thoughts and dreams for so many years. In her thirst for compassion, she had been one of the first to go and help. A wall had collapsed on her. Her lovely face no longer had either form or beauty when she was pulled out of the debris.

Mgr Godiot tried to recall those features, that smile, the lively sparkle in her eyes, the intensity of her gaze when she looked at him, that charm ... He remembered how he had sometimes stood behind the curtain at that self-same window and seen her on the footpath opposite. Before she crossed the street she would take a mirror from her handbag to make sure she was presentable. Mgr Godiot had never bothered to interpret or try to understand this shy humility in women, who are never sure of being attractive; that is until today, when the one who had so often performed these ritual gestures could no longer defend her lost beauty against any attack.

"She did it for me," he whispered. "All that care and preparation, all that attention to detail in little tricks to make herself beautiful, which were vain but so touching in their vanity."

He felt sobs rise in his throat.

"What harm would it have done me," he thought, "what harm would it have done the Lord, what harm would it have done to my faith if I had been kind enough to hold her close to me like a child, for in spite of what she thought she wanted from me, that was what she really needed, what all mortals need."

It was too late. He had heard of her death from local gossip. He had never seen her again after the fatal scene between them. He suddenly found the severity of dogma hard to bear. He stared at the moonlight, the trees, the street, a passing dog, everything untouched by the war.

Then, as if appearing out of his search for memories, he saw a dark figure trudging up the footpath opposite towards the bishop's residence, pushing a heavily laden bicycle. He recognized it from its strange appearance as the incumbent of some poor country parish. The priest crossed the road with his bicycle and His Grace heard the bell being pulled. Nine o'clock was striking at St Jérôme's.

"They'll turn him away," the bishop thought. "The nuns won't have me disturbed. They're very strict on that score, especially since they started to worry about my being so thin. Besides, I didn't summon him. Now, a person who turns up at nine in the evening without an invitation, in these difficult times, can only be driven by some urgent need. Let us go and see."

He arrived just in time to surprise the sister in the act of pushing the door shut on the intruder after having summarily refused him entry. But the priest had put the basket he had unloaded from his bicycle in the doorway.

"Let him come in," the bishop ordered.

"But it's nine o'clock Your Grace."

"Come now, Sister," the bishop said impatiently. "If this priest arrives so late and under these difficult conditions, he must have a reason for it."

"Yes Your Grace, I do," the priest said firmly.

"Come up to my study. But first, leave your basket. You can pick it up on your way out."

"Excuse me, Your Grace, but that thing is the very reason why I'm here. With your permission, I'd prefer to keep it with me."

"As you wish. Let us go upstairs," the bishop said.

"Wipe your feet!" the nun said crossly to the priest.

She was thinking that if His Grace hadn't recently taken it into his head to stand at the window and breathe the evening air, the man would already be on his way with his wretched wicker basket.

The country priest took some time scraping the soles of his shoes on the doormat. He was as gnarled as an alpine tree and his bony head had a stubborn brow. He appeared neither intimidated nor embarrassed. People who have a secret are always like that: sure and resolute.

When they had satisfied the rules of ecclesiastical small talk and the priest had sat down with his *toilette* basket beside him, Mgr Godiot said,

"Tell me your story!"

"This morning a man named Félix Austremoine from the farm at Fumeterre came to see me. He brought me a sack of bones which I transferred to this basket. Some time ago, a man called Séraphin Monge died in our mountains. He came from elsewhere and was buried alive in a landslide. I should mention that I minister, amongst others, to the remote area of Les Fosses-Gleizières, where a landslip of considerable proportions is taking place. Perhaps Your Grace knows about it?"

"Yes, I do," the bishop said.

"My flock has believed a superstition for some time, and still believes that this landslip stopped for the whole time that Séraphin Monge was buried there. Then, one day the bones were taken away and the earth began to slip again. I'm sorry, Your Grace, but this is the chronological, if not the logical order, in which these things actually happened."

The bishop made no reply, showed no surprise, no scorn. His old dog's face still expressed only sadness.

"This man Austremoine had three sons. His property is the one most exposed to the landslip, and the Austremoine men are the most miserly in the canton. They are also the most dull-witted. They have been proclaiming the unfairness of their fate long and loud. To cut a long story short . . . The three Austremoine sons believed that the war provided a good opportunity that would not come again. They took advantage of the events of these last weeks to go and get back these . . . remains, from the place where they were buried. Two women there ordered them off, then shot at them. The

Austremoines killed one woman. The men died, all three of them, by various means."

The priest of Enchastrayes had thought, throughout his difficult journey, that he would need a full five minutes to explain the matter before doubtless being shown the door. Excluding the time it had taken to catch his breath, he was fairly sure from watching the clock on the mantelpiece that he had been speaking for barely four, and that he had more or less covered everything.

"But," he pointed out, "the last one died only this morning from tetanus after bringing the sack back to his father."

"But if he believed that these . . . objects could stop the landslip, why did the father give them to you?"

"He said to me, 'What use are they to me now? Even if the land stops disappearing, I have no-one left to work it.'"

Mgr Godiot wondered at that moment why he was reluctant to tell the priest what he knew about the whole tragedy.

"And so," he said, "you have come eighty kilometres to bring me this sack of bones, in these difficult times, knowing the risks you might run . . ."

"By the grace of God, I don't have to tell you about those, since I got here safely."

"What made you do it?"

"The fear of scandal, Your Grace. These bones, which backward peasants believe to be endowed with some virtues or other, are a source of scandal to the Church."

"In that case, why didn't you have them buried in the normal way? With no fuss?"

The parish priest of Enchastrayes pondered for a few seconds before replying.

"Because the Austremoines, although the most dull-witted, are not the only ones to be quite convinced of the legend – and may he who has already seen the mountains descend on him cast the first stone – I even think that they all believe it. They simply would never have let me bury these remains in hallowed ground."

He hesitated for a moment before continuing.

"And then . . . Men and women have been killed. The story will get out.

The war is still on for the moment. It can hide many things in its shadow, but everything leads me to believe that it will soon be over. Then there'll be an inquiry. We won't have heard the end of these bones if we don't quietly put them back where the Austremoines stole them."

"That was your intention?"

"Yes, Your Grace, but I'm old. I'm seventy-seven. I'm worn out. It's another forty kilometres to the place Auphanie Brunel, our tobacconist, told me about before I left. I'd never get there. I've already been dragging myself from bush to bush since Barles, fearing for my life and my mission. Time and time again I thought I could never get going again. Our Lord has helped me . . . but for how long?"

The bishop looked closely at the priest who was trembling like an exhausted horse. "He's right," he thought. "He'll die before he gets there."

"Believe me, Your Grace, I never intended disturbing you," the priest of Enchastrayes continued, "but I knocked at the door of the priest at Saint Jérôme's, and he didn't answer, either through deafness or fear. I wandered all over Digne, where I know no-one. I came here out of desperation."

At that moment hunger made itself felt and, always a poor adviser, changed the mood of the bishop, who thought he had forgotten all about it.

"Why did you come and burden my mind with this absurd story?" he complained irritably. "I've been praying for the last twenty-four hours for the thirty-seven who were killed in the bombing. What am I to do with your bones?"

He got up and turned his back, annoyed at having his thoughts interrupted and, to top it off, his stomach felt as empty as a drum. He heard a dull noise on the floor behind him.

"Forgive me, Your Grace," the priest said, "but you are my pastor. You are the one who knows what should be done. I am in the shadows of faith!"

His Grace turned around quickly. He saw that the priest was kneeling, without having been asked to do so.

"Get up!" thundered the bishop. "Get up immediately!"

He reached out his hands to help the old man rise to his feet.

346

"Don't you realize that I am as humble as you?" he muttered. "But where, who told you about the shadows of faith?"

"Why, no-one, Your Grace!" the startled priest replied. "I simply feel that is the state I am in."

"That is the state we are all in," the bishop sighed.

He gave a sideways glance at the black-painted *toilette*, an appropriate colour for something to hold a priest's provisions. The bishop thought for a moment. Mgr Beckx must be on hot coals somewhere in his office or his bedroom or battling with the stubborn silence of the nuns. At that time, they were two portly women in billowing habits who came from the sisters of the Holy Trinity at Embrun. They had inherited the traditional antipathy that all the nuns felt – no-one knew why – for the long, pointed face of the vicar general.

"Just put that cumbersome *toilette* in the window recess and pull the curtain over it," the bishop said.

He had just made a decision and found the way to put it into practice without the presence of his vicar general.

"I needn't tell you not to speak of this to anyone. And I mean *anyone*," he insisted. "I'm saying this to you because I shall get Mgr Beckx to accompany you to Saint Jérôme's presbytery. They'll open the door to him. I shall give orders to them to feed and house you for the night. Tomorrow you will return to Enchastrayes with your mind at rest. Think no more about all this. Oh! Just one thing. Is your bicycle in working order?"

"It's twelve years old, Your Grace."

The bishop picked up the enormous bell sitting on top of his missal on the very tidy desk. He kept ringing it until one of the sisters appeared, after taking her time getting there.

"Ask Mgr Beckx to come and see me," he said.

The vicar general was there in the twinkling of an eye. His intense, anxious curiosity seemed to fill the room. The bishop told him what he wanted him to do and put the parish priest of Enchastrayes into his care.

He stood waiting until he heard the front door close before walking over to the window where he had hidden the wicker basket. It seemed heavy when he lifted it, but that was no doubt because his lack of food had weakened him.

He brought it over to the light. He took out the rod that fastened the lid and opened it.

He saw a pile of earth-coloured bones, which had obviously not been handled with any care. They were crammed together, many of them broken. Others were crumbling into dust, with the exception of a large sternum as big as a washerwoman's paddle and a perfect skull. The bishop picked it up in both hands.

"The shadows of faith," he murmured. "So this is it!"

He set Séraphin's skull on the marble mantelpiece above the cold fireplace and watched the flickering light from the candlestick dancing on the teeth, which sparkled as if they were still alive. The forehead was cracked like parched earth, and the everlasting smile of this creature who had never smiled in his life intimidated Mgr Godiot. He found himself turning away, as if those empty sockets were staring at him, expecting him to understand at last.

But where exactly did the enigma lie? In the imagination of those who firmly believed in the power of those miserable remains? In the guilty hesitation, which perhaps Mgr Godiot enjoyed instead of saying "no" to the doubt he continued to entertain? Or was it in that skull itself, or at least in what it represented: the infinite realm of the unknown?

What finally was Séraphin Monge's metaphysic, his essential nature and purpose?

Well, the devil whispered to him, there's a very simple way to prove it. Just give the pile of bones back to the people of Les Fosses-Gleizières and let them bury them wherever they like. If the landslip stopped its natural course for the equivalent of a grain of sand more or less in its weight and strength, when all human efforts had been exhausted, perhaps then (but would he ever allow himself to believe it?) there would be a small new hope in the mountain, and it would not be unwelcome.

"No!" he said quietly. "It's a risk I refuse to take."

He dared to look squarely at the empty eye sockets of the skull, which was at his height on the mantelpiece of the tall fireplace with its coats of arms. At the same time he seemed to hear the voice of the Baroness Ramberti, when she used to say to him, "Your Grace, you don't dare to go the whole

348

way, as usual. You take refuge behind the *non possumus* like a child behind its mother's skirts. You don't want to be free of doubt about yourself, other people or even the nature of the world!"

In spite of the love he bore her dear memory – he had finally admitted it to himself – his reply to this challenge was still the same. He obstinately shook his head. He picked the skull up firmly with both hands as if it were an ordinary object, put it back in the *toilette*, and threaded the rod through the two plaited handles.

"No, I don't want to be free of doubt! It's not the Church's role to be free of doubt!"

The priest from Enchastrayes showed him the way. With his simple faith, he didn't know it, he wasn't even aware of it, but his infallible instinct had unhesitatingly led him to make the right decision: remove these unimportant relics from the test of truth. He didn't want to be free of doubt either.

His Grace rang the large bell vigorously once again. He had to get away before the vicar general returned and started making a fuss.

The nun arrived, grumbling this time as she found His Grace very restless that evening. She found him holding the black wicker basket that had caused her so much bother when she opened the door to the priest from Enchastrayes. He almost bumped into her as he passed, wanting to take advantage of her surprise.

"I'm going out!" he said in a tone of voice that brooked no dissent.

"Your Grace is going out?" the sister spluttered. "Without waiting for his meal, without . . ."

"Yes! Without all that! And I won't be back tonight!" he added, cutting off further questions.

"But there's the curfew!"

"No-one is keeping it any more!"

"But, Your Grace. It's dangerous! Everything's in turmoil! It's not fitting!"

"Do you think, Sister, that last night was fitting? That what's happening around us is fitting? And do you really think that the coming of Christ on earth was *fitting*?"

He said these stern words as he was crossing the hall, still holding the *toilette.* They wanted to take it out of his hands, but he used all his authority to keep hold of it.

"You'll get yourself killed!" the sister cried, forgetting the niceties of ecclesiastical address.

"So what!" His Grace snapped. "Just hold the door while I take this wretched *toilette* outside!"

The priest's bicycle was there, thin, black and venerable, like a lady's companion. The moonlight gave a false appearance of youth to frame and wheels, which bore the marks of its many battles against mud, ice and flint.

Mgr Godiot efficiently attached the basket to the carrier, an action that took him back to when he was fifteen and his father, a peasant from Le Trièves, had him take crates of eggs to the Mens market. The nun could not bring herself to close the door again.

"Mgr Beckx won't be pleased!" she said.

"Oh! Mgr Beckx! Mgr Beckx!"

The bishop made the sweeping gesture of throwing salt over his shoulder. He took hold of the handlebars and got on the bicycle. He wobbled a little with the first few turns of the pedals, but soon steadied himself. The little peasant from Le Trièves came to life again on the black bicycle, which groaned under the respectable weight, despite his fasting, of this giant of a bishop.

When Mgr Godiot had crossed the waters of the Bléone at the ford, he found himself saying these words, which were to come back and back throughout that eventful night:

"Thinkest thou that I cannot now pray to my Father, and he shall presently give me more than twelve legions of angels?"

Where had he read that in his studious young days? Was he even sure it came from the Gospels? He had never dared look up those holy words, preferring to take their veracity on trust. But on that night, who knows if even twelve cohorts would have been enough to cleanse the land of the cruelty and madness that was raging through it.

Deathly, stinking smoke lingered in the air and, in spite of the moon, even blocked out some of the countryside. The water no longer made any sound, the birds had fallen silent, and it was as if the wind dared not shake the smallest branch. The only noise now was made by men, and there cannot have been anyone in that whole area who thought of love that night.

Coming from Mallemoisson, all the countryside around the Bléone had a soft halo of light from distant fires that reached almost to Brunet and the dry plain of Majestre. Above Thoard and the Col de Valbelle, in forests scarcely fifty years old, the uneven tops of the trees were red towards Sisteron, as if dawn was about to break over them. You could hear the dull sound of bombs exploding somewhere.

Dominating all of this was the carpet of planes rolling on and on, and sounding like a hive of angry bees. They had taken control of the sky all over Europe. The bishop had a vision of fountains springing up under the deluge of iron pouring down from the planes. But these fountains spouted red flesh, which fell in scattered, tangled and unrecognizable pieces, deprived of even the hope of inspiring either grief or fervour. He blessed the mission he had undertaken. Why should he have stayed cosy and safe in his study when everything was suffering or dying around him? He pushed his bicycle with its basket of bones as a small expiation. He was also judging himself. What part did pride play in this unseemly self-abasement, and what was his responsibility concerning popular belief? Was it "to stay immersed in the shadows of faith"?

He wove his way from one dark spot to another. Twice he had to cross the stream and hide under a bridge as the death machines passed overhead. He pedalled undisturbed for a full hour down sunken paths leading to isolated farms where even the terrified dogs no longer barked, and you felt that all the inhabitants were living in the greatest fear of their lives.

"Do they pray though?" Mgr Godiot wondered out loud.

He was certain that no-one in that dark night was thinking of Jesus Christ. He was sure that religion seemed as empty as this war-torn night, that the churches too were empty and the crucifixes nailed over every bed were never even glanced at. And the signs and signals that God had made to man, how distant they seemed! He heard the bones rattling in the *toilette*.

They were being reduced to fragments by the ruts and jolts as he rode along the country tracks.

"And what if I'd refused to cocoon myself in the shadows of faith," he thought, "if I'd wanted to be free of doubt, to be certain?"

He was on the point of turning back towards the dark mountains, but he was too faint-hearted not to blindly obey what the Church would have required of him, had it been able to give him orders at that moment. But it had implanted those orders in him a long time ago. He was surprised to find them so much in keeping with what his own love of logic and harmony dictated.

"The sin would be to attract attention by allowing the scandal of a false sainthood to spread in the diocese under my care. No-one has asked me to verify it. On the contrary, I have been strongly recommended to avoid scandal. By quietly taking these bones back to their normal grave (which won't be possible as soon as this indescribable chaos ceases), I am acting strictly according to good sense."

These thoughts were going through his mind as he neared the Chaffaut bridge, riding past the fine stand of aspens overlooking the Bléone which slumbered at low water between one little plateau and the next.

It was then he had the impression that the wicker basket on the carrier behind him was becoming heavier by the minute. He went on for about another 100 metres, but it would have been beyond him to go any further. He stopped, exhausted, and leaned his bicycle against a tree.

Then a whistling sound made itself heard above the continuous hum of the planes. The shining cross of a bomber, bathed in moonlight and looking almost translucent, suddenly appeared above the bridge. The whistling stopped abruptly as the plane rose up into the sky again. Mgr Godiot knew what that meant. He had heard that same silence twenty-four hours before when Digne was bombed. He threw himself down on his stomach. The ground beneath him shook twice, as it had thirty years ago in Argonne, when he was a stretcher-bearer. Earth and pebbles rained down on his cassock. A piece of gravel came to a stop after ricocheting off his tonsure. His Grace stayed hugging the ground for several minutes after the noise of the explosions had ceased. His eardrums hurt as if they were about to burst with the shrillness of the noise.

"Did I have time to be frightened?" he wondered. He felt his pulse. "No, I didn't have time for that. Did I have even enough to prepare to die?"

No. He hadn't had time to make the sign of the cross either, although it was an instinctive gesture in Christians.

He looked about him. The bridge seemed to be intact, but a car was silently burning half way across it. A horrible smell of tyres and human fat melting together in the fire enveloped the bishop in swirls of black smoke blocking out the moonlight. Men were running further away beyond the bridge. They were calling out to each other in German. Were they fleeing? Were they looking for a group of Resistance fighters to exterminate? The bishop was not sure which direction to take to avoid them. His bicycle looked strange lying there against the foot of the tree, where he had left it. He got on again and had as much trouble as before riding among the ruts on the track. He zigzagged for about 150 metres, but was suddenly confronted with a hole. The path no longer existed. The shell had blasted a wide hole more than a metre deep with part of a tree lying across it. Strange thoughts came into his mind as he stood there gazing at it, bicycle in hand,

"If I'd kept going," he thought, "if I'd been riding on this slightly sloping path at the same speed I'd been doing for kilometres, and if I hadn't stopped because I was exhausted, in all probability I would have arrived at the spot where the bomb fell at the same time as it did." "Perhaps not!" his critical faculties retorted. "You'd need to do a whole set of ballistic calculations to prove it!" "Perhaps not, but it's possible."

"Oh, come now!" he said, reproaching himself out loud.

He was about to untie the basket to check its weight, in spite of his inner convictions, and as he was looking for somewhere to lean his bicycle, he realized that it was bucking when he pushed it backwards. He leaned over and saw that the back brake was jammed on the rim.

"Well, there you are!" Mgr Godiot exclaimed, his face lighting up.

He was very pleased to be able to think that he had not been granted any exception in the small incident that had just occurred. For a moment he had feared that God had lost patience and forced him to be free of doubt in spite of himself. Fortunately, that was not the case. The weight of the basket had not varied, as he had so foolishly feared. He lifted it up to finally convince himself. So, if God had wanted to keep Mgr Godiot provisionally on this earth to continue doing His work, He had done it in the most reassuring and obvious way possible: by providing him with a mechanical accident.

In order to avoid stumbling into a German post or a Resistance ambush, the bishop did as he intended: he crossed back over the Bléone again, pushing his bicycle. Once there, he heard the happy sound of water in an irrigation channel, and found himself face to face with a lone man who smelled of honest sweat and earth. The farmer had just released the sluice gate to water his fields. He straightened up, singing a song.

This man was neither a torturer nor a victim. He did not lean towards either side. All he wanted was to make sure he could keep some food for himself and others whenever possible. The way he went about things was simple and unaffected. Just now he could have been lying face down in the channel, shot by some anonymous sniper, but there he was, happily singing. Yet his wife must have said to him,

"Do you really think this is the right time to go and water the melon bed?"

"It needs it," he replied.

That was reason enough. What did the Germans, the maquis and the endless sea of planes matter? The melon bed needed water, full stop. That long night when people looked up to the stars, trying to make sense of the world, would not have been complete without the appearance of that man and his reassurance of continuity.

"People like him will be there, a part of history until the end of the world," the bishop thought. "They will speak of the war as if it were merely someone who had run past their door."

"*Voï!*" the man said. "Is that you, Father?"

There was enough moonlight to make the religious habit visible, but he was a man who couldn't tell a priest from a bishop, even though he respected the cloth.

"I was passing through," His Grace said.

"Fine! I don't know what you're doing with your bicycle in the middle of my rows of melons, but I make it a rule not to ask anyone anything. Particularly the way things are these days. But since you're here, come with me. We're killing the pig. I'll give you two rounds of sausages and you can take the opportunity to bless the house. It must be thirty years since it was done last!"

"If it's in my direction," the bishop said.

"It's over there," the man replied.

He pointed beyond the town of L'Escale to the village of Les Mées, in the shadow of the peaks called the Pénitents. He led the way, swinging his arms.

The farm was notable for its rich smell of manure and the warmth of its stables, where a large number of cattle were stamping their hooves. It was a large severe building entirely without light. The house was hidden by a crowd of trees higher than the rooftops. It looked certain of surviving the upheaval happening all around.

"Come!" the man said. "Don't worry. The lights are covered by the black-out, but it's jollier inside. Come! Meet my wife and children. The way things are these days, as they say, they'll be happy to see a priest. Come and have a bite to eat with us!"

Odours of plentiful good food and wine hung in the air. Smells of feasting rushed outside through the black door leading into the corridor. The bishop's heart failed.

"No!" he said. "No! I have a mission to complete . . ."

He wanted to keep his vow of hunger intact for the remission of his sins and those of his fellow man. He turned his back on temptation, but his soul had been sustained by this chance meeting with simple life. As he left, the weight of the basket on the carrier felt lighter.

All around him, however, the war went on both near and far, as if the whole earth had been blighted by it. He came across a dead body. It was a civilian, still wearing a wing collar and a tie with a pearl pin. He had been killed cleanly, from in front, with a single bullet to the middle of his forehead. A red ribbon stood out on the lapel of his suit. His Grace propped his bicycle against a tree and said a prayer. After which, he set off again.

Weapons flashed, orders and threats rang out at all the moonlit cross-roads. The bishop wove a path between them. Memories slowly came back to him of the time when he dragged his boots through the Argonne mud, spurred on then by a strong will to survive.

And so it was that through the clear August night and longer still, Mgr Godiot made his way through the din of that strange war with no set boundaries and no front line, pushing his heavy bicycle through the ruts and hollows of sunken roads as some kind of penance. In the midst of fearful distant bomb blasts, the crackling of a farm burning as its beams collapsed, the occasional stifled cries of someone being shot against a wall or a tree, the war still allowed the clocks on village steeples to chime the hour. The faces on the clocks were blue, but the regular sound of the hours being struck was enough to recall sound sleep and peace restored.

The last thing he had to avoid was the main road from Les Mées to Oraison, which passed by Pontradieu. Consequently he discovered a good number of farms off the beaten track, sheltered by orchards and gardens. As he passed, he could breathe in the smells and perfumes that had been part of them through the ages, coming from whatever crop the people who lived there set out on trellis to dry.

He also had an unexpected encounter. From a distance he could see the shed of the La Destorbe property lit by the dull light of a lantern. Four German soldiers were harnessing the mare to the Count's barouche. The bishop's heart sank with fear. Had they exterminated the whole family in the house? The large Countess and her two skinny daughters she was having such trouble getting off her hands? No. The Germans were not carrying any visible weapons. When their baby faces passed in front of the lantern, the cold sweat of fear was visible on their downy skin.

While the bishop watched them through the branches of the tall vines which no-one had worried about pruning that year, they managed to harness the mare and put her between the shafts. The four of them were in a panic, jostling to get into the wedding barouche that would give up the ghost after 100 kilometres. Off they went at a gallop. That is the way all the armies in the world disintegrate when they are worn out with casualties.

"They're going home," Mgr Godiot thought, taking things philosophically.

He resumed his wandering through woods and fields. At last, at about two o'clock in the morning, he saw the high treetops of Pontradieu, the finest in the district. They were shining in the distance like the points on a crown.

He had heard and thought so much about the pink marble tomb, and had been obsessed by it for so long, that he went straight to it. He took no precautions crossing the moonlit forecourt pushing his black bicycle in front of him. He no longer needed to hide. Even if some fatal blow were to happen to him here, his mission had been accomplished, and he himself was of little importance. He intended to put the *toilette* on the ground in front of the tomb, where it would be found by the appropriate people the following day. Then he could go back to Digne by the main road and in daylight, arriving at the palace in time for the first office.

After putting his bicycle against the trunk of one of the cypresses, he began to untie the rope around the *toilette*. He took hold of the handle and found it heavier than ever. Then he heard the door of the tomb grating and saw it open. So much had happened that night and the ones preceding it, that Mgr Godiot was no longer capable of surprise. Moreover, the faith that had never left him protected him from inappropriate fear in any situation. And so, when he saw the door open, he was quite calm.

Two gaunt, dishevelled creatures came out, one carrying the other, who had blood on his face.

"I had to knock him out! They'd have caught us! I don't know what's wrong with him. He was howling! Howling like a dog!"

He repeated this sentence as if he was justifying his action.

"He was howling, I tell you!"

While still holding him, Laviolette was trying to staunch the blood still oozing from Ismaël's swollen nose with a dirty handkerchief.

"Come," the bishop said gently. "We'll go up to the house."

That was the moment when Marie, her two children and the Jew were coming out of the château, as there had been no further sound. The previous afternoon they had been visited by two cars full of Germans armed to the teeth. Rose had just been buried in the tomb when they arrived. The four of them just had time to shut themselves in the cellar behind the secret passage. The château echoed with the sound of the soldiers kicking all Pontradieu's carved doors and hitting them with their rifle butts. They bore the marks for a long time afterwards. The four of them had their hearts in their mouths when they heard footsteps pounding the flagstones on the cellar floor, and the cries of delight when the soldiers decided to break the necks of numerous bottles and empty them in a hurry.

"If they torture the farmer, we've had it!" the Jew said. "His daughters will talk!"

But they didn't know that the army was now sensing its own disintegration. The military machine that it had so carefully constructed had almost run down. Like worn-out robots, the soldiers left everything half-finished.

When Marie saw the huge priest advancing towards the steps holding Ismaël, she thought her son was dead and let out a piercing scream. They could not hold her back. She literally threw herself from the top step and ran towards the tight group walking slowly towards the house.

"Ismaël!" she cried.

"He was in the tomb," the bishop said.

"What have you done to him?" Marie said in a threatening tone.

"He was howling his head off!" Laviolette repeated. "They'd have caught us. I just stunned him a bit to make him stop."

Faced with the anger of this good-looking woman, the trained fighter felt like putting his arms up to protect himself from the blows that were going to rain down on him, as he used to do with his mother.

"Brute!" Marie said scornfully.

Then she suddenly remembered that Ismaël and Rose had been lovers for one night and since he had taken shelter in the tomb, he now knew that she was dead.

"Oh Lord! My poor boy! Forgive me. It was my fault she died! I arrived with my gun a moment too late. Forgive me! All I could think of was Séraphin and his bones, which they'd stolen!"

"I've brought them back to you," the bishop said, "and as for the three men, they're dead, all three."

"So much the better!" Marie cried. "Oh, my poor boy!"

She wanted to hold him close and protect him with her love. He pushed her away roughly. He also freed himself from the bishop who had a firm grip on him. Laviolette let him go, full of remorse for the punch he had given the young man.

"Leave me alone," Ismaël moaned. "I must go and weep for her! I must weep for her!"

He crossed the terrace and went up the steps. He went into the house and through the hall, then opened one side of the door to the drawing room, repeating over and over again,

"I must go and weep for her!"

The bishop said later that he went towards the piano and seemed to hold out his arms to her.

The electric light had been cut off for the past two days. When Marie came up from the cellar, she had lit the oil lamp and put it down in the most convenient place.

"Rose!" Ismaël moaned.

He could see her. On the night of the storm he had said to her, "Don't turn on the light!" In Ismaël's eyes, it was she who had just left the lamp on the side of the piano. Her breath, which had scarcely vanished from the room, had just made the heart-shaped flame quiver for the last time.

His hands felt heavy as he placed them on the keyboard. He felt then that the being who constantly haunted him had taken his place, considering him inadequate for such a moment, and it was he who was improvising for the dead woman, as he had done so many times and for so many others in the course of his miserable existence.

In the course of his own career, Ismaël often called upon this moment in his life when he had known real despair. But he called in vain. Despite his need and the longing for her which never faded, the despair of having lost his love never again came to aid his skill when he played.

If Ismaël had been a fifty-year-old with senses somewhat dulled by familiarity, he would probably not have chosen that piece of music to accompany his weeping. But he was fifteen. It was still her flesh he sought in the little of her remaining in that room, and not her soul, which he had not yet come to know.

He looked at the spot where she used to sit half-hidden, listening to him. The tears that had refused to flow at his birth now flowed down his cheeks.

They fell on the keys when he leaned over, trying to capture the consoling power of the whispers welling up from the music.

"What is it?" Laviolette asked.

"It's the *Pathétique* sonata by Beethoven," the bishop replied.

The Jew put his finger to his lips.

"Listen!" he whispered. "You'll never hear it played like that again!"

The three men remained standing close together in the shadows at the entrance to the drawing room. Their perspiration mingled in the air around them: from fear in the Jew and Laviolette, and unaccustomed exertion in the case of the sixty-year-old bishop.

"Why has no-one ever told me that something like this existed?" Laviolette murmured.

"Well, now you know," the bishop said.

Silently they went over and joined the family circle around Ismaël. His mother and his two brothers were crouched beside him, weeping with him, almost as an accompaniment to the movements of his hands and fingers.

When he had finished, the three of them clasped Ismaël, sharing his grief, and Marie could at last put her arms around her son while the hot tears were still running down his face. She rocked him with even more emotion than when he was a child and still blind. Laviolette took Ismaël's right hand, which was hanging limply by his side. He pressed his lips to the boy's wrist.

"I'm sorry," he said.

Then they noticed the sudden, unusual silence outside. It was almost unbelievable, as they could now hear the chirping of the crickets and the rustling of the wind among the leaves. The silence was heavy, as if the great body of the war was exhausted and had lost its voice.

It was at that moment that they saw a strange figure of a man enter the circle of lamplight. He looked almost like a marionette as he thumped his twisted foot on the parquet floor with every step. He seemed very angry, muttering words that were scarcely intelligible.

He was complaining about the fact that the law was a shambles these days, that it was a disgrace that Dr Jouve had, in a hurry and on the sly (those were his words), given permission to bury a body that had obviously been murdered.

"By the Germans!" Marie took the liberty of interrupting him.

He brushed this aside and continued his harangue: that it would be a disgrace if this house were left any longer without the protection of the law, *especially* as its contents were so valuable and anyone could just come in and walk off with anything.

"It's immoral and illegal!" he barked. But, in short, the bailiff was with the maquis, the gendarmes were with the maquis, like the public prosecutor and the clerk, and he too would also have been with them if nature had not given him a handicap which excluded him. "For," he explained sarcastically, "where there used to be a few isolated cases of people fighting with the maquis, now it was like an epidemic."

All he was doing was quietly going about his duty. However, seeing everything falling into chaos and wanting to protect his old friend Rose Dupin's property from being pillaged, as soon as the group of Germans who were in the area around the fountain at Peyruis had been made prisoner by the Resistance, he had rushed over on his old bicycle with its buckled wheel and no headlamp.

It was Maître Bellaffaire, the hunchback notary. The sight of the grieving family and the bishop had no effect on him. He asked everyone to clear out as he was going to close the place up and put on the seals immediately. But the bishop had the advantage of height and authority. He glared at the stunted notary.

"All right!" he said. "But my time is limited. Since you insist on putting on the seals, come and do it on the tomb first."

"Seals? On a tomb?"

His Grace nodded.

"Marie," he said, "I told you that I've brought back Séraphin Monge's remains. I'm not at liberty to tell you how I came by them. But, to restore order and give you complete peace of mind, we must give them proper burial. There are quite a few of us here to witness it, after which, this sworn official can carry out his task."

He stared at Maître Bellaffaire, who was not looking pleased.

"These remains are part of the family heritage," he added.

They all made their way through the park in silence. Their footsteps crunching on the gravel were muted, as if they were attending a funeral. When they reached the tomb, they saw the black *toilette*, which the bishop had placed there. With all of them helping, Marie not the least of them, they had soon raised the marble slab and transferred Séraphin's remains to the small box where Rose had originally put them. As Rose and the bishop had done before her, Marie could for a moment hold up the dead man's skull, the skull of the only man she had ever loved. She dared not put her lips to it in the presence of her sons.

"He has chosen her!" Marie whispered bitterly.

Neither her pain nor her grief could completely wipe out the wild notion that tormented her: while she was living out a useless existence on this earth, Rose and Séraphin were now together in eternity.

Day was breaking as they came out of the tomb. A noise, distant at first, then deep and strong like a river, came flowing down the highways and byways. The rumbling that had previously come from the skies was now on land, which resounded with an intermittent dull thud like a power hammer. A tidal wave of steel was surging over the countryside. In the early morning light, under the moon slipping away to the west, we could see what looked like shining tortoise shells jolting along, as if an enormous crowd of these creatures had invaded the plain.

"Them!" shouted the Jew. "It's them! They've arrived!"

When they reached the château, there, taking up most of the terrace, was an enormous, brand-new tank pointing its gun towards them. Green stars were dotted all over its sides. It was caught in a fishing net covered with box branches, as if it had just emerged from the sea. The turret went up, and they saw two human faces under helmets, also crowned with box twigs, that were looking at them in astonishment.

The little group all fell to their knees in the gravel, including the bishop. They all made the sign of the cross, except the Jew who prostrated himself in the dust and stayed there with his forehead in the gravel.

Marie, who was clasping all her children tightly to her, still managed to hold out her hand to Laviolette and give it a long squeeze. They looked at each other.

Her smile was saying, "I'll see you again soon!"

XIII

WHEN MAÎTRE BELLAFFAIRE HAD TO CONCEDE THAT IT WAS ROSE Sépulcre's sister Marcelle who inherited everything, he could hardly believe his diplomas at first.

For a moment there alone in his office, he thought he would choke with resentment, and pressed several nibs so hard against the large sheet of glass on his desk that they broke. Ugly Marcelle had rejected him when he was eighteen and already hunchbacked. She had rejected him quite haughtily, with the condescension of a princess in a fairytale, encouraged by her sister's example into thinking that she would find her prince elsewhere.

Admittedly Marcelle was ugly, but she had a magnificent behind and wasn't even aware of it. Maître Bellaffaire could have had it all to himself. It's well known in our part of the world that in ugly girls, the top safeguards the bottom. They are therefore saved from the desire of others.

But she didn't want it. That was a pity. He would have married for love, as Marcelle didn't have much else to offer. Instead, he had been obliged to settle for a rich heiress who was willing to disregard his hump for the income from all his land. For his part, he had never forgiven Marcelle for the nights he had promised himself with her. Finding her now the sole beneficiary of that fortune made him hate her all the more.

"Anyway, she hasn't laid her hands on the inheritance yet," he thought with a sneer.

He was mistaken. Despite all the legal obstacles he raised and the traps he constantly put in her path, he had to give in after only a year and a half, whereas, with the help of the court and bailiffs, he normally managed to hold on to the richest inheritances for more than five years. He was well known among his colleagues for his virtuosity in these matters.

He had made the mistake of underestimating Marcelle's character, as she had always managed to give the impression that she had none.

After waiting only two months, she would lock the door of her modest house on the Place Vieille in Peyruis at about eight o'clock every day and stand guard in the street outside Maître Bellaffaire's office. The clerk and the secretary would see her some distance away as they came to work. She would be standing there smiling, looking harmless and humble with her shopping bag hanging from her arm. Her first thought had been to turn up in the waiting room opposite the secretary's window after they had arrived, but on mature reflexion she found it more effective to disconcert them thoroughly by appearing before they started work.

She would slip in behind them as soon as they opened the door, and sit on the furthest and most rickety chair in the line provided for clients. At first, like everyone else, she had been overawed by the imposing atmosphere created by the green padded doors and the smell of violet ink and furtively opened tins of pastilles, but after a week she was quite used to it. She would take a piece of knitting from her bag and click away happily with the needles.

"But . . ." the secretary would say, "you don't have an appointment?"

"That's all right. That's all right!" Marcelle said. "I'll wait. I haven't anything else to do, you know. I'm sure Maître Bellaffaire will agree to fit me in between two clients. I won't take long."

He bustled in every morning in a bad mood, thumping his left foot on the ground as if he was trying to nail down a coffin. When he saw her, he would mumble "good morning" and walk on past her without slowing his pace.

Marcelle would stay there until midday and come back at two, except for Saturdays when she did her shopping. After two months of this, the smooth running of the Bellaffaire office began to show signs of strain. More and more often, the notary found the Dupin Inheritance file on top of the pile. Each time he angrily put it down to the bottom again.

364

In a rage one day, he upbraided the secretary, who burst into tears, revealing to the notary the seriousness of the problem.

"I can't bear the sight of her any more!" said the model employee whom Maître Bellaffaire had inherited from his father.

The clerk himself came and told him that he was at the end of his tether, as he was the one who usually received Marcelle's complaints. Her recriminations were always made in a particularly whining, whingeing tone. The clerk had no idea what to do, as one cannot with impunity show an heiress presumptive the door. This one stood to inherit a 500 hectare property, a metals business and a steam mill, not to mention two or three large bank accounts and some plots of land to be built on, which Gaspard Dupin had bought in Aix. Even if the tax department took the largest slice of it, there was still enough left to command respect.

Maître Bellaffaire took the bull by the horns. He summoned ugly Marcelle and roundly took her to task. Hers wasn't the only matter he had in hand; there were others more pressing that couldn't wait, and those clients had already been waiting for three years. Three years! And moreover, the procedure in her case was still in train, the law anticipated a reasonable waiting period for . . .

"A reasonable waiting period!" Marcelle groaned.

She was not sighted until the following Monday. When Maître Bellaffaire arrived that day, the secretary had red eyes and the clerk was chewing the ends of his thin moustache. They both looked at him fearfully.

"She's here!" the secretary whispered.

He indignantly flung open the door to the waiting room. And indeed she was there, but not alone. There was a man with her. They both stood up out of deference. Maître Bellaffaire started. There in front of him was another hunchback, but his hump was on the left, while the notary's was on the right.

"My solicitor . . ." Marcelle said, making the introduction.

She lowered her eyes modestly as she uttered these words, as if she had said "my lover". The two men shook hands firmly and smiled broadly at each other. Three months later, Marcelle Sépulcre marched into the château as mistress of Pontradieu.

*　　*　　*

For fully ten years we all savoured the pleasures of peace restored. It was a delightful sensation, like warming oneself in winter sunshine.

Of course there were still bodies mysteriously found in the bushes well after the general reconciliation had been proclaimed. In the end people tired of actually eliminating enemies, preferring to kill with stealthy looks. We continued, nevertheless, to murder our neighbour in the depths of our hearts, until the last actor in that wretched play had died a natural death. Then, as the next generation forgot the past, everything returned to normal.

We thought our imaginations would have nothing to work on for some time. Luckily we still had Marie.

When the Marquise de Pescaïré died at 104 with all her faculties, Marie was at her bedside. The Marquise didn't actually die; she just slipped away gently. She said it all the time, using the old peasant expression from her youth,

"I'm going, Marie. I'm going."

Marie was very upset, but kept stroking her hair. There was no-one left for her to love. A few months earlier, old Clorinde had fallen forward on to the Roberval scales, crushing both her chest and the scales. Thus the two trusty workers, who had watched over our communal appetites for more than sixty years, died at the same time.

"Godmother, I've made a mess of my life," Marie said, full of doubts about herself. "I can admit it to you."

"Don't blaspheme, Marie. You've had three lovely children who, thanks be to God, are alive, well and give you a lot of satisfaction."

"I've had someone else's three lovely children. It's Séraphin I wanted. I've never loved anyone but him."

"You'd have deceived him, like everyone else!" the Marquise sighed.

"I! I'd have deceived Séraphin! Now you're the one who's blaspheming!"

"My poor child, you don't know yourself. It's in your nature to be attracted to men, and it was in Séraphin's nature to suffer. Men made him suffer, and you would have made him suffer too. God would not have abandoned him."

"Godmother, one day you said to me, 'The expression in his eyes is not of this world.' Tell me, do you still believe that? Do you think that Séraphin . . ."

The Marquise used the last ounce of her strength to put her skeleton-thin hand over Marie's mouth.

"I'll soon know," she whispered.

With those last words she fell back in Marie's arms.

The Marquise made Marie her sole heir in her will, which was read out in Aix. This inheritance coincided with the end of passion for Marie.

One day, after making love, Antoine said to Marie,

"You know . . ."

"It's all right," Marie said. "You can marry and have a family if you want to."

"Yes!" Antoine exclaimed. "How did you guess?"

"Last night you told me I'd put on weight."

"Well, you see . . ."

"Yes, I see perfectly," Marie said.

He was a man who had now reached a certain position in society. With a good deal of backing and some money he had saved, he was able to buy back the Dupin business after Marcelle had to sell it to pay death duties. Thanks to his heroism during the Occupation, he had managed to get in with a whole group of leading citizens. He himself had become a county councillor, and was preparing to stand as a member of parliament. As such, he needed a family to give him credibility with the voters.

"That won't stop us!" he said hastily.

"Yes, it will," Marie replied. "It'll stop me!"

"You've become very strait-laced all of a sudden! You didn't worry too much about treating yourself to my deputy Laviolette, did you? And on Liberation Day!"

"Don't be crude! Besides, he wasn't your deputy. He told me, 'Private, second class! Never more than that! And above all, never in command!'"

"Well, you did make love to him, didn't you?"

"Of course! He was young and thin. He wanted me. And besides, he had his arms around Ismaël. I was in a very emotional state . . ."

"You didn't even have enough strength to wait for me to come back!" Antoine sighed bitterly.

"Not even that," Marie admitted.

Antoine took hold of her hands, which she withdrew. They were sitting naked on the bed, but a rift had deepened between them. It was invisible, but separated them nonetheless.

"It's no then?"

"It's no."

"You know that I'll miss you."

"You'll do more than miss me," Marie said, "you'll eat your heart out."

She didn't really believe it. That same evening, she slipped out of her clothes with the same deft movements she always used when undressing for her lovers. She had begun to doubt her attractiveness.

"Family or not," she thought, "he would never have dared to do it, he would never have had the strength to do it, if I was still my old self."

She looked at her naked body in the wardrobe mirror. She let down her chignon and her hair, now darker than it used to be, fell down to her waist. She looked at herself with the eyes of a jealous stranger. Not one fold of skin escaped her scrutiny.

"No," she decided out loud. "From now on I should live only for my children."

And make herself ugly she did. When you make an effort, nature responds quickly. Marie had thick legs and rectangular buttocks sooner than she wished. Her breasts sagged over her plump torso. She had the dreaded "fatty apron". Men no longer turned around to look at her, which they had done until she was more than fifty.

"Oh well, it's for the best!" she said.

For what she had to do, beauty and love would only be a burden.

Her three sons, it's true, had given her some satisfaction. Bertrand was an engineer in Cadarche. He had a nice life between the pool, the tennis court and casual breaches of the marriage contract, as there was no lack of opportunity. Knowing his mother was well, he hardly ever came to see her, but would often say with a sigh on the telephone, "Ah, Maman! I'd really like to have those gold louis you promised me when I was seventeen.

There's a marvellous Lamborghini for sale, which would help me get ahead in my job."

Ange, the eldest, was always struggling with business deals which were like the rock of Sisyphus: the bigger they became, the more their very weight threatened to send them rolling down to the bottom. He too sighed for Séraphin's box when he phoned.

"Ah, Maman! Those louis you promised us would be very useful to invest now."

But Marie knew how to hold a grudge.

"No! You should have taken them when I offered them to you!"

She made a gesture of throwing salt over her shoulder.

"They'll have to manage on their own! They have wives and children . . . And, by the way, they got fat pretty quickly, those Lucrèce girls! They've become what I thought they would when I saw them all pink flesh and dimples on the edge of the pool at Pontradieu. I'm not surprised their husbands are so unfaithful to them!"

She wrote to Ange, the eldest:

"Last All Saints' Day I put a pot of chrysanthemums on Stéphanie Aumusse's grave. You don't even remember who she was. Although she was a fascist like you, she may have loved you."

According to Marie, it wasn't good to let people we love forget secrets for which they should still feel remorse during this brief life of ours. She judged her two older sons with the same objectivity as she had examined the folds of her aging body in the mirror. She loved them, but had no illusions about their worth.

"They're in America," she would say to her neighbours.

She knew she was lying. Only one was in America . . . well, at least Ismaël was there, when he wasn't in Yokohama, Prades, Glyndebourne or Montreux. He gave recitals. Marie would say to the neighbours,

"His name is in letters thirty centimetres high on the notices. I have one of them pinned to the back of the door. You must come and see it one day . . ."

He wrote her very affectionate letters. He said that he hadn't forgotten anything, that he was not looking for a soul-mate, that he often wept when

369

he played certain pieces. "And above all," he wrote, "make sure that the tomb is properly maintained. I know that Marcelle is mean. Suggest to her that we'll pay for the upkeep."

One day he added the following postscript:

"Dear Maman, I have a favour to ask of you. Try to buy the lamp Rose put on the piano from Marcelle. Pay anything she asks. It's a simple oil lamp on a square copper stand with cherubs embossed on the base. The turquoise bowl had a honeycomb pattern. No doubt the mantle she touched on that last evening has disappeared, but who knows? Perhaps the lamp still has its mantle. If I could, I would like to put it on my piano at all my concerts, so that I would no longer be alone."

"*She* will never grow old!" Marie thought bitterly. "He will never love anyone but her."

The battle between Marcelle and Marie began over this lamp. We were used to these fights to the death. There were several within families at that time. As most of them were based on ordinary conflicts of interest, none fascinated us as much as the one that set Marie Dormeur against Marcelle Sépulcre, for there was passion at the heart of it.

Immediately after the Marquise's death, Marie sold all the property to pay for the death duties: The Phare du Soleil, Bel-Air, the mansion called Temps Perdu at Vauvenargues, which had been closed for 100 years. While she was at it, she sold her own family home plus the business.

When he knew the total of what remained after tax had been taken out, Maître Bellaffaire did not see Marie in the same way as she had seen herself in her wardrobe mirror, even though he was fifteen years younger. "Ah!" he thought. "Her beauty hasn't entirely disappeared." He had just lost his rich heiress who died still young, worn out by six pregnancies and fifteen years of boredom. His father was still alive in a wheelchair, but the woman who looked after him was a great expense. Strong, healthy Marie seemed suited to his particular problem. He put the proposition to her boldly: to combine two modest fortunes, by contract because of both their children, and face the trials and tribulations of approaching old age together.

Marie said no without a word of explanation but without any show of ill humour either. "I don't want to," full stop. Maître Bellaffaire, on the other hand, was very wordy as he spoke of his loneliness. Marie said to him,

"You should talk to Marcelle Sépulcre. She'd make a good catch and she's younger than me."

Maître Bellaffaire burst out,

"Marcelle? Let me tell you about Marcelle! Do you know what she did to me?"

"No . . ." Marie said.

"The other day she invited me to dinner to talk business. Do you know what she served me? A swan!" Maître Bellaffaire exclaimed. "A roast swan!"

Marie felt as if a cold draught had made the hair on the back of her neck stand up.

"It smelled atrociously of mud!" the notary said with disgust.

In the beginning, however, Marcelle crept around among the splendours of Pontradieu feeling somewhat overawed. She investigated all the nooks and crannies, hardly believing her eyes, for two full years. At first she just stood in the twenty-two rooms of the château, not daring to touch anything. Then she opened the first drawer, the second, then everything. Nothing had disappeared or even been moved: not the love letters of Patrice to his sister Charmaine, nor the dresses and furs in her wardrobes, to which Rose had just added her own. The chests of drawers and chiffoniers with their oval mirrors smelled of perfumed cigarettes smoked by women in the period between the two wars. Marcelle spent some delightful moments plunging her hands into the silks and the crêpe de chine panties and slips.

She scuttled around everywhere, summer and winter, tightly wrapped in a black shawl against the draughts. You could hear her coming from the jingling of the bunch of keys she wore on her belt. As soon as she arrived, she double-locked all the bedrooms in the house, all the doors apart from the main entrance, all the storerooms, the service rooms, the lofts and the cellars. After an enjoyable time doing the inventory of everything in it, she even shut up the summerhouse where Patrice played as a boy taking the insides out of clocks.

The tomb itself did not escape her vigilance. She did not replace the pane of crazed glass, but she did have a heavy safe-lock installed and kept the key in her pocket rather than on the ring with the others. She sometimes went anxiously through her pockets, thinking she had lost it.

Always accompanied by this gentle tinkling sound, like the bell on a goat grazing over the slopes, Marcelle tiptoed over Pontradieu, taking its measure.

She stuck her nose into everything, even the farmers' machine sheds and the rows of peach trees that disappeared into the distance. The swans on the pool saw her spend entire evenings enjoying the cool air stretched out on a deck chair. Looking at the mirror surface of the water, each tree in the park and the copper beech, the tallest of them all, she would put her hand to her open mouth, exclaiming,

"Heavens!"

She meant, "Heavens, it's so beautiful!"

This beech almost made her become more human. Well before the Dupins ever came to Pontradieu, two lovers had cut their names entwined into the bark of the tree. As it grew old, the bark had burst open all the letters as well as the heart above it. Marcelle was moved and spent some time gazing at these two names engraved by people long since returned to dust.

For a while a kind of hope made her less ugly. She had never had anything in her life. Nature had given her nothing to begin with, and people followed Nature's example. Then suddenly she had everything, even men. They came, attracted by the extent of her property, and were all the more easily charmed by the magnificent bottom which Maître Bellaffaire had fancied and which she still possessed, but never put to any use.

She did, however, try it once with one of the men who came to offer his services, hair slicked down and hat in hand, saying, "I don't want to boast, but . . ." During the whole thing, which lasted some time, she kept hearing the bed creaking and the clock ticking. She realized that it was either too late or that there had never been a right time.

It was then she began to wonder how she could rid Pontradieu of any trace of Rose – Rose who had been so beautiful and had the good fortune to die young enough so that all anyone remembered was her beauty. Whenever she thought of her sister, the same phrase had always summed up what she resented about her: "She thoughtlessly took everything."

She thought of Marie. Marie had immediately comforted her. Even though she was sick with worry not knowing the whereabouts of her third son, she had impetuously rushed over to Marcelle, tears streaming down her face.

"My poor Marcelle! There are only the two of us left now!"

"My poor Marcelle indeed!" Marcelle sneered. "She was hand in glove with Rose, and I'm not so sure whether at one time . . ."

The idea that there was still a woman left to torment revitalized her, although she didn't know how to exploit the situation, not having much imagination, even for malice. She put her mind to it, however, and when she had found the way to get her own back for Rose's beauty and Marie's condescension, she gloated well in advance over the pleasure it would give her. It was then, armed with her plan, that she asked the farmer's wife to wring a swan's neck and invited the notary to dinner.

This strange event also made Marie suspicious. She decided to buy the modest house in Les Mées, where she lived for the rest of her life, so that she could keep an eye on Marcelle. The property was small, with a two-storey building over a coach house, which you entered from an exterior staircase. Next to it was a garden looking over to the peaks of the Pénitents. There was a spring in the garden, and it was principally for this spring that Marie bought the property. Mint grew all around it and the water flowed through a little copper pipe into a basin scarcely two metres wide and the same in length.

"It's a very appropriate spring for the end of one's days!"

It flowed noiselessly into the basin on a level with the surface of the water. One day Bernard, the engineer son, filled a test tube with it at the end of a long drought.

"It's amazing," he said, "that your spring still flows at the same rate while all the others in the area have dried up."

He came back one day, astonished himself. He went and stood in front of the basin and the copper pipe spouting its little stream of water.

"Do you know how old this water is?" he asked.

"I don't know!" Marie said. "It's fresh and cool. What more do you want?"

"Four hundred years!" her son told her. "It fell on the earth as rain 400 years ago!"

From that day on, Marie looked on her spring with new eyes. During heatwaves she would spend many hours on her own reverently watching water that had fallen on the earth 400 years before. Had she not felt Pontradieu threatened by Marcelle, she would have been completely happy, despite the end of sex.

One day she had to have cataracts removed and dared not drive any more.

"I certainly did the right thing coming here!" she thought.

Having bought the house in Les Mées, she had no need of a car to visit the tomb of her dear departed, and she could pay frequent visits to Marcelle. She thought she thoroughly understood Rose's malicious sister, and that greed was her only preoccupation. For that reason, Marie never arrived empty-handed. Sometimes it would be a pigeon in aspic, at others a litre of oil from the olives she hand-picked in her orchard at Lurs.

Marcelle always greeted her with some bitter comment, as she did when she was young and had nothing.

"And what about me?" she said. "Did anyone ever bother to find out if I was happy?"

"Oh!" Marie replied. "You were like a dry apple! You didn't have enough juice in you!"

"You and Rose never stopped telling me that I was ugly!"

"You aren't any more!" Marie said. "You've been overtaken by lots of others since then. Just look at me with my thick glasses!"

Nevertheless, Ismaël wrote to Marie, "They pay me 50,000 francs per recital. The Jew has insured my hands for a million dollars. He says I can buy Pontradieu if I like. Suggest it to Marcelle. Sound her out."

The person he never called by any other name than "The Jew", out of the deepest affection, was his first teacher, the one who was there when he made love to Rose. He was very old now, but Ismaël looked after him himself, took him everywhere with him, as one carries a memory from one

374

place to another. When he felt tired or lonely, he would often say, "Talk to me about her. You were in her company for weeks on end. Make her come alive for me. I only had one night to love her."

Marie replied to her son, "If I suggest outright buying Pontradieu from Marcelle, she's capable of giving it to the Little Sisters of the Poor. I'll have to go about this in a roundabout way. Let's begin with small things first. You asked me to get Rose's lamp. I'm going to Pontradieu this afternoon. I think I'll be able to get it."

She arrived bearing a pot of raspberry jelly. She had discovered that Marcelle was extraordinarily greedy, so Marie made good use of that knowledge in her dealings with her.

The lamp had never been moved from the top of the piano where Rose had set it down. Marcelle had only to wrap it in newspaper, with no great care, the way she did everything.

"Goodness!" Marie said. "If you only knew how much this lamp will please Ismaël! If you knew how much it means to him!"

"Ismaël?" Marcelle said. "I thought it was for you."

"Oh no, Marcelle."

Marie placed her hand on her wrist.

"You know how silly lovers are! This lamp is the last thing Ismaël saw your sister touch. He wants to put it on his grand piano every time he gives a recital."

Marcelle felt the initial willingness to indulge this unimportant request from Marie beginning to fade. Once again she was forced to remember Rose as she was then.

So, at thirty-eight her sister had got herself a boy who could have been her son, and was still so much in his heart a quarter of a century later that a simple oil lamp she had held for a moment could bring tears to his eyes. Marcelle remembered the creaking of the bedsprings the only time in her life she had made love. What did the man who had shared this disappointing moment look like? Nothing. Nothing of him remained: not a single gesture or tone of voice. So, there were people who could experience this dreary event that she had experienced and get such joy that they still cherished it twenty-five years later? Where was the divine justice in that?

Marie nervously scrabbled around in her bag to take out as many notes as Marcelle might require.

"How much do I owe you for being so kind?" she said.

"*Oïe*! You don't think I'd want you to pay for that, do you? Here. Take it!"

She held the object out awkwardly and far enough away for Marie to think she had missed it because of her bad eyesight. Marcelle joined her in a long cry of distress when the lamp smashed on the floor. She watched the paraffin spread out from the broken bowl and slowly soak into the newspaper.

"Good Lord! My parquet floor!" she moaned.

Marie might not have understood the full import of this incident if she hadn't caught Marcelle's furtive look of triumph. How could you believe that someone could hold such a grudge against a dead woman because she was beautiful and loved? Is it possible to imagine anything more futile, Marie thought. She could scarcely believe what her heart was telling her. From that moment she began to look at Marcelle differently. Perhaps avarice was not the only passion driving the wretched woman.

"You know," Marie said the next day to be quite sure, "don't worry about the lamp. I found one almost the same in the second-hand shop. Ismaël will think he was mistaken about the detail."

She sank back in the deep armchair with a long sigh of satisfaction.

"The main thing is to make him happy," she said.

Marcelle was knitting a layette for a needy mother at the time. Her needles suddenly scraped against each other as she fumbled over a dropped stitch, and Marie knew then that the châtelaine of Pontradieu did not like other people to be happy.

"A keepsake!" Marcelle muttered when she was alone again. "If he needs something to help him remember, he can't have loved her as much as that after all!"

But still tormented by doubt and resentment, she bit her nails as she looked at the splendour of the heavy Venetian chandeliers hanging from the ceiling. They reminded her of Rose on her wedding day moving about under their light in her sumptuous gown.

The week before, a second-hand dealer from Forcalquier had come to see her, sitting timidly on the edge of a couch.

"What are you doing with all these old things?"

"They're memories," Marcelle protested. "And, anyway, they're valuable!"

"I don't deny it, but should you be burgled . . ."

He said no more but slipped her his card. Marcelle telephoned him one November afternoon when the rain was making people with no imagination die of boredom. He came so quickly with two helpers and worked so smartly that by sunset the room had been divested of a great slice of its past.

"And into the bargain," the dealer said, "in their place I've wired up 200 watt globes and three bead shades. No charge!"

He fled like a thief in the night. Marcelle wanted to surprise Marie with the change she had made. She invited her to lunch.

"Have you noticed anything?"

"Yes!" Marie said with a serious look on her face.

"He gave me 30,000 francs for them!" Marcelle said triumphantly.

"Each?" Marie asked.

"No! For the three . . ."

"Oh, Marcelle . . ." Marie sighed.

One day when she arrived, her arms laden with gifts, she came across four furtive-looking men pushing a cart to a truck parked just below the terrace. Marcelle was trotting along beside them. The piano had been slid into it on its back like a helpless cockroach, with its four legs in the air and its castors vainly turning.

Marcelle's mind had become a machine for destroying memories, and from that moment, it went into high gear. She realized very quickly that if she couldn't knife Rose, who was dead, she could do it each time to Marie, who was very much alive.

"Come and see this!" she said proudly.

She led the way, preventing her from going first to hide the surprise, as the scaffold is hidden from a condemned man.

"Look!" she said.

There, instead of the magnificent pool whose mirror surface had reflected so many family dramas, Marie found a gouged-out eye. The basin was empty. There was mud and slime three metres below the rim.

On that day Marie could not repress a cry of pain.

"I've sold the swans!" Marcelle exclaimed triumphantly. "You see, I've lost my court case against the commune. They've cut off my water from the spring. It's too expensive now. I can't afford it."

Marie quickly regained her composure. She was a fighter and she still hoped to make Marcelle give in by appealing to her weaknesses. She bustled in one day saying,

"Marcelle! I've seen a château for sale in Anjou. Twenty-two rooms!"

"The same as here!"

"With three hectares of gardens, and only 200 hectare of land."

"Less than here!" Marcelle said.

"Look at the price it fetched! Look at the advertisement. It's written there!"

"As much as that!" Marcelle said, impressed by the amount.

"I'll give you twice that if you like for Pontradieu!"

Marcelle never replied straight away. She let hope rise in Marie's heart, until she finally said a seemingly contrite little "no". It was enough to kill her.

Marie secretly clenched her fists, but Marcelle knew she was doing it, and that evening she added a mysterious little mark to those already in the margins of the Post Office calendar. They signalled the victories she had won over her dead sister through Marie.

From the moment she heard the cry of distress that Marie had not been able to suppress on seeing the empty pool, Marcelle's malicious fantasies knew no bounds.

She had never forgiven Floréal Lucrèce for having given his two daughters to Marie's sons. He had always maintained the property like a royal garden, but Marcelle made her farmer's life such a misery that in the end he gave up in despair and went to offer his priceless services elsewhere.

"You know," Marcelle said to Marie, "Lucrèce was starting to get a bit old for the job."

"But who will you get to replace him? You know how hard it is to find honest, competent people these days."

"I'm not getting anyone," Marcelle replied calmly.

Then we saw the horrible spectacle of 500 hectares of the plain left untended. Weeds and thistles grew two metres high under the unpruned peach trees where suckers sprouted at the foot of the gum-spotted trunks. Stubble as far as the eye could see grew up around the dwarf elders so that all you could see was a melancholy expanse of their black fruit. The peasants from the area said in the marketplace that they stopped their ears to block out the sound of the property calling for help. Maître Bellaffaire raised his arms to the heavens.

"She has a Sardanapalus[5] complex!" he exclaimed.

People turned their backs on her whenever she went out. Farmers spat with scorn after she had passed. The baker's wife in Les Mées, with a baby at her breast, burst into tears one day in front of her.

"Don't come here any more! Please! Seeing you treat the land this way is worse than if you had killed my child!"

She had to get Marie to fetch her bread, which she was not very happy about. In general, however, she was quite pleased with herself: she had done the major things, now all that remained were the minor matters.

When she received the bill for her heating fuel at the end of a bad winter, she complained so much that the supplier had to take off ten per cent on the spot, even if he lost by it. But that wasn't enough for Marcelle. She told him to go away and not come back again.

It was at this time that she installed a stove in the drawing room. It had a long pipe that led into the central point of the main fireplace, right in the middle of a family coat-of-arms. She cut off the central heating so that the frozen pipes burst the following winter, flooding the parquet floor. She claimed that she didn't have the means to have them repaired, and henceforth she had the trees in the park cut down and burned the wood in the stove.

---

5 An Assyrian king who is said to have ordered everything he owned to be burned on the funeral pyre with him, including his wives and his treasures. Cf. Painting by Delacroix.

In actual fact, the heating was only a pretext. The beautiful trees in the shady park kept whispering cruel love stories in the wind. Marcelle disliked this constant murmur.

Up to this point, Marie had never let down her guard, apart from the day when she had seen the pool like a gouged-out eye. She had never shown any reaction to the blows Marcelle dealt her. One morning, however, she arrived to see a patch of blue sky where the shade of two sequoias should have been. The twin trees were lying on top of the topiary box bushes shaped like young girls, which they had crushed and broken. On that day, Marie fell to her knees.

She wept bitterly and tried to put her arms around the enormous trunks of the two trees, as if to beg their pardon for being so powerless to do anything, and also to say to them, "I loved you!"

It was here at the foot of these two trees, in front of the box bushes that hid the beginning of their trunks, that Marie had found Séraphin on his knees, his bleeding hands clasped over the body of Charmaine, who had been savaged by the dogs.

In the following winters, down came the copper beech with the intertwined names of the lovers from the past, who had never done anything to Marcelle, who never even knew she would exist. Down came the two huge plane trees, which conversed with the wind and never let it be forgotten. And so Marcelle laid Pontradieu bare like a woman about to be whipped for misconduct.

But when she had made the gap at the end of the park, which could be seen from the drawing room windows as well as those in her bedroom, the pink marble tomb appeared in view. It offended her sight and she began to think seriously about it.

Sometimes a dark, shadowy figure would appear in front of the chapel, mostly of someone old, and often crippled. It would stay there for a long time, in quiet contemplation, kneeling from time to time. Marcelle registered this intrusion on her property with some displeasure. It nevertheless went against her miserly nature to fence in the park, which had never had any barrier between it and the surrounding fields. She hired two men for a particular job, then telephoned Antoine Maujac to order some

380

rolls of barbed wire and a certain number of posts, which she got at a discount price.

Within two days, the Dupin chapel was defended like a blockhouse by two rows of needle-sharp barbed wire. Marcelle went to make sure that her instructions had been followed to the letter. She was coming back from the tomb to the château, satisfied with her inspection, when she had a brilliant idea, which she thought would deal Marie the *coup de grâce*.

But, contrary to her usual practice, Marie didn't come for two days.

She was leaving her kitchen garden with her arms full of vegetables to make soup, when she saw a man with his hat in his hand who had come from His Grace the Bishop.

"He's at death's door," the man said to her. "He sent me in his car to fetch you. He begs you to grant his request."

Marie asked him to wait, tidied herself up and put on her astrakhan coat. His Grace was dying a natural death, due to his great age, but first he wanted to see Marie. It was the last thing he wanted to do on earth.

Mgr Beckx had greyed somewhat at the temples, but he was still faithfully hovering around his bishop. He was a man who had sacrificed all advancement and eminence to his curiosity. The fact that he was a holy man could be seen from his foot soldier's boots and his beret, which he wore perched on the side of his head like an alpine chasseur.

The whole of his theory was based on the fact that he did not think that His Grace had faith, at least, faith as he understood it: obedience to the Church first, and God second. And that is why he hovered over him with eager solicitude right until the last moment. He was watching for some lapse in the sybaritic prelate.

He was wasting his time. When Mgr Godiot summoned Marie, it was outside anything he owed to the Church and to God. He had made his confession to the priest at St Jérôme's church, omitting nothing, neither the Baroness Ramberti nor his reading of Ecolampadius nor his night journey with Séraphin's bones. He even smiled as he thought of it when making his contrition: "My soul was still young," he thought.

But he had filled a dossier with certificates and first-hand accounts relating to the case of Séraphin Monge and his bones. That is what he wanted to talk about with Marie.

His hand with the opal ring was hanging limply out of the bed. Marie knelt and pressed her lips to it for a long moment. He made a weak gesture for her to get up. He had sent his vicar general away the moment Marie came into the room.

"Marie," he said, "swear to me on your eternal soul that your son regained his sight in front of Séraphin's tomb."

"Yes," Marie said, "but I can't swear it. Perhaps I imagined it; perhaps I dreamed it. I often think of that day. I can see a hazy light around me, as in a dream. The air had no smell, no weight."

The bishop's eyes were closed as he nodded his head.

"No-one can swear," he said. "And yet . . . I've collected so many accounts that it's impossible not to harbour some doubt. Marie, do you think these testimonies should be made known?"

"No," Marie said. "The longer it remains secret the better."

"You're a good Christian, Marie," the bishop said.

He pointed to a desk with a cross on its flap standing in a dark part of the room.

"The key is under the base of the lamp," he whispered. "Open it. Open the drawer on the left. You'll find the file there. It's thick. Burn it in the fireplace a sheet at a time. It wouldn't burn all at once. I had the fire lit on purpose. It was no small matter, I can tell you! Burn everything! In front of me! In front of me!"

He raised himself on his elbows to see the flames dance higher as Marie did as he asked. One by one the sheets of paper glided high up above the hearth with a sound of ruffled wings, then slid down obliquely to the flames as if they wanted to gently settle there.

"The light of God does not need any new sign," the bishop said behind Marie, who scarcely heard him. "We have been given a sign once only for all eternity. And that should be enough for us. You're sure, aren't you Marie?"

"Yes," Marie groaned.

She was crying. She was doing something that meant that one day, when she was dead, there would be no-one left to remember Séraphin Monge. As she committed all those pages to the flames, she felt he had gone away a second time.

Mgr Godiot died only when the last page crackled in the fire. Before that, he took Marie's hands in his and said to her,

"You see, Marie, no-one should know that such things are conceivable; otherwise, what would become of our freedom?"

Marie remembered these enigmatic words for a long time. When His Grace's hands released hers, she let out a little cry. Mgr Beckx leaped into the room like a cat. He glanced quickly at the fireplace.

"*Quid tibi dixit*? Sorry! What did he say to you?" he asked.

"Nothing!" Marie replied. "He was delirious."

When she arrived back in Les Mées, she found a note from Marcelle asking her to call in. She went the next day, taking the kilo of bread the miserly woman ate every three days.

Marcelle was wringing her hands, apparently in despair.

"Sit down and listen!" she said to Marie. "A Dutch couple are buying Pontradieu from me!"

"For how much?" Marie asked.

Marcelle scribbled a figure on a piece of paper that she tossed to Marie.

Marie heaved an invisible sigh of relief. The price gave her plenty of room to manoeuvre.

"The only thing is," Marcelle added, "I have a moral problem. When the Dutch woman saw the tomb, she threw up her hands in horror. She won't buy the property with the tomb. She talks of turning the place into a hotel, putting in a swimming pool. So the tomb ... Anyway, this is what I've decided: I'm going to transfer the Dupin remains to the Dabisse cemetery. It's their parish and besides, they have a family vault there."

"Right!" Marie said sharply. "It didn't take you long to solve your moral problem!"

"My dear, the way things are in business these days, you have to act quickly."

"And Séraphin?"

"Séraphin! Séraphin! He wasn't even a member of the family! His name's not on any register! It's as though he wasn't dead, as though he wasn't ever born! I can't even mention him, or I'd be in trouble. Everything must be done legally, you know, and transferring Séraphin to another grave just wouldn't be legal."

She leaned over to poke the fire she had kept going during the cold October rains.

"I've booked the bulldozer for next Tuesday," she said. "It'll all be done at the same time, both the transfer and the demolition. I'm paying for it with the marble from the chapel, and I've asked the contractor to be discreet. Séraphin's ashes, because they're only ashes, and without a name . . . Séraphin's ashes will be . . ."

"Scattered . . ." Marie finished the sentence for her, aghast at what she'd heard.

She got up and went to the door, leaning her hands against the walls for support. She left without a word, without an insult, without a sigh. She got back to Les Mées by stopping and leaning her back against every poplar. Her ears were buzzing. She thought she could still feel Rose's hands around her wrists the day she said to her, "Marie, if I die before you, swear to me that you will never let Séraphin's bones be taken away from Pontradieu!"

She saw herself with her father's gun loaded with buckshot on that terrible night, firing at the fleeing figure, then dropping her weapon to help Rose, who was dying.

"No!" she said aloud as she walked. "No!"

She repeated this "no" the whole way home. Some people who heard her as they passed her in the narrow streets wondered if she was losing her mind, she looked so distraught.

Next Tuesday. She had a week. At the end of the week the bulldozer would rip everything out of the soil of Pontradieu, right down to the memory of those who had suffered so much there.

Marie wrote to Ismaël:

"Keep your yen, your dollars, your marks and your Swiss francs! She won't take them. Gold might be the only thing! It's my last hope. After that, it's all in God's hands!"

She went to Pontradieu with Séraphin's gold, plus everything she could find by selling the Marquise's blue-chip shares, some of which had increased tenfold in value. She was walking with difficulty, bent forward under the weight of a big canvas bag tied in the middle so that she could balance it over her neck. On one side was Séraphin's gold, and on the other the Marquise's. It dug into her neck as she walked.

"Make some room for me!" she said to the startled Marcelle.

She let the weight of the bag thump down on the drawing room table. She untied all the string and tipped it. As it emptied, the contents spilled out in a shower of golden light, brightening the dull autumn day.

"There you are!" she said.

"What is it?"

"It's to pay for Pontradieu! Everything's losing value, Marcelle. Times are bad! Now gold is really up at the moment and it'll go even higher in the coming weeks! It's the only thing worth having. Look! Just look at these $20 coins with the eagle! And these 100 Swiss franc coins! Aren't they beautiful!"

Marcelle nearly succumbed to the sheer profusion and variety of all that gold, expressly chosen by Marie. She blinked with curiosity at this strange source of light on a dull rainy day. It looked so much like a glowing fire that she was surprised it didn't crackle. She almost thrust out her hands to touch the fortune, if only with her fingertips. But hate kept her arms solidly clamped to her sides.

"The Dutch florin isn't going down either," she said.

She lifted a corner of the curtain and watched Marie departing in the fine rain, loaded up like a mule with all her useless gold. The paths in the park, ruined by all the wood that had been dragged out, were now nothing but potholes and puddles filled with water. Marcelle reflected that winter was coming and there were still about 100 trees that could be cut down. But it was a passing thought. All her attention was focused on the back of the old woman, four years her senior, who was walking with difficulty, despairing under the weight of her gold and her defeat.

"Oh! I'm ugly!" Marcelle said. "You wait!"

She let the curtain fall back again.

*   *   *

Marie was on the alert. It was one of those nights that warn you to watch out if you want to avoid nasty surprises, a night when you hold your breath, and when, in our part of the country, anything can happen.

She was boiling down herbs in a big pot bubbling over high heat, and there was already only a small amount of liquid left. She had also put a bowl of strawberries to macerate in Bordeaux wine. They had been picked covered in drops of October rain, and were no doubt the last for the year. These were the only ones Marcelle liked. She liked them soaked in wine with a lot of sugar.

Every year Marie prepared a jar of them, which she took to Marcelle as a sign of allegiance. She had to sit there while Marcelle set to and ate them in front of her with a good deal of satisfied slurping.

"Thank goodness I still have that to fall back on! Thank goodness she's as greedy as an old cat!"

Although the rain was beating down she had opened her kitchen window wide to get rid of the foul smell. Giant hemlock plants with their green hanging umbels had always prospered along the garden path, brushing against her in the breeze as she passed. It was perhaps this "forget-me-not" touch that invited Marie to make use of them when the time came.

Frowning with concentration, she looked at the juice thickening in the small saucepan into which she had poured it. She sniffed it. It had lost its odour. She tasted a tiny bit from a wooden spoon on the edge of her lips. It had lost nearly all its bitterness. The strawberries, the wine and the sugar hid it completely. For the first time in her life, Marie's hands were trembling.

"Since nothing has come to my aid . . ." she said aloud.

There was anguish and fear in her voice.

The rain had already been pouring down for four days when a storm started at about eight o'clock. Thunder claps now rent the sky following bolts of lightning that streaked out over the plain.

Marcelle smiled with satisfaction as she looked at the grand staircase at Pontradieu. It was stark and bare, reduced to nothing but the steps. With one blow she had stripped it of half its beauty. She congratulated herself on her cleverness: she had just sold the eighteenth-century banisters and ironwork, all scrolls and black birds' nests, to an ironware dealer for 200,000 francs. This wrought iron balustrade, which formed the stairwell and continued around the landing on the first floor, was 25 metres long. The dealer paid in cash, and that same afternoon he had taken the work of art to pieces, intending to put it together again in a house belonging to nouveaux riches somewhere near Gordes.

For several months, and especially in recent weeks, Marie had been saying how much she admired this work by a journeyman from long ago, so finely wrought that you couldn't see any of the joins. Despite the worries Marcelle caused her, she often went as far as running her hand over the balustrade, as she would with a beautiful animal. She did it even last week. Consequently, she had more or less forced Marcelle to deprive her of this thing she cherished.

Marcelle looked up at the stairs from the ground floor. They made one feel dizzy now that the whole mutilated side leaned over into empty space. The carpenter from Les Mées was coming the following day to replace the balustrade with a simple walnut-stained wooden rail. In the meantime Marcelle, who had a fear of heights, went up the steps nervous and panting, holding on to the wall. Lightning cracked twice as she made her way to the bedroom. It flashed in all the windows, holding Pontradieu in its crossfire.

Marcelle usually fell asleep immediately and slept soundly. She did so on this occasion, with a smile on her face because of the sheets with Rose's monogram, which always felt so soft against her body.

Suddenly she found herself sitting upright, with no memory of having done so. The echo of an enormous clap of thunder was still buzzing in her ears. Even when she was young and poor during the most violent storms back in the mill on the Lauzon, Marcelle had never woken up at night. She felt that someone had just shaken her by the shoulder, as Rose had done when she had made her come down into the courtyard to find that their father had been crushed to death. Heavens, how distant that memory was, and yet how quickly it had come to her mind that night.

She was frightened and pressed the button on her bedside lamp. There was no light. Lightning must have struck the transformer. The rain was now falling very lightly on the roof at Pontradieu, but it seemed to Marcelle that there was another noise rising up and growing louder through the whisper of the rain. She felt an urgent need to go and look. She opened her door. The long corridor was in complete darkness. Through the window at the end, she could see lightning on the horizon forking out like opening flowers and illuminating the valley, a sign that the storm was moving away. In between times, it was dark again. But Marcelle knew the open spaces in the house so well she could have gone there with her eyes closed.

She was not mistaken. At least she thought she was not mistaken. Downstairs, beyond the entrance hall, through the drawing room doors, which she never closed, she thought she heard quiet footsteps moving slowly across the floor. "A confident step," she thought. "A visitor." A clock at the end of the corridor calmly struck three.

"Who's there?" Marcelle called out anxiously. "Is that you, Marie?"

For Marie had become her only preoccupation. The isolation she had created around herself and the hatred with which she pursued her childhood friend meant that this was the only name left for her to call on.

She moved forward slowly, wide-eyed, hesitant and uncertain. The great space of the entrance hall was in a kind of murky darkness, the sort that let you know it was there.

The footsteps continued, but were neither approaching nor retreating. It was as if they were staying in the same place and the ground were moving under their tread.

Marcelle was trembling and felt the need to hold on to something for support. She took two steps forward with her hands out in front of her, as she had done so often. But she was also in the habit of leaning on the balustrade she had just sold.

As she fell head first over the edge into empty space, she let out the strange cry of someone who has lost everything in an instant.

When Marie made her way to Pontradieu the next evening with the poisoned food for Marcelle, the storm had passed, but it was still raining. The rain was taking revenge on us for seven months of drought. What had been withheld when we needed it for harvesting the crops and the grapes was now being dumped on us in a fury, as if the sky, sick of our recriminations, was saying,

"Right! There's your rain! Drink your fill!" Now of course it was no use at all, as usual.

During the night the Durance had sprung to life again. It was roaring from one side of its bed to the other, as it did in its prime, with that unmistakable sound made by the furious tumbling of its stones and pebbles. All the sluice gates on the dams from Serre-Ponçon to Miramas were raised to the last notch in an open invitation to the river,

"Come through, my girl!"

But the people in charge and those who lived on the banks thought that the bulimic river would never have enough space to contain the flow of water.

"All to the good!" Marie thought. "No-one will be out tonight. They're all huddling at home in fear."

With her basket on her arm like a good peasant woman going to market, Marie made her way slowly in the pouring rain. She was wearing an old shepherd's cloak that had been hanging behind her door for as long as she could remember. She had never used it and didn't even know where it came from. She was also sheltering under a big, cumbersome, blue umbrella, which usually just stood like an ornament in her hall.

She was thinking as she walked along that in 400 years the rain falling on the earth that night would come out of the pipe in her little fountain. It would still flow gently with its own little music. She also thought, not with any sadness, that no-one then would remember her, Marie, what she had thought, what she had done, and what she still had to do.

As she made her way to Pontradieu, the road at Marie's feet was quite visible in spite of the dark and the falling rain. The curtain of cloud could not completely block out the brightness of the moon risen high in the night sky: light still filtered down through it on to the countryside below.

Her heart was beating fast as she reached her destination. Although it was still early – hardly more than eight o'clock in the evening – she was surprised to see the château in darkness. She prepared to make the fatal strike with the hand-shaped knocker that had announced decrees of destiny many times already. She knocked four times. It sounded to her as if the blows were echoing inside in sombre emptiness. She tried to get an answer for several minutes. Then she called out,

"Marcelle!"

No answer. Then she remembered that at the bottom of her basket she had a set of keys to Pontradieu which Rose had given her years before. She found them among all the bits and pieces she never bothered sorting out.

The same dull light that had lit her path came in through the lattice window. As soon as she opened the door, Rose could see that the main staircase was bereft of its balustrade. She gave a bitter laugh.

"I knew she'd get rid of it if I showed her that I liked it," she whispered.

She looked down. There on the floor, next to the dilapidated old sedan chair with its peeling leather, she saw the small white heap of Marcelle's body in its prim nightgown. There was no need to go any closer to know that she was dead.

Marie knelt down with her basket beside her.

"Thank you, God!" she said, and crossed herself.

Then she heard, or thought she heard, slow, deliberate footsteps moving away down the main corridor on the first floor. She had already heard those steps more than sixty years ago behind the closed door of La Burlière. She instinctively cried out,

"Séraphin!"

Her voice rang out in an all-embracing moan that echoed through the vast emptiness of Pontradieu. She rushed, or thought she rushed, on to the unprotected stairs. Oh! If only she had the legs of eighteen-year-old Marie who struggled with her love when he wanted to throw the cradle in the fire! But no! These were poor old thick legs, which had swollen above the ankle with her bad circulation! Oh, how we change!

When she reached the landing, the moonlight had just broken through the clouds and poured in through the window and down the length of the corridor with bedrooms on each side. It was empty and all in order. No-one had just gone down it.

Marie left the château. She threw the food she had prepared for Marcelle into the irrigation channel running beside the house. She washed the container very carefully and put it back into her basket.

She marched over to the open shed where all the farming tools had been left to gather dust. She knew what she was looking for and where to find it. Despite her umbrella and basket, she managed to get hold of some wirecutters hanging on the wall.

From there she went straight to the tomb imprisoned behind its barbed wire. She cut through it methodically, one section at a time. With the strength of a young girl, she shook the posts loose and pulled them out.

Her chest was wheezing like bellows in a forge when she finally sank to her knees on the step outside the tomb, where Ismaël had hit his head as a child. She leaned her forehead against the crazed pane of glass.

"Sleep peacefully, my loves," she said. "I've watched over you!"

It was more or less then, perhaps a little later, that Marie received the strange visit no-one could explain.

She had just managed to buy Pontradieu for Ismaël thanks to money and sheer persistence. The Dutch couple did actually exist, but they thought it was charming to have a tomb on their property. They gave in at nine million, knowing that Marie had the backing of Ismaël Saille. The insatiable Maître Bellaffaire had also tried to come out the winner by resorting to all kinds of tricks.

"Leave it alone," Marie told him, "if you don't want to find yourself reduced to nothing. Your last land development deal was a disaster. If necessary I'll make sure that the next one goes the same way. Leave it alone. You just want Pontradieu out of vanity, but for me it's love. Ismaël will never have children. He'll leave Pontradieu to you. Well . . . to your children! You're nearly as old as I am."

Then she received that visit. She was in the middle of watering her fuchsias, as August had been very hot.

It was the time of day that Marie liked best, when the smiles of the summer evening were in harmony with her idle but pleasant thoughts. She still occasionally dreamed of herself clinging to one of her dear lovers, and thought of one or other of them with affection. Where were they? As old as her, if not already dead and buried. She saw them as they must look now: slow-moving and stiff in the joints. They would have that bewildered look which seems to be searching for something to cling to as they stand on the brink of that confusing time when the rest of their life is rushing by so fast. No doubt their clothes are hanging off them and the seats of their pants sag as they wonder, "Who is that?" when one of the wonderful loves of their youth passes by.

Even though she had held his bones in her hands, Séraphin was the only one Marie always remembered just as he was when she met him one morning sixty-eight years ago in 1921. She still saw his huge shoulders, his unsmiling face, and his eyes always trained on something invisible, beyond what we could see. He seemed to be saying, "I know how your souls will hammer on the lid of your coffins, begging the Father for them to be opened."

It had taken sixty-eight years for these words to crystallize in Marie's mind, and they helped her to face death. She was thinking of that while watering her fuchsias when the strange individual asked to see her. He found her standing near the spring with its fossil water, busily filling her watering can.

However, the man sitting on the seat who pointed out Marie's house could never describe him. He had had a cataract operation the previous year. Not very successful, it would seem.

But Marie probably recognized him immediately. She lied to him, but accepted his verdict with the best grace in the world.

After he left, she looked honestly at her life. Even the shadow of Tibère could not prevent her from finding it a full life. She had never asked others for more than she had received. Her children were far away. Having heard it often enough from others through the years, she knew what they whispered when they talked about her, in bed with their current lover, "Mother? What can you expect? She's 85!"

It was a clear, moonlit night, and the only thing remaining for Marie to do was quietly and peacefully to lay down that burden.

These things were told to me by intense, serious voices around many a hearth. Outside, the century went by, centuries went by, which no-one noticed, content to live the small scrap of all that time so parsimoniously granted us. While the fires died down deep into the night, we wavered between imagination and reality, sickness and health, suffering and joy. The *frisson* we felt on hearing about the misfortune of others reinforced our own humble, autumnal well-being.

For a long time now, there have been no visitors to the cemetery on All Saints' Day to tend the graves of the dead we talked about. The cypresses around the chapel are as high as those at La Burlière, though they may seem more slender for another hundred years. But already they give the impression of raising up the pink marble chapel on their roots and presenting it to the heavens. In any event, on summer days as their swaying treetops paint that striking blue, they moan in the wind of their loneliness and our pain. Children no longer come and sit in their shade. The *santibelli* they shelter has long ago lost his power. It would even seem that the legend of Séraphin has vanished into the mists of time. Nonetheless, an arthritic old man, who knew what happened in the past but never spoke of it, will sometimes come and sit with his cane between his legs on the threshold to the tomb, on the pretext of getting a little bit of sun. If one of them ever got up cured or eased of his pain, he has never breathed a word of it to anyone. Inexorably ground between the march of time and the movement of the spheres, saintliness too can wear out and fade away. The one who was revered three centuries ago for being able to make the plague disappear, now has not even enough power to relieve the stiffness in our old bones.

Those were the things we regretted in Lurs as we noted the passing of time. The world only brushed us with its wing from far away and not for long. Successive waves of modernism, always the definitive one and always superseded, caught us for a while, sometimes by force, then we came back to our olive trees, which were damaged by frost every seventy-five years. Their roots smoking in the hearth brought tears to our eyes.

We waited for the outcome of events to prove us right or wrong. We waited. We were well placed for waiting. Our young people growing old replaced us in this quest while we silently withered, disappeared and came to dust. Thus we were forever trying to work out the puzzles our lives had set us, and which we were never able to resolve.

When we had finished with the story of Marie Dormeur and, in silent affirmation, had put our open palms to the brightness of the fire to show that Séraphin's hands, unlike ours, did not have the stigmata of his fate, there was always someone waiting his turn dumbfounded, who now burst forth in passionate denial. He would say,

"*Bé qué diès*? What are you talking about? What are you saying about Séraphin Monge? You don't know. Séraphin Monge, the real one, is buried in the Vieux-Noyers cemetery. He's actually one of the last to be buried there. And I should know! In those far-off days I was assistant postman in the Jabron valley. I did the route on foot between Saint Vincent, Saint Martin, Saint Claude and the very same Vieux-Noyers. I'm talking of 1924! I heard the bell tolling just as I arrived. They told me that a man had swallowed a wasp and that his tongue had swollen up, one thing led to another and he choked to death, a senseless death. That's the story of Séraphin Monge! And besides, that cemetery at Vieux-Noyers is still there. You can go and look if you don't believe me! Just push aside the weeds and wild lavender. You'll find his name all right. Perhaps even his photo!"

He would sit down again with his hands spread out on his thighs and a triumphant look on his face, delighted at having shut us up in only three minutes, after we had been talking for hours.

But at that moment, waving a long arm in protest and denial, someone else from the smoky inglenook would insist on being heard in his turn, someone more consistent, more credible, who spoke gravely, who seemed to know.

It was always someone who claimed to hate falsehood, yet had it written on his face. His hair grew low on his forehead, but it was self-interest rather than worry which furrowed his brow. Owl's eyes, very deeply set, dominated his cheeks. He would then stand up, pray silence, and say . . .